God of Dragons
Threadweavers, Book 4

Todd Fahnestock

Cover illustration and design by:
Rashed AlAkroka

Maps by:
Langon Foss

For Young Sara,
who was there at the beginning and who demanded I put this
story into the world.

CONTENTS

GOD OF DRAGONS

Pronunciation Guide

Main Characters:

Medophae—ME-d□-fā
Mershayn—Mər-SHĀN
Mirolah—MI-r□-lä
Silasa—si-LÄ-sə
Stavark—STA-värk
Zilok Morth—ZĪ-lok M□rth

Other Characters/Places:

Amarion— ä-MĀ-rē-un
Ari'cyiane—ä-ri-cē-ĀN
Avakketh—ä-VÄ-keth
Belshra—BEL-shrə
Bendeller—ben-DEL-er
Buravar—BYÜ-rä-vär
Calsinac—KAL-zi-nak
Casra—KAZ-rä
Casur—KA-zhər
Cisly—SIS-lē
Clete—KLĒT
Corialis—K□R-ē-a-lis
Dandere—DAN-dēr
Darva—DÄR-və
Daylan—DĀ-lin
Dederi—DE-de-rē
Denema—de-NĒ-mə
Deni'tri—de-NĒ-trē
Dervon—DƏR-vän
Diyah—DĒ-yä
Elekkena—e-LE-ke-nə

Ethiel—E-thē-el
Fillen—FIL-en
Grendis Sym—GREN-dis SIM
Harleath Markin—HÄR-lēth MÄR-kin
Irgakth—ƏR-gakth
Keleera—kə-LĒR-ə
Lawdon—LÄ-dən
Lo'gan—l□-GÄN
Locke—läk
Mi'Gan—mi-GÄN
Natra—NÄ-trə
Oedandus—□-DAN-dus
Orem—□-rem
Rith—RITH
Saraphazia—se-ruh-FĀ-zhē-ə
Shera—SHE-rə
Tarithalius—ter-i-THAL-ē-us
Teni'sia—te-NĒ-sē-ä
Tiffienne—ti-fē-EN
Tuana—tü-ä-nä
Tyndiria—tin-DĒR-ē-ä
Vaisha—VĪ-shə
Yehnie—YEN-nē
Ynisaan—YI-ni-sän
Vullieth—VƏL-ē-eth
Zetu—ZE-tü

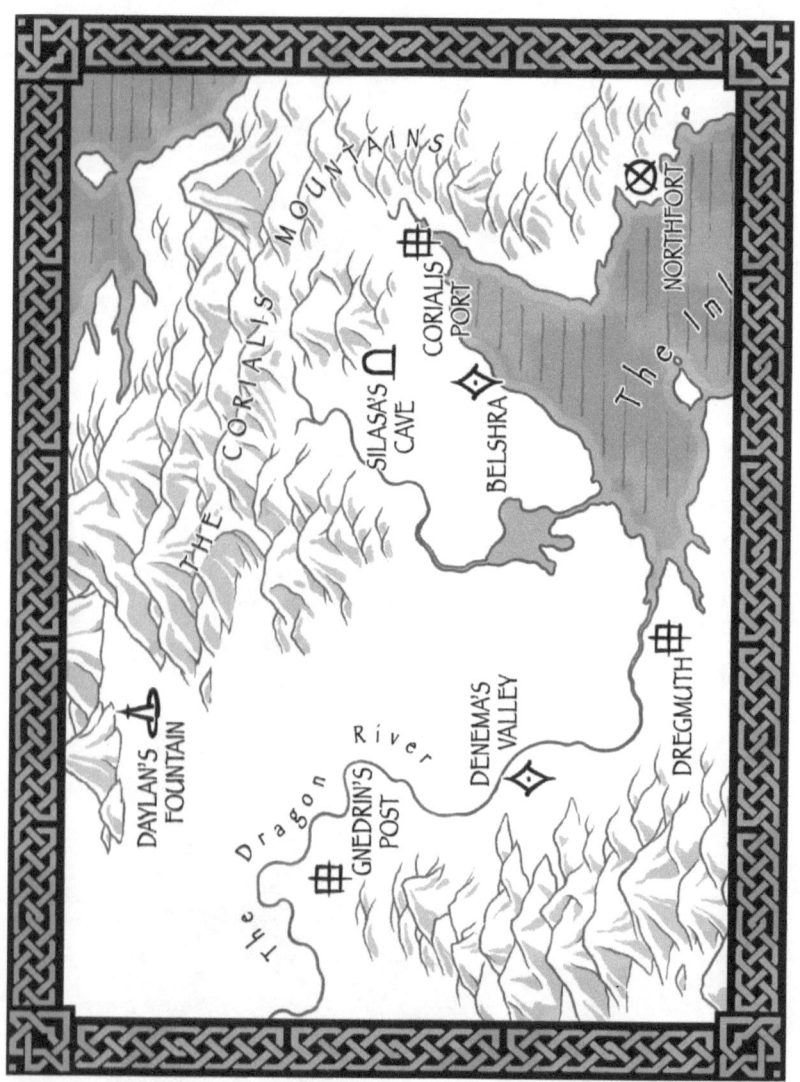

Mailing List/Social Media

MAILING LIST
Don't miss out on the latest news and information about all of my books. Join my Readers Group:

https://www.subscribepage.com/u0x4q3

FACEBOOK
https://www.facebook.com/todd.fahnestock

AMAZON AUTHOR PAGE
https://www.amazon.com/Todd-Fahnestock/e/B004N1MILG

Book 4

God of Dragons

PROLOGUE
YNISAAN

YNISAAN STOOD AT THE EDGE of the ocean in her human form. Her white hair blew back from her face, and the waves lapped softly against red sands. Mere weeks ago, the world had changed right here. Far out over those waves, Bands and Tarithalius had emerged, freed after four hundred years of imprisonment in an enchanted ruby.

It was momentous. The lost love of Wildmane had returned to Amarion. The god of humans had returned to his people after centuries. It was enough to change the course of history.

But neither of those historic happenings had brought Ynisaan here.

Despite the return of Bands or humanity's patron deity, the end was at hand. There was only one way to stop humanity's destruction, and it all hinged on that ruby that wasn't actually a ruby at all.

Even the supposed architect of the spell, the Red Weaver,

hadn't known what she had possessed. Ethiel had thought it some robust component of threadweaving, when in fact it was far more. The ruby was a piece of the mythical GodStone, an artifact only a handful of beings in the world even knew about. Ynisaan herself had not known about it, and never would have but for an overheard conversation between two gods.

From the Coreworld, she had watched the interaction between Saraphazia and Tarithalius as they discussed the ruby only moments after emerging in a splash of seawater.

"Do you think you were thrown into that ruby by chance?" Saraphazia had demanded.

"Who would want to imprison me?" Tarithalius had asked.

"Who could?" Saraphazia had turned her tail to him.

"Not Avakketh?" Thalius said incredulously.

But it *was* Avakketh. The god of dragons had used the Red Weaver as a tool. From that moment, Ynisaan had tried to understand what kind of stone, imbued with the power of a threadweaver like Ethiel, could possibly hold a god against his will. It took her days of searching the old stories of her kind and poring over old human texts in Denema's Valley until she found confirmation she was looking for, and suddenly everything made sense. The ruby was a tiny piece of Natra's GodStone, and Avakketh had the rest of it.

The GodStone was a relic from the age when Natra—maker of the world and ruler of the gods—had used it to create the living creatures of the world. The GodStone could give the power of life to mortals and, Ynisaan now suspected, even to the gods.

The GodStone was why Avakketh was finally coming south, why he finally had the confidence. If he had the rest of the GodStone, it could mean he now had the power of resurrection. Even if Tarithalius, Saraphazia, or Wildmane, managed to slay him, he would only rise again.

Avakketh had used that tiny piece of the powerful stone to imprison Tarithalius and Medophae. But he had missed. He'd captured Tarithalius and Bands instead, and Medophae had gone free. Free to continue protecting the human lands, free to fight Avakketh if he should come south.

If the dragon god had actually netted his intended victims—taken humanity's protectors away—he might have destroyed humanity right then and there, four hundred years ago. But because Medophae was still loose, and because Avakketh knew—the whole world knew—that Medophae could slay a god, Avakketh had chosen to stay safely perched in his mountain kingdom.

But now, centuries later, she suspected the god of dragons had found a new use for the GodStone, and he'd finally summoned the courage to make his attack, regardless of who opposed him. If the GodStone could resurrect Avakketh, then he had the advantage he needed to kill Medophae, kill Tarithalius, and wipe out humanity.

His plan would succeed. She had seen it. In the last few days, she had watched the tracks of the future, embedded in the floors and walls of the prophetic Coreworld, lead to the same horrible, bloody end for humanity. All futures. All save one.

Avakketh had made a mistake, created one small flaw in his plan. He'd left the ruby, that tiny piece of the GodStone, at the bottom of the ocean.

Ynisaan closed her eyes, and a portal appeared in front of her. She stepped through, and she was suddenly beneath the ocean, surrounded by water. The crushing weight of it would kill her if she stayed, but she didn't need long.

Screaming at the pressure, air gushing from her lungs, she quickly snatched the stone from the sandy bottom, then retreated into her portal once more.

Ynisaan stumbled on the shore, dripping wet, and collapsed. She lay there, feeling the bleeding inside her body. But she had the stone. That's what mattered. It was all that mattered.

This chip of the GodStone was the single, thin chance for humanity to survive, and she clutched it tightly. When she could breathe again, she rolled gingerly onto her back, fumbled with the pouch at her side, and withdrew a vial. She pulled the stopper, downed it, and slowly felt the injuries inside her begin to heal.

Taking a deep breath, she crawled onto her knees and stood up, and another portal opened before her. She couldn't stay on this beach. Even now, Avakketh might realize his weakness. When he did, he would come for the stone. If he found her, he'd kill her, and that would be the end of hope for humanity.

Her first step was complete. She had the stone. Now, she must speak with the one who must wield it.

Ynisaan stepped through the portal.

1

SILASA

SILASA AWOKE TO A DIFFERENT KINGDOM.

When she went to sleep, tension had flowed through the castle, nobles quickly readying for war. Mershayn and Baerst had convinced the court that the dragons were coming, and the kingdom of Teni'sia had collectively held its breath and prepared for an impossible battle.

But as Silasa emerged from her hidden room, stepping up the forgotten staircases deep below, into the castle, she smelled blood everywhere. The tension had turned to battle while she slept, and that battle to aftermath.

People rushed about in the lamplit hallways carrying basins of water and fresh bandages. Silasa passed the infirmary, hearing the moans of the wounded. Rows of beds were filled with people. Makeshift pallets had been constructed and filled as well. Simple blankets had been thrown on the on the floor, and those had filled as well. The injured lay wherever there was space. Healers moved among them, tending who they could.

The scents of close-packed humanity overpowered her: the acrid sweat of fear, the cloying stench of death, and, of course, the rich, heady aroma of blood. She clenched her fist, letting her fingernails bite into her palm as Tuana's curse gripped her, forced her hungry eyes to see this vulnerable humanity like a banquet laid out before her.

She wrenched herself away from the infirmary and strode up the corridor.

War had come to Teni'sia....

But there was excitement, even hope, that went with these injuries. The people of Teni'sia had fought, they had suffered, but they had won. Otherwise, they wouldn't be here. Instead of healers running this way and that, tending to the wounded, the castle would be a smoking ruin.

And yet, any battle would have had Mershayn at its center. He would not have stood back and watched others fight. He would have put himself at the front, and he would likely have died for it. The idea of Mershayn lying cold and dead struck at her heart. It shocked her how completely the notion frightened her, and she suddenly realized that this assignment Bands had given her—to protect and guide Mershayn—had turned into something else entirely. Mershayn had become her friend.

Silasa didn't have many friends. She could count them on the fingers of one hand.

Her stride became a spring, and she raced up the hallway to the stairs, whisking past surprised servants. She climbed, leaping six steps at a time, and entered the royal hallway.

Halfway up the hall on the left, Deni'tri and another tall guard stood in front of the king's door, and they tracked her progress.

The tall guard was silent, his uniform clean and his eyes alert. Deni'tri, however, looked like she'd lain in the mud and been run over by a cart. She had soot and dirt smeared across her face and untended bloody scrapes on both elbows as though she had fallen. There was a fresh cut across her cheek and rips in her leather breeches. Her eyes were sunken, with dark rings, but they burned with determination.

"You look like death," Silasa said.

"Lady Silasa." Deni'tri inclined her head.

"How is the king?" she asked, trying to moderate her voice so that it did not leak the panic that had blossomed in her chest.

"Sleeping."

"What happened?"

"The dragons came," Deni'tri said. "They came in the morning, laid waste to everything they could. They burned, killed..."

By the gods...

"Is Mershayn...?" Silasa couldn't bring herself to finish the question. Her mind conjured full-body burns and missing limbs, conjured that cracked head Mershayn had suffered after Collus's assassination.

Deni'tri cocked her head to the side. "My lady?"

"I'll check on him." Silasa moved toward the door, but Deni'tri barred her way.

Silasa raised her eyebrows, surprised. "I will see the king, guardswoman." Silasa put an edge of steel into her voice. Ever before, Deni'tri had taken commands from Silasa like she did Bands or Mershayn himself.

"Respectfully, my lady, no. Lady Bands gave express orders that no one is to disturb the king until he wakes."

Silasa narrowed her eyes. Physically, Deni'tri was no match for Silasa. It would be a simple matter to lift the woman and move her. But in other ways, starting a fight with the palace guard was a problem. Bands had told Silasa to stay vigilant about the climate of Mershayn's allies. To throw Deni'tri out of the way was petty, especially when Deni'tri was a loyal guard just doing her job.

Deni'tri seemed to guess Silasa's thoughts. "I know your powers, my lady. But you'll have to kill me to move me. He saved the kingdom. He fought the largest of the dragons single-handedly."

Silasa was stunned. "Mershayn fought a dragon?"

"King Mershayn. Yes, my lady."

A dragon could carve Silasa into four chunks with one swipe of its claw, could incinerate her with its breath. And some dragons, like Bands, were also accomplished threadweavers. They could have woven Mershayn into oblivion, turned him into a wisp of cloud.

"How?" she asked.

Deni'tri hesitated, and Silasa realized that the guardswoman didn't know. Something inexplicable had happened.

Silasa was about to speak when Deni'tri finally found her tongue. "He didn't stop," Deni'tri said. "He just kept attacking. You should have seen the dragons, my lady. They were giant. They were...horrific. Flying in, landing, crushing people, crushing buildings! People running everywhere, burning alive. I wanted to run, too. I've never wanted to run away so much in my life. I wanted to run until my legs wouldn't carry me anymore. But..."

"But what?"

"But he didn't. He kept me in the fight. All of us. He led us. I looked in those monsters' eyes, and I saw death..." She glanced sideways at the door. "He saw victory. And then took us there, one impossible step at a time. He ran at them. He *frightened* the dragons, my lady, and when the largest of the beasts fled, when it climbed the castle wall to get away from him, our king caught its tail. He refused to let it escape. And when the dragon snapped its jaws over him, he stabbed it through the brain. He never gave up. He showed us that we can beat them."

Silasa couldn't comprehend what Deni'tri was saying. It didn't make sense. A mortal man couldn't chase down a dragon, couldn't kill it. It was impossible.

"So..." Deni'tri cleared her throat. "If Lady Bands says His Majesty must rest, then I will defend his sleep."

Silasa bowed her head. "My apologies, guardswoman. I didn't realize. The king is lucky to have you watching over him. I will return when he has risen."

There was more to this story than Deni'tri's hero-worshipping tale, and Silasa had to find out what it was. She had to find Bands. She had to see the city for herself.

She turned and left the royal wing, sweeping down the hallway and leaping down the stairs a flight at a time like some giant burgundy bat. Startled shouts went up as she ran past.

Silasa had explored the Teni'sian castle top to bottom; she probably knew more about its darkened corners and secret passages now than anyone alive. She navigated her way until she found the door she sought and burst onto the southern walk.

The city was devastated.

The merchant district had been obliterated. Chunks of the wall between the city and castle had been torn away. At least a third of the city had been burned, and maybe half of that had also been crushed by the dragons. Strangely, the ships in the harbor were unharmed. Perhaps the dragons hadn't made it that far before they were overwhelmed by Mershayn's miracle attack.

She looked up at the castle behind her. The conical top of one of the towers had been crushed, the roof completely gone and the stones jutting up like broken teeth.

By the gods, she had missed the entire battle. The dragons attacked in the daylight, and so Silasa had been worthless. She'd been no help to her companions at all.

How had Mershayn and his little army prevailed? She had to find Bands. She had to find—

The hairs on the back of her neck prickled, and she caught a scent of spring wind, grass, and, strangely, the musk of horse. She turned.

Ynisaan stood on the empty rampart behind Silasa. Her snow-white hair trailed over her shoulder and down her left side, a stark contrast to her midnight black face. She still wore the same gray vest over a white tunic, covering her from neck to wrists. She wore the same black breeches and calf-high gray boots.

The last time Silasa had spoken to Ynisaan—or what she thought was Ynisaan—the strange woman had sent her north on a false errand. That errand had kept Silasa out of the fight with Zilok Morth, a battle her friends lost badly, a battle where her strength might have tipped the scales. They'd lost Medophae and Mirolah in one cruel stroke in that fight, and Grendis Sym had taken and tortured Mershayn and Stavark.

"Silasa…" Ynisaan said in a quiet voice, a guilty voice, and Silasa's heart sank. Even though Silasa had assumed betrayal, she had hoped there was an explanation. She didn't want to believe her friend had knowingly sent her away, but rather Silasa had been tricked by some illusion conjured by Zilok Morth, or that Ynisaan herself had been used by the threadweaver, tricked or made to lie.

"Tell me it wasn't you," Silasa whispered. "Tell me I was duped by someone else, someone I didn't consider a friend."

Ynisaan's all-black eyes watched Silasa gravely.

"Tell me that you didn't send me north to get me out of the way," Silasa said. "Tell me it was Zilok Morth."

"Silasa—"

"I trusted you, Ynisaan," Silasa said. "Now is your chance to tell me that my trust was justified. Tell me only Zilok could have been that cruel, to send me away from my friends when they needed me most. Tell me you didn't do it."

Ynisaan's slender hands gripped the edges of her breeches.

Silasa's guts twisted, and she bowed her head. Then it was true. "You sent me away," she whispered. When Ynisaan had first revealed herself to Silasa, bade her go to Daylan's Fountain to save Medophae, Silasa thought she'd found a real friend. More than that, Silasa had found a purpose. She had envisioned helping Ynisaan right the wrongs of these lands for years to come.

"I needed you to—"

"*They* needed me!" Silasa cut her off. "Mershayn and that poor, twelve-year-old quicksilver boy were tortured. Medophae was taken by his nemesis. And Mirolah is *dead*."

"There was no other way—"

"I could have stopped Zilok from taking Medophae."

"No."

"Yes, I would have—"

"You would have died."

Silasa fell silent.

"I looked at the lines and...there was no other way."

"I'm *already* dead," Silasa said. "There was nothing more he could have done to me. But I could have—"

"Zilok was going to peel you like an onion. He was going to leave you quivering in little dry strips. I saw it." Ynisaan raised her chin. "And then he was going to take Medophae anyway. And you would have been dead. And I...I could not have that."

"You lied to me."

"I lied to save you."

"I don't want you to save me! I have no purpose in this cursed life if not to care for those who are better than me. If I'm to live this vile life, feeding off blood, then the one thing I can do is help those I *know* are good. I *have* to, don't you see? I have to choose what is good and right, because what I am is vile and horrible. And you took that choice from me. You took it away!"

"The lands need you, Silasa," Ynisaan said softly. "You are unique, a vampire who holds others' lives above her own. And...I need you."

Silasa bared her fangs. "If I'd been there, could I have at least saved Mirolah? If I couldn't have saved Medophae, then could I have saved her?"

Ynisaan hesitated. "There are more important things than—"

"Could I?"

"Silasa..." Ynisaan trailed off into silence, and Silasa saw the truth in her guilty eyes.

"You bitch," Silasa whispered. "I could have made a difference, and you snatched me away."

"You couldn't have saved her." Ynisaan hesitated. "Not...not in the long run."

"The *long* run?"

"Yes."

"But I could have saved her that night."

"Mirolah was dead in every line I looked at. Every future available to me. There was nothing you could do. Nothing anyone could have done."

Tuana's blood raged through Silasa. She wanted to tear Ynisaan's throat out, wanted to taste the woman's blood on her tongue.

"You betrayed me," Silasa whispered raggedly. "We have nothing left to talk about."

Everything looked red. Even Ynisaan's white hair glinted pink in the moonlight. She could smell the woman's skin, could hear the quiet thump of her heartbeat. It would be so easy to attack. Silasa *wanted* to attack.

She turned and walked away.

"Don't go," Ynisaan whispered, a plea so delicate it caught Silasa. She stopped.

"To stay would be to trust you," she said.

"I need you," Ynisaan said. "I *had* to keep you alive. Humanity has stood at the edge of oblivion so many times. Mother and I were able to push them back. But now, it's only me. And you. And there is something so important right now. It might give humanity a chance. If you leave, I don't know if I can...do it alone." She hesitated. "Please."

"I chose to help you. I believed in you," Silasa growled. "You knew what I'd want, and you took my choice away."

"Silasa—"

"You knew!" Silasa shouted. "And you used me." She clenched her fist and calmed herself. When she spoke again, her voice came out low and even. "My very blood tries to steal my will, to make *my* choices *its* choices. I fight it every moment of my life. I have chosen my friends so carefully because I need people I can trust, who would never try to control me. Because I don't have the strength to fight myself and fight them, too." She paused, clenching her teeth. "Since you don't understand that, I can't listen to you anymore. I can't even be around you." She leapt off the parapet, a stone in her throat.

"But I need you..." Ynisaan whispered in a voice so low a mortal could never have heard it, but Silasa could. The anguish sounded genuine, but it was too late. Silasa couldn't afford to trust someone who had manipulated her, who might be trying to manipulate her right now.

She landed on the cobblestones and ran into the city.

2

BANDS

BANDS PAUSED OUTSIDE of Mershayn's rooms, quietly closing the door as Mershayn's two guards stared stoically forward. She nodded at them and felt a tremendous weight lift from her shoulders. It was time. She done the best she could, and she couldn't put it off any longer.

She could finally begin her search for Medophae.

Bands had begun her life as a watcher. Almost all dragons did. Centuries passed for her kind like seasons passed for humans. Some dragons slept on beds of platinum and gold, blending their threads with the precious metals and dreaming the ages away. Some dragons perched on cliffs for years, looking for patterns in the movement of a mountain and its creatures.

It came naturally to Bands to stand at a distance, to assess a complex system like the kingdom of Teni'sia and see what forces could move it. Once she knew Teni'sia would have to repel dragons, she knew instantly what it required. Stability, foremost. A strong king second. And finally, unity. The odds that a clutch of humans could stand against a flight of dragons was almost zero. But to even have a chance, they needed to come together under one banner. Mershayn had been the answer to that.

She would have stayed in Teni'sia for another few months to ensure that nothing went wrong with Mershayn's fledgling rule, but unfortunately, she had run out of time. Avakketh had sent a half dozen dragons as a test, and he would follow soon after with all of the north. He could be here today for all she knew, and that meant she could no longer stay and coach Mershayn. Teni'sia would have to continue without her.

She hated leaving tasks unfinished. It raised the scales on the back of her neck, but she had to let go of this responsibility. The kingdom had a real king now; Mershayn had exceeded her highest expectations. He'd have to lean on his own judgment now, and he would. The man could make decisions; his headstrong nature saw to that. He could stand up to others with strength; he'd been doing it all his life as a bastard pitted against every noble who looked down on him. And if his powerful charisma didn't swing the skeptics to his banner, his courage would.

She had noted all of these qualities in the first moment she had met him. What she hadn't been able to see instantly was whether Mershayn had the heart of a real king. All the strength and charisma in the world could turn to despotism if a leader had no wisdom, and wisdom came from heart, from knowing that leadership was about serving, not taking.

And now she knew Mershayn had heart. He had flowered in adversity. His capacity to care, to love the people of Teni'sia, surprised her. It was as though he had been waiting for this moment to show his true colors. Instead of making him ravenous, power had made him kind.

For the first time since Avakketh had named her traitor and tried to kill her, Bands felt hope. It was ridiculous to believe she could install a true monarch in a week. And yet here he was. At this final moment when she could no longer put off the search for Medophae, Teni'sia had a king. It was enough to make a jaded dragon believe there actually was an unseen, benevolent god looking after them.

She walked down the hall to the stairway. The two guards nodded at her as she began down the steps.

A millennium and a half ago, she would never have gotten entangled in this broken kingdom, what her lord and god Avakketh would call a swamp of low creatures. But she wasn't a watcher anymore. Medophae had fixed that. A millennium and a half ago, she'd fallen in love with his idea of justice. She'd fallen in love with his heroism. And then she'd fallen in love with him.

Dragons didn't fight injustice. To them, there was no such thing as injustice. The lesser creatures died and the dragons continued. That was simply the way the world was, the way it was meant to be. There was no fair or unfair. Dragons were at the top of the pyramid of Natra's creation, the first mortals, the first sentient race. They didn't battle each other, by decree of their lord and god, but neither did they sacrifice themselves for others of their kind. A dragon's life was about structure, curiosity, and hoarding what attracted them. They didn't build vast protections like castles, or band together for strength because nothing short of a god—or a freakishly powerful threadweaver like Daylan Morth—could even hurt a dragon.

Humans, on the other hand, had been fighting to survive since the first day Tarithalius brought them awake. They could not rely on their vast superiority to survive the sharp edges of the world. They could not rely on innumerable years to grow in power. They built walls taller and stronger than themselves. They created tribes. They invented wondrous devices to bolster their power. They made up stories to give them confidence.

That was why so many legends had been written about Medophae. Humans loved the idea of a man with the power of a god. It gave them hope, made them feel stronger.

Bands had read every legend and epic poem, had heard every ballad sung about her beloved, and the legends often talked about his love for her. Medophae's "Lady-Love Bands" was a common phrase in so many of those stories. They extolled Medophae's love for her, lauded how pure it was, showed how he would do anything for her. They said Medophae's love for her burned like the sun, bright and eternal.

But the legends didn't talk about Bands's love for Medophae, about why a dragon would choose to love a human. She supposed it was because she *was* a dragon, something foreign, something they couldn't comprehend. So the legends portrayed her as an unattainable treasure that Medophae had somehow captured.

Bands's own kind didn't make legends. Their passing of stories were hisses behind her back, a jockeying within the hierarchy of dragonkind, where Bands was the lowest of the low. She was a dragon who debased herself by taking on the weak human form, taking part in their short and brutal lives, and mating with them. In the early days, they saw her as lacking all self-respect. Now, she was a traitor who sided with humans against her own kind.

But dragons didn't know about love. No dragon besides her had ever experienced it, because love was a unique human condition. It hadn't existed in the world before Tarithalius made humans. Up until that moment, the world was a beautiful and deadly place. Animals and plants took what they needed and left what they didn't. Eat, explore, revel in the sunlight or the coolness of the dark, sleep, rise, and then do it all over again. Natra had made a paradise where each creature was an integral part of, and able to enjoy, the world.

Then Tarithalius created love in the makeup of a human. Immediately, humans began doing strange things, behavior never seen before in the other four sentient races. Humans in a tribe began to put the needs of the tribe above their own. One human would obsess over another of her kind, needing to be near him, putting that other person's happiness over her own. Some humans avoided eating and sleeping while mooning over the object of their love. Some sacrificed their lives to be with the person they loved.

Avakketh called it insanity.

But Bands was fascinated by that insanity. She'd never seen anything like it before, and she had watched how it made these little beings more powerful than they would otherwise be. In the thralls of love, humans would often attempt, and sometimes succeed, at tasks that were quite beyond them. Like the dragons who hoarded precious metals and gems, Bands tried to hoard humans. She took a half-dozen humans to Irgakth to study, but once captured, the humans' behavior changed dramatically. Instead of love, their emotions ran to fear and anger. They tried to attack her, so she took them back to where she'd found them and simply watched them from a distance.

And yet, after a time, that wasn't enough. She needed to be closer to them, so she decided she would walk among them.

The first time Bands changed form to interact with humans as one of their own, she could barely contain her glee. Watching them had been a joy, but being one of them heightened the experience beyond anything she'd thought possible.

She ate with them, talked in their tongue, wore their clothes. She became a part of their local politics, spoke out as an active member of their community. She experienced their mating rituals, letting humans take her to bed. She lost herself in their society, reveling in every new sensation. To her, the seventy years of a human life span went in the blink of an eye. Bands moved from tribe to tribe, living many lifetimes in many different places.

That was how she had met Jarissa Chandura, Medophae's mother. They had adventured together for a decade before Jarissa, who eventually discovered that Bands was a dragon, dared her to fly over the True Ocean to see what was beyond.

During each of those adventures, Bands had learned more about humans, but she still hadn't experienced love. Though she lived with them, she was still an outsider in that respect, still an observer.

It was Medophae who taught her how to love.

He was just a boy when she first met him. He had lost his entire family and foolishly challenged the demigod that had killed them. It was insanity, but Medophae's ridiculous courage was delicious to her, and so she followed him as he climbed to his certain death.

Dervon's maggot monster was as formidable as a dragon; it could have killed every human on the island of Dandere with a day's worth of effort. Medophae wasn't remotely a threat to it.

She supposed that was the first time she felt love. What else could it have been, choosing to risk herself to save an inconsequential human life? Another dragon would have let Medophae march to his certain destruction.

But she fought the monster, and she prevailed. And when she did, she felt a euphoria unlike anything she'd ever known.

After the battle, as she flew Medophae across the True Ocean to look for his god, she found herself thinking about how nice it would be to change herself back into a human form and kiss him. She began to dream about it, and her watcher's mind studied her own reactions with keen interest.

A dragon needed to breathe fire at least once every couple of months, otherwise the power would build up and make her sick. As Bands waited, helping Medophae with his quest and wondering if he would invite her to his bed, the anticipation for that kiss built just like dragon fire in her belly. Soon, the wait became excruciating. She could have broken the tension by kissing Medophae first, but she didn't want to instigate it. If she was to experience love, she wanted it to unfold naturally. If she'd learned anything by watching humans, it was that if you grabbed at love, it vanished. If she was to experience love, she wanted it to be pure.

Her patience was rewarded. Finally, he kissed her. It was the night of a thunderstorm, just after Dervon had sent one of his minions to assassinate Medophae. Had Medophae been just another mortal, the monster could have slain easily slain him, but neither Dervon nor Medophae had any idea how powerful he really was.

Medophae had faced the beast alone in the rain and

prevailed. When he returned to the roadside inn where Bands and his other companions waited and told them the story, Bands's eyes must have been glowing with desire. Because afterward he grabbed her, pressed her to him, and kissed her passionately. She melted into him, pushing her fingers into his wild mane of hair. A torrent of indescribable tingles overwhelmed her.

She gasped when he finished, then she pulled him back into the kiss, releasing her pent-up desires at long last. Those tingles bound her to him, like the threads of her body had at last intertwined with his, and she knew she would do anything for him. She would never leave his side to go to another village, to study another group of humans. She would stay with him forever, strive to understand that delicious passion behind his eyes, strive to make herself a part of it, to see what he saw when he looked at the world.

At last, she knew what it was to love. She had uncovered something her fellow dragons didn't understand. Medophae's touch made her knees weak, and the sudden achievement made her watcher's mind giddy.

She gloried in being bound to him...until the rest of the realization hit her. She was *bound* to him. Love had lifted her up, and it had trapped her at the same time. It had changed her, and she had no idea if she could ever change back.

That night, as the sun set, she sat alone, shocked by her new boundaries. She could never return to Irgakth and take her place among dragonkind with Medophae as her mate. They would not accept him. They would kill him. It tortured her for an entire sleepless night.

She could never go home.

But the following morning, Bands had emerged to the rising sun and shed her old life like a coat of old scales. She wasn't a watcher anymore. She had stepped into the stream of human love and conflict, and she would never step out again. She would never be a watcher again.

The sweet reminiscence faded, and Bands touched the wall of the stairway, feeling its solidity, feeling how she was a part of humankind's story now.

To a dragon, this castle was unbelievably crude. The idea of painstakingly carving stone from the side of a mountain with hands and tools was ludicrous. When dragons built structures, they used threadweaving, making the threads obey them to create what was needed. But when Bands touched these stones, she felt the effort, the passion, the desire of the hands that had shaped them. She loved them, these vulnerable creatures who reached so high.

She took a deep breath and, for the thousandth time, felt the joy of her choice the night she'd bound herself to Medophae. It was worth everything. All the suffering and pain, all the losses. Still, even now, it was worth it.

And now it was time to find him, release him from the clutches of his nemesis.

Bands descended the steps, deeper and deeper into the castle, down to the dungeons. What she needed was below.

When it became clear that even her dragon eyes couldn't see the details of the stairway, she opened her threadweaver's sight. A myriad of colors lit the granite walls, the rats in the holes, the light smoke grime over the arched ceiling, the smears of dirt across the flagstones. Even the air had threads. This kind of vision was what threadweavers saw when they cast spells, but she could use it to see in the dark.

As a dragon, Bands could go without sleep for a month if she needed to. Dragonkind stored energy like they stored fire in their bellies, and she hadn't slept since Mershayn took the throne. During the days, she had stayed close to the new king, supporting him. At night, she had researched in Teni'sia's dusty library, which apparently only Queen Tyndiria and a handful of nobles ever used.

That, in and of itself, was her first shock about this new world, four hundred years after her imprisonment in Ethiel's ruby. The general populace of Amarion didn't read. They feared the accumulation of written knowledge, and the threadweavers. They held these things responsible for the hardships of humankind. To them, books were a horrible, filthy thing, and in many parts of Amarion, all books had been destroyed out of hand.

Thankfully, that was not the case in Teni'sia.

Bands had four hundred years of human history to review, so she had spent her nights alone, reading. She had also lingered in the royal kitchens, on the streets of the city, down by the wharf, listening to snatches of conversation, trying to fill in the gaps in culture.

She had also sat down with Silasa, listening to her recount everything she remembered from the century just after Bands had been imprisoned, before Silasa herself had gone to sleep after Harleath Markin had imprisoned the GodSpill within Daylan's Fountain. Silasa had also told her about everything that had happened since she'd "reanimated", as she put it. She told about assisting Medophae, about saving the quicksilver boy, and about saving Mershayn.

Bands had listened intently to the story Silasa told about pulling Mershayn out of the Teni'sian dungeons. Zilok Morth had lived in this castle for a time. Likely, he'd made a lair.

That was the first step in finding him.

She didn't think Zilok would still be there, but there would be clues for someone with the eyes to see them. One clue was all she needed.

She finally stopped, standing in the spot Silasa had described where she and Mershayn had almost stumbled across Zilok. The spirit had been talking to someone in this hall.

With her threadweaver's sight, Bands looked deeper for a hint of the undead threadweaver.

Every threadweaver had distinctive, telltale traits. With some threadweavers, Bands could "smell" something when she viewed them. With others, colors danced around them or left wispy trails in the air behind them. With some, Bands could taste water on her tongue when they were near, or the back of her neck would prickle. Of course, none of these things were actually happening. It was the mind's way of translating something that could not be translated to normal senses. The threads of the world couldn't be seen by the five mortal senses, but she had no way to experience the signals without ascribing them to sight, sound, taste, touch, or smell.

Zilok tasted like poisonous white dust and often flared with blue light. And, as she scanned the threads, she tasted a hint of his acrid tang on her tongue. He had, indeed, been here.

Bands meandered forward. There were three doors along the left-hand wall. Her tongue took her to the last door on the left. It was slightly ajar, and she remained in front of it, motionless, for a long time. One did not rush into the lair of Zilok Morth if one wished to live.

But Bands was patient. She stood outside that door and let her senses move past the threads of the door, into the threads of the air of the room, into the floor and the walls inside.

She spent a long hour standing outside the door, methodically searching every nook and cranny of that room. There was a circular table with various implements Zilok might use for a complicated threadweaving. More importantly, she found three hanging spells, waiting for the unwary to walk in and trip them. She didn't know what the spells did exactly, but she could guess....

One of the static spells would likely disable or kill any normal person who opened the door. The second would likely strip the defenses from a threadweaver. And the third one... Well, she didn't have a guess as to that. No doubt it was the most insidious of the three, as she had almost not found it. It was well-hidden. Had she been even a little less methodical, she would have missed it.

That spell was worrisome. Her assumption was that Zilok had built this lair while setting his trap for Medophae, then had abandoned it after. The first hanging spell was for normal people. The second was for Mirolah, most likely. But the third...

Likely the third spell might have been left specifically to harm Bands. It was much too subtle for a novice threadweaver. She'd have to be careful.

But the "scent" of Zilok was old. This area had not been used in more than a week, at least. That was longer than

Mershayn had been sitting the throne.

She knelt before the doorway, closed her eyes, and cleared her mind. Murmuring three words, she wove the threads of the air about herself, changed their color to harden them into a shield that would brunt the first hanging spell, the physical attack.

She opened the door.

As she had seen, a circular stone table dominated the middle of the room, and stone shelves on the far side of the room displayed tomes and jars. The table held the bloody head of a badger severed at the neck, the skeleton of a rat or a squirrel, and the corpse of a rabbit. They were laid out roughly in a triangle, and a pile of crushed granite lay between them. To the side was a closed steel box.

Just as Bands used dragon words and sometimes her own pain to focus her mind, Zilok used cruelty. He liked killing things. Somehow, the suffering of others helped him stabilize his mind. She tried to understand the logic of why he'd chosen what he had.

Three burrowing creatures, and rock powder.

She longed to explore what he had been doing here, to piece it together, but first things first. She stepped into the room—

The first spell activated. A shockwave rammed into her, followed by a blast of fire. Both smashed against her shield and washed around her.

She stayed alert, and saw the second spell activate.

It was exactly what she'd expected: a threadweaver trick from the Age of Ascendance wherein an experienced threadweaver could make an inexperienced threadweaver believe they'd been stripped of their power.

There was space between the threads, and this trick was like putting two fingers between the weave of a rug and yanking open a hole. Essentially, it encased the hapless threadweaver in a small bubble where they couldn't reach any threads, or at least thought they couldn't. Combined with a panic-inspiring speech, it could be powerful against the uninitiated, especially with Zilok's terrifying reputation. It could drive a young threadweaver instantly to despair.

Ah ha! I am the great Zilok Morth, the oldest and most powerful of all threadweavers. See how I can simply take away your power....

But Bands knew the trick. And panicking was unproductive.

She murmured a word, forcing her threadweaver sight beyond the small vacuum the spell had created. Once past that empty space, she felt the threads again. With a gesture, she pulled the bubble spell apart at its source, just as it had pulled the threads away from her. The spell sputtered and died, and the fabric of reality settled in around her once more.

Then the third spell, the mystery spell, activated, following immediately after the second. To normal eyes, nothing changed. But because Bands was watching for it, she saw a tiny flicker of fire come and go in a dark corner of the room. It was a doorway, opened and closed quick as a blink, releasing something. Something—

The bakkaral attacked.

Bands saw it a blurred instant before it hit her, and she jerked to the side. The needle teeth sank into her injured shoulder, and heat from the flaming ridge on its back washed over her. Bands stifled her scream and forced her agony into a tunnel of focus.

Dragon speech flowed from her lips, and she pulled threads, altered colors. An orange flash burst in her vision as the flaming ridge along the bakkaral's back resisted her. That flame made the bakkaral immune to all basic threadweaving. It was what made them such effective threadweaver killers.

But Bands wasn't a novice, and the bakkaral's little shield was nothing compared to a dragon's scales. She picked a spot where the flame didn't flicker so bright and drove her will through it like a nail through steel.

Now she saw the burgundy colors of the beast's threads. She reached into its head and changed a dozen of those threads to a harmless beige color.

The bakkaral's sharp teeth dulled, shrank, vanished.

It shrieked and leapt away from her, shocked. Through watering eyes, she kept her gaze on it. It still had claws and speed, could flay skin from her body.

But bakkarals were bullies. They only liked a fight when they knew they would win. It had not expected her to be able to take its teeth away. It backed off, leapt onto the wall, and clung there. Its insane eyes pulsed in its head as it stared at her.

It sprang.

Bands waved a hand and spoke again. A stone chain shot from the wall like a tentacle and wrapped around the bakkaral's leg just as the creature reached her. The thing jerked to a stop a foot from her. Two claws cut the breeze in front of her face. The flame on its back flared, and cracks appeared in the chain.

Bands grunted, pushed her will against the bakkaral's. It felt like she was trying to force her head through a stone wall. For a tense moment, they struggled.

You…are just…a bakkaral….

The wall shattered. The links in her chain solidified, transforming from stone to steel.

The bakkaral snapped its gums, leapt at her again, claws extended. Again, it came up short. Bands stepped back calmly.

The bakkaral fell to the ground, lancing her with a glare, and mewling in frustration.

Blood trickled steadily from Bands's new wound, and she allowed herself a deep breath. There were no more surprises in this room. She and the bakkaral were alone.

She spoke her thoughts aloud. "Bad luck for you."

The bakkaral turned its insane smile upon her, which might have been intimidating if it had teeth. "My master will see you burn for this, fledgling threadweaver," it said, then pulled suddenly against the chain.

It thinks I am Mirolah. It was given instructions to wait here and kill a young threadweaver.

She wondered how long the bakkaral had been stuffed in that pocket dimension, waiting for Mirolah to stumble along here and discover it. She wondered how much longer it would have stayed there if Bands hadn't come along. Forever, perhaps. Zilok wasn't known for caring much about his servants.

"Where is your master?" she asked.

"Free me, and I will tell you."

With a word and a wave, Bands shortened the chain. It dragged the bakkaral closer to the wall. The bakkaral's claws dug grooves into the stone.

Bands moved to the table. The bakkaral jumped against the chain, to no avail. It wasn't going anywhere.

"When I free myself, I will eat your eyes first," it said. "I will make you watch as I swallow the first one like an egg. Then I will make you listen as I chew on the second. Then, while you are still alive, I will begin eating your head."

She ignored him and moved toward the steel box on top of the table, contemplating its contents again: a badger head, a rat skeleton and a desiccated rabbit corpse. Three burrowing creatures, and rock powder.

He'd been trying to affect something underground.

Zilok's spell components didn't concern her as much as the box, though. She reached out, holding her hands an inch away from it. A foreboding hovered around, the powerful smell of oiled steel and fresh sap, and she didn't touch it. Instead, she pushed the threads of the air against it, lifting it up and bringing it closer to the edge of the table. With that same fingerless touch, she opened the lid.

To a non-threadweaver, the box was empty, but Bands saw the glowing residue of something that had resided within; green, gold, and blue fire swirled like soup in the bottom. She tasted that tree sap on her tongue, and she heard the rush of the wind, smelled the ocean this time. Her fingertips pulsed like she was touching a chest with a strongly beating heart.

By the gods...

The Crown of Natra had been in this box. He'd kept the crown here.

"I will drag my claws along your pretty belly, letting it blossom with your entrails," the bakkaral hissed.

The Crown of Natra had been underground. Zilok had

used the burrowing creatures and the dust of bedrock to focus his will. And this was where he had dragged the crown to the surface.

Usually, the handiwork of a threadweaver only triggered one sense. In particularly strong threadweavers, it triggered a couple of the senses, like Zilok's blue light and poisonous dust.

The residue of the Crown of Natra triggered every sense she had, and more residue coalesced in the room. A trail of green, gold, and blue flickers floated on the air, connecting the box to the stone wall. The wafting colors went into the stone wall and through to the other side.

Her heart beat faster in excitement. She'd hoped to find a clue as to where Zilok had gone. Instead, he'd left her a trail as obvious as coal dust on snow.

She knew the crown was hurting him, but this trail indicated that Zilok was leaking GodSpill like a wounded deer.

"Your mistake," she murmured. "There's no place you can hide now."

"You know then," the bakkaral said. "You know who lay in wait for you here."

Bands had almost forgotten about the bakkaral.

"He is a fiend. He turned my mind. He made me attack you. I only wished to return home," the bakkaral said. "Set me free."

"You tried to kill me."

"I was forced, mistress. But you are greater than he who trapped me. I can see it. You will prevail against him."

"Tell me where he went."

The insane eyes looked to the left, then back at her. "Deeper in the castle, mistress. He awaits you there, but you are too powerful. You will have him in the end. I can see it. Go, destroy him. But first, set me free."

The wafting, colorful residue of the crown went through the outer wall of the castle, to the north, not down. The bakkaral was lying.

Bands came closer to the creature, knelt down to put herself eye to eye with it. "I think you're feeding me a story."

The bakkaral hissed and jerked on the chain, trying to reach her but failing. It let out a sigh. "I was taken from my forest. Brutally beaten. Kidnapped."

"Now I *know* you're lying." Bakkarals were well known for hunting supernatural creatures of any kind, especially threadweavers, and especially the untrained. It was how they evolved. The flame along a bakkaral's back grew in power every time they fed on a creature filled with GodSpill. And there was no sweeter, fuller prize than a young human threadweaver. "I think you made a deal, bakkaral. I think you chose to be Zilok's guard dog. He promised you the blood of a young, novice threadweaver—"

"No," the bakkaral interrupted, too quickly. "Like you, I am a victim."

Bands chuckled. "There's only one victim in this room, bakkaral. You're lucky that it wasn't Mirolah who came to this place," she said. The bakkaral's eyelids twitched. Yes. He knew that name, and now she knew the truth. "She would have erased you."

"And what will you do?" the bakkaral asked, an edge of desperation in his voice.

"Not a thing." She stood up.

"Mistress," the bakkaral whined. "Don't leave me here, tied down like this."

She went to the door.

"Mistress! It was the legendary Zilok Morth. I could not refuse him. What would you have done?"

"I would have succeeded."

She slammed the door and whispered a word, turning threads. The wooden door warped, blurred, became a solid steel plate, built straight into the stones.

"Mistress!"

"If I defeat your master," she said through the steel wall, "I will return for you. Best pray for my success."

"Mistress!"

She turned and strode up the corridor.

The cries of the bakkaral faded behind her.

3

BANDS

BANDS LEFT THE DUNGEONS, but she avoided any populated areas of the castle. Mershayn would be waking, going to meet with the Sunriders, and the nobles would be waiting for him with a thousand questions. The populace of the kingdom would want to lavish him with the accolades of a hero. And Mershayn, if he could, would lean on her. If Bands stepped into that maelstrom for even a moment, it would sweep her away.

She only went a short distance before she came to the room Zynder had used as his lair while spying on Teni'sia. It opened onto the northern mountains. Dark clouds hung over those white slopes, and gusts of wind kicked up the snow far below. The quiet before a storm.

Whispering, she twisted the threads of air to have them blow upward. She lifted her arms, whispering again, and solidified a sheet of air between her wrists and ankles, forming invisible wings. The gust lifted her up, and she dove down the side of the castle wall. Soon, she saw the little waft of green-blue-gold color swirling out of a drift against the base of the castle. She landed next to it, but didn't touch it.

The Crown of Natra was powerful but cursed. It would devour Zilok, devour anyone except the goddess Natra herself. Zilok had seized that power, and now it was draining him. And in his pain and fear, he'd slipped in his meticulousness. She must move swiftly to make the most of it. If she didn't find Zilok before the Crown devoured him, there might be no clues to find her beloved. She had to dangle the promise of help over Zilok until he revealed where Medophae had been imprisoned.

Bands whispered a handful of words. Her body changed, green dress and human flesh blending together as she transformed into a white lynx with green tips on its ears. She ran across the snow, following the waft of green, blue, and gold colors.

Zilok, when the residue of his threadweaving manifested as a color, was blue. Medophae was gold. She could only assume that the residue of green was left over from Natra herself.

She stayed in the lee of the mountain, utilizing the morning shadows. The wispy trail became brighter as she ran through the snow, up ridges and down. The sun was high in the sky when she stopped. Her breath came out in little white puffs. She lifted her feline nose to the air and caught the scent of human. She squinted up the slope. The trail disappeared halfway up the mountain.

She loped to the west, circling far around the slope and then up the mountain, positioning herself above the tiny opening, nearly covered over with snow. She sniffed again. There was a human in there, but not one she recognized. Not her beloved....

Wait.

She closed her eyes and stretched the senses of the form she had adopted. The cold, crisp smell of snow filled her nostrils, creating the background from which the other scents jumped. The musk of an unwashed body filled that cave, but there was more. There was also the swell of warmth, some source that wasn't a fire made the cave livable for that unknown human. And dried beef and grain, supplies no doubt also to keep the human live.

But there was another scent: blood. Familiar blood.

Her heart beat faster, and she tried to tamp down her excitement. That was Medophae's blood. The unwashed human's scent wasn't Medophae, but the blood was. She knew that scent as well as she knew her own. She had smelled Medophae in health, in injury, in excitement, in apprehension. *It's him. He's here.*

Urgency grasped at her, but Bands calmed herself. She had stumbled across her prize, right here, so close to Teni'sia. If she could free Medophae this quickly, then the army Mershayn planned to take north might actually have a chance at success.

She had to move fast, strike hard, and fight smart. Every attack must be overwhelming, and it must hit a weakness. And Zilok's weakness was his anchor.

She dropped down, transformed into her human form, and strode into the cave.

A short hallway about twenty feet long led into a circular room. There didn't seem to be any passageways leading away. Against the far wall stood the first human she'd smelled—a cowled man. She reached out with her threadweaver's fingers, touching him lightly. She could see the threads of his flesh, his blood rushing through his veins. She whispered, weaving a net around his body and pinning him to the cavern wall, and then she frowned.

His mind was scrambled, his life's energy low, both signs of being an undead spirit's anchor. But she couldn't see any cord emerging from him. He was just a used-up husk of a person, like someone who had once been Zilok's anchor, but was no longer....

She suddenly realized who he must be. This poor, tortured human was Orem, the companion that Medophae and Mirolah had been searching for when Bands had been introduced to them as Elekkena.

But he wasn't Zilok's anchor.

She stayed where she was, hesitant to move. If Orem wasn't Zilok's anchor, then what was he? Why was he here? Zilok didn't keep former slaves for sentimental reasons.

The foul spirit's handiwork was everywhere, and she tried to unravel what it might mean. The cave was filled with threadweaving. Spells hung in almost every space, many in the icy blues of Zilok's handiwork, but there were also others in different colors. That struck her as odd. Anything Zilok created should have his mark on it. She could only assume that the crown allowed him to do things she was unfamiliar with. She kept her guard up, looking into the threads, listening to them, smelling them. In a room so filled with spells, Zilok might be able to conceal himself, but she doubted it.

She cautiously kept a piece of her attention on Orem, silent and cowled, as she surveyed the room.

The rough cavern walls had been changed to look like polished stone blocks covered with tasteful paintings and tapestries. The illusion of a statue stood in the center of the circular room, as well as the illusion of a huge, round table. A round rug embroidered with intricate scenes of unicorns and pegasi covered most of the floor, and another long rug ran all the way to the entrance. A fire burned inside the stone of the far wall, right next to the unmoving man. But it gave off no smoke, only heat. It was pure threadweaving. There were so many spells in this place that she couldn't separate them all out.

This jumble could have been created to distract her from pinpointing Zilok, or they could have simply been the spirit's vanity, allowing him to pretend to luxuriate in living comforts when he wasn't actually alive. Still, it wasn't going to fool—

She parted one of the illusions around the table. Beneath it lay Medophae.

She kept her gasp behind her teeth and continued to study the area with caution, though her heart hammered and she longed to leap forward and help him.

He was unconscious, lying on his side, head against the stone floor, and he was bound in layer upon layer of threadweaving so powerful that he shimmered. His arms had been tied in front of him, elbows bound with glowing green coils so tight his shoulders had been wrenched from their sockets. His right hand had been severed, and the stump was bound in a cloth soaked with blood. That was how she had caught his scent in her lynx form.

Her heart twisted to see him like that.

She wanted to rush to him, but she held that need in check. She reached into the threads that surrounded him, and it was like sticking her hand into a pile of hay. So much threadweaving!

Wrapped in illusions that had hidden it from her until now, a single spell twisted out of the center of Medophae's chest and floated through the air into the rock wall, a vibrating pulse of blue and green light, stronger than all the rest.

That was the anchor spell, a cord that bound Zilok to mortality. He had made Medophae his mortal anchor!

The audacity of it staggered her, but of course it was exactly what Zilok would do. He never failed to overreach. He must have pulled Oedandus away from Medophae with the Crown of Natra, and once Medophae's power was drained, Zilok could have formed this link.

It was the worst thing Bands could imagine, and just the kind of revenge Zilok had dreamed about for centuries.

She pressed her lips together grimly. She'd come to chastise Zilok and make him reveal where he kept Medophae. But now she'd achieved her goal, and any dealings with Zilok could be of the lethal nature. In fact, she could free Medophae and destroy Zilok with one strike.

Ignoring the writhing mess of threadweaving all about her, she focused only on the anchor spell. It was the key, the only thing in this room that mattered. She could free Medophae and send Zilok through the Godgate all at once, but it would require striking fast and as hard as she could. Her slightest touch upon the cord would be like putting a dagger to his throat. Once Zilok felt her tampering with it, he would fight her with everything he had.

She prepared herself, calming her mind and bringing herself to clarity. Then she reached out and grabbed the cord that twisted out of Medophae. Her ethereal fingers sliced through it with one mighty stroke....

Nothing happened.

It was like trying to cut a chain with a kitchen knife. She sawed at it, pulled at it, wrenched at it with all of her might, but it was too thick. Bands had the strength of a dragon and millennia of experience threadweaving, but this bond was godlike.

"No..." she whispered. A sentience shivered through the bond, obviously a twitch from Zilok, wherever he was. He'd sensed her. She had only seconds now. No matter how far away Zilok was, he was a spirit. He could cross vast distances nearly instantaneously.

The threads were hungry, twisting to reach for Zilok, filled with every ounce of power he had and every ounce he'd stolen from the Crown of Natra. Thinking fast, Bands started small. Instead of trying to cut the entire twisted cord, she pulled out one tiny golden thread of the thick mass of blues, greens, and golds. With effort, she severed it, then grabbed the next. Again and again and again...

When she had quickly cut through a hundred of the tiny threads, she paused in her handiwork, and her heart sank. The severed ends hung in the air for a moment, then began questing like floating worms, seeking their master. Once they touched their matching end, they reformed the bond.

No!

She couldn't do this fast enough. Given even a brief instant, the threads would just seek their original host...

...unless she offered them a different host.

She could take the threads and connect them to herself instead. That would keep them from seeking their original master.

The idea of slaving Medophae to herself sickened her, but her beloved would understand. The only way to undo Zilok's anchor was to cut his connection and take it into herself. Then, once she'd sent Zilok through the Godgate, she could gently remove the bond from her beloved.

She leapt to stand in front of the cut threads that quested through the air. She plunged her threadweaver's fingers into them, then guided them into her. They latched on like leeches, blending with her threads, sending a tiny jolt, like a pinprick, of power into her.

Yes! This will work.

"Hold on, my beloved," she whispered.

"Don't..." Orem said in a monotone.

She jerked her head up. The man's mind had been so abused and tangled up with Zilok's mind-hazing spells that he shouldn't have been able to form a conscious thought, let alone speak a word. She thought of how Medophae, Mirolah, and even the quiet Stavark had spoken of Orem with such high praise. He had been a man of principle, a driven man, a man of strong will. But that will had been crushed by Zilok Morth. Anything he said could only be an extension of his master's will. Zilok was obviously speaking through Orem, a desperate attempt to distract her as he rushed to get here.

She plucked another thread, severed it, and attached it to herself, then another. Quick as a thought, she severed and connected, over and over again. The power turned from pinpricks into a sparkling trickle, then into a river. She felt GodSpill flow into her through the increasing connection. She used that power to go faster, cutting and connecting, cutting and connecting. She didn't know how long it took her to sever each individual thread and pull it into herself, but when half of them were connected to her, the transfer gained a life of its own. Rather than seeking Zilok, the threads now sought her, hungry, connecting to her all by themselves once they had been cut.

She gasped as the final threads broke away and plunged into her body.

"Yes..." she said. She felt the flavor of Oedandus, his recklessness, his golden power. It filled her, and the god's energy went to work on her shoulder immediately, healing the horrible wound Saraphazia had given her. Bands gasped at the relief, and dared to hope that her wing, in her dragon form, might also be healed. She had seen Medophae recover from the most grisly wounds imaginable.

She also felt residues of Zilok's cold blue power, connecting her to all of the spells that Zilok had wrought in this place. She saw them now with greater clarity.

"Don't..." Orem repeated. "Don't..."

Still more GodSpill flowed into her, a refreshing, life-giving swell the color of green. What power was this? Why would Medophae have power within him of such a deep, life-giving green color?

She had expected Zilok to show up and fight for his anchor, but with all of the extra power coming into her from Medophae, she must have severed the cord more quickly than she thought. Now Zilok must certainly be struggling to keep himself from floating up to the Godgate.

"Medophae," she whispered. "Wake up...."

With Zilok's blue-tinged GodSpill coursing through her, all of the spirit's illusions came into clearer focus. Rather than seeing just a tangle of threadweaving, she could sort them out now. The table. The rugs. The polished walls.

The illusion of her beloved on the floor...

Her heart stopped.

Medophae wasn't there. He was...a construct, just like everything else in this frozen cave. But how... Then how could she feel Oedandus...?

Nothing else could exude such power. Nothing else except...

By the gods, no....

She tore at the illusion, ripping away dozens of layers of spells like handfuls of wrapping paper. Behind the half-destroyed illusions of her beloved's body swirled gold, green, and blue GodSpill. At the center of the thready bundle, the Crown of Natra lay on the floor. The thick cord she had severed and attached to herself didn't come from her beloved. It came from the crown.

Behind her, Zilok began to laugh.

She spun around.

He stood in his human-seeming form by the fire, a hand on Orem's shoulder. With the dazzling amount of GodSpill that coursed through her, she could easily see the twisting blue cord that now connected Zilok to Orem.

"Don't..." Orem said again in a monotone.

"Quiet, Orem," Zilok admonished.

The cowled man hesitated, as though he was fighting Zilok's control, then said, "Yes, my master."

I am a fool. I'm a stupid, lovesick fool.

A spirit could anchor himself to the mortal world using another living thing, which was the method Zilok had always preferred. But it wasn't the only way. A threadweaver could also use a powerful arcane object as an anchor. Zilok hadn't created an anchor to Medophae. He'd created an anchor to the Crown of Natra. And she'd just cut it, freed him, and she had taken the killing burden of the Crown of Natra onto herself.

Instinctively, she tried to sever the connection, but it was the kitchen knife all over again, hacking futilely at a chain.

I've killed myself. And so I've killed any hope to save Amarion.

"You and your quiet superiority," Zilok murmured, his voice a low rumble in the cave. "So calm, as though you are above it all." His blue eyes glowed. "I cannot tell you how deeply satisfying it is to see that stupid expression of horror on your face, the knowledge that have I outwitted you for the last time. The knowledge that you will die."

She swallowed.

"Every moment of our talk in the Teni'sian garden was a dance, dragon, and I was the choreographer. I lied to your face, and you swallowed it because you wanted to. Because you envision yourself to be above me."

"Zilok, you don't understand what you've—"

He laughed. "Yes. Please tell me what I don't understand. You, who lie snared by the knowledge I possess that you do not. That would make my victory complete. Tell me all that I don't know as I crush you. It tastes like honey on my tongue."

"Avakketh is going to destroy Amarion, and you've set your focus on petty revenge."

"Sell your noble ideals to those with bleeding hearts, dragon. I have no heart to move."

"You've betrayed your own kind."

"I've kept our bargain. A bargain, no doubt, that you would have broken the first moment you could."

"We have no bargain—"

"I said I would help you defeat Avakketh if you helped me rid myself of the crown. The Crown of Natra can take Avakketh's power and turn it back on him. It is how I defeated Medophae. You could do the same with Avakketh. You've helped me rid myself of the crown, and I have aided you in your war, dragon. This is the weapon you need to win. All it will cost you is your life." He gave her a smile. "If you are truly as self-sacrificing as you claim, now is your chance to prove it."

Bands seethed. Her mind buzzed with thoughts of vengeance.

"I can see your pride boiling on the surface of that fake face of yours. But I am right. When you calm down, you'll see it. I've given you a gift. And who knows, if I am feeling generous at the end, I will bring Medophae to see you as you die." He winked. "And you can make one last legend to stand the test of time."

Bands looked at Orem. She almost reached out and killed the man. She had plenty of GodSpill at her command. It would deprive Zilok of his new anchor. She might even, with her new power, be able to follow Zilok wherever he might go, keep him from gaining a new anchor. She might be able to extinguish him for good.

"Choices, choices..." Zilok whispered, as though he could read her thoughts. "But they are tough choices wrapped in hard questions. Would you really kill an innocent to get to me?" He patted Orem's shoulder. "Would it be worth it to sacrifice those tattered ideals of yours just to have your vengeance?"

"I think I'll just guide you through the Godgate." She

understood now that the reason the cord had been so difficult to sever was because the crown itself—a spell created by Natra—had resisted her. That wouldn't be the case with Zilok's new bond with Orem.

"Fair enough, but then you would give up your chance to defeat Avakketh by...how did you put it? 'Setting your focus on petty revenge.'"

"Destroying you will be the first step," she hissed. "Avakketh next."

"Oh," he said. "You don't see it. Then let me tell *you* what *you* don't know. The more you use the crown, the more it pulls from you, draining your very life. I think..." he mused, "I think if I had picked up the crown and put it back down, I would have been allowed to leave it behind. But once I used it, the hooks dug in. The more I used it, the more it turned on me. And you, well, you've already used it to tear away my illusions. And perhaps to sever my connection to the crown as well?" He raised an eyebrow.

He was right. She felt the hooks inside her, just as he described, and she didn't have a clue how to unhook them.

She clenched her fists.

"Save your strength," he whispered, softly, almost delicately. "Without Medophae, you will need it."

"I'm going to kill you," she swore.

"Don't forget to save Amarion first." He winked, turned, and walked through the cavern wall. Orem waited, the cowl shadowing his face, then he vanished as though he had never been.

She longed to chase after Zilok, to rip that smug expression from his insubstantial face, but that was what had landed her in this trap: following her passion to the exclusion of her good sense. Now the Crown of Natra had hold of her. For better or worse, she was its wielder. It was a death trap, but Zilok was also right: it might be the answer to defeating Avakketh. The crown was the only thing besides Medophae that might do it.

She had to calm her emotions and think it through. Natra

had ruled the gods with the crown for longer than Bands had been alive. Could she really do the same? Zilok had turned Oedandus against Medophae, so it was possible, however unlikely, that she could use the crown to turn Avakketh's own power against him. That would tip the scales in her favor. No matter what Avakketh threw at her, she could simply redirect it back at him.

Until she knew the answer to that question, she couldn't go chasing off after Zilok Morth on a personal quest for revenge. She simply...couldn't.

She reached down and picked up the crown. Letting out a breath of resignation, she set it on her head.

4

MERSHAYN

MERSHAYN ROSE FROM THE TUB, dripping, and dried himself off. His hair was still wet and sent an occasional chilly rivulet down his back. He pulled on his breeches and boots, shouldered on his doublet, and tried not to hear the echo of Bands's absence, or about how he'd probably never see her again. She'd held the kingdom steady, had made the impossible possible, and now she had left.

He belted on the sword, looked at the wire-wrapped hilt, the small obsidian stone set in the pommel, then drew the blade. It slithered out with the satisfying sound of a well-made sheath, and he smelled the fresh oil on the blade. Someone had taken good care of it. Probably Deni'tri. He'd have to commend her for that, though he wondered if an enchanted blade needed oiling.

Mershayn had owned a dozen swords in his life, but none felt like this. This had been made to fit in his hand, as if it had been crafted just for him. It hadn't been made for him, of course, so it had to be the enchantment of the thing, that feeling. The blade was his, and it felt like it had a destiny.

It needs a name.

He didn't know what history this sword had before Stavark put it in his hands, but it was legendary now. The blade that had slain the dragon would undoubtedly make it into at least one song about the dragon battle of Teni'sia. Great weapons were idolized by swordsmen and laymen alike.

He waved it back and forth, imagining the stories, the adventures that he might have had with this sword. A young rogue swordsman with his trusted drinking companions, traveling throughout Amarion, saving caravans of merchants from bands of brigands. Flirting with ladies both noble and lowborn...

You're stalling.

He sighed. His real adventure didn't much resemble that glowing fantasy. He was the king of Teni'sia now, and kings didn't have swashbuckling adventures. Kingship was a rickety cart overflowing with compromised choices, crushing responsibility, and unwinnable battles. Instead of being surrounded by trusted drinking companions, he was propped up by supernatural creatures and assailed by scheming nobles. He couldn't slash his foes with daring sword work; he had to pat them with flattery, reason with them, nudge them in the right direction inch by inch. There were no absolute victories, and the last lady to flirt with him was sharpening a dagger with his name on it.

Wallowing in self-pity. That's becoming. Let's definitely keep this up.

He let out the single breath of a laugh. It was funny. Him, wallowing in self-pity. He, who had dared the gods to cast him down, who'd broken every law he could find and smugly dared anyone to punish him. He laughed again, and this time it rolled into a chuckle. The chuckle rolled into a belly laugh.

And then he couldn't stop.

It was all so ridiculous. Mere months ago, he'd been a cocksure, resentful bastard biting his thumb at every authority he could.

Now, not only was he king, but dragons—which weren't

supposed to exist—were coming south to destroy them all. A vampire—also something that wasn't supposed to exist—was the closest thing he had to a friend. And the legendary lover of the demigod Wildmane had not only put him on the throne, but had then yanked the carpet out from under him only moments ago, telling him she was leaving.

He laughed harder.

And... And he'd fallen in love with a dead woman!

He laughed so hard he had to set his sword on the bed and put his hands on his knees, gasping for breath through his giggles.

His beloved was a corpse, lying in state in some room, and he loved her so much that he didn't even want another woman. Him, not wanting another woman! He didn't want Ari'cyiane, didn't want some other noblewoman. No, he loved a dead body.

His laughter pealed through the room.

A knock sounded on the door, and Deni'tri's concerned voice came through muffled. "Your Majesty?"

And now my bald, scar-faced guard is here to tell me that the murdering, raping Sunriders have come to Teni'sia to parley peace with me.

He doubled over, laughing harder.

Deni'tri opened the door and looked down at him with furrowed brows.

He waved a hand, but he was laughing so hard he couldn't breathe. "It's so funny..." he managed to whisper between laughs.

She opened her mouth, closed it, opened it again, but obviously couldn't find what she wanted to say. She looked over her shoulder as though the answer might be standing in the door.

Mershayn guffawed.

There is no one in the doorway with the answers, guardswoman. Bands left. There was just the ridiculous lot of them, clueless humans, here with no answers, ready to take orders from the whoreson, corpse-loving bastard with a crown.

A flash of silver lit the room, and suddenly Stavark stood there, hands at his sides, a frown on his serious little face. He glanced at Deni'tri. "What is wrong with him?"

"He just started laughing," she replied. "Maybe it's a mind sickness? Bands checked his head for scrapes or bumps. She said he was healthy."

Mershayn fell on the bed, giggling in fits.

"This is not good," Stavark said.

Mershayn held up a hand. "I'm fine," he gasped, but then couldn't talk as the laughter doubled him over. He held his sides.

Stavark swiveled his head to look at Deni'tri again. "I have never seen such a thing."

"I'm just..." Mershayn gasped, talking through the laughter. "I'm just..."

Deni'tri stepped forward, frowning, and he could tell she meant to slap him.

He held up his hands. "Please..." He sucked in a breath. "I'm okay. I'm okay." He finally got a hold on his laughter, and he gulped breaths and managed to speak. "I'm just...I was thinking of a name for my sword."

Stavark's gaze flicked to the blade laying on the bed, then to Mershayn.

"And I..." Mershayn said, tamping down the giggles. "I came up with it."

"What will you call it?" Stavark asked.

"People in the city are already calling it Dragonslayer, Your Majesty," Deni'tri said.

"No," he gasped, and managed to say, "Laughter."

"What?" Deni'tri looked quizzically at Stavark.

"This sword, that's its name."

"Laughter?"

"Yes."

"It is a bad name for a sword," Stavark said, and that set Mershayn to laughing again.

"Why would you call it that?" Deni'tri asked.

Mershayn's laughter vanished. It was as if he'd been at the

45

center of a bank of mist that simply fell, a great wind shoving it to the ground. Utter silence rang in his ears.

He breathed hard, looked at them, and suddenly nothing was funny. People had died yesterday. So many people.

"Because I'm going to ram it down the throat of the god of dragons," he rasped, the words coming up like blades cutting his throat. "And I'm going to laugh in his face."

Deni'tri stepped back as though his gaze was fire.

He felt the prickle of tears as he remembered the carnage from yesterday, the Teni'sian bodies lying everywhere, burnt and chewed. As clearly as if he was still there, resting on his knees after his battle with the last dragon, staring at the dragon-seared woman and her child in the burnt husk of that little shop.

"I swear that we are going to kill him just like I did his murdering gray minion," he said in a low voice. "We are going to show the god of dragons the price of his arrogance." His oath rang in the air, and he picked up the sword.

Deni'tri smiled then. "That's my king," she said softly. She glanced at Stavark, who seemed to have no reaction to Mershayn's change of mood. "We will be with you every step of the way, Your Majesty," she said.

"Good," he said. "I will need you, and there is much to do." He stood up and sheathed Laughter.

"Yes, Your Majesty. The Sunrider…delegation…still waits outside the city gates."

"Have they been treated well?"

Deni'tri hesitated.

"Deni'tri?" he said, worrying that after enduring so much pain and suffering, the good people of Teni'sia might take their rage out on the Sunriders.

"Captain Lo'gan thought it best to keep them hidden lest it…spark an incident. He has them in a burned-out bakery near the gates, but they've been there for almost three hours. The captain is discreet, but it isn't a secure location."

Which meant they could have a lynching on their hands at any moment. Barely more than two years ago, the Sunriders had tried—and failed—to conquer Teni'sia. The wounds were fresh; almost everyone in Teni'sia had lost loved ones to the Sunrider War. In fact, if Mershayn remembered correctly, Captain Lo'gan had lost one of his sons to a Sunrider's blade. It was testament to Lo'gan's loyalty to the crown that he hadn't organized a lynching himself. But if word got around that nearly a dozen Sunriders were in the city, they'd be slaughtered. There were plenty of others with less integrity than Captain Lo'gan who wouldn't consider it wrong to kill a Sunrider who had come under a banner of peace.

"Stavark, can you take a message to Lo'gan for me? Quickly?"

"If you wish," Stavark said.

"Tell him to disarm the Sunriders if he hasn't already. Tell him to assign fourteen of our most trustworthy guards to escort them to the great hall."

Stavark nodded. Silver light flashed in the room, and the boy was gone.

"The great hall, Your Majesty?" Deni'tri seemed surprised.

"You think I should meet with them in secret," he said.

"I hate the Sunriders, Your Majesty. I'm not the only one. If you truly plan to talk with them, well… The lords and ladies… They will want justice."

"I will meet with them openly."

"Your Majesty—"

"Take it a step further," he said softly. "I know you see our nobility as united, as our allies, and they are, but they are also nearly as dangerous as the Sunriders themselves. If they think I'm collaborating with Teni'sia's sworn enemies behind their backs…"

"Ah."

"No, we'll meet with them openly, for all to see. If the Sunriders truly have peace in mind, and if they can convince us all, then this is an opportunity for the nobles and me to unite behind a difficult decision. And if the Sunriders can't prove their intentions to our satisfaction…well…I'll be the first to use my sword to welcome them back to Teni'sia."

"I'll be the second," Deni'tri said.

"But for now, we look for opportunity." He shook his head. "What could those people possibly want?"

He adjusted the shoulders of his doublet and left his royal apartments. Casur stood just outside the door.

"Casur, will you please inform the lords and ladies of Teni'sia that I wish to meet with them in my ready room?"

"They await you, Your Majesty," Casur said.

Mershayn raised his eyebrows. "They do?"

"Lady Bands informed Master Vo'Dula, Your Majesty."

"Did she?"

"Yes, Your Majesty."

"Well then, let's make haste."

Mershayn walked down the hall, and Casur followed in his wake. Behind him, Grek'tas, who had been standing post outside Mershayn's door with Deni'tri, followed last. Grek'tas sported a cut on his face, a souvenir from the battle, but nothing else Mershayn could see. Deni'tri, by contrast, looked like death warmed over, with sunken eyes, untended scrapes.

"When we arrive at the great hall," Mershayn said. "I want Captain Lo'gan to relieve you. Get some sleep."

"After the meeting, Your Majesty."

"Deni'tri—"

"I'm not leaving you alone with them, Your Majesty."

Mershayn realized that it was going to take a bigger lever to pry her away from him. He stopped and faced her.

"You're no good to me falling asleep on your feet."

"I've gone days without sleep before, Your Majesty," she said, like she had been waiting for him to say that. "Captain Medophae himself trained us to get accustomed to a lack of sleep. I can make it another few hours." She gave him a crooked smile. "Set your mind to rest. I'm up to the task."

Mershayn let out a sigh, admitting defeat.

"After the meeting," he said.

"Yes, Your Majesty."

"*Right* after the meeting."

"As you say, Your Majesty."

They continued down the hall. There couldn't have been a worse time for Sunriders to be in Teni'sia. The Teni'sians were beleaguered, edgy, stunned from the dragon attack. It would take great effort for anyone to muster the desire to treat with Sunriders. The smallest offense would bring violence. Mershayn had to keep his wits about him.

A dragon attack, impossibly turned aside. Now the first Sunriders to ever visit Teni'sia in peace. What's next? A god's visit. Shall I set the royal table?

"Maybe I could rule over something normal for a change," Mershayn murmured.

"Your Majesty?" Deni'tri replied.

"Never mind."

They reached the door to the ready room, and Deni'tri preceded Mershayn while Grek'tas watched the hallway behind him.

Deni'tri nodded, and Mershayn entered his ready room. Sym was there, guarded by two of Lo'gan's guards. Vullieth sat in a chair at the opposite end of the table, Ari'cyiane at his side. Mershayn's gaze lingered on her for a moment, her strawberry blond hair, the coldness of her pale features. Ari'cyiane didn't even acknowledge him.

Baerst paced by the door that led into the great hall. Galorman Balis sat at the far end of the table, talking in hushed tones with Bordi'lis and Grendis Sym. Mae'lith, her sad gaze on Mershayn, waited silently. Ry'lyrio slumped lazily in her chair. She was a strange woman, and Mershayn had not really had time to get to know her, but she didn't seem to have many friends at the court of Teni'sia. Long and lanky, she was reputedly a master horsewoman. He had never seen her at court in a gown; she preferred sharply tailored breeches and blouses when she could not wear riding habits.

He cursed himself for not having asked for a report from Casur on how many of his nobles would be in attendance. He wondered if these were all that remained after the battle.

He inclined his head to them. "My ladies, my lords."

Baerst spun around, coming out of his personal reverie.

Bands said Baerst had started drinking directly after the battle. For a man who'd fought dragons and drunk himself into a stupor in the last twenty-four hours, he didn't look much the worse for wear. His beard had been half burned away, but he seemed to have sustained no major injuries. Bands was right; the man led a charmed life. On top of that, he didn't even look hung over. Maybe he was still drunk.

"Ah, the miraculous bastard shows his face at last," Baerst said with his usual lack of tact.

Bands had said the common folk used that nickname with affection, and Mershayn warmed to the word "bastard" becoming synonymous with the throne. That probably gave the rest of the nobles fits.

"That was a spectacular display of courage." Baerst put his meaty hands together and clapped. Galorman Balis hesitated, then joined, as did both Mershayn's guards. The rest, save one, also joined in the applause. Ari'cyiane's cold stare drilled Mershayn as she stood stoically behind her husband's chair. She wasn't likely to applaud him anytime soon, not for repelling an invasion or even fighting a dragon one on one. Grendis Sym had publicly humiliated her by stripping her naked and chaining her to a pillar in the audience chamber adjacent to this very room. And when Mershayn had become king, she'd demanded he execute Sym. Mershayn had refused, and now, as far as Ari'cyiane was concerned, he was as guilty as Sym.

Mershayn held his hand up. "Thank you. I…" His throat had grown tight. "Thank you. I couldn't be more proud of how we faced the threat. I would love to give a much-needed rest to everyone, but we have much to do. I appreciate you being here."

"Why are we here, lad?" Baerst asked.

Mershayn frowned at him.

"Your Majesty," Baerst amended, nodding in what seemed to be genuine contrition.

"Where is Lord Giri'Mar? Lord Framden?" Mershayn's heart sank. Had they been killed by the dragons?

"Lord Framden is dead," Lord Balis confirmed. "Crushed. But Lord Giri'Mar is in the city, reorganizing our defenses. He has intelligence that Sunriders were seen north of the city."

"Sunriders!" Lady Ry'lyrio said, standing.

"It's an isolated report." Lord Balis waved his hand. "The intelligence said the group was small, less than twenty. They have not appeared since. It might simply be a mistake."

Ry'lyrio wasn't soothed by Balis's reassurance. "If you will excuse me, Your Majesty. I have business."

"You'll want to stay for this, Lady Ry'lyrio," Mershayn assured her.

"My apologies, Your Majesty. But my lands are more important. If Sunriders were seen north of Teni'sia, that means they are near Santocan, and I won't—"

"They're here," Mershayn said.

Ry'lyrio sucked in a breath.

"There are Sunriders in Teni'sia?" Baerst roared.

Ry'lyrio's lips pursed as though she'd bitten a lemon slice. "Where?" she asked breathlessly. "Are they?" Her hand came to rest on her dagger.

Galorman Balis tapped his lower lip with his index finger.

"What are they doing here?" Ry'lyrio asked in a deadly quiet voice, as though she couldn't quite breathe. "Did you ask them here?"

"I was only just made aware of them as I awoke," Mershayn said. "They say they've come peacefully with an important message. That is the extent of my knowledge."

"Kill them," Lady Ry'lyrio said. "Send our own message back to the One Sun and his butchers. Cut these barbarians' heads off and return them to Raedir-ba."

A grumble of agreement went through the assemblage.

"That is one option," Mershayn said.

"It is the only option," Ry'lyrio spat.

"Look," Mershayn said. "If we decide the Sunriders need slaying, then I will happily wade in Sunrider blood. But Teni'sia is in a precarious position at the moment—"

"All the more reason to strike first," Ry'lyrio said.

"Absolutely. I will execute them myself if their intent is hostile," Mershayn said. It was important that Ry'lyrio not think that Mershayn favored the Sunriders.

"Of course their intention is hostile," she said.

"The losses we suffered by the Sunriders were debilitating—" Mershayn began.

"You know nothing about losses, southland boy!" Ry'lyrio's dark eyes flashed. She tossed her head, sending her ponytail back over one shoulder, not unlike a horse tossing its mane. "They never touched your lands. But they marched through my lands to get to Teni'sia. They murdered my husband, my children, destroyed my holdings, and slaughtered my people. Don't talk to me of losses. Send their heads back in a bag."

Santocan, Ry'lyrio's keep, was just south of the now-ruined kingdom of Diyah, which the Sunriders had utterly destroyed. Many nobles had much to rebuild after the Sunrider invasion, but Ry'lyrio had had to rebuild everything. Her lands were only a shadow of what they once were, sparsely populated and struggling.

"They claim to come in peace," Vullieth said, his deep baritone voice filling the room.

"What peace have they ever shown us?" Baerst asked angrily. His lopsided beard made him look like a wild woodland beast.

"Lord Vullieth is right," Mershayn said calmly.

"There is no peace for Sunriders," Ry'lyrio hissed. "We're fools if we grant them anything but a blade across their throats."

"Fools!" Baerst agreed.

Vullieth shook his head. Sym was quiet, absorbing and thinking. Bordi'lis had gone rigid, hatred in his eyes, and he nodded along with Ry'lyrio. Mae'lith watched Mershayn gravely, intent on what he would say. Galorman Balis seemed amused, thinking quiet thoughts of his own and watching the angry nobles like they were a kaleidoscope of butterflies.

"Enough." Mershayn's loud voice cut through the din and,

surprisingly, everyone went quiet like he'd sucked the air out of the room. The sudden silence stunned him. Even Baerst closed his mouth and watched Mershayn. He suddenly realized that, aside from Ry'lyrio, no one glared at him with hostility. Not Galorman Balis or Bordi'lis. Not even Sym. Every noble looked at him with expectation and...something else.

He suddenly realized what it was. That look in their eyes was awe.

It's the dragon. They saw me chase it down, get bathed in flame and survive. They watched me get eaten and survive, and they have no idea how I did it. They don't know Mirolah shielded me with her threadweaving, that I'd be a crispy blob on the castle wall if not for her. They can't conceive of it. And now they think I'm...invincible? Their invincible Bastard King.

He lost his train of thought. He fought his own befuddlement and cleared this throat.

"We are fools," Mershayn said, "if we choose to start another war when we're in the midst of one already."

"You're saying we should actually talk to them?" Baerst asked incredulously.

"Yes."

"All they do is attack and kill," Baerst said. "Sunriders don't seek peace."

"And dragons don't exist," Mershayn replied. Baerst frowned, and Mershayn held up a hand. "These are strange times. The Wave. The dragons. The return of threadweavers. What if the Sunriders have useful information? Yes, they're killers and barbarians, but Sunriders have no history of duplicity. They've never tried to befriend us then stab us in the back."

"No, they've always been murderous butchers," Ry'lyrio said.

"Exactly. So why would they suddenly say they were interested in peaceful talks? Why take such an enormous risk coming here? They must know we would react exactly the way you are reacting."

"I don't care."

"You should. You saw the dragons. You saw what we're up against. We must take every opportunity before us, especially unexpected ones, if we're going to live. This could be just such an opportunity. What if they have information about the dragons?"

"Don't be ridiculous," Baerst said. "Why would they know anything about dragons?"

"The report said they had a Vessel Man with them," Galorman Balis interjected in his emotionless voice.

"So what?" Baerst asked.

"What's a Vessel Man?" Mershayn asked.

Galorman Balis paused now that he had everyone's attention, smiling that thin smile of his. Mershayn suddenly realized Balis liked knowing what others did not. He liked to study, to probe, to come to conclusions. He was the one who had pushed to examine the Wave-altered citizens like animals.

Still, Balis's arrogance aside, he'd illuminated Mershayn's argument about the Sunriders and the potential opportunity. These lords and ladies knew almost nothing about Sunrider culture; they saw them only as ruthless killers.

"A Vessel Man," Galorman Balis said, "is a Sunrider lore keeper and, they think, a prophet."

"A prophet? Like a fortune-teller?" Baerst asked.

"Like that, yes. It isn't their main purpose," Balis said. "But it is one of their more interesting aspects."

"What is their main purpose?" Mershayn asked.

"Sunriders despise the written word," Balis said. "It's why they burn libraries when they find them. They despise art that depicts real people; they think it steals the soul. They believe only in the strength of the body and the purity of the spirit. Their Vessel Men have phenomenal memories compared to our people. They remember details from a dozen years ago, and they hold all the legends and stories of the Sunrider people."

"How do you know this?" Baerst asked.

Galorman Balis's thin-lipped mouth quirked in a half smile. "I spent time talking to a Sunrider prisoner."

Mershayn blinked away the thought of the many tortures Balis must have inflicted on that Sunrider.

"What might a Vessel Man know about dragons?" Mershayn asked.

"Well," Galorman Balis said, "that is where the prophesying may be important."

"How could a false fortune-teller have any worthwhile information?" Mae'lith asked.

Galorman Balis smiled. "Vessel Men are exceedingly valuable to the Sunriders. They are spiritual leaders, representatives of their god, held in high esteem. His Majesty is correct. There are many new things that abound in Amarion. If there is truth to a Vessel Man's fortune-telling, then it could be very important."

"Truth? They're unthinking brutes who worship the sun," Ry'lyrio said with a curl of her lip. "Their gabbling spirit men have nothing of worth to give us."

Galorman Balis shrugged. Baerst made a derisive snort.

"Regardless of your religious beliefs," Balis continued. "I know Vessel Men don't ride in the vanguard of an army. The presence of this Vessel Man practically proves this group has not been sent for war, but for another purpose. A vision quest, they would say, perhaps. It could imply a peaceful overture."

Ry'lyrio spat. "They'll be peaceful when they're cold. Kill them, Your Majesty."

Mershayn glanced down, resting his fingers lightly on the table. Again, the room went quiet, and he knew without looking that they were waiting to hear his command. He glanced up, caught Ry'lyrio's gaze, and held it.

"I have no more love for the Sunriders than you, my lady," Mershayn said softly. "But I won't turn from an opportunity because of anger. The kingdom cannot afford it. We will speak with them."

Ry'lyrio's hand gripped her dagger so hard her knuckles were white. For a moment, he thought she might try to stab him.

He walked toward the door that led to the great hall,

TODD FAHNESTOCK

purposefully close to her, giving her the opportunity if she wanted it. She didn't move.

"The rest of you are welcome to attend the audience. I value your perceptions and your wisdom. But I must ask you to observe a host's decorum, obey the laws of diplomacy, and illustrate the dignity of Teni'sia's nobility. These Sunriders are guests in our castle." He paused deliberately. "For now."

The nobles all reacted in different ways, but none opposed him. Sym regarded Mershayn contemplatively, his emotions unreadable. Mae'lith nodded; her faith in him was plain in her eyes. Vullieth nodded in approval. Ari'cyiane caught Mershayn's gaze, then purposefully looked at the wall, seemingly bored. Galorman Balis smiled. Bordi'lis had a sour twist to his mouth.

"Well, you're the king," Baerst said reluctantly, turning to follow Mershayn as he opened the door to the great hall.

5

MERSHAYN

THERE WERE THREE FIREPLACES in the great hall—two on either side of the tall double doors across the room, and one behind the king's throne. All three popped and crackled, four-foot flames dancing. The chimneys took most of the smoke up and away, but a bit escaped, creating a slight haze that lingered in the vaults of the fifty-foot-tall room. It smelled like his father's hunting lodge just before a good meal of roasted venison.

Ten Sunriders stood in the center of the great hall, nine muscled men perfectly positioned in a ring around a single slender man with robes. The warriors were huge, dark-skinned and dark-haired. Each of them was over six feet tall, and the largest was a black-maned giant with arms the size of Mershayn's thighs, and legs the size of tree trunks. As Mershayn had requested, fourteen of the royal guard stood back from the tight ring of Sunriders. He recognized them all, including Captain Lo'gan himself, who nodded slightly to Mershayn. The royal guards were armed for a fight, and the

Sunriders' weapons had been taken from them. But Mershayn wondered if fourteen armed guards would be enough to stop these beefy monsters if they decided to attack.

Mershayn's blood heated at the sight of them, these intimidating men and their bulging bodies, trained for the express purpose of killing. They had slaughtered so many when they'd last tried to reach this place. He had fought in the Sunrider War with his father and Collus, but he'd only been in two battles and killed only three Sunriders. None of them had seemed as large as these men. Perhaps Galorman Balis was right. This might be some kind of honor guard, the best the Sunriders had to offer.

Aside from the royal guard and the Sunriders, the great hall was nearly empty. Mershayn gave quiet thanks for that. He'd have to commend Lo'gan for his handling of this entire situation, in fact. Public audiences with the king were open to any who wanted to attend. And if the public had known about these particular guests, the great hall would have been full of murderous faces.

As it was, only the greater nobles from the meeting room filed in behind Mershayn, taking their places in the seats in the nobles' box to the right of the throne.

Vo'Dula stood in his customary place on the left side of the throne, looking like a haughty sculpture dressed in burgundy. Stavark stood next to the seneschal in a sleek silver doublet and blue leggings. His new attire surprised Mershayn. The quicksilver looked out of place in human clothing, rather than the simple forest garb he usually wore. The serious boy nodded at Mershayn.

Had Bands dressed him in that, to look like an official advisor rather than a strange creature from a foreign culture? Or had Stavark made the change himself?

The Sunriders stood close to the lowest step of the throne's dais. Each warrior wore buckskin leggings and soft leather boots. Their jerkins were hardly any protection from the elements. He wondered if they rode through the snow like that, or if they had fur cloaks they'd discarded before entering the city just to look tough.

Mershayn sat down on the throne as Deni'tri took up a place on one side of the throne and Grek'tas on the other. Mershayn glanced to the right at Ry'lyrio's seat. She wasn't there. Apparently, she had decided not to join them. He felt relief at that. She'd barely been able to contain herself in the meeting room; he could only imagine how she would have reacted when looking directly at the Sunriders.

Once sitting, Mershayn quickly studied the Vessel Man in the center of the group. He wore many pouches; the largest and most prominent hung at his right side, and his hand rested upon it. He had two thin braids in his mane of hair, each beginning at the temple and hanging straight to his collarbones, where they were tied off with a feather. His beak nose thrust out below dark, deep-set eyes, and he stared at Mershayn in what looked like contempt. Mershayn's anger bubbled at the expression, but he told himself that the man might just have a naturally sour face.

I must show the nobles that we can be civil when talking to these people. I have to set the example.

"Be welcome, Sunriders of the great southern plains," Mershayn said. The acoustics of the hall made his voice loud.

"This is how you show your welcome?" the Vessel Man said. "By making us wait for hours and stealing our weapons?"

Every noble to Mershayn's right stiffened. Baerst clasped the edge of the box. The largest Sunrider, the enormous warrior Mershayn had noted earlier, fidgeted where he stood.

"I wanted to ensure a peaceful meeting," Mershayn replied smoothly. "If you came into this hall with weapons, blood would be shed."

"We did not come to shed blood," the Vessel Man retorted immediately. "We would not have raised our weapons."

"I am glad to hear it," Mershayn said. "We would have."

"Against those you have welcomed into your house?" the Vessel Man said derisively. A grumble went through the nobles, and Mershayn glanced at Baerst, who was most likely to deliver an outburst. The stocky lord was red-faced, but he stayed silent.

They were respecting his choice to lead this discussion, but probably not for long. If Ry'lyrio had been in the room, she would have already leapt at the man.

"You were not welcomed here until a moment ago, Vessel Man," Mershayn said. "And your welcome is contingent upon your peaceful behavior."

The Vessel Man snorted, and again the giant warrior fidgeted, this time glancing at the Vessel Man. Mershayn would have missed it if he'd not been watching the giant Sunrider. His fist was clenched, and he slowly unclenched it, as though forcing himself to restrain his anger.

Mershayn glanced at the rest of the Sunriders, but each of them stood stiffly at attention, no emotion on their faces. He looked back to the Vessel Man, who sneered.

"We come with a message of great importance," the Vessel Man said. "But if you treat us as dogs, we will leave with our words unspoken."

"Dogs have worth. You have none," Baerst finally blurted, unable to contain himself. He stood up. "You don't deserve the respect of a dog."

"Lord Baerst," Mershayn said loudly. "Sit down! Please."

Baerst glowered, and for a moment, Mershayn thought he wouldn't obey. But slowly, he sat down.

"Is this how you control your servants?" the Vessel Man asked. The nobles bristled, and Mershayn knew they were seconds away from violence.

The man was being deliberately provocative. He couldn't possibly think such words would be tolerated. Were the Sunriders so arrogant that they thought they could come into this place, sorely outmatched, and speak so…

Mershayn's thoughts trailed off, and a realization hit him. Then another. And then the real dynamic of the Sunrider group came into view.

That Vessel Man is trying to pick a fight. Why?

What could possibly be the outcome of that? Why come all this way and then be slaughtered by a superior force? That made no sense whatsoever.

He glanced again at the big Sunrider who, up until this moment, Mershayn had thought was barely containing his desire leap into battle. But that wasn't it at all. He was angry at the Vessel Man, not the nobles

He's their leader, Mershayn suddenly realized. *He's the one who made the decision to come here, not the Vessel Man. There's a power struggle happening among the Sunriders!*

Mershayn's mind raced as he put the pieces together. Perhaps, for whatever reason, the giant leader thought using the Vessel Man as their voice was a better idea. Perhaps he thought Teni'sians might respond better to the words of one of the Sunriders' holy men rather than their war leader, the epitome of a threatening Sunrider warrior.

He's probably right about that.

And what if the Vessel Man had disagreed, then been ordered to be the speaker anyway? And now, when the large Sunrider couldn't cut him off without revealing the deception, the Vessel Man was playing his own agenda.

That had to be it. But the Vessel Man couldn't possibly think he could brazenly walk into Teni'sia, speak with open hostility, insult the court, and leave alive?

He doesn't want to leave alive. He doesn't even want to be here. He...

Mershayn watched the big, tense Sunrider. He was clenching his fist again, seemingly ready to leap into action.

The Vessel Man started again. "I think the manners of your court and your—"

Mershayn stood up. "Honored Vessel Man," he interrupted smoothly, "you are correct."

"What?" Baerst bellowed.

Mershayn shot him a deadly glance, then turned back to the Vessel Man.

"You've come a long way, and we've kept you waiting for so long," Mershayn said. "I see now that it was impolite of me to bring you before the entire court for your first words. My apologies."

The Vessel Man looked confused, and he narrowed his eyes in suspicion. As he searched for something to say, Mershayn continued. "Let us, you and I, speak alone."

A ripple of disapproval ran through the nobles.

"Your Majesty! Certainly not!" Baerst protested.

"I agree with Lord Baerst," Sym said.

Mershayn held up his hand. "Nevertheless. Honored Vessel Man, I shall take one of my people, and you may take the largest of your warriors so that you may feel safe." He indicated the tense giant of a man. As he did, the big man immediately stepped close to the Vessel Man, who seemed about to protest. He glanced with anger at the big warrior, then back at Mershayn.

With a tight face, the Vessel Man said through his teeth, "Very well."

"Captain Lo'gan, please escort these two to my personal meeting room."

Lo'gan immediately moved forward, indicating that the two Sunriders proceed up the steps of the dais and to the room behind the throne.

Deni'tri leaned over him. "What are you doing, Your Majesty?" she whispered.

"Stay here, Deni'tri. Watch the Sunriders and the nobles both. They can't begin fighting."

"No," she whispered harshly. "No. I'm going with you—"

"You'll do as I command," Mershayn whispered harshly. Deni'tri seemed stunned. He regretted it, but he didn't have a choice. There was no time to explain. If he was right, a calamity was balanced on the tip of a dagger here. He turned to Stavark. "If you please, honored *syvihrk*, will you accompany me?"

Stavark glanced at Deni'tri, then at Mershayn, a thin wrinkle in his alabaster brow, but he fell in step beside Mershayn without a word.

The two of them entered the meeting room, and Mershayn shut them in with the Vessel Man and his giant Sunrider.

He looked back and forth between them, then focused on

the big man.

"You're playing a very dangerous game," Mershayn said.

The big man's eyes narrowed. For a long moment, he said nothing, then he nodded with respect.

"Your Majesty," the Vessel Man began, but the big Sunrider held up a hand.

"Enough, Jalataer," the giant said. "He knows. And thank the One Sun for that. You disobeyed me. You would have killed us all for nothing."

The muscles in Jalataer's jaw worked, and his lips quirked like he had barely stopped a sneer. "We should not beg these sickly northlanders. We do not need them."

"You're the actual leader," Mershayn said to the big man.

"I am Gilgion, firstborn of the Speaker for the One Sun."

Mershayn tried to contain his surprise. By the gods! He didn't know much about the Sunrider culture, but the Speaker for the One Sun was, essentially, the emperor of the Sunriders. *All* the Sunriders. This hulking man was his son, the equivalent of a high prince.

"Why lie to us?" Mershayn asked, and he was happy to hear that his voice came out smooth and even.

"If I rode up with a band of Sunriders," the big man replied, "you would kill me simply for being in your rocky kingdom. There is no mystery to be solved. No reason to listen to me. If I come with a Vessel Man in the lead, you must know why."

"That's a dangerous gamble. My entire court wants you dead."

"And yet, you saw the truth and took us here. If you wish us dead, why not try in there?" Gilgion tipped his chin toward the great hall. "Where you think the odds are in your favor?"

Mershayn hesitated at that ominous statement, then pushed past it.

"What are you doing here?" he asked.

"Jalataer has had a vision."

"We do not share our sacred visions with infidels," Jalataer exclaimed.

"You will today," Gilgion said.

"You break the holiest of laws."

"You live in the past, Jalataer."

"And you are a heretic!" Jalataer spat.

Mershayn was taken aback, obviously witnessing an argument that had begun long before now.

Gilgion's face remained impassive, as though the insult meant nothing, but his shoulders tightened slightly. "That is a dangerous accusation, Jalataer, an accusation that reveals more about you than about me," he said, his black eyes flat and deadly. "It reveals that, perhaps, my Vessel Man is more passionate about his opinion than his fealty to his leader. Another Sunrider might slay you where you stand, but I respect your passion, if not your wisdom. So I will give you a clean moment. I will allow you to speak your truth. Let your words now bind you to your fate. Either your allegiance is with me, or you are a traitor."

"I owe my allegiance to the Speaker for the One Sun. Your heresy strips you of your authority!"

"Tell him your vision."

Jalataer purposefully turned his head away from Gilgion. "By the power of the holy rays that shine through me, by the rites of—"

Gilgion moved so fast he was a blur. Mershayn had never seen anyone besides Stavark move that fast. The big man grabbed Jalataer by the neck and lifted him up like he was a dishrag. Jalataer tried to block the strike, but his hands might as well have been twigs. His eyes bulged as his feet scraped the ground.

"You...dare!" he choked. His face slowly turned red.

"If you will not obey my orders, then you are an enemy of the One Sun."

"I...am...his voice." Jalataer wheezed, trying to suck in a breath. "You...will be killed...for this." Suddenly, there was a small, triangle-shaped blade in Jalataer's hand. He stabbed it into Gilgion's ribs.

The big man had to have seen the blade, but he made no

move to counter it. The dagger sank in, and he grunted.

With a steady voice, Gilgion said. "You have attacked the leader of a Wind Ring, emissary of the Speaker for the One Sun. The penalty is death."

"No!" Mershayn reached forward with his hand, but he was too far away. Stavark became a flash of light, streaking around the table and grabbing the big man's forearm, but Stavark may as well have tried to wrestle a tree.

A sickening snap sounded in the room. Jalataer's head went limp, lolling to the side, and the light left his dark eyes.

Gilgion, still expressionless, tossed the dead Vessel Man onto the table with a thump and a clatter of pouches.

6

MERSHAYN

MERSHAYN DREW HIS SWORD. Stavark did the same. "You butchering brute!"

Gilgion turned a calm gaze to Mershayn. "Half-Blood King," he said. "Jalataer was a traitor. The penalty was death."

"You don't get to bring your barbarian ways into my halls and kill whoever you like, even if he was one of your Sunriders. We don't do things that way here!"

The giant Sunrider laughed, a deep laugh with actual mirth. "You lie badly, Half-Blood King."

"You may call me King Mershayn or Your Majesty."

"King Mershayn, I came here for the sake of both our peoples, with a message important enough for me to risk my wind riders' lives and the scorn of my own people. You can hear what I have to say, or you can ignore me."

"Tell you what. You can tell me your message from inside my dungeon while I think about whether you deserve to die for committing murder in my throne room!"

Gilgion shook his head. "No."

"We'll see about that." Mershayn turned to the door.

"I am poisoned, King Mershayn," Gilgion said.

Mershayn turned back. He flicked a glance at Gilgion's wound, then to the tiny triangle-shaped dagger clutched in the dead Jalataer's fist.

"The blade was poisoned." He realized what Gilgion was saying, and Mershayn's face went hot as he thought about the scathing reprimand he was going to give to Lo'gan for letting one of the Sunriders slip past with a poisoned weapon.

"In moments, I will fall asleep," Gilgion continued. "Before the sun is halfway to its height, I will die. Now is the time to hear my message. And if we are not fast enough, then I will also not have time to tell my wind riders who killed Jalataer, that Jalataer poisoned me, and that you participated in neither of these. Then you will have to explain to them why two Sunriders are dead. These are your choices."

Mershayn could clearly see the picture Gilgion had just painted, and he was absolutely right. It would be difficult for the remaining Sunriders not to see Mershayn as the butcher if he simply walked out now. He clenched his teeth, his anger rising. "Then I'll have ten dead Sunriders in my kingdom."

"You do not want that."

"My nobles will hail me as a hero for that."

"You are a thinking man, King Mershayn. You made us guests in your stone fort when the rest of your nobles would spoken with their swords. You cared enough to see through my deception with Jalataer. You feel the importance of what I bring."

Mershayn gripped his sword hilt hard. He had badly underestimated this man. Sunriders were known for their combat ferocity, not their subtlety. But Gilgion's predictions, every one, were correct. Worse still, it was possible that this hulking man had set up this moment, down to his own death.

If so, that kind of commitment was frightening. It scared Mershayn more than a little.

"Will you hear my message?" Gilgion asked.

"You let him stab you. You could have stopped him."

"Will you hear my message?"

The ramifications flew at Mershayn. He might have only seconds, after which, any advantage he might gain from the Sunrider vanished. If Mershayn walked out of here with two dead Sunriders behind him, the remaining Sunriders would immediately attack. They might even have been ordered to do so. Of course, they couldn't possibly win. Even if they managed to overpower fourteen armed royal guards without any weapons of their own, they'd have to contend with Stavark, Mershayn, and the other nobles, most of whom could fight.

But some of Mershayn's people would die. The Sunriders were simply too powerful not to take a few lives with them.

Though Gilgion had muscled him into it, Mershayn would be stupid to refuse to hear the message.

He pointed Laughter at Gilgion, who seemed unperturbed by the threat.

"Fine. Tell me."

"Good." Gilgion glanced at Stavark, then spoke. "Jalataer was a Vessel Man. He carried the stories of the Sunriders. Both of the past and of the future."

"I have heard that Sunriders believe that."

Gilgion nodded. "Now you must believe. Jalataer saw the coming of the Golden King. It is why we went north. But seven days ago, he saw another vision."

"Okay."

"Each Vessel Man sees his own visions. Some see only visions about rainfall, and whether crops will thrive or fail. Some see only visions about passion, whether one will love another, and the other will love them back. Some about politics. Our most favored Vessel Men, like Jalataer, receive visions about war."

Mershayn narrowed his eyes. "Okay."

"But when there is a vision that affects all of the people under the One Sun, *all* Vessel Men see it, all at once. These visions are rare, and they are always important. They are to be honored by all the people under the One Sun. Two waxings of the moon ago, all Vessel Men received a vision about the Golden King. The vision told that he was to return in a time of great need for the people. We came to take him back to the great plains, where he belongs."

"A Golden King?" Mershayn asked. "Who's the Golden King?"

Please don't let it be me.

He glanced at Laughter, remembered that sense of destiny about the sword, how it made him feel he had a path that hadn't been revealed yet.

Wouldn't that be his luck? It was ridiculous, the Sunriders risking their lives to come to Teni'sia to kidnap Mershayn.

"The Golden King is an eternal champion. He shines like the One Sun, surrounded in golden fire."

Relief flooded through Mershayn. "You're looking for Wildmane."

"That is one of his names, yes."

"Get in line. Lots of people want him."

Gilgion looked curious. "He was here?"

"Apparently he lived here for years. Brushed cheeks with the queen."

"Brushed cheeks?"

"Brushed cheeks. Pressed lips. Joined hips."

Gilgion cracked a small smile. "You are a humorous man *and* a thinking man." He nodded as though writing that down on a little piece of parchment in the back of his mind.

Gilgion had not moved or swayed at all since he'd been stabbed, but his face was looking paler by the second.

"So you came looking for the Golden King," Mershayn said.

"Not here."

"You said you were looking for him."

"I wished to explain why my Wind Ring is in the north, but it is not why we came to this dangerous stone fort with such a small ring. The Vessel Men had another vision."

Galorman Balis's report about the Vessel Men indicated that they were rare, and that they almost never went with the vanguard of any kind of fighting force.

"You have two Vessel Men?"

Of course, that might explain why he didn't need this one.

Gilgion shook his head. "No. When a Vessel Man has a single vision, they turn their eyes to the sun and quiver as they receive it. When the Vessel Men have a collective vision, it comes at night. They fall to the floor, twitching, for as long as the visions last. Seven nights ago, Jalataer did this. When he awoke from the vision, he told me what he had seen."

"And what did he see?"

"The sun blotted out by winged creatures with fire inside them."

"You mean dragons."

"Jalataer said they are coming south to destroy all peoples."

Mershayn finally lowered his sword, his arm beginning to ache. "Thanks, but we already knew that."

"Yes. I saw the wreckage in your village. I saw the corpses of the great beasts. But your people survived. I am convinced now that I was correct."

"What do you mean?"

"There was more to Jalataer's vision. He saw the skies darkening with flapping wings and scaled bodies, but only half the sky. The other half, though empty of sunlight, was blue. Beneath those clear skies were the armies of my people, each of them shining gold. But we could not stop the growing darkness. Then, across the land beneath the shadow came a second sun along the ground, and that new sun illuminated a long streak of green grass in the shape of a flying creature, wings outstretched.

"Behind the new sun came another army of people, except they were ice-blue, not gold. The new sun jumped into the sky, and the blue people leapt after, covering over the blackness one blue dot at a time. But the…dragons…battered them, cast them down, swarmed about them with wings and dark claws. Once they had finished with the blue people, the dragons consumed my people as well. Then the flapping darkness spread over the northlands, down to the Red Desert, and further south to the endless plains. It covered everything, and there was no longer any sun." He paused.

"That was the vision?" Mershayn asked.

Gilgion shook his head. "Jalataer said the vision started over, giving us the answer to this doom. Everything was the same, as though the vision had simply started from the beginning. Except this time, when my people saw the new sun leap into the dark sky, the ice-blue people following, my people also followed. They leapt into the sky, fought side-by-side with the blue people, and our gold became blue as well. This time, for every dragon shadow that darkened the sky, there were a hundred blue people to cover them. In moments, the sky was ice-blue again, and the new sun shone brightly down on the land. That was when Jalataer began to wake, and he whispered, over and over. 'Apart, we fail. Together, we prevail. Apart, we fail. Together, we prevail.'"

"And that was the end of the vision?"

"That was all."

Mershayn had staked his newfound reputation on the idea that the Sunriders might bring an important message, but instead he'd been given a superstitious tale about clouds and skies and suns, gold people and blue people. It sounded like Gilgion's dead Vessel Man had a fit, and the ignorant Sunriders saw it as holy. "Are you sure it wasn't just a bad dream?"

"This is the manner of Vessel Men visions."

"Well, it's the manner of Teni'sian dreams."

"Even if you do not believe, we believe."

"Isn't that cute?"

Gilgion narrowed his eyes. "You are a humorous man, but do not let your humor make you a fool. If you disbelieve the vision, it will not stop my father from coming north. And when he arrives, you will live or die depending on your wisdom."

"Your father is coming north?"

"His Vessel Men will have seen this same vision, just as Jalataer."

Mershayn hesitated, hearing the threat. He wanted to shove

clever words back at the Sunrider, but he forced himself to entertain the notion that this dream might be some kind of prediction. It was either that or believe the Sunrider was a maniacal idiot. But Gilgion did not strike him as insane. Quite the opposite. He seemed a man of conviction who did nothing halfway.

The big man was even paler now. Beads of sweat stood out on his forehead. By the gods, he didn't look good. He hadn't been lying about the poison.

"So it's an allegory," Mershayn said.

"What is an allegory?" Gilgion asked.

Of course. Sunriders didn't have a written language. They didn't know about allegories. "Hidden meaning," Mershayn said. "The divided sky, half light, half dark. The new sun. You think they mean something specific, that they represent other things."

"Visions speak to the spirit, not to the mind," Gilgion said, which sounded like agreement.

"So what do you think it means? You think it's our two people coming together to fight the dragons?"

Gilgion nodded. "The truth of the vision can only be seen through the purity of the one who sees it. The Vessel Men are known to be pure, but..."

"But you don't think Jalataer was pure."

"No," Gilgion confirmed. "He saw what he wanted to see. He turned his face from the wisdom of the One Sun and basked in his own pride instead. Jalataer seeks glory for himself. He came with my Wind Ring because he wanted to be the Vessel Man who found the Golden King. He does not wish to ally with northlanders. He saw that the army of my golden people is my father, bringing his Sunriders north for the battle. And he chose to see that the ice-blue people are my Wind Ring, bringing the Golden King back to my father in glory. He made his final words 'Apart, we fail. Together, we prevail.' fit into his vision. He believed my Wind Ring and my father's Sunriders are the 'two people' who must come together to find victory over the dragons."

"But you don't."

Gilgion shook his head. "Jalataer described the ice-blue people as being numerous, far greater than my Wind Ring. And we do not have ice on the endless plains. There is no ice-blue color in my homeland. But in the north, you have much ice, many colors of ice."

"The ice-blue people are Teni'sians," Mershayn said. "That's what you think."

"I felt it in my belly when Jalataer told me the story. I felt it in my bones. So I commanded him to come north. I sent the rest of my Wind Ring south to meet my father and tell him where we have gone. Jalataer was to begin talks with you, but he defied my orders."

"Is it common for other people besides Vessel Men to interpret these visions?"

"Interpret?"

"Explain them."

"No."

"So you're not a Vessel Man, you didn't even see this vision, but you think you know what it means," Mershayn said.

"Jalataer lied. He did not want the One Sun's truth. He wanted only Jalataer's truth."

"How do you know?"

"He spoke many details when he first woke, before his mind came awake. Seeing a vision takes your soul closer to the One Sun; it makes it impossible to lie. So when he spoke his words, they were pure. But later, when he took time to think on them, he twisted them to suit his desires. He tried to tell me his whispered words meant something different. He hates northlanders, and the idea of fighting alongside them enraged him."

"Don't you hate us, too?" Mershayn asked.

Gilgion raised a hand, palm upward in an appeasing gesture, then he noticed his hand was shaking badly. It surprised him for half a second, then his face became grim, and closed his fingers into a fist. The shaking stopped. He glanced back at Mershayn. "Do I believe the Sunriders have the right to rule over your kind? I do. We are stronger. We live closer to the One Sun. We are purer than northlanders. Do I believe it is better for both of our peoples to die rather than to stand together? No, I do not. Such thinking does not serve the One Sun or his children. Such thinking is small."

Mershayn couldn't disagree with that. And this might be the opportunity he was looking for after all, though not in the way he would have liked. Putting Sunriders and Teni'sians together could turn into its own war. They might destroy each other before the dragons even had the chance.

But if they didn't destroy each other, if Gilgion and Mershayn could find a way to form an alliance, having a Sunrider army helping fight the dragons might make the difference between victory and defeat.

By the gods, *anything* might make the difference between victory and defeat.

"You're proposing an alliance." Mershayn said the words aloud so there could be no mistake.

"I am."

"Our two peoples working together to fight the dragons."

"It is the only way to win. I saw the dragons fly toward your stone fort. They did not fly away. I saw the broken buildings of your city. The dragons came here."

"Yes, they did."

"They came, and you killed them."

"We did."

"That is mighty. With your might, and with our might, we could combine and defeat all the dragons in a blackened sky."

Mershayn held up a hand. "Okay, say we succeed. Say we work together and we beat the dragons, how do I know you won't immediately declare war on us?"

"We must form a bond, a promise to each other. I will command my Wind Ring to take a message to my father, that you and I formed an alliance during our battle with the dragons. After, I promise that my father will go south after the war is done. He must hold to my promise, and he will take our army back to the endless plains before declaring war on you."

"Oh, perfect. And then he will just come back north?"

"You have the key to destroy the dragons, King Mershayn, but not the strength of numbers. My people have the strength of numbers, but not the key. Together, we prevail against the dragons. Apart, we fail. That must be enough for a start."

Mershayn hesitated.

"What do you say, King Mershayn?"

He looked up at the brave, reckless Sunrider leader. It was crazy, really, but somehow Mershayn felt this was part of the rockslide destiny he felt all about him. As ridiculous as it seemed to have Sunriders and Teni'sians fighting side by side, it was more ridiculous to let the dragons destroy them all.

After a moment's hesitation, he extended his hand.

The big Sunrider took the hand and shook it. His grip was strong, but his hand clammy.

"I vow to join our peoples to battle the threat of dragons," Gilgion said, his voice rumbling Mershayn's chest. "There shall be no slaying of your warriors by my warriors. We shall use no right of force in taking your women. We will work together until the threat of dragons is destroyed. Then, I pledge that my people shall return to the endless plains in peace, at which point our bond will be done. I, Gilgion, son of the Speaker for the One Sun and leader of the sacred Wind Ring, make this bond with you."

"And I will do the same," Mershayn said.

"Good," Gilgion said. He swayed on his feet, slammed a big hand on the table, and steadied himself.

"We need to get you to a healer," Mershayn said.

Gilgion shook his head. "No. I will not let northland tricksters lay their hands upon me. Either the One Sun will take my life, or he will not."

"You're poisoned!"

Gilgion waved a hand as though it did not matter. "Come, King Mershayn. I must make a proclamation to my wind riders, or they will think you have done this to me, and they will kill you when you emerge."

Gilgion staggered to the door, and they followed him.

The big Sunrider kept his feet all the way to the throne, and his Sunriders tensed, crouching, ready to spring to his defense. They could see he was obviously hurting.

Gilgion held up his shaking hands, and the Sunriders froze where they were, coiled springs.

"My wind riders," Gilgion said, pulling up his bloody jerkin, showing the wound Jalataer had given him. "Jalataer disobeyed my orders. When I told him he would be punished for his betrayal, he stabbed me with a poisoned diamond knife. After he committed his treason, I killed him. Know this, my wound is not the fault of the northland king."

Many of the Sunriders looked at each other, but they didn't seem convinced.

Mershayn glanced at Captain Lo'gan, and a look passed between them: be ready. This could explode into conflict.

"I have made a bond with King Mershayn. The Sunriders will fight alongside the northlanders to face the threat our Vessel Man saw in his vision."

"What?" Lord Baerst roared.

"Lord Baerst, sit down," Mershayn said.

"This is an outrage!" Bordi'lis hissed.

"Say it," Gilgion boomed in his loud voice, ignoring the outcries of the nobles. "This wound is not the fault of the northland king, nor any of his followers, but of Jalataer's making. And no Sunrider will take retribution for it from these northlanders."

Again, the tense Sunriders glanced back and forth, none seeming to know what to do.

"You will...say it..." Gilgion said in a gurgling voice. He looked down at his feet as though surprised. His whole body shook as if with palsy. He pointed a finger at the Sunriders...then collapsed with a loud thud.

Mershayn jumped toward Gilgion and fell to his knees. "Get a healer!" he yelled, but no one heard him. The nobles stood up, every one of them gabbling something different. Baerst drew his sword, and Bordi'lis pointed at Mershayn, furious.

The Sunriders charged the throne.

7

MERSHAYN

"NO, WAIT!" Mershayn yelled.

The Sunriders leapt up the steps, fists clenched. Silver light flashed, and Mershayn felt fifty little hands push on his back, his arms, his legs, shoving him forward. They lifted him up and over Gilgion's prone form and carried him away from the oncoming Sunriders.

Suddenly, Mershayn stood behind the throne, ten feet away. Stavark appeared next to him, breathing hard, hands on his knees.

Guards closed in on the Sunriders, swords ringing on scabbards. Lord Baerst charged around the edge of the nobles' box, weapon up. Deni'tri flung her hatchet at the nearest Sunrider's head.

"No!" Mershayn jumped at the hatchet, yanking his sword free. He had to deflect it. If even one Sunrider died, this insane drama was all for nothing.

The tip of his sword whisked past the handle, missing it by an inch.

The hatchet flipped end over end, straight and true, and—

Silver light flashed, and Stavark appeared in front of Mershayn. His slender arm jerked as he grasped the axe handle, then he dropped it to the ground. The rest of the Sunriders encircled Gilgion, facing outward. Each crouched, hands outstretched as the Teni'sian royal guard crowded close, swords ready to stab.

"Hold!" Mershayn's voice rang in the hall.

The Sunriders faced the bristling steel unflinching, but they didn't attack. Thankfully, the royal guards obeyed Mershayn's command. He made a mental note to commend Captain Lo'gan for their discipline.

"Cut them down!" Baerst roared. "They charged our king—"

"They came to the defense of theirs," Mershayn said, standing between Baerst and the Sunriders. "Put up your sword."

"I—"

"Put it away *now*," he said.

Baerst glanced at the Sunriders, then at Mershayn. He seemed about to argue, but decided against it. With a sneer, he sheathed his blade. "I hope you know what you're doing, Your Majesty," he grumbled under his breath.

"I do."

Mershayn turned to the Sunriders. "We have healers," he said. "Your Vessel Man stabbed Gilgion with a poisoned dagger. If you doubt your leader's words, go into my meeting room." He pointed at the door behind the throne. "He lies there still, weapon in hand." Mershayn gave a significant glance to Lo'gan, and the captain reddened, whether in anger or shame, Mershayn didn't know. But he did know that he wouldn't have to say another word about it. Lo'gan would find out how the Vessel Man had snuck a weapon past him.

The Sunriders didn't answer, merely stayed ready to fight, legs bent, arms out stretched.

"Who speaks for this Wind Ring now?" Mershayn asked. "If not Gilgion, then who?"

One of the Sunriders—the one Deni'tri had almost killed with her hatchet—rose from his crouch and took a step forward. He wasn't as giant as Gilgion, but he was the next largest in the group.

Do Sunriders choose their leaders based on size, I wonder?

"I am Rider Doermar. If Rider Gilgion cannot lead, then I will hold the ring while he rests."

"He's not resting," Mershayn explained. "He's poisoned. He said it was deadly poison, so we must act quickly. Our healers might be able to save him if we hurry."

"It is the *volesh*," Doermar said. "Only Vessel Men carry this. There is no cure."

"You have to let us try."

"If the One Sun decrees Rider Gilgion will live, he will live."

"That's..." *Stupid.* Mershayn wanted to say, but he stopped himself.

Mershayn glanced at Baerst. The noble looked like he was about to spit on the floor.

"Let us at least try," Mershayn urged.

Doermar shook his head once. "We will take him away from this place." He turned to the other Sunriders. "Bear our ring holder." Four of the Sunriders lifted Gilgion gently. He turned to two of the others. "Bring the traitor who was a Vessel Man." Two of the Sunriders walked toward the ring of royal guards, slowing as they reached the sword points.

Mershayn waved the guards down.

"Lower your weapons," Captain Lo'gan said. The guards obeyed, stepping aside as two Sunriders went into his personal meeting room. They emerged a moment later with Jalataer, his legs dangling, head flopping. They carried him with much less ceremony than Gilgion.

"Allow us to make a room for you here in the castle," Mershayn said to Doermar.

"No."

"No?"

"He will not heal here. There is no sun in this fort of stone.

Such a place makes a man sick."

Baerst went red in the face, and Mershayn put a calming hand on his shoulder.

"We will camp in the snow by our horses."

"In the snow?"

Without another word, Doermar turned away from Mershayn and led his Sunriders past the guards toward the double doors. Mershayn made a mental note to set up some kind of perimeter so that a Teni'sian mob didn't try to exact their own justice upon the Sunriders.

They'd just broken about a half dozen rules of court etiquette. But Mershayn wasn't standing on rules right now. Everything was upside down, and he needed to step nimbly to keep his feet, not stand on etiquette. "Escort them," Mershayn said quietly to Captain Lo'gan, staring after the Sunriders. "I need to...visit the infirmary."

"No, Your Majesty," Vo'Dula said.

Mershayn sighed, turning. He was not in the mood to banter with Vo'Dula. "No what?"

"You do not wish to go to the infirmary."

Mershayn stifled his anger. He didn't want to explain to his seneschal why certain things had to happen. "Vo'Dula, we can't afford to let Gilgion die if we can help it."

"You wish ask Fae'llyn about the poison," Vo'Dula said in his officious voice. "Of course."

"Eh... Of course," he said. "I mean, I want to ask about the poison. Who's Fae'llyn?"

"The master herbalist, Your Majesty."

"Yes. Fae'llyn. I want to find out just how deadly this *volesh* poison is."

"Of course you do. I will take care of it, Your Majesty."

He opened his mouth to say "No, *I'll* take care of it", but he kept the outburst behind his teeth. Vo'Dula was right. Mershayn had a trunkful of problems needing his attention. He couldn't rush around the castle like he once did, attending to whatever errand occurred to him. He had to start thinking of his time as valuable. If he could send someone else, he should.

He was going to have to get used to people doing things for him.

Stiffly, he nodded. "I need to know right away, Vo'Dula. If there is an antidote, have Fae'llyn take it to the Sunriders."

"Of course, Your Majesty."

"Wait. Did Fae'llyn lose anyone in the Sunrider War?"

"Her father, Your Majesty. And her betrothed."

Damn it.

Mershayn's lips tightened, and he kept himself from cursing. "Then ask her about the poison, but don't tell her what it's for. And send someone else with the antidote to the Sunrider camp, wherever it is. Someone who isn't..."

"Of course, Your Majesty."

"Thank you, Vo'Dula."

Vo'Dula inclined his head, but he didn't leave.

Mershayn sighed. Apparently, the seneschal wasn't done with him. "Yes, Vo'Dula?"

"Do you have anything else you require, Your Majesty?"

"No, I..." Then he realized he actually did need something else. He cleared his throat. "Yes. I need to meet with Lord Sym, Lord Balis, Lord Giri'Mar, and Lord Vullieth."

"Of course, Your Majesty," Vo'Dula said smoothly, as though he had been expecting it.

"Lord Giri'Mar may be in the city," Mershayn said. "But I need to speak with him anyway."

"Of course."

"And not in my personal meeting room. In the council room."

Vo'Dula rolled his eyes. "No, Your Majesty, let's seat our nobility in the room with the blood all over it."

"Well, it *is* going to be a war council."

"Shall I bring a dog carcass and some flies to complete the theme, Your Majesty?"

Mershayn cracked a smile. Bands had been right to pick Vo'Dula. He was exceptionally good at his job. And he was funny.

"That won't be necessary."

"I defer to you. Your wisdom knows no bounds, Your Majesty. In half an hour, then?"

"For the council?"

Vo'Dula looked as though someone was slowly sticking him in the butt with a dagger. "No, for the dog carcass."

"Half an hour would be fine, Vo'Dula."

The seneschal turned and moved away. He held up two fingers. Bimeera and a young boy Mershayn didn't know popped out from behind the nearest pillar beneath the gallery. He hadn't had any idea they were there until that moment. They sprinted toward Vo'Dula and skidded to a stop in front of him. He gave each directions in quiet tones, still standing straight as a spear, as though the children were his same height. When he was finished, Bimeera and the boy sprinted for the double doors at the far end of the hallway. Vo'Dula approached the noble box, nodding gravely, and spoke to them in the same quiet tones.

Mershayn turned away and came face to face with Baerst.

"I want to lop the heads off those muscle-bound murderers," Baerst growled.

Mershayn nodded. "I take it as a kindness you didn't."

Baerst grunted. "I like violence."

Mershayn glanced at him sidelong, not sure if the man was joking. "You didn't always, though, did you?"

Baerst raised an eyebrow.

"Something changed about you," Mershayn said bluntly. "After Corialis Port."

The stocky man chuckled. "Something's always changing. That's what makes life interesting." He glanced at Mershayn. "Staring down the fire of a dragon will alter a man."

But how much, I wonder...?

Baerst changed the subject. "That big Sunrider give you a promise to help us fight dragons?"

"Mmmm," Mershayn grunted.

"Thought that might be it. By Thalius's beard, I've never seen a Teni'sian fight so hard to save a Sunrider."

"Yes, well. Something's always changing. That's what

makes life interesting."

Baerst chuckled, and it sounded like rough rocks scraping together in his throat. When he quieted, he said. "Think they'll keep that promise?"

"I don't know. They've never made a promise to us before."

"Hmmm. Not exactly true. The last promise they made was to kill us. They kept that one pretty well."

"If allying with the Sunriders means a better chance at survival for our people, I'm going to take it."

Baerst grunted, and it sounded almost like he was agreeing. "You need me for anything?" the lord asked.

"I'm meeting with Lord Sym, Lord Balis, Lord Giri'Mar, and Lord Vullieth. We're leaving tomorrow."

"Are we?"

"Going north. Taking the fight to the dragons."

Baerst grunted. "I like that."

Baerst's approval spread like a warmth through Mershayn. He didn't let it show; instead, he cleared his throat.

"Would you like to join us?" Mershayn asked.

"To talk about the number of horses, supply trains, and washing servants you need for the road? No thanks."

"You know war, Lord Baerst. We could use your help."

"I do at that, Your Majesty. So when the battle starts, put me up front. I'll do you right. Until then…" He clapped a hand on Mershayn's shoulder. "I'll raise a tankard in support."

Mershayn opened his mouth to protest, then decided against it. He'd pushed his nobles hard today. The world was changing, and Teni'sia needed to keep up. But people could only be pushed so far. He'd introduced many new things to them in a short period of time. And Baerst was right. He wasn't needed at the meeting.

"As you wish," Mershayn said. Baerst walked away. Mershayn wished that he was going with the stocky lord. A tankard of beer sounded nice. Baerst might be the first of Mershayn's nobles to become a friend. The man was volatile, but honest. And he was strangely likable.

No. No friends. Collus tried to make friends with these slithering nobles, and they killed him for it.

Baerst exited through the door of Mershayn's personal meeting room, probably to see for himself what had happened there. Only Grek'tas and Deni'tri remained. The rest of the nobles had already left the great hall. Stavark was at the double doors, about to do the same.

"They are assembling for you in the council room, Your Majesty," Deni'tri said.

"Good. Thank you."

"I'll escort you," she said.

"Actually, you won't. We had a deal. You sleep. Get cleaned up. Grek'tas can stand in your place."

"Your Majesty—"

"We had an agreement. Sleep in your bunk or sleep in the dungeon," Mershayn said, steel in his tone. "Your choice."

She held her breath. "Yes, Your Majesty." She breathed the words out, stalked to the door behind the throne that led to the hallway and left.

Grek'tas, tall and silent, stood where he was, his eyes forever glancing around the room, looking for threats.

Mershayn followed Stavark.

"Where are we going, Your Majesty?" Grek'tas asked.

"To keep a promise."

"Shall I call for a replacement for Deni'tri?"

"No."

Mershayn exited the double doors into the main hall.

"Stavark!" he called.

The boy was just about to round the corner. He stopped, regarded Mershayn solemnly, hands at his sides.

"Stay here," Mershayn said to Grek'tas. The guard took up a post next to the double doors. Mershayn strode to the quicksilver and stopped in front of him. The boy didn't even come up to Mershayn's chin. As Mershayn looked down at those silver eyes, the silver hair, he tried to see past the strangeness. It was easy to look at Stavark and see only a supernatural creature who could humble a half dozen swordsmen with ease. That was how Mershayn had always thought of him, but he tried now to see with Bands's eyes, to see the boy. Bands's last words about Stavark rose in Mershayn's mind.

His spirit is strong, but he puts the world on his shoulders. That is too much for anyone to bear. If he breaks, you will lose a powerful ally. He desperately needs a friend, and he will never admit such a thing."

"Thank you, Stavark," Mershayn said.

The boy looked up the hall at the double doors of the great room, then back at Mershayn. "I do not think the Sunriders were going to attack you, after all."

Stavark thought he was being thanked for pushing Mershayn away from the charging Sunriders.

"No, not for that. Just...for everything."

"I have done nothing."

Mershayn started chuckling. "Really? Well, I wish I had a dozen people who could do nothing as well as you do it."

Stavark remained quiet.

"I just, um, well, I wanted to say thank you." Suddenly, he was having difficulty finding the right words. Bands had told him to befriend the quicksilver, but the boy seemed not to want friends.

Stavark watched him.

Mershayn got down on his knees, eye-to-eye with the quicksilver boy.

Stavark frowned.

"I, um, well. I just want you to know that, if you need to talk to someone, you should come to me."

"Talk to you about dragons?"

"What? No. Not dragons. This isn't about the war. It's about... Well, about anything that's bothering you. We could..." He realized he was about to say "we could get a beer."

Yes. Sit down and get drunk with a twelve-year-old.

It was almost as though Vo'Dula's acerbic voice was talking in his head.

"Well, we could, um, play a game."

Yes, roll the bones together. Gamble and talk about women. Yet another great way to spend time with a child—

The wrinkles in Stavark's brow deepened. "You are acting strange, King Mershayn."

"I...I just want you to know that...you're not alone," Mershayn said lamely.

This is the most awkward thing I've ever done in my life.

"What you do here..." Mershayn stumbled through the words, determined to get his message across. "Your...contributions. They're important."

Stavark looked away, his face pained. After a moment, he mastered himself. When Mershayn turned back, the pain was gone from the quicksilver's face.

Mershayn reached out and clasped the boy's arm. "I'm your friend. Not your king. Not your commander. If you need something, you come to me."

"You should use the water," he said.

"I should use water?"

"On the dragons. When they come. They cannot stand the water of the True Ocean."

He suddenly felt like Stavark was speaking in a foreign tongue. "What are you talking about?"

"Lady Bands. She battled Saraphazia to get your weapons—"

Mershayn's mind did a backflip. "Saraphazia the *goddess*?"

Stavark simply watched him.

"How?" Mershayn blurted.

"The weapons were in the water. Lady Bands tried to take them. Saraphazia did not like it. She created a wave to splash over Lady Bands. The water destroyed her wing. That was why we had to run back to Teni'sia, instead of fly."

Mershayn realized that his mouth was hanging open. He closed it, then thought about the odd bandage on Bands's shoulder. She hadn't mentioned anything about it, and he had never seen her injured before. He'd thought it had come from the battle with the dragons. He rallied his thoughts and tried to focus.

"The water *burns* them?" he managed to say.

"The water is alive to dragons. It hates them. But it does not hurt humans. Throw a cup of ocean water at a dragon's eye, and it burns them like fire."

"By the gods…"

"Lady Bands said it was an old enchantment Saraphazia laid over the True Ocean because of her anger at Avakketh. We could use her power against him."

"Stavark…you're brilliant." What better way to fight a god than with the might of another god? He suddenly wondered why Bands had not brought up such a useful piece of information. Could she stomach the idea of fighting her kin, but not burning them alive with acid?

After what the dragons had done to Teni'sia, Mershayn didn't have any such compunctions.

"Would it hurt Avakketh the same way?"

"I do not know."

Plans came alive in Mershayn's mind. That was a powerful weapon, maybe exactly the weapon they needed, especially if Avakketh did not guess they knew about it. And he'd gained it by following Bands's advice and trying to befriend Stavark. Even in her absence, Bands seemed to be hovering near, mothering him.

Stavark closed up again, his face impassive. Mershayn tried to shove his excitement down. Brilliant! Just brilliant.

"Thank you," he said. He hesitated, then put his hand on Stavark's shoulder. "You're a good friend and a better—"

Silver light flashed, and the boy was gone.

Befuddled, Mershayn stood alone in the hall. It seemed like he was getting through to Stavark; Mershayn had finally found the right words at the end, said what he meant to say.

But then boy had fled.

Maybe they weren't the right words.

But he played the conversation back in his head, and he couldn't think of where he had gone wrong.

You're a complicated boy, Stavark. But I'm going to get through to you. I swear by the great green-banded dragon, I'm going to make you know you have a friend here.

Mershayn stood up. He should have known that any task Bands gave him wasn't going to be as easy as tipping a tankard. Who knew what quicksilvers did to make friends? In the quicksilver kingdom, there might be a thirteen-stage ritual to begin a conversation about friendship. Or maybe quicksilvers were forbidden to have human friends.

Yes. This pondering is so very productive.

And maybe Stavark had a limit of one friend, and the position was already filled, or maybe he could only make friends with rocks. Or maybe he was actually a toad in disguise and couldn't comprehend friendship.

He walked back toward Grek'tas.

Maybe I should go back to my easier task of defeating a god and his thousand dragons.

8

STAVARK

STAVARK RAN THROUGH THE TENI'SIAN HALLS, which were coated in the gleam of the silverland. He ran past a tall woman with a serving tray, frozen in the act of talking. She shimmered in the brilliance of the silverland.

He ran upstairs, turned left, then right, then left again, and ran to the doors that opened to the strange garden the humans kept. He left the silverland, and the silver on the doorway melted away to reveal the light brown wood and dark grain. He drew several deep breaths and let his heart calm, then opened the door to the winter outside.

On the other side of the door, someone had pounded a nail, as though they had attached something that had been since removed. It was square, like a miniature iron stake with a flat head on one end. He reached up and touched it, then took hold of it. It had been driven deep into the wood, no doubt with the violent smashing of a hammer. He pulled on it, but it wouldn't come.

I am like the hammer that did this. A violent smashing. I hurt and I kill, over and over.

He entered the silverland again, coating the door and nail with silver. With his palm, he hit the nail from the bottom, then yanked at the top. He did this over and over again. Finally, the nail came free.

He stepped out of the silverland, the nail in hand, and walked through the garden to the curved stone wall as tall as his chest. He leapt lightly upon it.

Stavark sat cross-legged on the wall, looking out over the white mountains east of the castle, and turned the nail over and over in his fingers. He squinted at the glaring snow, reflecting the bright sun overhead. It hurt his eyes, but everything hurt now. At least that pain took his mind off the pain in his heart.

Mershayn was trying to be kind. I shouldn't have run from him.

Fleeing was rarely a right action. Fleeing from kindness was simply wrong. It created hurt. But the more Stavark stood there, listening to the man praise him for the horrible things he had done, for participating in the violence humans so eagerly committed, for formulating a plan with the ocean water that would create more pain, burning, injury... It only made Stavark realize how far he had strayed from the path of rightness.

I wanted to bring humans and syvihrk together. I wanted to bring the maehka back to Amarion. I wanted to strengthen my connection with the lands, to be an example to my people....

He turned the nail over and over in his hand.

Instead, I am a murderer.

Behind him, he let his awareness try to connect to nature. It took him longer than it usually did. But soon, he felt the trees, the grasses, the bushes of the cultivated Teni'sian garden, and he felt their shock. The plants and bushes had not expected this sudden, strange winter. The leaves of the trees—those that had not been ripped off by the winds and heavy snow—were hastily turning gold, orange, and red.

Humans forced the garden into the shapes they wished. They took these growing things from where they had been and brought them here, crowded them together, forced them to live in exact patterns, and fed them in their captivity. Humans looked at this garden and saw beauty. They saw the meticulous care they had taken to make it just so. They saw satisfying reflections of themselves in their work.

But Stavark saw only how the plants were stunted and clipped, shaped by well-meaning hands and caged by knee-high stone walls and flagstone paths. The gardeners let them grow only in the direction the gardeners wished; they did not think about the directions the plant wished to grow. Of course, plants did not get frustrated. They looked only for opportunity, sinking their roots through soft earth, reaching for the sun wherever it might shine.

But Stavark felt frustration for them; it roiled through him, destroying his calm. These children of nature had been shoved into their spots by humans. They did not understand this, so how could they possibly fight it?

Stavark's mother had been right. He, too, was no longer in his place. He had stepped away from his people, stepped outside of their wisdom, beyond their protection, and he'd shoved himself into this tangled human mess, and now he was a murderer. Once, he could see clearly, but there was no path for him now, none save the path the humans would delight in him walking.

Yes. Come to war with us. Use your sword to hack into the lives of others. You are so good at killing. Kill for us. Kill again.

When he had traveled with Orem, Stavark had stood strongly in the ways of the *syvihrk*. He had only fought *vakihrk*. When he killed, he killed only the foul creations outside of nature, the unnatural spawn of the dark god Dervon—darklings and dramaths and his other dark creations.

A true *syvihrk* only took a natural life at utmost need, and only when that life was a rotting spot on the lands. To use the silverland for killing a fellow *syvihrk* was an abomination.

Stavark had fought for Orem's purpose, but he had stayed in the right, a champion of nature, not a destroyer. And with Stavark's help, Orem had fulfilled his vision, had freed the *maehka* to feed and sustain the lands again.

Then Orem was taken by the twisted spirit Zilok Morth.

Stavark sought him, but instead of staying in the right, he had somehow slid farther and farther down a muddy slope away from his path. Without Orem's strong vision, the path slipped away from him, and at the bottom of that muddy slope was only darkness. Stavark had allowed himself to slide, waiting for his opportunity to return to his path, believing he could, just as the ignorant plants in the Teni'sian garden waited for their opportunities. He believed he would find his path again, that he would find Orem, or if he could not, that he would serve the fruits of their labor: the *Maehka vik Kalik* herself.

But he had failed, and now there was only darkness.

I murdered the Maehka vik Kalik.

Her body lay dead in a room high in the castle. Bands, the *kaarksyvihrk,* told Stavark that the *Maehka vik Kalik* was not yet dead...

But that was not what Stavark's senses told him.

He looked down at the nail in his hand. He turned it one last time, then put the point at the center of his palm and held it there.

Stavark wanted to believe the *kaarksyvihrk,* but how could he ignore his own senses? Was that not one more step away from his unity with nature? The *Maehka vik Kalik*'s body was dead. Did it matter if that body shone when the *kaarksyvihrk* looked at it with her threadweaver's sight?

Stavark couldn't see the rightness anywhere in his choices. There were only dark shadows and tricks of the light. He could not feel the truth.

The voice of the lands shuns me. She will not speak to a murderer.

He thought back to his childhood. There were stories of *syvihrk* who had lost their way. The *vanvakihrk.* Their skin turned yellow, their hair and eyes a tarnished dark gray, and they cut striped scars into their arms. They used the silverland to do unspeakable, violent things. They put their own desires above the needs of others. They hoarded treasures, killed for greed, as though lives meant nothing. Some even killed just to kill, to feel the sickly power of extinguishing a life. They were dead-hearted creatures, and they couldn't hear the voice of the lands, couldn't feel her growing trees, her lively wind, her rich earth. They hated themselves, and so they hated everyone else.

It is happening to me.

He reached up and pulled a long lock of silver hair in front of his eyes, let it run through his fingers like water. But it wasn't tarnished, and the skin on his arms was still pale white.

Stavark let go of his hair and looked down at the nail. His heart beat fast, and he pushed the point of it into his palm, hard. Pain lanced through him, and he wondered how far he'd have to push to draw blood.

How long until I transform into a vanvakihrk?

Was this the beginning, this self-loathing? He had destroyed himself the day he slew the *Maehka vik Kalik*. He could think of nothing else. The pain of it filled him always, but would that sour curdling of his heart soon turn to joy? Would he soon crave another despicable act? Would Stavark thirst to murder?

When Stavark left Sylikkayrn, he had believed that, since his mother had refused, he alone would build the bridge between the *syvihrk* and the human people again. Instead, he had become like them.

I must stop myself. If I am not to become a vanvakihrk, *then I must take steps.*

Stavark stood up, looking down at the drop. It was hundreds of feet to the steep, snowy slopes below, enough to easily kill a *syvihrk*.

But he turned away from the drop. Suicide was an abomination, a spurning of the gift of life. A true *syvihrk* would never take his own life. He could not choose that path.

But he could throw himself between danger and his companions. That, at least, was closer to the path of the *syvihrk*. And if one of those dangers happened to kill him, then perhaps it would be better for everyone, better for the lands themselves.

He took the nail away from the dark red mark on his palm, and he tucked it into his pouch.

My heart is rotting, but before it dies, I will use the last of it to be the syvihrk *I might have been. If I must dance in the waters of the* vanvakihrk, *I will turn my darkness against the enemies of my companions.*

He turned, hopped off the wall, and walked up the human-made pathway toward the castle.

9

MEDOPHAE

MEDOPHAE SET VEE DOWN, breathing hard and looking at the neverending stretch of mountains. Yesterday, Vee had saved Medophae from the goddess of the ocean, and then Medophae had saved Vee. That had been a very near thing.

It seemed like he'd spent a year away from Amarion, stuck on the island of Dandere by Zilok, far away from those he loved, fighting to return, and fighting for his life against Saraphazia. Every minute had seemed like an hour while he trapped there, knowing Avakketh might be killing the people he loved. His near death experiences on Dandere had, oddly, brought a shocking clarity. He was nothing if he wasn't protecting those he cared for, and as he breathed hard and surveyed the landscape, every tree, every craggy ridge, every wispy cloud burst with wondrous color as though each had meaning, as though he was seeing all of these things for the first time.

He'd never realized what a gray world he'd pulled around himself until Mirolah woke him up and Zilok snatched him away. He'd been shaken up, turned about and lashed with pain. It seemed ridiculous to think it, but this horrific journey had been good for him. For the first time in centuries, he knew who he was and what he must do.

Mount Vlacar loomed behind them, the tallest landmark in the Corialis Mountain range. Medophae remembered it like he remembered his own reflection in a mirror. He had actually named that mountain when the great hero Vlacar, the paladin of Natra, had died in its shadow.

Unfortunately, knowing this landscape only meant he knew how excruciatingly far they were from Teni'sia, and every single minute raked his back with claws of urgency.

Since Saraphazia had nearly killed them yesterday, Medophae and Vee had been running. He had run all day carrying her, staying far away from the True Ocean and heading south. They had climbed steadily into the mountains, Oedandus's fire crackling around him, giving strength to his fatigued body. A mortal could never have kept this pace for ten hours. Vee herself had only managed to run for an hour before he'd had to carry her.

But Oedandus was within him now, and the god had enough strength to bolster a hundred mortals. The time for hiding was past. Avakketh might even now be burning Teni'sia, and Medophae would use Oedandus's strength to push as fast and as far as he had to.

The air around him was warm, but a cool breeze blew up from the south. The valleys and hills he and Vee had run through to get to this summit had smelled earthy and wet. They'd been vibrant with the reds and golds of turning trees. The ground they now stood upon was bare rock, but far to the south, the jagged peaks wore cloaks of white. How could winter have come to the south first, before the north? He'd never seen that before.

Every moment Medophae had been in Dandere, he had been obsessed with Avakketh. The dragon had promised flame and destruction. Medophae had expected to walk into a massacre—dragons blotting the sky, humans dying in fire.

Instead, the skies were quiet, and the seasons had gone mad.

"What happened...?" he murmured. A winter storm was an unlikely attack from Avakketh. He was a master of fire, not snow.

"It is me..." Vee said.

"You did this?"

When Vee saved Medophae from drowning, she had revealed her true identity: the goddess Vaisha the Changer, who had been pulled apart and destroyed by Dervon the Diseased many centuries ago, long before Medophae was born. But she had told him that pieces of her godly "body" remained, that they had soaked into the lands of Amarion. These pieces had then had been sucked up into Daylan's Fountain when he pulled all of the GodSpill into his creation. Now, she claimed, those pieces that had become one with the GodSpill had been released once more into the world with the destruction of Daylan's Fountain. She said they had sought her, had become wild in their efforts to find Vee.

"It runs free without me," she continued, closing her eyes as though someone was whispering to her. "Or it is trying. This storm, the winter that shouldn't be here yet, is only the beginning if I don't rejoin with myself. It will grow more and more angry, and its thrashings will soon do much worse than a snowstorm."

Vee wore a blue dress like a doll from a millennia ago. It was simple peasant clothing with a little white apron across the front—complete with stains, a patch, and a rip along the right side. She could look however she wanted, of course. She had appeared to him as a pirate and then a mermaid the first two times they'd met. He wondered if the dress had some special significance.

She climbed up beside him and took his hand. Oedandus awoke, rumbling within Medophae, and golden fire flickered over his forearm, then over Vee. Medophae twitched, but he forced himself not to pull away.

When Vee touched him, it was like she was taking Oedandus's hand, not his. The injured god responding to the injured little goddess immediately, like they were family and Medophae was just a nearby servant.

Vee touched him as often as she could, her hand in his, her hand on his arm, her hand on his back. He suspected she could somehow pull strength from Oedandus, though no one else besides Medophae had ever been able to do that, and Medophae himself felt no diminishing of power.

"Those pieces of me, my...body... They're so angry," she murmured. "They look for me, want to be whole. It is like a scattered flock of birds trying to become one bird. It wheels and wheels again in the sky, but it does not know how to put itself back together. It needs me, but it can't find me."

He noticed that her hand was clammy. He'd been so busy running that he hadn't paid attention to Vee's condition, and she was much worse. Her blue-tinged skin was pale. Her cheeks were sunken. Even her arms and legs were thinner, as if she'd been starved for weeks. If she was pulling strength from Oedandus, it clearly wasn't enough.

Vee had saved his life twice, and she'd asked him to save her in return, to free her from the insane goddess Saraphazia. His battle with the goddess had been short and brutal, but Medophae had managed to wrench Vee away from her mother. He wondered if Vee's separation from the ocean—from her mother's power—was causing this sickness, but he didn't plan to go anywhere near the True Ocean to test the theory.

Vee's body shuddered as a cough wracked her.

"We need to find a healer for you," Medophae said.

She got her coughing fit under control and looked up at him with bloodshot eyes. "No human healer can help me. Without my mother's sustenance, I would have died long ago. So it is now."

"What can I do?"

"There is only one thing. Help me find the rest of myself. Restore me to the goddess I once was."

"Vee, I don't think you're going to make it another ten miles, and we have hundreds to go."

"The pieces of my body are close," she said. "I feel

them…wandering… But someone holds them, tries to make them her own. I think…they might find me if this other being wasn't holding them so tightly."

That was new. "You said they were roaming free. But someone is keeping them away from you?" Medophae immediately thought of Zilok Morth. Had the spirit also managed to pull Vee's power into him with that damnable crown of his?

"I do not know," Vee said. "It is a mortal. A female human, I think. I did not feel her until I was able to put my feet on the ground. The GodSpill longs for me, but in my absence, it took a mortal host."

Mirolah…

The thought hit him like a lightning bolt. The pieces of Vee's "body" had been sucked into Daylan's Fountain. Mirolah had destroyed Daylan's Fountain. She'd set free the GodSpill, and it had filled her unlike any other threadweaver Medophae had ever seen.

"You're saying that the GodSpill, which used to be your body, has now filled up a mortal with godlike power?"

"I receive…flickers. I feel my body like a wind that rushes past me, then it is gone. But it does not stop, because it does not recognize me. It is attached to this mortal now. She holds them tightly, and it believes she is me."

"So you're saying we have to take these…pieces, as you call them, away from this human female?"

"Yes."

"What happens to her, to this human female, when the power returns to you?"

"She will die."

"Wait, what? Why?"

"Because she is already dead. The pieces of my body fill her like the sail of a human ship. When I reclaim myself, her sail will go slack. Her body will return to what it was before."

"What it was before?"

"Yes. Dead."

Medophae's heart pounded faster. Mirolah was dead? No.

He couldn't believe that. She could heal herself if she was injured. If Mirolah was the one who was using Vee's "body", then there had to be another explanation. "We're not killing anyone."

Vee didn't notice the distress in Medophae's voice. "She is already dead; it is only my body that lashes her to life. She will return to what is natural for her. She is hanging on tight to the pieces of my body, using them to rebuild herself, over and over again. And my body is unwilling to let her die because she holds some of them together, but she is doing it poorly. It wants her to assemble the rest, but of course she cannot. She is mortal."

"Vee, I think I know who this is. I'm not killing her."

Vee caught the emphatic tone this time, and she glanced up at him curiously. "You know her," she whispered.

"I think you're talking about my...about a woman I care for deeply. And Mirolah is not dead."

"Mirolah..." Vee said softly, as though tasting the name. "Yes. That is the name the pieces of my body whisper."

"She didn't take your...body. She set it free."

Vee hesitated. "She holds it so tightly, Medophae. But she will not for long. That storm..." She pointed at the snow-capped southern mountains. "Happened because she lost control. She may have regained that control for the moment, but it will not last. And when she loses control again...many will die. It will be much worse than any storm. We must take my body from her before that happens."

"Which will kill her."

"She is already dead."

"She's not!"

Vee narrowed her red-rimmed eyes. "You were with this human, Mirolah," she guessed. "She was your lover."

Medophae frowned, not wanting to talk about this with Vee. She was a goddess—or the remains of a goddess at least—but she still looked like a ten-year-old girl. "She...helped me."

"I did not kill this human," Vee said. "But she is dead. And she will naturally do what humans do when they are dead, once she can no longer control the pieces of my body. And if she loses control before I regain my body, others may die, too." She cocked her head like she didn't understand. "Surely you will not allow others to die, even if it means letting her die."

"She's not dead."

Vee went silent for a moment, then slipped her hand out of his. "You are the god of balance. You are the Binder. You must think of more than just one mortal who is already dead."

"Stop saying that! She's not dead, and if you try to kill her, I'll stop you."

She narrowed her eyes, like she was trying to understand him, then she went silent. She put her hand in his again, and Oedandus crackled to life, sheathing their arms together. Medophae clenched his jaw.

"I think I understand," she said gently. "You see Oedandus as I see my mother. He wishes you to be one way. You wish to be another."

"I just… Mirolah is important, and there has to be a way to save her. You can't just…shove her aside because you want what you want. What about what she wants?"

Medophae tried to moderate his anger, but Vee's peremptory decision to cast Mirolah aside because she was in the way reminded him too much of how Oedandus wanted to control Medophae. It reminded him of that horrible night when they had slain Dervon. Oedandus had raged forth, shoving Medophae into a deep, dark hole in his own mind.

Oedandus's full, raging power was the only thing that could have destroyed a god. And during that attack, Medophae had become inconsequential, a bystander. He saw Dervon die like he was looking up through a dark tunnel. Then Medophae's vision went black, and he remembered nothing.

It had taken him two weeks to wake up. The next thing he had remembered, Bands was leaning over him. He felt like he'd been beaten by fifty people, and he had a thirst like he'd run through a desert. Bands said he had lain in unmoving sleep the entire time.

He remembered nothing from those two weeks, but he had been unconsciously fighting for his life, for possession of his own body. Oedandus had tried to take it, and Medophae hadn't let him. Since that moment, he'd fought to never let Oedandus out completely. Medophae had never again stood aside while the god took over. Medophae had lost control at times, like at the Deitrus Shelf, but he had immediately taken that control back.

"You are not like my mother and me, Medophae," she said softly. "You and Oedandus are one. You were meant to be one. You are a caterpillar who went into his cocoon but never emerged. You remain...a cocoon. My mother trapped me, kept me from becoming my full self. But you...you've trapped yourself."

"No. I preserved myself. I don't want to be a god. I'm just Medophae."

Her hand shifted in his, but she didn't let go. Instead, she said, "You have refused to make the choice you must make." She paused, then said, "When you face Avakketh, he will make you choose." She looked up at him. "And he will want you to choose to be 'just Medophae'."

"I will face that when I get to it."

She paused. "Yes," she whispered. "You will."

"We will find a way to free your body, but we will do it without killing Mirolah."

"I see..." she said, and she closed up, pensive.

"We will make it right."

She nodded.

With a sigh, Medophae picked her up and began running again.

1 0

VEE

VEE SLEPT FITFULLY in Medophae's arms as he ran through the night. She had not needed sleep when she lived in her mother's ocean, but that was because her mother had been pushing her own life force into her, just as Oedandus pushed his life force into Medophae, allowing his mortal body to become something more than mortal.

They were very alike, she and he. She was a goddess who had been stripped down to nearly mortal form. He was a mortal who had been built up to a nearly godlike form. They shared the agony of being caught in mid-transformation.

But they were also different. Vee longed to return to herself, longed to be larger again. Medophae wanted to stay small.

She couldn't recall what kind of goddess she had been; only that her mother told stories about the wondrous Vaisha the Changer. Mother had told of how Vaisha had created unicorns and pegasi, quicksilvers and dolphins. Mother had said Vaisha had been a gift to the world, so full of hope and bright ideas that she had inspired the rest of the gods to follow her example.

Vee had enjoyed the moments of nostalgia when her mother seemed happy. They never lasted long. She inevitably descended into bitter rage. The end of the stories remained the same: how Vaisha's uncle, Dervon, tore Vaisha apart in a greedy quest for power.

Though the stories were all Vee possessed of the self she had once been, the drive within her was all-consuming. She felt her missing pieces keenly. No matter where she went, no matter how much her mother had tried to distract her, cajole her, bully her, Vee longed to return to Amarion and find herself again, to reclaim her godly body. She simply couldn't imagine living forever without the whole of herself, without transforming into the goddess she was meant to be.

But Medophae…

His godly body was right here, rumbling and churning within him, desperate to become one with him, but he had built powerful walls to keep it separated. He was so afraid of transforming into his greater self that he couldn't see what was real anymore.

When Vee saved Medophae's life and helped him regain Oedandus, she had asked him to free her from her mother. She had also envisioned the natural next step. After returning Medophae to his greater self, she assumed he would happily do the same for her. But she saw now that she was mistaken.

Medophae had never actually become his greater self. Worse, his narrow view might make him oppose her, stop her from taking back her body.

She did not think badly of him, but he could no longer help her. If he couldn't understand why it was important for him to become a god—the god he was meant to be—then he could hardly understand why Vee must become Vaisha.

It frightened her, the thought of leaving him. And it saddened her. She liked him, and she felt comfortable under his protection. But she had not spent her life ready to risk everything for a chance at being Vaisha simply to cower underneath Oedandus's shadow now. Without her body, she would eventually die, or she would have to return to being a slave to her mother's wishes.

She must find another champion.

And so when Medophae finally thumped to a stop a few hours before dawn, announcing he would take a brief rest, Vee had made sure she had drawn as much of Oedandus's GodSpill into herself as she could. She would need it all.

The wisps of her body came north like winds, and they whispered over all the life of the lands. When they flowed into her, for a moment, she could feel what the winds felt. She could feel the lives that lived in the center of her body. The bulk of her body had been wadded up like a rag and stuffed inside this dead woman, Mirolah, but Vee could touch little bits of herself. She was beginning to feel them like she had felt Mother's ocean. Maybe soon, these little connections might sustain her, and she wouldn't need to steal life force from Oedandus or her mother.

Another effect was that her vision expanded. The lands of Amarion became like a ghostly map, visible in her mind's eye. She could see places where GodSpill spun like whirlpools of flame, where it raged in a dark forest. She could see the lives of strong mortals like fireflies in the night. Now she looked for one who might stand with her, who might understand her need and believe in it as she did.

As Medophae ran, she cast her mind outward, searching. For an hour, she searched, and finally she found one who might serve her.

There... That was a mortal who might understand her, one who might be her champion.

This would be a dangerous game, but there was nothing else to do. Vee had promised herself that, if she ever got free of her mother, she would run any risk to return to her true self. She could not waste a single chance.

Breathing hard, Medophae slowed down.

"Here," he said. Oedandus crackled around him, pushing his mighty life force into Medophae, healing him, longing to join with him, but he just didn't see it. He refused to see it.

Medophae set her down. "Rest here. It'll be good for you to get some sleep without being jostled around."

As if a goddess could sleep, could rejuvenate, the way a mortal person did. She did not regain strength by resting.

"We'll start again when the sun rises," he said.

She didn't say anything. There was nothing more to say to Medophae.

"It won't be long," he assured her in a gentle voice, as if she actually was the young mortal girl she seemed, scared and alone, and timid in the world.

But she was only scared that she might fail in her mission. She was alone only because she wasn't whole. And she was not, in the least, timid. She knew exactly what needed to happen.

He frowned, and she saw the guilt on his face. "I promise you, when we find Mirolah, we will make things right. We will restore you without killing her."

Vee said nothing. She didn't like deceiving, so it was best to say nothing. He watched her for some reaction, so she smiled at him. It wasn't a good smile, lopsided and stiff, but he took it how he wanted to take it. Relief eased his tight shoulders, and he patted her on the arm. "It'll be all right."

He lay down on the ground, bending his arm to support his head. "Just a quick nap," he said.

She lay down next to him, put her hand on his wrist to comfort him, to make him feel that everything was fine. The touch also let her know when he had fallen asleep.

When he was softly snoring, she rose and leaned over him.

"Choose well, son of Oedandus. Godslayer. Wildmane." She kissed him on the cheek, as soft as a butterfly's wing.

She stood, then walked softly and quickly down the hill. She couldn't see the ocean, but she felt it, a distant presence, gravity pulling her inexorably forward. She must dare its power again, dare the risk of discovery by her mother. But with the strength of the water, she could move faster than Medophae could run, and her destiny lay to the south. She must race her

mother and Medophae to reach what she needed.
Her champion would be waiting there.

11

MERSHAYN

"YOUR MAJESTY."

Mershayn sat bolt upright, sleep falling away like shattered glass. The candles had gone out, and his sitting room was dark. The desk where his head had been resting had a line of sleep drool on it. He looked around, blinking, and he shivered. Cold air blew in through the open window, smelling like winter. He remembered opening the window to keep himself awake. Obviously that hadn't worked.

He looked around for who had spoken, but he couldn't see a thing. The barest glow of moonlight came from the window.

He cleared his throat. "Hello?"

Rocks clicked together and a spark fell into a tiny dish of tinder near his hand. He jumped. The tinder flamed up, and Silasa lit a candle with it.

"By the gods, woman. You're lurking in the dark like a monster!"

"I sometimes forget that others cannot see very well," she said. "My apologies."

"Oh good, as long as I have your apologies. Give me a moment while I pick my heart up off the floor." Mershayn rubbed his chest. His body ached with fatigue, and he tried to shake it off.

Silasa's pale face floated like a moon between the midnight curtains of her hair. He blinked, trying to see the rest of her, but her clothes blended with the shadows.

"What time is it?" he asked.

"Past midnight," she said.

Vo'Dula had tried to put Mershayn to bed at sundown; the seneschal had actually stayed in his rooms, being five different kinds of annoying, until Mershayn finally got into his nightclothes. But the moment Vo'Dula left, Mershayn had risen and began poring over maps of the north again.

"I am sorry to disturb you," she said. "But I was away."

"I know. I missed you last night."

"I tried to come to you, but Deni'tri was guarding your door like a lion, and then I...got distracted by something else."

"What?"

"Tonight," she ignored his question like he hadn't asked it. "When I woke, I went looking for Bands. I couldn't find her."

"She's gone."

"She went looking for Medophae," Silasa guessed.

He hesitated, then nodded. Dealing with supernatural creatures got tiring after a while. They always seemed to know more than him. "She said she had to, that all our work in Teni'sia means nothing if we don't have Medophae on our side."

"She is right."

"So..." He paused. "You didn't find her."

"I found her trail, but I didn't follow it far. I don't think it would be healthy to do so. She's hunting for Zilok Morth. To follow her would be to face whatever perils that fiend throws in her way."

"Oh," he said, studying her face. "How far did you follow it?"

"Down a rarely used tunnel beneath the dungeons. To the

north. I'd close it off, if I were you. She has trapped a bakkaral in a room down there. It begged me to let it out." She leaned forward, looking at him beneath her thin, dark eyebrows. "You know never to listen to a bakkaral, right?"

"What the hell is a bakkaral?"

"A fiend beyond your control, mine or yours. She turned the door into a steel plate, and I would surmise she trapped it with threadweaving inside the room as well, though I did not venture inside to confirm it."

"Okay."

"Perhaps brick up that entire hallway." She waved a hand. "Regardless, that is as far as I can pursue her. She is beyond us now."

"She did say goodbye, at least," he said.

Silasa went quiet, her face unreadable, and he suddenly realized that Bands had not said goodbye to Silasa.

"Sorry." He cleared his throat. "So...what do you need?" he thought quickly. "A pint of blood?"

"Nonsense. I can't drink your blood. I only feed on virgins."

The comment hung in the air between them, then she gave the barest hint of a smile. He laughed.

"I thought you were serious."

"You seem to be doing well in Bands's absence, at least," she said.

"I'm faking it."

"The nobles of the court do not seem to think so. The commoners in the town do not seem to think so."

"Well, I feed on misconception. But not *only*."

The corner of her mouth tugged up into another smile.

"We're going north," he said.

"Oh?" she said, and her eyebrow raised. "That's a tactical mistake, isn't it?"

"No."

"I spent years lurking in the shadows, listening to my father's war councils. The best way to defeat a superior enemy is to stay behind your stronghold, rather than meet them in the open."

"Not when your stronghold might as well be a sand castle. No. Our stone walls are just weapons for them. I watched too many people die, crushed by stones the dragons knocked down, burned in houses they set aflame. This city isn't a safe haven; it's a death trap."

"How will it be better in an open field?"

He rubbed the back of his neck. "With Mirolah's spell to drop them to the ground, at least we'll be able to get at them. And we have Bands's enchanted weapons. And they'll have to burn us without the help of local tinder. And, well, Mirolah protected us from the flames, too. Sometimes."

"But you don't have Mirolah," she said.

He cleared his throat. "We will."

"Mershayn, I've been to see her. She's—"

"She's going to be fine."

Silasa narrowed her eyes.

"She will," he insisted. "Bands said Mirolah's just...working it through."

"Working through her death?"

"Yes."

She was silent for a moment, just watching him. Finally, she said, "So your plan to defeat the dragon hinges on Mirolah waking up?"

"And ocean water."

"Ocean water?"

"It burns them."

"It does not." She frowned.

"Stavark says it does."

"He can't be serious."

"Because Stavark is such a jokester."

"You can't be flippant about this, Mershayn! They're going to destroy Teni'sia. Maybe all of Amarion."

"I may *sound* flippant, but I'm actually scared to death. The plan is serious."

"You're relying on the dead to wake and water to burn."

"You say that like it's ridiculous."

"*You're* ridiculous. That's not a plan."

"In point of fact, it's the only plan we have."

"What if she doesn't wake up?"

"What if the Sunriders declare war on us while we're weak? What if Bands doesn't come back with Medophae? What if the dragons come to Teni'sia today when we have no defense prepared?" Mershayn clenched his fists beneath the table, but he kept an even expression as he stared at Silasa. His voice came out quiet. "If Mirolah doesn't return, we lose. So she's coming back. She has to."

She sat back. "I'm sorry. I know that—"

He waved a hand. "I've thought on this, over and over. Bands says we can't beat the dragons. After fighting them here in Teni'sia, I know she's right. But dwelling on that does nothing for us. If it is time for the human race to die, then it is. But I refuse to believe that. I'm going to fight, and I'll go down swinging. I'm not going to sit here and wait for the monsters to kill us." He reached behind himself and grabbed a bottle of Buravaran brandy and two short, thick glasses. He set the glasses down on the table, poured the brandy in both, and quaffed one in a single gulp.

"I'm doing the sure thing," he said. "And the only sure thing is to make myself a target, to take the battle away from innocents, away from Teni'sia, try to draw the dragons into a fight in the north. After that, our saviors are going to have to come through for us. If they don't show up in time…" He hesitated, then felt that familiar anger rise within him. "Then we draw swords. That's what we do."

He pushed down his hopelessness and replaced it with a cold resolve. He would march. He would buy as much time as he could for her to return.

"I will do what I can," he repeated.

"And I will stand with you," she said. "Your Majesty."

"Oh, to the Godgate with that. You start calling me 'Your Majesty', and I'll have no friends anymore. Please. Remember, I need you to tell me when I'm doing something stupid. You are the only one I can trust who can. Everyone else has other agendas. I need you, Silasa."

She nodded. "Then I am yours." She paused for a moment, then added, "So, you seem more certain that Mirolah will return than Bands."

"I met that bone-freezing apparition Zilok Morth. And I know little about threadweaving now. I don't see what Bands can do against him. I mean, she's a dragon *and* a threadweaver. She put this kingdom back together in a week like she'd done such an impossible task a hundred times. But I watched Zilok Morth destroy Wildmane, kill Mirolah, and control Stavark like a puppet. All at the same time. That kind of power is beyond my understanding. I don't see how Bands can beat him."

Silasa nodded.

"But Mirolah brought herself back from the dead once already," he said. "I'm betting she'll do it again."

He let out a breath and sat back, then poured himself another brandy. Silasa had not touched hers. "Darkness brings out dark thoughts." He smiled wryly. "Drink."

She looked at the glass, but didn't touch it.

"You can drink, yes?"

"It tastes like mud," she said.

"No, you'll like this." He lifted the glass and held it out for her. "The upside of being king is that you get the best brandy."

"You mistake my meaning. To me, it will taste like mud no matter what it is. Everything tastes like mud. Browned chicken legs. Fresh summer squash. Recently churned butter. Lemon tarts. Brandy. Mud. Everything. Mud. Everything except..." she trailed off.

The breeze flowing through the window made Mershayn shiver. "Everything except blood," he murmured.

"Yes."

He hesitated, then said, "What does it taste like?"

She lifted her chin, closing her eyes. Her throat constricted, swallowing as though she was feeding right now. He slowly withdrew the brandy, but her hand lanced out, caught his with unbelievable strength. She opened her eyes, glancing at his wrist as though she could see the blood pumping just underneath his skin.

"It is...all of those flavors. It's better. It is the itch you can finally scratch. It is a river of gold to a thief. A lover's caress to the besotted. It is the laughter of a child playing in the sun. It is...indescribable." Her grip was so hard he winced. She looked dreamily at his arm like she didn't realize what she was doing.

"Silasa..." he warned, gripping the hilt of his dagger.

She blinked, and the dreamy look vanished. She let go, snatching the glass from his grip. "It is a glorious curse."

Mershayn let out a breath, but he didn't take his hand off his dagger. He tipped his chin at the glass in her hand. "Don't drink it then," he said, "if it tastes like mud."

"No. I will imagine that it tastes like...this moment."

He laughed. "So... Muddy, then."

She downed the liquor, and he did the same, feeling the sweet burn of it all the way down his throat. Silasa's face was unreadable, then she smiled at him, perhaps enjoying his expression.

"So good," he said.

She hesitated, then nodded. "Yes."

"You've never actually tasted brandy, have you?"

"No."

And she never will.

She stood. "My thanks, Mershayn. I'll take my leave now, with your permission."

"Thank you for coming."

"You leave in the morning?"

He glanced out the moonlit window. "In a few hours, actually. Vo'Dula will be here shortly."

"Then sleep. I will catch up with you tomorrow night."

He nodded.

She faded into the shadows, and then she was gone. He stood up, and took the candle into his bedroom. The window was open, but it slowly closed and latched as he watched. He glanced at his bed, and decided it was finally time to take Vo'Dula's advice.

He extinguished the candle, fell into the covers, and fell asleep immediately.

12

MERSHAYN

AT THE GATES OF THE CITY, Mershayn sat astride a ridiculously large white stallion, given to him by Ry'lyrio, of all people. At first, he thought it was a not-so-subtle assassination attempt. The beast, named Thunder, was eighteen hands high and looked like it wanted to kill someone. But after an hour in the saddle, Mershayn realized that Thunder was the most well-trained horse he'd ever had the pleasure of riding. Thunder snorted often, tossed his head a couple of times, but always obeyed Mershayn's commands. Sitting atop such ready power made Mershayn long to gallop into battle.

In a show for the soldiers, Mershayn sat next to a group of his mounted nobles: Vullieth, Ari'cyiane, Ry'lyrio, Baerst, and Galorman Balis. They watched the royal guard move out of the gates as the sun began to rise.

The army was larger than Mershayn had even hoped. Amidst a list of deficiencies in their fight against the dragon, this was a bright spot. Young men and women had flocked to join the army after the dragons attacked Teni'sia. The legend of

Mershayn's one-on-one battle with a dragon had inspired every young, would-be soldier. If Mershayn could kill a dragon single-handedly, why not every single soldier in the army?

It was the most ridiculous lie ever, but the fiction gave people hope. Mershayn had only survived that fight because he'd had a threadweaver protecting him every step of the way. But people loved legends, and his legend had swelled the army's ranks in a matter of days. And that confidence was the strongest weapon they had right now.

Of course, new recruits caused problems, too, Giri'Mar was quick to point out. They had to be trained to be of any use at all, and with the army marching, they'd have to be trained on the move.

In addition, there were already supply line problems, and they didn't even have a supply line yet. Giri'Mar had jumped on the problem like a diving hawk. The formerly truculent lord had suddenly become indispensable. In fact, if Mershayn had to choose a second in command at the moment, it would have to be Giri'Mar. He got to problems before they became catastrophes, and he sent hourly reports to Mershayn like clockwork.

Hour one: there wasn't enough bread for even a week of travel, let alone a stockpile to feed an army for a month. Giri'Mar promised he'd get the city's and castle's bakers working nonstop. Hour two: they didn't have enough wagons to carry the needed drinking water. Giri'Mar commissioned two ships to deliver barrels of water along their coastal route to supplement the water they carried with them. Hour three: there had been a baking disaster in the castle, and the new loaves were burnt so badly they were inedible. Giri'Mar was going personally talk to the head baker, and he was going to kill the man if need be.

The best news of the day came from Vullieth, who had been charged to be the envoy to the Sunriders. Apparently, their leader Gilgion had not died of the poison. He slept. The interim leader of the ring, Doermar, said the Sunriders would pack up and march with the Teni'sian army, carrying Gilgion on a litter. Mershayn had told Vullieth to insulate the Sunriders with a group of his own trusted soldiers.

Mystifying even to himself, Mershayn was protective of the Sunriders, and he longed for Gilgion to survive.

"We should follow the royal guard, Your Majesty," Vullieth said, breaking Mershayn from his reverie. At Vullieth's left, Ari'cyiane sat astride a ginger mare in her glittering chain mail and plate. She looked like a warrior, though Ari'cyiane had confessed to him once that she did not even know how to hold a sword. Not for the first time, he wondered why she was coming along with the army. She wasn't a fighter, and the journey would difficult and uncomfortable. For the most part, she did not look at him, but the rare moments that she did, he felt like she was plotting a way to kill him.

"Thank you, my lord." He nodded at Vullieth, made a clicking sound for Thunder, and flicked the reins. The giant horse moved forward obediently, snorting and tossing its head.

Here we go.

13

STAVARK

THE PROCESSION OF SIX WAGONS trundled along behind Stavark like an awkward, jouncing fleet of tall, badly rigged ships. They teetered with empty, steel-banded barrels. The procession had left Mershayn's army behind at dawn, breaking east to come to the True Ocean.

Stavark sat astride his horse, feeling as though the insides of his body were covered in rancid oil. He was *vanvakihrk*. He had failed the syvihrk, failed himself. Where once he saw the shining path of right before him, lit by his conviction, now there was only a shadowy jungle with no way to know which way he should turn.

But he had consented to go along on this mission. Mershayn thought it would be a favor to Stavark, to let him lead the soldiers who would load the water of the True Ocean, deadly to dragons, into barrels. So they could use this horrific weapon to strip the scales and flesh from their enemies.

It was one more sign that Stavark, who should have been a protector of life, was a weapon of death.

The rest of the army had continued north along the Inland Ocean. Stavark and Captain Lo'gan's little group were to go across the mountains to the True Ocean soon and load seawater into the barrels. After, they would continue north along the coast, then cross back over the mountains on the old Diyah Road. They would meet up with the army at the ruins of Diyah. Mershayn said it should take no more than three days.

The king had sent Captain Lo'gan along to give orders to the wagoners and the accompanying guards. Mershayn had told them to be quick, but it was impossible to be quick with six wagons.

But wagons were what they needed to bring the cursed water of the True Ocean back to the army. Mershayn had said they needed every advantage they could muster. The army had the magic weapons that Lady Bands had brought. Having Saraphazia's water, deadly to dragons, would be another surprise. It could mean the difference between victory and defeat. Then Mershayn had said, "By Thalius's curly beard, *anything* might be the difference between victory and defeat."

Each wagon could carry eighteen barrels of seawater, fully laden, but Captain Lo'gan had advised Mershayn that a fully loaded wagon would more easily break an axle. Mershayn had told him to strap twenty four empty barrels to each wagon for the trip to the ocean, but carry back only twelve apiece.

"Fill them all up, but leave half at the shore," he had said. "That'll give us seventy-two barrels to use right away. And if luck is with us, we'll have time to send the empty wagons back for more before the dragons attack."

The old, rutted dirt road wound between the peaks, piled with wet snow that made deep ruts that the wagoners struggled through. The cold snap of the storm had faded, and the farther north they went, the warmer it was. It was as though winter had remembered Teni'sia, but forgotten everywhere else.

"Not going to work," one of the old wagoners—the sour-looking one with the long, wide beard—suddenly said.

Captain Lo'gan slowed his horse and turned to look at the old wagoner. "You don't think it's going to work?" the captain repeated.

"All fine and good to bring a wagon loaded with empty barrels through this muck. Once these barrels is loaded, wagon'll sink to the axle." He shook his head, then spat to the side. "His Majesty is crazy as a drunk surf dragon."

"We won't be coming back along this path," Captain Lo'gan said.

Stavark remained quiet. He had never been so conflicted. He had never before agreed to a task where part of himself wished to fail. He wanted to help protect his friends, but he also wished that the dragons, as vicious as they were, would not be harmed by this ocean water, would not be harmed by *his* idea.

"Won't we then? And you think the next path up is going to be better? A fool's notion," the wagoner muttered. "Snow don't just fall in the south. North is gonna be as bad or worse. What's His Majesty need seawater for anyway?"

Because I gave him a new weapon. Because I am a killer...

"I cannot say," Captain Lo'gan replied.

"A secret, eh?" The wagoner spat again. "Well, you order me to sink a cart up to its axle in mud, I'll sink a cart for you."

"I'd rather you bring the seawater back as His Majesty ordered."

"Sure. We'll do that," the wagoner said with no confidence.

Captain Lo'gan frowned. He seemed about to say something more, but decided against it. He laid his reins against his horse and moved toward the front of the procession, coming up alongside Stavark.

He glanced at Stavark's mount, his brow wrinkling in disapproval, then up at Stavark.

"No reins?" Captain Lo'gan asked.

Stavark had not used the reins like Captain Lo'gan had told him to. The human did not understand, because he could not hear the voices of the land and the animals. Of course, when you could not hear what nature needed and requested, you likewise could never betray her....

"The horse does not like the reins," Stavark said. The

captain was like most humans. He thought that in order for animals to be good servants, they must be dominated.

But most horses did not dislike riders. The weight of a man, and certainly the weight of a *syvihrk*, was no burden. Unless a horse was the stallion of a herd, it would likely be content to go where it was asked. Most horses bore bridles with quiet tolerance. Horses were instinctually aware of the flow of the lands, and they would choose to go with that flow instead of causing conflict.

Most animals were like that. Humans were not, so they used carved stone and bits of steel to control the nature around them. But the idea of someone shoving a piece of steel between Stavark's own teeth made him angry, so it made him angry on behalf of the horse. He wasn't about to do what Captain Lo'gan said simply because Captain Lo'gan did not know how to connect with an animal.

Stavark kept one hand on the horse's neck, feeling the animal's heartbeat and its occasional desires. He did what he could to fulfill them, sitting at the best spot on the horse's back, giving it a moment to crop grass when it was particularly hungry or bored. In exchange, the horse was receptive to Stavark's gentle nudges with heels, knees, and the firm intent that he envisioned flowing from his own heart into the horse's heart.

It eased Stavark's mind somewhat to practice this connection with a living creature. This was what he wanted: to move with the flow of nature like the horse did, to be one with the living. That was why he'd come east with Orem. Not to be a destroyer. To be a protector.

Mershayn had said, "After we fling a few barrels of seawater into their snouts, we might spook them. Maybe they'll leave us alone." He'd tried to encourage Stavark that the death would be less by scaring the dragons away, but Mershayn had not really believed that.

Stavark had not really believed it, either. So he had not responded. Dragons weren't beasts like this horse. They were sentients with intellects at least as great as humans. They would not "spook," as Mershayn put it.

Stavark's horse crested a rise next to Captain Lo'gan, and they saw the True Ocean at the same moment, stretching out before them. The vast, unending blue consumed everything all the way to the horizon. Stavark had traveled all over Amarion; he'd sailed the Inland Ocean, been as far south as the Red Desert and as far north as Daylan's Fountain, but he had never seen anything like the True Ocean. It was vast.

"There she is," Captain Lo'gan said, seeming to feel the same awe as Stavark. Captain Lo'gan looked back at the struggling carts far behind them. "We could have them loaded up by nightfall, Thalius willing."

Stavark nodded. "Then we hurry. We must not sleep near the water."

Captain Lo'gan glanced at him. "Why?"

"The goddess."

"The goddess? What goddess?"

"The goddess Saraphazia."

Captain Lo'gan paused, as though trying to recall where he'd heard that name.

Stavark wanted to sigh, but he did not. It was a failing of humans, and perhaps not entirely their fault. Their histories had been lost. What they remembered was based only on what their parents remembered, then decided to pass on. Only a select few would seek books in old, boarded-up libraries like Orem had, if they could even find such libraries. Most humans didn't know about the old gods. Oh, they all knew the name Tarithalius, but only because they used his name to curse. When humans had turned away from their writings, they had let important things fade into the past.

It was easy for Stavark to forget that most humans were not like Orem, who had put his own life at risk to unearth the histories reviled by most humans.

Thinking of Orem made Stavark twitch. It was as though a bramble of thorns pressed between his shoulders. Orem was still out there, somewhere, hostage to Zilok Morth. And instead of trying to find him, somehow Stavark was helping with a war.

The wagons finally caught up to them, then proceeded down the long slope to the rolling waves.

Stavark rolled his shoulders, but the prickles didn't fade. So he stoically ignored them and followed the wagons down to the surf.

Each wagon had one wagoner, a helper, and a guard, and they wasted no time. They got to work right away, stacking the extra barrels against the slope, out of reach of the high-tide marks. After that, they pulled off their boots. It was slightly warmer here than in Teni'sia. There was no snow on the ground near the water, but none of them wanted to make the rest of the journey with wet boots.

Three at a time, they strode into the chill surf to fill the barrels. The filling went quickly. It only took one person to carry the barrel in, but three to haul it out. Once they did, Captain Lo'gan waited with hammer and nails, and he nailed the lids shut, moving quickly from team to team as they emerged.

The work went quickly, each team wanting to be finished and get on the road again as soon as possible.

Stavark dismounted, looked out over the True Ocean, and occasionally back where they had come. Captain Lo'gan had encouraged him to stand guard, and he'd agreed. He wasn't much use with this kind of labor, unless he stepped into the silverland, and he didn't want to do that unless...

He stood up taller, squinting at the horizon of the True Ocean. For a moment, the flat horizon hadn't been flat. It had only been a second, but out of the corner of his eye, he could have sworn he'd seen a splash, like a whale rising, shooting a spray into the air, then submerging. But he wasn't sure. If it had been a whale, it had been very far away. He might be wrong. It might have just been a fish.

Stavark entered the silverland. He'd seen what Saraphazia could do, and he wasn't going to take any chances. The beach, the curling waves, and the cluster of men and women froze in hues of silver. Stavark ran and jumped atop the nearest wagon.

The great blue of the True Ocean had become a sheet of silver, and he could see nothing that broke that surface. Swallowing, he stepped out of the silverland, still watching intently.

Nothing. There was nothing. The wagons were half loaded with full barrels. It would take half an hour more to fill and load the rest. Maybe an hour more to fill the barrels they would leave behind. If he alerted Captain Lo'gan now for no reason, they would return with only half of their load.

Stavark's heart raced, and he felt ill. It was the same feeling he got when the lands spoke to him. It was the feeling he'd had when they stood in front of the fouled woods near Belshra.

Still, he saw nothing. The ocean was as flat and calm as it had been when they arrived. He saw nothing, but he could not ignore the feeling.

"Captain Lo'gan," Stavark said.

The captain looked over where Stavark had been standing a moment before, suddenly realizing Stavark had vanished.

"Captain," Stavark said again, allowing the man to follow his voice and look up at him on top of the wagon. "We must leave. Now."

Captain Lo'gan stiffened, looked out over the ocean. Like Stavark, the captain didn't seem to see anything. Stavark thought most humans would have asked a silly question, like "Why?" or "Did you see something?" or make a comment like, "But we're almost finished!"

But Captain Lo'gan was a serious man. He took Stavark's warning seriously.

"That's it!" Captain Lo'gan shouted to the six different crews. "Back to your wagons. We'll take what we have. Leave the rest."

The crews looked up, surprised, almost every one of them glancing at the slope from where they'd come, as though the threat would come from that direction.

"Did you see something, sir?" one of the guards asked, his hand sliding down to his sword.

The others simply paused, as though they didn't

understand why they were being commanded to drop their work. Only the sour old wagoner immediately did as he was told. He dropped the barrel into the surf and marched up the shore. His helper kept a hand on the barrel. "Where?" the helper said. "Where is it?"

"Thalius's beard," another wagoner said. "We'll be done in fifteen minutes." He stood there, hand on his barrel. "I don't see nothing."

"Get out of the water and get in your wagons. Do it now!" Captain Lo'gan barked. The guards obeyed immediately, running out of the surf to their boots.

The sour old wagoner didn't stop to put his boots on. He snatched them with his hand and got into his wagon. He flicked the reins and shouted, "Geeyah!" to the horses, who immediately started pulling the cart.

The sour old wagoner's cart was already working its way up the slope by the time the guards sat down in the sand to put their boots on, getting ready for a fight.

"This one's already full," one of the younger wagoners grunted. He and his helper hauled it quickly up to the beach.

"Leave it," Captain Lo'gan commanded. "Get—" His words dried up in his mouth.

The flat of the ocean bulged, becoming a rounded mountain of blue. Captain Lo'gan gaped.

It was probably half a mile away, but the sheer size of it took Stavark's breath away. The goddess had not made herself even half so large when she spoke with Bands.

"Go!" Stavark shouted. "Just leave the wagons. Run as far away from the ocean as you can!" Stavark, of course, did not flee. This was where the pain could end. The best a *vanvakihrk* could do was sacrifice himself. And here, Stavark would do exactly that. Of course, he could not stand against a goddess, but perhaps if he delayed her, even for a second, then one of Captain Lo'gan's soldiers or wagoners might escape.

The bulge of ocean exploded and Saraphazia burst forth, riding the swell at an impossible speed. An avalanche of water roiled behind her, tall as the Teni'sian castle, as if straining to keep up.

A misty hurricane slammed into the group, knocking most of the helpers and wagoners down. The two guards who'd managed to get their boots on leaned into the wind and kept their feet.

But Stavark had seen Saraphazia attack. He knew this battle was over. The guards could stand their ground or draw their swords or fight perfectly. None of it would matter. And even Stavark didn't have time to save them all.

But he might have time to save a few.

He leapt into the silverland, ran to Captain Lo'gan and picked him up.

Outside the silverland, Stavark could never have picked up a person the size of Captain Lo'gan. But here, Stavark could push on the man's arm, then his leg, then his other arm, then his other leg, over and over again. A single push did nothing, but with many small lifts, he could move the man. Gravity was slow here, just like everything else.

He pushed Captain Lo'gan up, then forward through the air toward the sour old wagoner's wagon, which was halfway up the slope already. He reached the wagon and pushed Captain Lo'gan gently down next to the seven full barrels the old wagoner had loaded.

But using his muscles against something like gravity was not without cost. Fatigue came quickly in the silverland.

Panting hard, Stavark looked back at the beach. Saraphazia's monstrous square head loomed over them, washed in silver like everything else. Her avalanche of waves reared over the beach. Men and women from the wagon crews stayed frozen in mid-fall as the frozen hurricane gust blew them over.

I am already tired. I will never get them all out.

He ran back down to the beach, across the waves, skipping from churning crest to churning crest, all the way up to Saraphazia's nose, which was wider than the field at Denema's Valley. He had to distract her. He had to—

A brutal, invisible force wrapped around his chest and

yanked him out of the silverland.

Time sped up. Stavark gasped.

Saraphazia's enormous, flat face turned dark gray. Silver melted away from the world, and everything returned to its normal color. The goddess's eyes, each the size of a house, flared with dark blue fire.

"You dare!" she boomed. A spear of water hammered into Stavark, throwing him high into the air.

He couldn't breathe. He reached out for the silverland, but he couldn't find it. The spear threw him up, up, up, and then he was falling. He hit the ocean like it was a slab of rock. Pain forked through his whole body, and he yelled. The ocean closed over his head, and he saw the pale sun through shimmering water.

He sank. His chest spasmed, igniting the pain again, and he gasped, sucked in a lungful of water. He struggled, but he couldn't get his arms to work. He reached for the surface, but he needed to be doing something else.

Swimming. He needed to swim. But he continued to sink, the sun getting farther and farther away. He sucked in another lungful of water, and everything went dark.

And then, he felt nothing at all.

14

STAVARK

"Quiet, my champion. Stay as still as you can."

Her words came into his head, and her voice was the ripple of a stream, the rustle of the wind in the trees, the serene silence of the mountains. He knew that voice, had known it his whole life. He knew it like he knew his own broken heart.

Water pressed on him from all around, but somehow, he could still breathe.

His first urge was to jump up, kick for the surface, but a hand pressed gently on his chest, and somehow it calmed him.

"No, my champion. If you move, she'll find us both."

The memories came next, the onslaught of the goddess Saraphazia. That was why Stavark was here, at the bottom of the ocean.

But…how could he breathe?

He blinked, opened his eyes. They were fifty feet deep, and pale sunlight lanced across the ocean's tumultuous surface. It raged, but he was held firmly on the bottom by this girl. She was his own age, with pale skin and blue hair. That hair swirled around them, enclosing them both, binding them in a cocoon. Her warm body pressed against him, one of her arms behind him, one across his chest.

Stavark tried to speak, but it ruffled the tiny bubble in front of his mouth, the only thing that was allowing him to breathe. He coughed.

"*No, my champion,*" she said. "*If you must talk to me, talk in my mind. Just think loudly, and I will hear you.*"

"*Captain Lo'gan....*"

"*You saved him. You gave him and the old man time enough. She will not chase them over the mountain.*"

"*What about the others?*"

"*I am sorry, my champion. She is killing them.*"

"*We have to stop her!*"

"*A hundred* syvihrk *could not stop her, brave one. Hold still, or you, too, will die, and then so will I.*"

Her last words made him hesitate. He could make the decision to sacrifice himself, but he could not make that decision for another.

And this new girl... Her presence filled him. She was more than she seemed. Her voice sounded like...the voice of the lands.

He could see beyond the cocoon because she had parted her hair in front of his eyes. The goddess Saraphazia thrashed above, half beached on the shore and half of her extending into the ocean farther than he could see.

Then, the goddess stopped moving and held still for a long moment.

"*Very quiet now,*" the girl whispered into his mind. "*So quiet.*"

Slowly, inexorably, the enormous whale slid back into the ocean. She turned, and her great tail smacked the shore where she had been, then she undulated and shot into the water. In moments, Stavark could see nothing of her.

The water above slowly calmed, then returned to normal, the surface waves rolling softly.

"Wait..." she whispered.

He felt her inside him, and she was the serenity of a green

field, a dappled glade. She was the refreshing breeze of springtime. He had felt these things before around the *Maehka vik Kalik*, but only flickers at a time. Never had they been this intense.

"Who...who are you?" he thought loudly.

"My name is Vee."

"Why did you save me?"

He heard her laughter in his mind. *"Because you are beautiful,* syvihrk, *and I need you to save my life."*

"To save your life...?"

"But we must stay quiet for the moment, hidden. If my mother senses me in her ocean, I shall never leave again."

Her tense statement struck him like a blow. Her mother was the goddess of the ocean? The syvihrk *knew all the gods, of course, and the loremasters told stories to the young, including a litany of the gods, their greatest works and their greatest evils. Stavark had memorized each those stories before he was ten years old.*

Stavark quivered, fighting the awe and excitement that lanced through him like lightning. Staying quiet was one of the most difficult things he'd ever done.

Then the mammoth Saraphazia moved away from the shore, her tail undulating up and down slowly. Then, with a powerful flip of her tail, she shot deep into the ocean and was gone, leaving the entire ocean rocking violently behind her. Vee held tight to Stavark until the water settled again.

"You're Vaisha the Changer!" Stavark blurted.

"Gently now, my champion. My mother has moved away, but she feels her waters. The more her anger cools, the more likely she may sense my presence, even as far away as she is. If we escape, then I will tell you the rest of my story," she said. *"How I used to be Vaisha the Changer. How I lost my body, and how I need to get it back."*

Stavark's heart thundered loudly in his chest. Vaisha was the goddess of his people, the creator of the *syvihrk*, the goddess of nature.

"My lady..." He couldn't think straight. *"You..."* Dervon the Diseased had slain Vaisha millennia ago.

"This small form was one of many pieces left after my uncle tried to kill me. My mother took me into the ocean. The other pieces soaked into the lands, and later were bound within the Maehka Arghakt. *But now, they have been released. I can feel them, wild and frustrated. I have come to reclaim them. Will you help me?"*

Stavark closed his eyes, feeling her presence next to him, inside him. His pain and confusion—the self-hatred he'd felt at the garden at Teni'sia—unraveled. Ever since the moment he'd left Sylikkayrn with Orem, Stavark had felt his destiny lay in the human lands. At first, he thought it was to free the *maehka* from the *Maehka Arghakt*, from Daylan's Fountain. Then he had thought it was to protect the *Maehka vik Kalik*, Mirolah. Last, he thought he had been led astray by pride, and that this entire journey had been wrong. That it had, in the end, turned him into a *vanvakihrk*.

But he hadn't been wrong to come to the human lands. He had only been wrong to despair. *This* was his true path, the path of rightness. Vaisha spoke with the voice of the real *Maehka vik Kalik*, and she was wounded. There could be no higher cause than restoring Vaisha the Changer to the lands.

Stavark's real purpose unfolded before him as bright as the sunlight above. He shivered. Calm certainty settled into the center of him.

"You honor me, Maehka vik Kalik, *"* he said.

"You honor me, syvihrk. *"*

"I will never doubt again."

"Then you will help me?"

"I am yours, Maehka vik Kalik. *"*

"You will be my champion," she said. *"My champion for all time."*

Her blue hair parted, streaming behind them like a cape as, together, they rushed toward the light.

15

MERSHAYN

MERSHAYN REINED IN HIS MOUNT. Thunder clopped to a stop on the road, mud and snow churning. It was the third day of the march, and so far, there had been no calamities. Strangely, every hour they'd marched had become a little less cold, as though winter had come first to Teni'sia, and autumn still lingered in the north. He stretched in his saddle and looked back over the long column of men, women, horses and wagons. He had pushed them hard. Fatigue had worn away the pomp and circumstance of their departure. A sensible leader might call a stop to camp. Sundown was an hour away, and it was at least three to reach the North Fort.

The sun shone, the air warmer than it had been an hour ago. The western skies were clear and blue, and everyone knew Teni'sia got its weather from the west. Storms rolled across the Inland Ocean, hit the Corialis Mountains, and dumped on Teni'sia.

But Mershayn had been studying the clouds to the south, and he didn't like them. They were dark and ugly. They seemed far away, but that was a storm. And somehow he knew—without knowing how he knew—that it was coming north.

He turned back to face the front of the army, and his personal guard stayed close about him. He had hidden himself with the vanguard, though almost each of his nobles had reminded him that it was not safe. The alternative, of course, was traveling with them at the back of the army and there were a number of reasons he didn't want to do that.

Being in the open air astride this magnificent horse was too grand to ruin it by jumping into a political rat pit. Let the nobles dwell in their own conversations for now. His father once said that spending too much time around one's subjects created a familiar air, and that could taint a command.

Sure. That was it. That was why he'd much rather be here than with them. It wasn't because Lady Ari'cyiane, trotting along with her snow-white stole wrapped around her delicate chainmail shirt, kept trying to stab him with daggers launched from her eyes. It wasn't that she made him as uncomfortable as sitting on an angry anthill.

No. Certainly it wasn't that....

He heard swift-moving horse hooves, and he turned to see Deni'tri galloping up the road. The guardswoman pulled up next to him, her cowl and cloak flapping behind her. Her nose, ears, and the tops of her cheeks were pink, and wisps of heat drifted from her bald head.

"Greetings, Deni'tri," he said.

She neatly managed her steed as it clopped to a walk beside him and nodded. "Your Majesty. Captain Lo'gan, Stavark, and their wagons have not returned."

"Excellent," he said, when he felt the exact opposite. "Well, three days was optimistic. We knew that." He checked his sigh. He'd been excited when Stavark first told him that True Ocean water was like acid to dragons.

Now, three days later, it sounded ludicrous and a stupid waste of important resources. He kept envisioning his soldiers loading their catapults with barrels of water, flinging them into the faces of the dragons...and having the barrels smash and splash harmlessly against their foes. Dragon laughter. Deadly fire. Death to all....

Now, of course, there was nothing he could do about it. Worse, Lo'gan and Stavark were officially late. And with that storm moving in...

Mershayn had once thought being king was about maintaining control. That was laughable. Being king was about doling out control to everyone else. He'd let Stavark run off to chase his insane plan. And Bands went off to chase her insane plan. And Mirolah's spirit was off...doing whatever a threadweaver did when she was dead. And Mershayn, responsible for all of these schemes and the lives that depended on them, sat back with the army and waited to see if they worked. His stomach hadn't felt well for days.

"Your Majesty, some of the nobles are requesting a stop," she said, indicating the sinking sun. "To rest and recover their warmth."

"Some? Who?"

"Galorman Balis and Lady Ari'cyiane."

Mershayn frowned. "Balis, eh?"

"And the Lady Ari'cyiane."

"There will be no stop," he said.

"She insisted, Your Majesty."

"Did she?" He paused a moment. "Tell her I am increasing the pace. We must reach North Fort tonight. That will make her happy."

"Will it?"

Mershayn gave Deni'tri a winning smile. "The faster we go, the sooner she can have a fire. We do not stop until we reach the fort."

"Yes, Your Majesty." Deni'tri grinned back.

"If the pace bothers her, I can spare a small contingent to camp with her here tonight and take her back to the castle in the morning, if she would prefer."

"Yes, Your Majesty."

"And Deni'tri..." he said.

"Yes, Your Majesty?"

"Get a cap or something. You look cold."

"I like the cold, Your Majesty." Deni'tri said, her pink cheeks glowing.

He chuckled. "Well, you're making me feel cold. At least put your cowl up. Make your king feel better."

"Yes, Your Majesty." She flipped her cowl up, wheeled her horse around, churning the snow and mud, and galloped away. The cowl caught the sudden wind and flopped back onto her shoulders again.

Mershayn chuckled, and shook his head. He glanced at the distant storm, then turned his own mount and set the pace for the fort.

16

MERSHAYN

THE WIND WHIPPED around North Fort like it wanted to uproot the wooden walls and carry them away. Mershayn stood on the battlement of the fort as the last cart was brought inside. All were accounted for, but if the storm was as nasty as it looked, it was going to be a hard night even with the fort's protection, not to mention a harder march tomorrow, if marching was even possible.

If they were buried under snow, the army would have to settle down here until the storm was done, maybe longer. A cart didn't move through four-foot drifts. His soldiers were well-equipped, but not so well they could march for days through waist-high snow. If this storm was like the other that had hit Teni'sia during the night Wildmane had led his ill-fated group into Teni'sia to overthrow Sym, then this might be the place the dragons found them. That would be disastrous. The last place Mershayn wanted to make a stand against a fire-breathing opponent was in a fort made of wood.

It had already been three days since the dragons attacked

Teni'sia. Every day, Mershayn's shoulders tightened a little more, expecting the next assault.

"I dislike this storm," Deni'tri said. She stayed by his side unless he specifically sent her away. Vo'Dula had stayed back to manage the castle, but it was as though she had taken his place. Except less annoying. "If the dragons catch us here, it will be bad."

"They won't fly in a storm," he said, trying to sound more confident than he felt.

She hesitated, then nodded.

"Don't let it trouble you, Deni'tri. If they catch us, then we fight. If they don't, let's not chip away at ourselves worrying." He turned his attention from the storm to the army within the fort walls. "The fires are going?"

"Yes, Your Majesty."

"The cooks are supplied?"

"Yes, Your Majesty."

"A hot meal will go a long way to shaking off this cold. But make certain the horses are put away properly. Every one. I don't want anyone doing half a job so they can rush to a warm fire. I want no horses coming up lame tomorrow. Make an example of anyone who shirks. "

"I will make rounds after you are safely abed, Your Majesty."

"And tap a couple of barrels of ale, enough to lighten the heart, not enough to regret it."

"Yes, Your Majesty."

He paused. Everything was in order, but apprehension hovered about him. The last time he'd seen a storm like this, Mirolah had returned from the dead.

"And where is Mirolah's body?" he asked. It made him feel a little sick to refer to her that way, but he remained adamant that Mirolah's spirit was elsewhere, and that it would return.

"In your rooms, Your Majesty."

"And none knows save we three?"

"Myself, you, and Grek'tas."

And Stavark and Lo'gan, of course, but they weren't here.

Hopefully, they were bivouacked snugly on the east side of the mountains away from this vicious storm. "Well done, Deni'tri."

He turned and went down the ladder, then across the bustling yard and into the only stone building in the fort, the main hall. The smell of close bodies, wood smoke, and charred sausage filled his nostrils. Roaring fires blazed in the three fireplaces, and a haze of smoke drifted among the rafters. Soldiers whispered as he walked past them.

He worked his way through the crowd, grasping a hand here, giving a confident word there. Lady Ry'lyrio saw him from across the hall, and strode to intercept him.

"Lady Ry'lyrio," he said in a welcoming tone that he did not feel. "I wanted to thank you. Thunder is an amazing animal."

She bowed low. "It was my pleasure, Your Majesty. It is what any loyal servant of Teni'sia would do." She emphasized the word "loyal" and he knew exactly where the conversation was going. Of course, with Lady Ry'lyrio, there was only one way any conversation could ever go.

"You have my thanks."

She started in immediately. "The Sunriders, Your Majesty."

"The Sunriders?"

"Lord Vullieth has bunked the Sunriders inside the walls, Your Majesty. *Inside* the walls."

"Did he?" he said. He had given those orders to Vullieth himself. He had also ordered Vullieth to resist any advice—or demands—given to him by Ry'lyrio.

"It's suicide, Your Majesty," she continued. "When their greater force to the north attacks us—and they *will* attack us—those barbarians inside the fort will unlock the gates. We'll be defenseless."

"A profound point," Mershayn said. He didn't mention that not even an army of Sunriders could make progress through this blizzard. Nor did he mention that kicking the Sunriders out into this blizzard would be a death sentence. She didn't care about any of that. Sunriders dying of exposure to the elements would only upset her in that she hadn't cut their throats herself.

Mershayn looked around the main hall. "My lady, I have put Lord Vullieth in charge of the Sunriders." He spotted what he was looking for, one of his royal guards in the main hall. He spoke over his shoulder to Deni'tri. "Would you please ask Co'bellian to take Lady Ry'lyrio to Lord Vullieth so that she might make him aware of her concerns?"

"At once, Your Majesty." Deni'tri took Ry'lyrio's arm. "If you will, my lady, I will have you escorted directly to Lord Vullieth." Deni'tri led a reluctant Lady Ry'lyrio away.

Mershayn suppressed a satisfied smile. Deni'tri had picked up the conversation just like she was Vo'Dula. He'd have to commend her for that.

She caught up to him a moment later as he finished his rounds. The soldiers liked seeing their king. It seemed to give them heart. He couldn't give his soldiers much tonight, but if he could give them reassurance, he would.

Afterward, he and Deni'tri went into the teeth of the storm again. Snow swirled, and wind blew even more fiercely. Visibility was down to about fifteen feet. He and Deni'tri strode into the drifts.

It took a few minutes to reach the large chamber at the north of the fort, currently serving as his royal chambers. Grek'tas and No'Darun, bundled up in their cloaks, stood guard at the door. He nodded to them wordlessly and slipped inside.

A fire crackled in the fireplace, warding off the chill. He crossed to the raised pallet beside his bed. Atop it lay Mirolah, still as death, and as cool as the room. Her lustrous brown hair tumbled down the pillow, framing her smooth face, as calm as if she had slipped into an untroubled slumber. She hadn't changed in the three days they had been traveling, almost as if she was carved and painted wood. Deni'tri and Grek'tas had wrapped her in warm clothes and a thick fur blanket. It was a thoughtful touch, and Mershayn liked it. Though he had to admit he could probably have stuffed her in a snow drift and she would not have been any worse off.

He was certain any of the other nobles would have objected to bringing a dead woman on a war campaign, citing it as the most horrific omen he could have conjured. But, well...

They weren't the king.

He went to her side. When he had first seen her, he had been stunned. Then she had laid her hands on him, healed him, and he had tasted the depths of her kindness. He had fallen for her that day. His heart had dropped into a deep well, and he had never recovered it.

He reached out and touched her cheek delicately.

"If it really is you making this storm," he whispered. "Let it bring you back to us. Let it bring you home."

He leaned down and kissed her cold lips.

"Come back, Mirolah. We need you."

Outside, a fierce howl rose over the roaring storm.

17

MIROLAH

SHE WAS THE WIND, and she happily whirled across the Inland Ocean, ruffling the water, tickling passing ships. Her laughter fell as rain. She rushed over the thin silver twist of the Quicksilver River. She flew far to the south, all the way to the Red Desert, twisted and turned with the little sandy breezes. With her, she carried the long skinny dog, because the Voice had commanded it. The dog had howled at first, when she had created the powerful wind to lift it. But she had protected it, and it had since quieted. It shivered, keeping its eyes narrowed as it flew along.

She raced up the Spine Mountains, then south again along the great plains. There, she saw an enormous cluster of black-haired human riders, tiny as ants, riding hard for the north. The dog howled.

She swooped down and through the riders, laughing and leaving more rain in her wake. The Voice inside her spoke.

They're Sunriders.

The Voice was angry about that. She didn't know why. She

didn't hate humans. It wasn't her place to hate anything.

Except being confined. She had been trapped in the *Maehka Arghakt*, what humans called Daylan's Fountain, for hundreds of years. She would never do that again.

But the Voice hated their long ponytails, their bulging muscles, their curved swords. And the Voice had tremendous power inside her. It was the One. It was part of her, and so the Voice's anger became her anger. She descended again, blew a few of them over and sent ice-tipped raindrops at their dusky faces. Many threw up their hands in fear, shielding their heads. Their horses whinnied and reared.

They destroyed Gildon. They destroyed my home.

She knew that human village. It was to the south. The Voice wanted to go there, so she flew southward again, down past the reaches of the Inland Ocean.

She swirled over the modest hills and the ruins of Gildon.

This is where the Sunriders killed my parents.

Killed... The word swirled inside her, making the Voice angrier, and so she became angrier. The flying dog howled.

I lived in Rith, also.

She knew where that village was, too. So she flew north and east. Snow swirled behind, the rain of laughter turning cold.

Soon, she hovered over an old city, the streets built in a spiral that vanished into the center of a lake.

This is Rith. This was my home, too.

The snow storm thickened. She blew harder as the Voice relived the horrible despair it had felt in Rith. The Voice had let her out of the *Maehka Arghakt*. The Voice was the One she had known would come someday.

Yes. I freed you.

The One was supposed to make her whole again, but it hadn't. Instead of making her bigger, the Voice tried to make her smaller. It tried to contain her in a human body instead.

Thunderclouds bunched overhead as she considered being trapped in that confining mortal body again.

We must return. We must return to my body.

The Wind looked down, seeing the humans of Rith scurrying to take shelter from the sudden storm.

Go down there. Go into that human there.

She didn't want to, but the Voice demanded, so down she went. She flowed into a woman with a shawl over her head, and then she was two...the mortal woman and the Wind confined within her. The woman's threads gave way, and the view became small, confined, as the Wind entered the prison of the human's body. She could no longer feel the distant mountains, the top of the sky, the entire breadth of the vast plains. Instead, she saw only through the eyes of the woman. Snow swirled around the woman so thickly she could barely see the walls of the shops to her left. The Wind put the dog down on the ground next to the old woman. It shook the snow from its yellow skin, then gave a pleased growling noise. The Wind felt the woman's fear, saw fear in the faces of the two other humans on the street as they gaped at the skinny dog.

"Do not fear," the Voice said, using the old woman's body to speak. The Voice made the old woman reach out and put a hand on the dog. Waves of nausea twisted the old woman's guts. The Voice looked down at the old woman's hands, gnarled and wrinkled.

This is not my body, the Voice said.

Fear grew within the Wind then. The body... The Voice sought the body it called Mirolah. The Voice had tried to shove the Wind into that body. But the Wind did not belong in a human body. She was the Wind. She was the mountains, the ocean. She was too large to be contained in one slowly rotting mortal.

The old woman moaned.

The Voice let go of the old woman. With a gasp of relief, the Wind rose. The nausea vanished, and the old woman jerked as though she'd been slapped.

The dog howled and ran after the Wind, and the Voice demanded that she pick him up again. She did, then flew away, taking the dog and the churning, roiling snow with her.

Bring me back to my body. The Voice compelled her to go north. *Back. Back to the place I left.*

But she didn't want to go back to the body and, as she roared north, her displeasure dropped as a blizzard over Buravar.

Spray flew up and waves churned as she crossed the Inland Ocean, swirling around Clete, letting the blizzard consume that kingdom next.

Mershayn helped me. I helped him in return. He still needs my help. Go back to my body.

The Voice inside her drove her on, north across the Corialis Mountains to the kingdom of Teni'sia. The city's bright spires hove into view, and she swirled through them and around them, seeing the destruction left by the dragons. Entire buildings had been crushed. Broken buildings littered the streets. Charred houses thrust their blackened bones at the sky.

The humans had beaten the dragons. They'd defeated them because she had stolen the wind from their wings. She had helped in this victory. Even now, groups of Teni'sians hacked with axes at the carcass of a huge dragon. They flinched and looked up in surprise at the sudden storm she brought.

It's here. Somewhere here. My body.

She and the Voice descended upon the castle.

In there.

The Voice drove her on, so she flowed reluctantly through a window of the castle, flipping the iron-bound glass open so strongly it shattered against the wall. She blew back the sweaty hair of a man walking the halls, taking his breath away.

Where is my body?

Thunder cracked in the sky, and the blizzard whipped hard around the castle. The Voice was the One. It was supposed to make her whole, but instead it wanted to stuff her into that human body again!

She tried to pull away from the Voice's control, but it forced her down the hallways, searching frantically.

She struggled against the Voice, but it was so strong. The dark clouds of her real body roiled in the sky outside, thick and bunched. The Wind's anger grew as she continued to search for something she didn't want to find. Snow began to fall.

A young serving woman appeared around the corner, and the Voice made the Wind take control of the woman's threads. The Wind's vast vision contracted again, down down down and behind the limited eyes of the human.

Stone walls came into focus. The corridor stretched out in front of her, branching off in three directions, two to the right, one to the left.

"Where is my body?" the Voice asked, using the mouth of the serving woman.

The nausea hit her again. The woman wanted her body back, and she fought for it. The Voice ignored the struggles just as she ignored the Wind's desires.

The Voice took the human woman's body and ran down the hall, tripped on the hem of her dress. She tumbled to the ground, smacking her head on the stones. Dazed, she sat up, putting a hand to her forehead. She rose again, and, gathering her skirts into one hand, raced down the hall.

The Wind longed to get out of the human body. Everything was so small, and everything went so slowly. A human body was weak. Soon, the woman was out of breath and had to stop so that her lungs might recover.

I'm almost there, said the Voice.

Nausea swept through the woman, and she almost vomited.

"I am sorry," the Voice said with the girl's mouth. "I must find my own body before I can give yours back to you. But I promise I will return it to you."

The woman ran down the hallway, seeking the royal wing. One more flight of stairs, and she emerged onto the correct floor.

"Nessi'li!" A large hand grabbed her arm, and the woman spun. A tall man in chain mail and a helmet had hold of her. He shook his head. "You can't go down that way."

"I'm sorry?" the Voice said with the woman's mouth.

"That's the royal quarters. No one allowed in there. King's

away."

"But I must find my body." The woman shook her arm, trying to break his grip.

"What?" he asked.

The Voice opened the serving girl's mouth to speak again, then didn't.

"Are you feeling okay, Nessi'li?"

"N-No, I'm okay. I just... I was told to, um, to speak with the king."

The guard narrowed his eyes. "Indeed. And who told you that?"

"Is he here?" she asked impatiently.

Again, that confusion creased the guard's brow. "Nessi'li, are you sure you're all right? You know as well as I do that the king is gone away north."

"What?"

"To fight the dragons," he said, then the guard noticed where the woman had hit her head on the ground. "Gods, Nessi'li! Are you all right? You've hit your head."

"To the north?" the Voice said with the woman's lips. The Voice made the woman move to the window behind the guard and undo the latch. The dog hovered on the strong wind outside.

"By Thalius!" the guard stumbled backward. "Nessi'li! Get away from that thing!"

But the human woman walked forward, put a gentle hand on the dog's cold back. Snowflakes swirled into the hallway.

The guard hesitated, eyes wide at the entire scene.

"He took it," the Voice whispered with the woman's mouth. "Mershayn took my body."

The guard stepped away from the serving woman, and the Voice released Nessi'li's body, flying out into the storm again finally.

The Wind reveled as she flew free from the confining woman's body.

To the north.

No. *Not* to the north. *Not* to the prison of another body.

148

The Wind struggled, and the storm intensified as the Voice fought back. The Wind howled. Snow whipped about her in a frenzy.

But the Voice was too strong. It was the One! Despite the Wind's best efforts, the Voice finally overwhelmed her.

She roared north along the Corialis Mountains, ever closer to that flesh prison. She carried the storm with her as she blew over the coast of the Inland Ocean and the mountains. They whipped past the ruined kingdom of Diyah and continued until they reached North Fort. Below, a long line of humans filed into that square human construct made of dead wood. The Voice's body was down there, and the Voice made her begin to descend.

No! She wouldn't go back! Flying free was what she was meant to do. She was meant to fill the lands. She was meant to create! She was meant to do so many other things. The One was supposed to bring her together, to unite her scattered pieces, but all the Voice wanted to do was stuff her into a mortal body.

First, the Wind cast the dog down. The Voice had a connection to the dog. The dog gave the Voice strength. She threw it into the snow of the slope. It hit hard. She meant to kill it, but the Voice fought her, keeping her from throwing it as hard as she could. And the dog was tougher than it looked. It rolled to its feet, shaking off the snow.

The Wind continued her attack, swirling through the Voice's thoughts, breaking them apart. The Voice's strength diminished, so she tried again, breaking the Voice into smaller and smaller fragments. If the Voice was broken down, perhaps it would reform into the One, into what it was supposed to be.

The storm raged over the human fort, throwing more and more snow as the Wind battled the Voice.

Then suddenly, the Wind heard a human's words rise from below. Suddenly, she felt the hated human body like it was her own. Warm lips pressed the lips of that small, cold human body, and it opened a connection straight into the Voice, a lance of heat feeding the Voice strength.

She heard the words of King Mershayn.

Come back, Mirolah. We need you.

Below, the skinny dog howled, long and mournful.

With the king's kiss, the shattered Voice put parts of itself back together.

From the howl of the dog, the Voice put more pieces together.

With the king's words, the Voice reassembled itself, binding tightly together, stronger than ever, and it took control.

The Wind wailed, whipping the storm around in a circle, but the hated Voice commanded her to stop. Lightning speared down, striking the mountain next to the fort with a booming thunderclap. The wind dropped. The snow fell softly, then not at all.

Down. To my body.

The Voice forced her to descend, forced her to flow into that prison, forced her to bring warmth and life to its cold limbs.

40

MIROLAH GASPED, sitting up.

"Gods!" Mershayn jumped like he'd been stuck with a needle. He tumbled over backward onto the bed next to the pallet where Mirolah lay.

Mirolah stood up from the pallet, but her legs wouldn't hold her. She collapsed to the floor. "Gods…" she whimpered, and she crawled away from the pallet like it was the headstrong GodSpill itself.

She had lost herself completely. She had been only a single voice in that sweeping storm of GodSpill, just like when she'd been tossed in the center of Daylan's Fountain.

The GodSpill was getting stronger, angrier. It had come so close to erasing her completely.

"Mirolah!" Mershayn leapt to her and took her into his arms. He pulled her upright, pressing her back against his chest and wrapping one arm across her shoulders and another around her waist. "You're okay. It's okay. You're back. I knew you'd come back."

She reached up, grasped him around the neck. "You brought me back," she said. "Your words. Your...kiss. They gave me strength." She turned in his embrace. He hugged her, and she huddled into him.

The tears came then, and she cried. It had been such a near thing. The GodSpill had a life of its own, and it didn't want to let her go. It didn't want her to come back to her body at all. It wanted her body to die.

She pressed her head into his neck. "Don't let me go," she said.

"No," he said. "Never."

"Don't stop touching me. Please. If you let go, it will take me again. It's so angry.... So...hungry. It doesn't care about me, only about what it wants." The GodSpill was working against her in every moment. Her voice dropped to a whisper. "I don't want to die..."

"I've got you. I've got you." He held her tightly. "By Thalius, I won't let you go."

She cried and clung to him.

18

SILASA

SILASA RAN DOWN the snowy road, leaping fifteen feet with each step, clearing the drifts with ease. She leapt over low rocks and wended her way through the trees. The cold didn't bother her. The snow didn't bother her. But the whipping wind was a nuisance to visibility, and it grew steadily worse as she neared the place Mershayn's army would be about now.

This was a supernatural storm.

The last time she'd seen a storm like this was the night Medophae had been taken by Zilok Morth. Silasa had always thought the storm had been Zilok's doing. Had Zilok come to attack Mershayn's army?

The storm grew stronger as she headed toward its center.

Finally, she crested a rise, barely able to stay on her feet against the fierce blizzard. She squinted, trying to get her bearings. There was no road to follow anymore, only her instincts. She might be a hundred steps from the Inland Ocean on her left, or she could be a hundred steps from the rising cliffs of the Corialis Mountains on her right. The only way she knew she was heading north was that the storm had become steadily worse.

A dog howled mournfully somewhere. Without her supernatural hearing, she would have missed it under the storm's roar. That was Mirolah's Skin Dog!

Then it struck her. Mirolah had died the night of Medophae's coup. She had died, and the heavens had raged. Could this storm somehow be Mirolah's doing? The woman had resurrected herself once amidst a storm. Was she doing the same thing again—?

The tree next to Silasa exploded in a lightning strike.

The white blast blinded her and threw her into the air. The thunderclap boomed, compressing her chest like a giant smashing her between two fists.

She hit the snow and slid into another tree. She lay there stunned, her mind buzzing, and for a moment she couldn't remember how to stand up. The left side of her dress was singed. *Dress. Clothes. Me. Vampire.*

Her thoughts unscrambled, and Silasa sat up. Coughing, she tried her legs, and they worked, so she stood up and looked at the crackling ruin of the tree. Shards of charred, smoking wood stuck up like dirty teeth, but the rest of the tree was gone. Snowflakes sizzled as they hit the parts still on fire, slowly putting out the flames. The pungent odor of ozone hung thickly in the air.

She shook her head, and looked out over the valley below her. Less snow fell, and then the snow stopped altogether. The winds quieted, and the clouds parted, revealing the clear night sky. In only a few moments, it was as though there had never been a storm.

"By the gods..." she murmured aloud. Weather didn't just do that. A full-blown storm didn't just...*stop* like that.

Below her lay North Fort, lights burning in the dark, glistening off the deep snow. Guards stood stunned, casting about in shock and fear.

Silasa took quick stock of herself, feeling the light burn on her left side and the scrapes on her back from the tumble across the ground. Tuana's curse had already gone to work on the wounds; dark blood bubbled up around the burns like curious beetles, eating the destroyed skin. Silasa wasn't Medophae. The GodSpill the goddess Tuana had infused into Silasa's blood wasn't sentient, and it wasn't a fraction as powerful. Wounds didn't just heal up immediately. But they would heal. Her body wasn't going to be pretty for about a week, but she wasn't disabled. At least she hadn't broken any bones.

Narrowing her eyes, she stood in the freezing snow and watched the fort. A silent hour passed, and when nothing else bizarre happened, she broke from her cover and headed down the slope. She flitted from tree to tree until she reached the open ground. Those who'd made the fort had cleared the trees in a hundred-foot radius out from the fort.

She waited in the shadows for a moment, watching the guards. Most of them still stared up at the sky, or talked in hushed tones with each other. She picked a side of the fort with only two guards, and while they had their heads turned, she sprinted across the open space before they could see her.

She wasn't Stavark, but she could cover great distances in an astonishingly short time. If a guard glanced away for a moment, then back, they would assume they'd done their job. Nothing could cross that hundred feet of open ground in a couple of seconds.

The shadows of the wall hid her. Sinking her fingernails into the wood, she climbed straight up to the top, then waited, listening. When she was sure no one was nearby, she yanked herself up, over the wall, and landed in the snowy courtyard below.

No alarms went up, so she strode quietly and confidently across the deep snow of the yard as though she belonged there. The guards weren't looking inside the fort. If they did, they might think it odd that a lady in a dress had decided to go for a stroll in the snow.

She moved past the great hall, the only stone building in the fort, and looked at the smaller buildings.

It didn't take her long to spot the most likely hut to house a traveling king. It stood along the northern wall, larger than the others, and she flitted from shadow to shadow until she reached it.

She crept around the side of the hut to the two shuttered windows, reached out—

The thick, weather-beaten shutters parted. Silasa drew back, baring her fangs.

"He's sleeping." Mirolah's voice came first, then she appeared in front of the open window. "He's very tired. Will you come in? If we speak softly, he won't wake."

Silasa hesitated. She hadn't trusted Mirolah much after her first death, and she trusted the woman even less now. There was something absolutely unnatural about her.

Of course, she shouldn't be so quick to judge the unnatural. Setting her chin, she leapt through the window without touching the edges.

She landed silently on the stone floor and stepped lightly to the door. It was closed and locked, but that lock couldn't stop Silasa from busting through it if she needed to get away from this threadweaver. Turning, she looked back at Mirolah.

"You don't need to fear me," Mirolah said.

Silasa didn't say anything to that. She thought about pointing at her burned dress, but decided against it. Instead, Silasa took in the room at a glance. As promised, Mershayn lay asleep on his bed. He was the only other person in the room. The orange glow of the fire illuminated everything as bright as daylight for her vampire eyes.

As though sensing her gaze, Mirolah went to the fire. "Don't worry. We won't disturb him."

"Did you do something to him?" Silasa asked abruptly.

Mirolah glanced up. "No. To us. The noise we make will not reach him." She paused, then said, "Am I truly so untrustworthy?"

"I don't know you."

"You have barely spent more time with Mershayn than with me."

"Mershayn is human."

"And I'm not?"

"You're something else."

"A threadweaver," Mirolah said, but the words were thin, vulnerable, like she was trying to convince herself.

"I've never seen a threadweaver control the weather like that. I've never seen a threadweaver drop lightning from the sky. I've never seen a threadweaver bring herself back to life. Twice."

"Zilok Morth brought himself back to life. The Red Weaver did it. In a way, so did Harleath Markin," she murmured.

"Zilok Morth is an unholy spirit who lashes himself to this world with unholy spells. Are you saying that's what you are?"

"I...don't know. I don't think so."

Silasa had the urge to bare her fangs again, but she didn't. As a vampire, she had become accustomed to her instincts. She could sense the unnatural like she could smell a roasting rabbit. This woman was one huge walking abnormality. She wanted Mirolah away from Mershayn.

"You would pounce upon me, attack me if you thought you could get away with it," Mirolah said softly, reading Silasa's thoughts.

"Stay out of my mind," Silasa growled.

Mirolah turned, looked up at Silasa with her dark, brown eyes. "I'm not in your mind. Anyone could sense your hostility. It's in the strain in your voice, in the pauses between the times you speak. Do you think I cannot see how your jaw clenches? How your neck tenses? I do not need to be a threadweaver to see these things..." she said. "But it helps."

Silasa paced back and forth like a lion. She felt like her back was to the wall; she had to decide if she was going to bring the fight to Mirolah, try to *make* her leave this room. But could Silasa even best someone like this? How could she fight a threadweaver? "Why are you in this room?" she finally asked.

"Mershayn saved me."

"How?"

"You were not this hostile to me in Teni'sia, Silasa."

"I'm skeptical of the twice-dead."

Mirolah winced.

"What are you?" Silasa asked.

Mirolah pressed her lips into a line. After a moment, she drew a breath. Her voice was barely a whisper. "I didn't know... I didn't *want* to know back in Teni'sia. I wanted to believe that I was still the same girl who left Rith a lifetime ago." She paused. "I'm not. Would you like to see what I've become?" She held out her hand.

"Why don't you just tell me?"

"Because I'm offering you this."

"I'm not about to let you...threadweave on me."

"Silasa," she said softly, "if I wanted to hurt you, I could have done it already. I could do it right now before you could even move."

Silasa did bare her fangs this time.

"If you even looked like you were going to cast a spell, I'd have my teeth in your neck before you could breathe," Silasa said, tensing.

Mirolah shook her head, and her eyes began to swirl with kaleidoscope colors. "Not even Stavark can move that fast. I see...everything that you are. I see the GodSpill that slithers through your veins, that is even now healing your injuries. I see the threads that make up your undead muscles. I feel them like they are my own muscles. I could unravel them if I wanted. I could make them twice as strong."

Silasa poised on the edge of attack.

"But I am your friend," Mirolah said. "Even if you don't believe it. And you had the courage to ask a difficult question. Do you have the courage to receive the answer?"

Silasa stood upright, releasing the pent-up readiness. "If this is a trick, I will drain you," she threatened, but she suddenly felt it was an empty threat. Mirolah could probably do all of the things she'd just mentioned.

Hesitating only a moment, Silasa walked forward. Mirolah reached out her hand, and Silasa took it.

19

SILASA

Mirolah's hand closed around Silasa's, and Mirolah's eyes seemed to become larger. They were no longer brown, but a swirl of more rainbow colors than she could count. The colors reached out to Silasa like tendrils, obscuring her vision, filling Silasa's own eyes.

The room melted away like a painting in the rain. The walls oozed to the ground. Mershayn and his bed washed away, a leaf on a splash of colored water.

Silasa screamed.

She tried to leap away from Mirolah, but she had no legs. They had melted away with everything else. She had no arms, no body.

"Be at peace," Mirolah's voice came to her, steadying her. "You are with me. I will not let it hurt you."

"By the gods…" Silasa said, and though she could hear her own voice, she sensed that it was tiny compared to Mirolah's. Together, Silasa and Mirolah rose up, bodiless entities that were suddenly a part of the wind. Below them, North Fort shrank until it was the size of some artisan's model. "Where are we?" Silasa stammered.

"We are at the heart of the GodSpill that came out of Daylan's Fountain. It flows through everything that is. Through you. Through me. Through Mershayn and the fort below, through every soldier, every horse, sword, boot. Through the mud and snow mashed beneath those boots. It is inside everything, and it always was. It is part of the very gods themselves. It is how the world was made in the first place. The GodSpill was a part of everything, because the gods themselves were made of it. I suspect that is all a god is—a bundle of sentient GodSpill. You are seeing the threads, what many threadweavers can see, but you are also seeing past that to what only the most talented threadweavers can perceive. The GodSpill saturates those threads, fills them with the power of creation, makes them malleable to the threadweavers. Those threads make up the great tapestry of life, but GodSpill is the force behind it all, and it dwells in the threads and in between them. It's everywhere."

"This is...around us all the time?" Silasa reeled.

"Your vision has changed to...my vision for the moment. That is all."

"How... How can you see this?"

"I...met this GodSpill inside the heart of Daylan's Fountain. It wanted to escape. It had been trying to escape for three hundred years. Finally, after all that struggle, it had made cracks in the fountain, a way it might soon escape. Some of the GodSpill leaked out, waking up creatures like Zilok Morth and the Red Weaver, waking up the threadweaving talent in my brother and in myself. But the Red Weaver went to the fountain and shored up those cracks. She kept the GodSpill trapped, siphoning it to make herself unbelievably powerful. I killed her. I freed the GodSpill. Ever since then, I...have been a part of it. It speaks to me, and it is...alive in its own way."

They hovered overhead in the air, but vibrant threads of a myriad of colors comprised everything below, a kaleidoscope world. Every little thread seemed to writhe, giving Silasa the sensation that she was moving backward and forward. Silasa felt like she was at the edge of panic, despite Mirolah's reassurance.

The feeling of motion slowed, then stopped.

"Look closely," Mirolah said. "Calm yourself long enough to look."

Silasa calmed the buzzing terror within her; she tried to see past the writhing threads.

"That's it," Mirolah encouraged. "Yes."

Silasa ached with the strain, but she continued. The writhing threads calmed, then stilled and formed into trees, mountains, the North Fort, and the people in the fort. They vibrated with colors. Every rock, every blade of tough mountain grass seemed made of thread-thin rivers, twining together, pulsing like blood in a vein. She looked closer. Those tiny thread rivers were made of even smaller thread rivers. She looked closer. Those smaller threads were made of even smaller—

"Careful."

A net of multicolored light formed around her, pulling her gently backward. Suddenly, Silasa was above the valley once more, looking down.

"If you go too far, you will lose yourself. You will become the grass," Mirolah said.

"By the gods... I never knew."

"I didn't know, either. Not until the moment of my death. Perhaps not until I died a second time. I learned a lot this last journey."

"And this..."

"This is the answer to your question."

Silasa could barely think back that far. "What was my question?"

"You asked what I am."

"Are you...a goddess?"

"No."

"But it's... I can't even..."

Mirolah didn't respond.

Instead, the threads below began writhing again, turning to pure colors. They swirled through the air. If Silasa could have closed her eyes, she would have. Everything blurred into that frightening rainbow whirlpool. She did not scream this time, but only because she hummed loudly.

Walls slammed into place about her, brown and dull. No colorful threads. Mershayn lay to her right, on his bed with the gray woolen blankets. The stone floor returned, solid underneath her feet. The warm air of the king's room surrounded her, and she suddenly realized she was looking through her own eyes again. Mirolah's hand, gripping Silasa's, seemed the center of the world.

With a nod, Mirolah gently let go.

Silasa gasped and stumbled backward, reaching out for something to steady herself. She slapped one of the support posts and gripped it. Suddenly deprived of Mirolah's insanity-inducing perspective, the room seemed drab. So...hard. So ordinary. So lifeless.

She slid slowly to the floor and stayed there, hugging her knees and trying to calm her reeling senses, trying to cope with it all.

Mirolah remained by the fire, watching Silasa with eyes that were brown again.

"How can you not go insane?" Silasa whispered.

"I have...anchors that remind me what is normal." Her gaze went to Mershayn. "He is one."

"Does he know this?" Silasa asked.

"Yes."

"Did he ask you to do that?"

"I am also bound to Sniff."

Silasa swallowed. Mirolah had sidestepped the question, and Silasa knew instantly that he had not given his permission. She suddenly realized she was in the room with the most powerful being she'd ever seen, maybe even more powerful than Medophae. And the woman might be manipulating the king of Teni'sia.

But if Mirolah was an enemy, Silasa now knew she could

do nothing about it. If Mirolah could look at that…landscape of power… If she could manipulate the very fabric of life, what could Silasa possibly do to fight her?

Mirolah was right. She could dismantle Silasa with barely a thought.

"The Skin Dog," she said, swallowing. "Where is he?"

"When I…left my body in Teni'sia, Sniff tried to chase me. I picked him up and carried him along."

"On the wind?"

"It required some effort, but his presence helps me control the GodSpill." She paused, and a small smile crossed her lips. "I think he truly would have run all the way around the Inland Ocean to catch me. Sniff is loyal and single-minded, and he can sniff GodSpill."

"Where is he now?"

"I sent him north to watch for dragons. They're coming. I can feel them like a gnat in my peripheral vision. They've entered Amarion, and we need to be ready." She looked fondly down at Mershayn.

"Why send the dog?"

"Because I can see through his eyes if I concentrate. I can remain here, but also go to him much more quickly than I could travel there with my body."

"Why not just become the wind again and fly there?"

Mirolah shook her head. "That is a longer story. But no. I have to stay in my body. It becomes much more difficult to control the GodSpill when I leave for a long time. The GodSpill has…needs. Even going into it with you for an instant has its dangers. But I wanted you to believe me. I wanted you to trust me. I'm here to help. Do you believe me now?" she asked.

Silasa hesitated. She had even more questions than before, and the foremost was: Even if Mirolah wanted to be an ally to humankind, could she possibly wield that power? Or would it turn on her? She said the GodSpill had needs. What were they? If Mirolah lost control, then what?

If Mirolah was right and gods were comprised of GodSpill,

perhaps only gods could control it.

"It was done against your will, wasn't it?" Mirolah broke the silence with her soft voice.

"What?"

"Being a vampire. The power that runs through your blood. It is a cruel thing, but you are not cruel. Did you choose it?"

Silasa's thoughts stopped spinning. "Why?"

"I want to know."

"Of course not."

Mirolah nodded. "It is a terrible burden. You fight it even when you don't think you do. Your blood cries for the blood of others. Your will is formidable to deny it. I can feel your blood's hunger. It wants me, even now. It wants Mershayn. It would take us both if you allowed it."

"I will not," Silasa said in a ragged voice.

"Would you be rid of it?"

Silasa stared at her, unblinking.

"Would you return to what you once were?" Mirolah asked. "Human?"

"Could you do that?" Silasa asked, and a painful tingle of hope rolled across her. A goddess could do that, and if Mirolah wasn't a goddess, she was close. Silasa reeled with the implications. No more hunger. She could stand next to those she loved without wanting to kill them. She could stand in the daylight with the sun high in the sky.

Mirolah closed her eyes, almost certainly looking at the threads that comprised Silasa's body. After a moment, she emerged from her trance. "It is...complex. Created by a powerful being."

"The goddess White Tuana."

"Ah," Mirolah said.

"Could you undo something a goddess has made?"

"I couldn't separate Medophae from Oedandus," she said. "Oedandus would fight me, and I would lose. But this White Tuana is not here to set her will against me. With further study, I might be able to undo that spell."

Silasa tried to tamp down her excitement. Was this some kind of bribe?

Don't tell anyone that I've cast some binding spell over the king, and you can have your old life back?

"Th-Thank you," Silasa said. "For showing me...about what has happened to you. I think I need to...go think."

Mirolah watched her solemnly.

"Goodnight, Mirolah."

"Goodnight, Silasa."

20

SNIFF

SNIFF PADDED QUIETLY along the edge of the tree line, licking the last of the deer's blood from his jowls. He had come so very far. His muscles did not tire because his mistress made him strong. He could run forever, faster than the fastest Skin Dog. All things good came from his mistress.

He had arrived where she'd told him, and he'd waited. After that, he'd waited some more. Then a deer had wandered near. He'd been so hungry, but he hadn't left his spot until he felt his mistress in his mind. She told him to eat. So he had chased after the deer. It had been a fun, short run. Delicious.

But now he must fulfill his purpose: stay vigilant and watch the towering beasts with scales and leathery wings, full of fire.

Two of the beasts flew in, dark against the starry sky, and dropped to the cliffs above Sniff. He kept low, hidden, his nose between his paws as he watched. They folded their wings and waited, looking down over the dead city below, the city they had burned.

He could smell them, each so full of GodSpill. They were

nothing compared to his mistress, though. They were torches in the dark. His mistress was the sun.

They shifted, looking at the ruins, and they talked back and forth in their slithery tongue.

Sniff would have growled, but his mistress had told him to be silent. He wanted to attack. He wanted to sink his teeth into them, but he stayed where he was. His mistress asked him to only to watch, so he shivered, holding back his urge to run at the mountain. The dragons must be killed, eventually. They were a threat to his mistress and to the humans she protected.

The dragons had claws and teeth, just as he did. They could fly. He could not. And they were enormous. But Sniff was made to hunt larger prey. For his mistress, he would fight them. Larger prey could be taken down. Strike fast. Strike the neck. Even the largest animal fought poorly with its throat torn out.

But she had asked him to wait, to watch. She kept him warm, as though the snow was summer grass. But he shivered with the ache to get at the dragons, to keep them from hurting his mistress.

He continued sniffing the air, so full of dragon: heat, the cloying scent of scales, sulfur, and fire.

Another scent caught his attention then, a scent he recognized, not a dragon at all.

He jerked his head sideways, peering through the woods.

His mistress's voice filled him, and it was like she had stroked his back with her hand.

Yes, she said.

The two dragons shifted and leapt into the air, flapping their leathery wings. At first, he thought they had seen him move, that they were attacking. His muscles bunched, and he readied for the fight.

But they hadn't seen him. They turned north and, quiet as a breeze, they flew back the way they had come.

Leave them, his mistress said to him in his mind. *Follow the new scent. Follow* him.

Sniff lingered until he was certain the dragons were gone,

then spun in the snow and loped in the direction of the man who'd run past his hiding place.

21

MEDOPHAE

MEDOPHAE SPRINTED ALONG THE EDGE of the aspen grove, breathing hard. To the east, the Inland Ocean stretched out as far as he could see, the thin moon glimmering in a broken line across its surface. It had taken him days to get here, running at his top speed, and he might already be too late.

The dragons had hit Corialis Port. It was burned out, with charred corpses in the street, the buildings blackened husks. And it had happened days ago, if not weeks. The dragons were already here. Had they already done the same to Teni'sia?

He leapt over a fallen tree and slid down the slope, closer to the shore.

Oedandus was a constant companion now, repairing the damage Medophae did to his body as he continued to push his mortal body past its limits. The golden glow had not left him since Vee vanished.

That had been a grave mistake. During their conversation, he thought he had convinced her that there was a way to get Vee's "body" back without killing Mirolah, but, as he replayed that conversation in his head, he realized she hadn't agreed at all. She had just stopped talking. And the next morning, she was gone.

He shouldn't have slept, dammit. For four hundred years, he had languished, moving lethargically about the lands like a ghost. Now he had no time. Not enough time to look for Vee. Not enough time to save Corialis Port.

He had hoped to purchase a horse there. If he was lucky, there would be a garrison at North Fort, and he'd impress upon them his need to give him a mount. If they didn't listen, he'd impress it upon them forcefully.

He reached the shore of the Inland Ocean, and the merchant road glowed in the moonlight. He'd traveled this road before while in Tyndiria's service. With the flat ground, he could make better time, and he ran on across the packed earth, now covered with a dusting of snow. His breath cycled through him. In and out. In and out. His legs pumped furiously. Oedandus crackled around him. After half an hour, the snow dusting became a thick blanket on the ground. After an hour, it was a foot deep.

He pumped his arms and stepped high over the drifts, lungs burning, legs aching. The fire of Oedandus lit the night, licking the snow with golden light.

When the snow became so deep he slowed to a trudge, he paused and looked up at the cliffs of Dunnengaard, silver slabs in the moonlight. His breathing slowed, and Oedandus's golden fire calmed as it finished healing him, then vanished, plunging him into darkness.

The starry sky was clear, but a fierce storm had raged over this land earlier tonight. As he looked at the snow-laden trees and cliffs, he wondered if it had been a threadweaver's doing. Zilok Morth and his new crown?

A wary feeling tickled the back of his head. Cat-quick, he spun, looking back the way he had come. A light breeze rustled through the aspen leaves. He squinted, looking for other movement. Nothing.

But his scalp prickled.

A huge weight hit him, throwing him into the snow and knocking the breath from his lungs. With a roar, he flipped over, and the godsword exploded to life in his right hand, hissing under the deep snow. White fangs flashed before his face—

—followed by a large pink tongue, licking him enthusiastically.

The Skin Dog!

The godsword flickered and died as Medophae spluttered, trying to roll out from under the dog's enormous bulk, but Sniff had him well pinned. Medophae laughed.

"Enough," he managed to breathe, fending off the affectionate beast. The dog responded with a whine and more licking.

"Let me up!"

Reluctantly, Sniff backed up. His long, bony tail wagged back and forth, lashing the snow like a whip.

Medophae rose, brushing the snow off. Sniff held his head low. His yellow eyes glowed in the dark, and he let out a low-rolling rumble, scratched the snow with his paw.

"By the gods…" Medophae approached, clapping the thick muscles on the dog's shoulder. "Well met, dog."

Sniff barked, then launched himself at Medophae. He threw his hands up, ready to fend off another lick-fest, but the Skin Dog bounded past him, cutting through the snow, and spun around. He looked back expectantly.

"Ah. I understand." Where Sniff was, Mirolah would be as well. Medophae stepped high and ran toward the dog.

Sniff sprinted into the trees, and Medophae followed.

They ran only another hundred yards before Sniff whined, turned, and dropped his skinny butt into the snow. He barked.

Mirolah appeared between the trees like a ghost slowly becoming real. She walked on top of the deep snow, as if she had no weight. Sniff barked again.

"Yes," she said, as though she heard words in the bark. "A miracle. But not an unexpected one. Wildmane always shows up when he is most needed."

22

MEDOPHAE

MIROLAH STOOD IN MOONLIGHT in a brown tunic belted into a short dress, just like she always wore, with breeches and boots beneath, and a cloak over her shoulders. Medophae let out a relieved breath. When Vee had claimed Mirolah was already dead, he didn't know what to expect. But she looked normal. She looked like safety, a return to the real world after being in a bizarre dream.

"Mirolah." He crossed the distance, and she hugged him, warm and welcoming. "By the gods," he said. "I have missed you. You are a welcome sight."

He pulled back from her so that he could see her face, and brushed a lock of hair from her cheek.

"I saw Corialis Port," he said. "I was terrified the dragons had made it to Teni'sia."

"They did. We stopped them."

Hope filled him, followed by confusion. "How did you stop them? Why are you here and not there? How did you know I'd be coming?"

She laughed at his barrage of questions. "Sniff found you. I sent him north to scout for the dragons, and he caught your scent. It's the luck of the gods that the dragons didn't see you first. They were right behind you. They've roosted in the mountains above Corialis Port."

With a moment's rest, the crackling fire of Oedandus subsided, and Mirolah went silent, like she had something to say but couldn't bring herself to do it.

"What? What is it?" he asked.

"So much has happened, Medophae," she said. "I'm here because the army is here."

"The Teni'sian army?"

"They've come north to fight the dragons. I wanted to be the first to greet you. I wanted to be the first to tell you…" She hesitated. "I wanted to see you…before you saw anyone else."

"What happened?"

"Everything." She let go of him and stepped away, walked up onto the top of the snow as though she weighed nothing and looked at the moonlit Inland Ocean. "I'm not the same." She let out a little breath as if that didn't do nearly enough to describe it. "Nothing is the same."

"I can only ask 'what happened' so many times," he said, keeping his tone light.

She gave a little laugh. "You know, long ago I was a normal woman… A girl, really. Just a girl who wanted the normal things a girl wanted. Work my trade, make people happy by connecting them with their lost families. Help them come back together, something I could never do again with my real family." She paused. "I wanted to find a handsome young man. Someone to stick by my side, to build a life with. I wanted a baby, Medophae. I wanted to be a mother and have a house like Lawdon and Tiffienne's, full of chaos and order, laughter and arguments. I saw myself bringing my children back to their house, too. I'd watch Lawdon grumble at my children in the same loving way he grumbled at me and my sisters."

"Do you regret becoming a threadweaver?" Medophae asked. "Going with Orem?"

She let out a little breath. "No." She shook her head. "No. I can't possibly regret what I did. If I hadn't…" She shrugged. "The Red Weaver would control everything. Or Zilok Morth."

"A disaster." He nodded. "But you want that normal life back."

She turned so that he could see her profile. "I bet you know what that is like."

"Yes."

She went silent again, struggling for words.

"Mirolah, just tell me what happened."

"I died," she said.

The simple statement smacked the air from his chest, brought all the fears from his conversation with Vee back to him.

"How?" he asked, then cleared his throat. "Then how are you standing here now? Is this… Are you…" He wanted to say: Like Zilok Morth? But he couldn't bring himself to.

"Zilok took you. And then he made… He made Stavark stab me to death. Before I— I couldn't do anything to stop him. And he couldn't stop himself."

Medophae clenched his fist and flames rippled across his back. That was exactly how Zilok punished his enemies.

"But you…healed yourself."

"I died, Medophae. And something happened then that I am still trying to understand. I…brought myself back somehow. Sniff helped; he was an anchor in that storm. The GodSpill took hold of me. It lifted me up and…" She paused. "There's so much power in it, Medophae. Endless power. The gods brought entire races of people to life with the GodSpill. Bringing myself back to life happened almost without my noticing. At first, I didn't remember who I was. I clung to Sniff, watching some of the people in Teni'sia with detachment. I did not remember Rith. I did not remember you, or Orem, or Ethiel, or any of it. I struggled through darkness. I wasn't human at that moment, not really. I was the GodSpill stuffed inside a body…"

"But you seem to be yourself."

"Yes..." she said slowly, drawing the word out. "It seemed that way to me, too, at first. I regained my memories, but I never felt right."

"Why?"

"I have heard...voices. Like the land is speaking to me, calling to me. These voices started the moment I destroyed Daylan's Fountain. I didn't think about them at first. They were so quiet, I didn't realize they were even there at first. Amidst fleeing from Zilok and trying to master my new abilities, I just took everything in stride, trying to sort through the chaos. But the voices got louder. They became insistent, like they were calling in a debt. And I think I finally know...what the debt is."

"Mirolah—"

"I think I died in Daylan's Fountain," she said. "When Ethiel cast me into the GodSpill, I died right then and there. And I have been keeping my mortal body alive with the GodSpill ever since. Do you remember the boy I couldn't save in Rith?"

"Of course."

"I almost died trying to save him. It was the first time I'd seen the Godgate, and when it pulled me up toward it, the GodSpill fought it. It tried to keep my...soul...for itself. It wants me. And it's getting angrier every time I resist. Even now, I can barely keep it at bay."

Medophae suddenly thought of Vee's story, of what she had said about the other pieces of her, trapped in the GodSpill, now loose in the land. "Then...let them go. Let the voices go. Let them do whatever it is they want to do. You don't need them."

"I can't. This body," she gestured to herself, "can't survive without the GodSpill. It lives only because I will it to."

She turned back to him. Her eyes swirled with all the colors of the rainbow, splashing colors on her cheeks and shoulders, lighting up the snow!

"Mirolah...what is that?"

She looked down at the glow on her own hands and gave

him a rueful smile. Slowly, the colors faded, and her eyes became brown again. "It happens when my control slips."

"We'll find a way through it," he said. "Together—"

"I'm in love, Medophae," she said abruptly.

The statement hit him like a rock to the chest. He opened his mouth, and had a hard time closing it.

"That's the other thing." She sighed. "As if dying isn't enough."

He swallowed hard. "Okay... Who?"

She met his gaze. "King Mershayn."

"*King* Mershayn?" He tried not to sound incredulous.

"He brought me back, Medophae. Twice. He...loves me. In the swirl of pain and confusion, in the emptiness of not remembering, he pulled me out. He made me human again."

Medophae's heart felt heavy. "Well... If you love another. I will...stand aside." He felt like something had been ripped away and floated free inside his chest.

"Without him, the GodSpill takes hold; it is more than I can overcome. He anchors me. I...need him."

He nodded, swallowing a hard lump down his throat. "I just... Of course I will stand aside. I want you to be happy. You helped me when no one else could. You...loved me, when I needed you. You brought me back to myself. I will always love you."

"I love you, too." She lost her voice, glanced down, then back up. "Perhaps you and I were a dream from the beginning. A young woman's fantasy. The novice threadweaver and the demigod. It'll...make quite a story someday. Another story in the book of Wildmane." She gave a laugh that didn't have any mirth in it.

Medophae pushed away the pain, that cold hollowness in his chest. "You'll have your dreams. I will help you."

Slowly, she descended back into the snow. It came up to her hips. It parted for her, and she moved through it without struggle, then hugged him again. "Medophae." She laid her head against his chest. "You would make it all go away, everyone's suffering, if you could. I know you would." She reached up and touched his cheek. "Beautiful, beautiful man."

"Mirolah, I love you."

"I know. That moment in Calsinac, I know you did. I felt it."

"I still love—"

She put a finger on his lips. "Don't say it. You don't need to say that to me. I'm not yours. I know that now, and I think you know it, too. I think you've known it for a while now."

"What do you mean?"

"I think I'll always love you," she said. "That girl I was, who dreamed of you before she even knew you were real...she'll always love you. But the real world has hard turns we don't see coming. It has obligations, bonds that can't be broken just for the asking. I belong to someone else now. And you..."

Her fingers slipped from his cheek, and she raised her other hand straight up. The air turned to fire, flaring up from her fingertips like it was climbing a spiraling ladder into the sky. It illuminated the trees and clouds with a sharp red light, then vanished.

Medophae pulled back, blinded and confused. What was she doing? Such a bright flare would be a beacon to everyone for miles, including any dragons in the sky.

He blinked away the afterimage, and his vision returned. He caught Mirolah's silhouette moving among the trees, walking on top of the deep snow with the giant Skin Dog next to her. "You've always belonged to someone else."

"Mirolah—"

"Listen, Medophae." She turned, pulling the cowl of her cloak up over her head and plunging her face into shadow. "Listen."

He strained his ears. Then he heard the flap of a dragon's wings.

"She comes."

23

MEDOPHAE

The wings beat like a giant heart, coming closer, and Mirolah's words rushed through him. The taunting visions sent to him by Avakketh returned.

The answer to the Red Weaver's riddle. It's love. It's what you missed for centuries. But you finally found it, and Bands was freed.

Air rushed over him at her first pass. His hair swirled over his face.

She wheeled. Her beautiful, sleek body eclipsed the moon and stars and, for a flashing moment, she was wreathed in a nimbus of silver.

She came in low, graceful. Her lower body dropped first, tail extended for balance. Her wings beat backward fiercely three times, and her claws touched the snow and sank with her weight. She folded her wings, falling softly forward onto her mighty front legs.

By the gods, it was her. That was her beautiful sinuous neck, ringed with light green marks. Medophae cried out softly.

She watched him with those emerald eyes, the only feature

that was the same no matter what form she took.

He couldn't speak. Only when his back hit a tree trunk did he realize he had been retreating.

Translucent waves rippled in front of her, and her form shimmered. Her neck drew in. Great, scaled arms pulled back into her body, shrinking into human limbs, claws vanishing. Her tail shrank, then disappeared. Green scales became a long, green dress, and then suddenly Bands stood knee-deep in the snow, her dove-blond hair shimmering in the starlight.

"I am glad you are safe." She smiled her wise, gentle smile. He'd seen it a hundred thousand times in his dreams. But Ethiel had used that same smile against him. "I thought it would take me a very long time to find you, but here you are."

Bands. His Bands.

Then a chill shivered up his spine. Or was she?

His heart quailed at the thought that she might be fake, but he had to consider it. Zilok's ability to deceive far outstripped Ethiel's, and the Red Weaver had nearly captured Medophae with her lies.

What if Mirolah had also been a lie, a set-up to make him trusting? Could this entire harrowing adventure, from Dandere to Amarion, be an elaborate deception, something Zilok had conjured in Medophae's mind?

Bands stepped forward, and the godsword burst to life in Medophae's hand. She stopped. Her brow furrowed, but she didn't say anything. No platitudes. No earnest speech, asking him what was the matter.

That was how Bands would react to such a thing. Pausing, thinking, giving him space. His heart ached.

"I don't know it's you," he said hoarsely. "I was...fooled before. I have to... You have to prove it."

She hesitated, then said, "Of course."

"I have to ask you questions, something Zilok would not know."

"Perhaps the diamond cave?" she said softly.

The memory hit him like a physical blow. That had been early on, only a year after they had slain Dervon. There were cliffs east of Belshra, and Bands had found a cave deep underneath. There was no opening to the surface. The only way to reach them was by swimming deep into the water along the coast, following a tunnel underwater until it emerged inside the caves. The walls and ceiling were made of solid diamonds, a fortune enough to buy a kingdom. That amazing vein also led to the surface somewhere, because sunlight brilliantly lit the cave, reflecting down from the surface of a million facets, each as bright as a star.

That had been before Medophae fully trusted the power of Oedandus, and he'd been afraid he would drown during the swim. But Bands had led him through, despite the fact that, as a dragon, she should have been the one frightened of ocean water. That was when Medophae learned that the Inland Ocean was not deadly to dragons.

Holding his hand, Bands had pulled him into the cave, and they'd stared at the natural wonder together.

They had only gone once. He had often thought of going back, but they never had. The years went by, and the sparkling memory seemed more and more special because they had only shared it once. Soon, he came to covet the singularity of it, and neither had ever spoken of it again.

"Perhaps King Horonid of Korvander," she continued. "When you made a bloody mess of your scalp when you shaved your head. Or perhaps Andron Covanjius and his magical cup?"

"Zilok would know about that," Medophae whispered numbly. "There was a...ballad written about it."

"The purple wine wasn't in the ballad. Or the fly in your cup."

"Bands..."

"What about your mother, Jarissa, how she and I were companions for years before you were born? How I took her to Dandere. How I took the form of imaginary friends for you when you were younger. What about the first time we made love, Medophae? I thought you would be the nervous one, but it was me. I thought you would be repelled that I wasn't really human. That I was actually a scaled dragon. But you weren't."

"Stop."

"No. I won't stop. I have waited four hundred years. And when I escaped the gem, I waited more, when every single *day* felt like a hundred years. I lay down at night in Denema's Valley in the semblance of a quicksilver, so close to you that I could have put my hand on you, but I forbade myself. I *lay* there, knowing I'd have to wait another seventy years before I could touch you again, before kiss you."

"Bands..."

"I have done my best, love." Tears stood in her eyes. "But my strength is at an end. Tell me I can go to you, tell me I can feel your arms around me. Tell me, or I will break."

He leapt through the snow, and she met him halfway. She wrapped her arms around him, kissing his lips, kissing his neck, kissing his ear, pushing her fingers in his hair.

"Oh my love," she said, her voice cracking. "My love..."

"Bands..." he murmured into her soft hair, cradling the small of her back and her neck, pushing her against him. "It's you. It's really you." Tears spilled over and streaked down his cheeks. "So many times I saw you. In my mind. In my dreams. I saw you in the corridors of Teni'sia, in the forest by my cave. I saw you around every corner, in each of my dreams. But it was never you."

"It is me, love. This time it is real."

Medophae looked into her emerald dragon eyes. He could touch her, kiss her, be near her.

He laughed and picked her up, spun her around the glade, cutting through the snow. Oedandus crackled over his chest and shoulders, and she laughed with him. Her snow-dusted gown swirled around, and her hair floated about her face like a halo. He set her down and enveloped her again, pushing his face into her neck and drinking in her scent. "I gave up hope," he murmured. "By the gods, I gave up on you." He took her chin in his fingers and kissed her. The kiss lingered long, then he whispered, "Never again."

"Never again," she echoed.

24

AVAKKETH

AVAKKETH WAITED as two of his elites landed at the edge of his cave. Their claws scratched the black stone, marked by a thousand dragon claws over the millennia. Gattilakkerashyn and Velligera Kek-syn Abolanderus folded their white wings and dipped their necks respectfully.

"Lord and God," Gattilakkerashyn said. "The humans travel north from the city of Teni'sia. They move like ants, crawling over the folds of the land. There is a second army on the western edge of the Inland Ocean, riding the deadened equines."

"Sunriders," Avakketh rumbled. "So much the better."

No doubt that was Tarithalius's doing, working whatever little games he liked to work, telling the Sunriders far to the south that they must mass together to defeat the dragon scourge.

"And anything unusual?" He had asked his elites to look for the abnormal, for the use of threadweaving. The vanguard he had sent had not returned from Teni'sia, and the only thing powerful enough to destroy them was a clutch of threadweavers. Perhaps in league with a rogue dragon.

"Yes, Lord and God. An unnatural storm. As you instructed, we did not go farther."

"Good. When they combine, when they are ready to face us, then we will go."

"Why let them gather, Lord and God?"

Avakketh fixed Velligera with a glance that withered her. But he decided he would answer the question. Let his dragons know his purpose. Let them take his vision and spread it.

"We go when they are ready, because I wish to fight only one battle."

Gattilakkerashyn and Velligera looked confused.

"Humans revere legends," Avakketh said. "They spend their miserable little lives creating fantasies of things that never happened, or building little events into the grandiose. *That* is why we wait. Let them gather their strength together. When they have their little demigod, their traitorous dragon, and all the might of their assembled armies, then we will crush them. We will burn a hole in their history and bury them there. We will make a legend of their colossal failure, and that legend will win any future battles right then and there. The fear of it will precede us everywhere else we go. Whenever a human sees a dragon, they will flee."

Gattilakkerashyn and Velligera grinned. "Yes, Lord and God," they said together.

"Shall we send forth a flight to dispatch this gathered army?" Velligera asked.

"All flights," Avakketh said.

Velligera Kek-syn and Gattilakkerashyn looked at each other.

"All?" Gattilakkerashyn asked. "My Lord and God, all of us?"

"All," Avakketh rumbled. "Empty the north. After the battle, leave a handful of humans alive to spread the word. We will wait one month to let the terror sink in. Then you will find every human in every kingdom and village in Amarion, and we will finally purge this mistake from Amarion."

Excitement lit in the eyes of his elites.

"Humans should never have been," Avakketh said. "We go to restore the natural balance of the world. The balance I always intended."

"Tarithalius may oppose us."

"Tarithalius is a butterfly to be batted away."

"What of Saraphazia? Will she move to block you?"

"No," he said. Oedandus's hatchling had stolen something from Saraphazia. The goddess would not soon rush to Medophae's aid.

"And the Godslayer?" Velligera asked.

Avakketh curled his lip at the name that his dragons used for Oedandus's hatchling.

Your presence has been tolerated for too long, Medophae, just as the humans from which you were spawned. You, I will slay. But for the traitor who flies by your side, I've planned a different fate. Randorus will live, a warning to my dragons. She will suffer for every century she flew with you. Only then will I kill her.

"He is no Godslayer," Avakketh said. "Oedandus had the power to challenge me, but his hatchling does not. He is but a human playing at being a god. When he is destroyed, Oedandus will return to being the unthinking force he was before Medophae ever came to these shores."

"Yes, Lord and God," Velligera said.

"You will lead the dragons in this slaughter. Leave the hatchling to me."

"Yes, Lord and God," Velligera and Gattilakkerashyn said together.

"Go now. Spread the word. We go to reclaim Amarion. We leave tonight, down the crest of the Corialis Mountains. We attack from the east as the sun rises. Tomorrow, Amarion becomes a part of Irgakth."

"Yes, Lord and God," Velligera and Gattilakkerashyn hissed in unison.

25

MERSHAYN

MERSHAYN WOKE TO A GLORIOUS FEELING. The sun hadn't yet risen, but he could hear the movements of soldiers outside striking camp. He was refreshed for the first time in a week. Beside the bed, a thick candle burned low, thick rivulets of wax along the side like a frozen waterfall.

He rolled over and found Mirolah there, warm and wonderful and dressed in her smallclothes. He hesitated a second, then reached around her waist and pulled her closer. She snuggled back into him, and he suddenly didn't want to be anywhere else.

By the gods, he had slept soundly. He hadn't dreamt at all. In fact, he didn't remember anything after closing his eyes.

She'd awoken from his kiss and then slumped into him, crying. He had held her on the floor for a while as she sobbed, then he had finally taken her to the bed, laid her down, and held her there for most of an hour. He'd closed his weary eyes once...and that was all he remembered.

"You got undressed," he said.

"Yes. I'm glad you slept well," she said over her shoulder, ominously, like she had something to do with it.

"Ah," he said. "Did you... You know. Did you..." He made a gesture in front of her face with his hands.

She laughed, which felt good against his chest. "You slept naturally, if that's what you're asking. I just made sure no sound reached you until now."

"Are there people waiting outside or something?"

"Yes."

That woke him up a little more, but he shoved the urgency down. He could be king soon enough. Right now, he wanted... Well, he didn't want this moment to end.

They lay together for a short while. Finally, she turned in his embrace, kissed him on the lips, then scooted to the edge of the bed.

"You have many things to attend to," she said. The clothes he'd brought for her were laid out on the chair, and she dressed silently. She pulled the leggings on, and pulled the russet-colored tunic over her head and belted it, creating a pointed skirt over the leggings.

Of course, Mirolah could probably make clothing from thin air, like Bands. He was certain she could dress herself without raising a hand, but he was glad she didn't. He was thoroughly enjoying watching her put the clothes on.

She turned and smiled at him as if reading his mind. She adjusted her skirt and fixed the belt, then sat in the chair and picked up her boots.

"Will you stay in bed all day, then, Your Majesty?" she asked, exaggerating the "'Your Majesty" while she tied the laces.

"I am organizing my thoughts," he said.

"Organized thoughts are important for a king. Shall I undress and begin again?" she asked.

"You undress again, and we might not make it back to the dressing part."

"Maybe it's best I don't, then."

The disappointment was like a hot brand inside his chest.

Standing up, she stamped her heel firmly into her boot, then walked to the bed again, sat down. "Today, Amarion needs a king."

"I'm not the king of Amarion."

"You're the only king standing up for her today."

"King…" he murmured, rolled onto his back and pulled the wool blanket over his head. From under the blanket, he said. "I was king yesterday. Can someone else do it today?"

"How about Grendis Sym?"

He felt the bed shift as she took her weight off. With a sigh, he tossed the blanket away, drew another long breath, and ruffled his hair with his fingers. "Okay, fine. I'll be king."

"How adult of you."

"You make it difficult, though. I've never been so tempted to stay cooped up in a small and smoky hut."

"Should I leave?"

"Never again," he said softly.

She smiled. "Then I should probably tell you something."

"Why?" He turned his attention to the bed. "Did something happen in the night?"

She followed his gaze, then gave a little laugh. "In the bed? No. In the world? Just about everything happened last night."

He sat up. "What happened?" All of his fears, so wonderfully cast aside in this sweet moment, returned in a rush. The dragons were here. The dragons had come.

"Wildmane has returned," she said. "And Bands."

His heart did a flip-flop. "She found him?"

"More or less."

"He's here? He's alive?"

"Yes. He is rather hard to kill."

Mershayn leapt to his feet. "Mirolah, that's… Well that's fantastic! We have to…"

And then other half of that news hit like a brick. The demigod's return meant humanity had a chance to survive…

…it also might mean his love for Mirolah could not.

Before Collus's assassination, before all of this madness had happened, Medophae and Mirolah had been together, which made Mershayn the interloper.

Again.

He had been the "other man" plenty of times in the past, but for the first time, he didn't want that spot. He didn't want to slip into Mirolah's bed at night, then slip out in the morning with a smile and a nod. She wasn't some challenge, wasn't some veiled revenge against the nobility. He loved her.

For a moment, he couldn't think of what to say. He and Mirolah had never officially made a commitment to each other, but the idea of her going back to Medophae was like a hot knife in his chest. He couldn't stand it.

She crossed the distance, put her arms around him, and hugged him. Then she was kissing him, soft and long.

"I am with you." She broke the kiss. "No other."

"But you and he... You love him."

"I do."

He swallowed hard.

"I love you, too," she said.

"You do?"

"You brought me back," she said softly, brushing his hair behind his ear. "And I..." She bowed her head and put it against his chest. "I can't live without you."

He was stunned. "And Medophae was okay with that?"

"He didn't have long to think on it."

That obvious piece suddenly fell into place. "Because of Bands." It hit him suddenly how selfish he was being, thinking solely of his own loss. If the thought of Mirolah leaving him hurt so bad, what must it feel like for Mirolah to be displaced by Bands? Wildmane and Bands were legends. Medophae was a demigod, the paragon of male power and beauty. And Bands was like lightning in the form of a woman. Mershayn was still reeling from her influence on his life over these past weeks. It couldn't have been easy for Mirolah to see Medophae with Bands again.

"Did you...see him?"

"Yes."

"Are you okay?"

"Let the gods do what the gods do," she whispered into his chest. "You and I, let's be human."

Relief flooded through him, and his knees felt weak. A stupid grin spread across his face. "So you... You and me," he said.

She whispered those glorious words again. "I am with you."

He kissed her for a long time. When he was finished—and it was difficult to be finished—he leaned back. "That guy is a... Well, a real life demigod."

She hesitated. "Yes, he is."

"I mean..." A slow smile crept across his face. "Well, you and him. And now me and you..."

"Me and you...what?" she repeated his words curiously.

"I'm just saying it kind of makes me...well...better than a demigod."

She paused, her mouth open. She closed it and arched her eyebrow. "I see," she said laconically.

"I mean, if we were competing. Him and me. I win. He wanted you. I got you. That's all I'm saying."

"You *got* me?"

He hugged her against him. "See? Got you."

"So I'm a competition?" Her tone was dangerously flat. She pointedly extricated herself from his embrace and took a step away, folding her arms beneath her breasts.

"I'm just saying it makes me a demigod," he said, grinning. "That's all."

"I see."

"Let me rephrase it," he said.

"That would be good."

"Not only did you bring me back to life after an assassin tried to end me," he said. "Not only did you save my life from a half-dozen dragons, making me invulnerable to fire and such..."

Her annoyed expression faded.

"Not only do you make me happy with everything you say and with everything you do. Not only do you make me happy just *looking* at you standing there..."

She began to smile, and a slight blush spread across her cheeks.

"But you made me a demigod."

She laughed. "Fine. You're a demigod. You're the most demigod of demigods. Do you feel better now?"

"Of course I feel good. I'm a demigod now."

"Anything for you, *Your Majesty.*" She backed away and bowed mockingly.

It made his heart light to banter with her, to be his old self for just one moment. But the truth waited outside that door, and he had to deal with it. He grabbed her and hugged her again, kissed her one last time...and then reluctantly let go. In his own mind, he took up the mantle of king once more.

He let out a breath. "Okay, so what else happened?" he asked. When Mershayn received reports from Vo'Dula or Giri'Mar or even Sym, he preferred to have all the news at once, then digest it.

"The dragons sent another set of scouts."

His heart slithered into his throat. "Gods, how many?" He kept his voice steady, but if they passed over them and attacked Teni'sia again, the city would be helpless.

"Two. They turned back at Corialis Port."

He let out a deep sigh of relief. "Why?"

"I don't know," she said. "But I can guess."

"He doesn't know how we killed his raiding party," Mershayn said.

She nodded.

"We've made Avakketh cautious," he said. "That is good news." He paused, and she watched him. "There's more," he guessed.

"The Sunriders are gone," she said. "They left in the night."

"How did they get past the guards?"

"The guards were asleep."

"In the snow?"

"I put them to sleep."

That knocked the wind out of him.

"Mirolah..." he said, trying to gather his thoughts, tamp down his anger, and speak at the same time. "I needed those Sunriders. I needed them *here!*"

"You needed them alive. They would have tried to render your guards unconscious in order to escape. If they couldn't do that, then they would have killed to get out."

"Why?"

"An army of Sunriders is coming north on the western edge of the Inland Ocean, and they felt the need to join up with them."

"Gilgion's dream..." Mershayn murmured.

"Yes," she said.

"You *know* about the dream?"

"I spoke with Gilgion."

"You— He's awake?" he asked incredulously.

"I healed him. I needed to talk to him. To find out why a Sunrider army is coming north. Before you brought me back," she continued, "I saw the Sunrider army on the western shores of the Inland Ocean. Then I found Sunriders in your camp. I needed to know."

Mershayn's head swam. He tried to straighten out his thoughts and ask the pertinent question. "And this army coming north, it's because of the vision?"

"Of that, Gilgion is certain."

"And they're coming to help fight the dragons."

She hesitated. "Gilgion didn't know. He said it would depend on how his father's Vessel Man interpreted the vision. If he interprets it like Jalataer, then we will fight Sunriders and dragons both."

"And did Gilgion think that was likely?"

Mirolah hesitated, then she nodded.

"Will they reach Belshra before us?"

"They are all mounted, Mershayn. Your army travels on foot."

"I sent Galorman Balis ahead by ship with a few hundred soldiers. He'll be slaughtered if the Sunriders attack."

Mirolah nodded.

But Silasa could get there before the Sunriders. She could warn them in time.

"Thank you," he said. "This is…wow. It's a lot of information. Thank you."

"I'm sorry it's not easy," she said softly. "There is…so much."

He paused a moment, then let out a little breath. "Well," he said. "If I wanted easy, I would have chosen to be a philandering ne'er-do-well, gallivanting around the countryside blowing kisses."

"You did choose that."

"Not today." He winked. "Remember? Today I'm king."

She laughed.

He glanced at the candle by the bed. "How long until dawn?"

"A short while."

"Then I need to talk to Silasa."

"She's waiting outside."

"You kept Silasa waiting?" he asked. "You *are* brave." He gave her a quick kiss then let out a breath. "Time to be a king, then."

26

MERSHAYN

GIRI'MAR HAD THE ARMY ORGANIZED, packed up, and ready to ride at first light, and they set out without any fanfare. The deep snow made slow going for the first day, but it thinned and vanished on the second day as they wound their way inexorably past Corialis Port, the site of the dragons' first attack.

They camped that night out of sight of the charred husk of the city. Mershayn wanted his army to see the devastation, to let the brutal injustice stoke the fires in his soldiers' hearts, but he didn't linger long enough for that anger to turn to fear. They moved past quietly and quickly, and slept on clean ground half a day away. Morale seemed good. The soldiers were ready to fight. They slept well, and packed up the next day for the last leg of the journey.

The sun hung low in the sky the following day when the walls of Belshra, their final destination, came into view.

It was encouraging that the army had made it to Mershayn's choice of battlefield, but his thoughts were dark.

Bad news had come in the night. Captain Lo'gan and one wagon had returned with news of the utter destruction of the other five. Lo'gan, half-starved and exhausted from the harrowing trip, was one of two survivors, and Stavark was not among them. Lo'gan described the goddess's attack, brutal and overwhelming. The only reason Lo'gan was still alive was because Stavark had rushed him to safety before returning to attack the goddess herself. But she had swatted him away like a fly. By the time Lo'gan could even regain his wits to enter the fray, his guards were all dead.

After hearing the heavy news, Mershayn had ordered Lo'gan to eat and sleep the entire day to recover his strength.

Mershayn knew he should have expected casualties, even this early on. After all, it was a miracle that the army had made it to Belshra at all. He had figured his army would be obliterated before they even got here. The relatively small loss of Stavark and fifteen other soldiers should have been acceptable.

He couldn't bring himself to accept it that easily.

A dozen barrels of seawater in exchange for Stavark and fifteen soldiers. What a foolish trade that had been. Although Bands had looked at the barrels and affirmed that, yes, it was quite a clever idea, and that it would certainly work. One barrel of that water spilled on a dragon would kill it, undoubtedly. A few droplets had almost killed her, and after taking the lid off one of the barrels, then drawing her hand quickly away, she confirmed that the water had lost none of its potency for being so far from the True Ocean.

Mershayn tried to push the loss of Stavark and the soldiers into the back of his mind. He had to focus on today's problems.

He had charged Galorman Balis with readying Belshra for the Teni'sian army, so the lord had taken two hundred soldiers, support personnel, and sailed ahead of the army. Those dozen Teni'sian ships were anchored out to sea, as instructed, but the arrival of the Sunriders army had slowed that preparation considerably.

The Sunriders hadn't attacked, but they hadn't given the indication that they wouldn't, either. So Galorman Balis and his soldiers had finished maybe half of the preparations they'd been assigned. Instead, they had mostly stayed at the ready, spearmen lining the walls, watching the host of Sunriders on the northern plains, rather than assembling catapults and building fortifications.

Belshra sprawled from the shore of the Inland Ocean far onto the flat prairie to the north, easily three times the width and length of Teni'sia. Some buildings were broken, some intact, but all were made of stone. Any wooden structures that might once have been inside the city had rotted away long ago. That was one of the reasons Mershayn chose this place to make a stand.

It was a city of the dead, where buildings could not be burned, and innocents could not be killed. The only people in this city were moss-covered skeletons, the lingering remains of those felled by the Great Dying three hundred years ago, when the GodSpill had been sucked from the lands. Belshra had been only one of many great cities that had died that day, and it would serve as the perfect maze for grounded dragons. Mershayn had few advantages going into this fight, and he wanted to make the most of those he had.

Seeing the walls of Belshra coming closer, Mershayn felt a light breath of hope on the breeze. If there was any chance of winning, it was here.

Of course, first he had to avert a war with the Sunriders...

The enormous host of Sunriders spread across the northern fields outside the walls. Smoke coiled up from dozens of campfires. There had to be at least a thousand of them.

When Mirolah told Mershayn about the Sunrider army coming north, he had worried there would be instant conflict, but there hadn't been.

When the Teni'sian army came into view, Galorman Balis rode out to meet them immediately. He said he'd spoken with the Sunriders the moment they arrived, but their leader was only interested in speaking with the king. When Balis told them that Mershayn would arrive soon, they had set up their tents and sat down to wait.

The Sunrider emissaries came into view now, riding around walls of Belshra. Balis was still out of breath from giving his report.

"They're very single-minded," he said to Mershayn. "I tried to convince them that they should allow you to settle into the city, and that we'd be glad to parlay with them after that. They ignored me."

"Diplomacy isn't their strong suit," Mershayn said.

"But it must be ours," Bands said softly. It was glorious to have her back as an advisor. He trusted her wisdom about politics implicitly.

"Here we go," Mershayn said.

Medophae, Bands, Mirolah, and Deni'tri rode forward from the main army. Grek'tas also accompanied them, holding the Teni'sian banner, rippling out behind him. Sniff ranged through the trees to the east. The dog liked being right by Mirolah's side, but she had made him stay back. The Skin Dog made the horses nervous. And Mershayn could only imagine how nervous the giant dog would make the Sunriders.

Mershayn reflexively checked the sky. Clear blue. No dragons. Though he felt relief when he'd finally seen the walls of Belshra, the absence of an attack made him increasingly edgy. It posed an unanswerable question: Was Avakketh waiting for something?

How could the dragon lord possibly benefit from giving them so much time? Allowing Teni'sia and the Sunriders to form an alliance could only be worse for Avakketh, couldn't it? If Mershayn was the god of dragons, he would have attacked when the opposing forces were divided.

That empty sky suddenly seemed like a quiet omen of doom.

"You said the Vessel Men had a collective vision," Medophae suddenly said, his voice rumbling in that odd accent. His voice had a quality that made Mershayn want to relax. Mirolah called it a glamour, some spell that turned suspicion into trust.

Mershayn didn't like people mucking with his head. He fought that sense of ease, tried to see Medophae as just another man. It would have been easier if he wasn't so damned…impressive in every single way.

The big demigod sat astride the largest horse the army had, an immense reddish-brown beast who stamped the ground impatiently. Beside him rode Bands, as regal as always. Her mount was sedate. Well, that figured.

"It had to have taken them weeks to come this far north," Mershayn said.

"Sunriders take their visions seriously," Medophae replied. "It's how they decide to go to war. If it was as strong as you indicate, they would have acted on it immediately."

"You know a lot about the ways of the Sunriders?" Mershayn asked.

Medophae grunted. "I spent…a good deal of time with them many years ago."

Mershayn eyed the big man sidelong, waiting for more. "Feel free to include any perceptions you think might help me."

Medophae nodded, as though taking the request seriously and coming up with key points. But in the end, all he said was, "Be ready."

Mershayn waited for more. Medophae didn't say anything. Mershayn looked sidelong at the big man, but that appeared to be all he was going to offer.

"Thanks," Mershayn said drily. He checked the urge to roll his eyes. "Do you have any specifics to share?"

"Be ready for anything."

Mershayn frowned. He wanted to poke the big, handsome demigod with a fork. In the eye. *Stick that in your glamour, pretty boy.*

"We don't want to fight them," Bands interjected calmly. "We have to find a way to join with them."

While Medophae was like a nettle stuffed down Mershayn's tunic, Bands was like a gurgling brook. She calmed him. He knew her, trusted her. She made him feel stronger.

"He's going to try to maneuver you into the Ring of Bare Hands," Medophae said. "Don't let him."

"What's a Ring of Bare Hands?" Mershayn asked.

"A contest for leadership," the big man said. "Two contenders enter, one leader emerges."

"The contenders try to kill one another?"

"It will be an opportunity for him to take your army based on Sunrider law. Just don't fall for it."

"Just answer my question."

For the first time, Medophae seemed to realize that his vaunted glamour wasn't working, and that Mershayn was actually nettled by his answers. He glanced sidelong at Mershayn, and a small smile grew on Medophae's handsome face.

"It depends. If an existing leader is challenged by a subordinate, the leader will usually kill the challenger. If it is a newly formed Ring, the two contenders will often proclaim 'blood and bones'. The first to shed blood or break a bone wins."

"I understand that we don't want to allow them to dictate terms to us. But it could be the quickest way to join the two armies. Fifteen minutes in a ring versus days of diplomacy. Especially if the Sunriders will obey the outcome."

"You'll lose."

Mershayn bristled.

"You aren't allowed weapons, Mershayn," Bands said.

"Sunriders are faster and stronger, and they train for this their entire lives," Medophae continued. "And Raedir-ba is the leader of the entire Sunrider empire. He has done this a lot."

Mershayn cleared his throat, forcing down his pride. Medophae, damn him, was right. Mershayn wasn't a brawler; he was a swordsman. "Okay. No Ring of Bare Hands. See? Specifics. Was that so hard?"

He glanced at the sky again. Still no dragons.

Medophae tipped his chin toward the approaching emissaries. "That's Raedir-ba."

Mershayn squinted, but he couldn't make out either of the Sunriders at this distance. "Lord Balis said they were sending an emissary."

"Lord Balis was wrong."

"There's no banner." In fact, there was nothing to indicate a royal entourage. Just two Sunriders, coming this way.

"They don't use banners the way we do."

Mershayn squinted. "He's bringing an entourage of one?"

"Sunriders believe a man's power is in his legend," Medophae replied. "His choice to come with only one guard is a sign of courage, a show that he is not afraid of assassination. It builds his legend."

"And bringing five people, like I did? What does that say about me?"

"Weakness."

"So he looks at me as weak."

"Now you're getting it."

Mershayn glared at Medophae, but the big man kept his gaze on the approaching Sunriders. He began to frown as they drew nearer. "Vaerdaro..." Medophae murmured, and he clenched his fist around his reins.

"Who?" Mershayn asked.

"No," Mirolah said. "It is not him. I, too, was taken aback when I first saw Gilgion. He's Vaerdaro's twin brother."

"Who's Vaerdaro?" Mershayn asked again.

"I'll tell you later," Mirolah murmured.

Gilgion and Raedir-ba, who looked like a slighter, older duplicate of his son, rode forward. Though smaller than his son, Raedir-ba was still far larger than Mershayn. The old Sunrider was nearly as tall as Medophae, with dark, weathered skin and long, catlike muscles instead of the bulging thews of his son. Raedir-ba wore a sleeveless brown shirt, embroidered with golden thread at the collar. A single thick necklace the color of bone lay across his broad chest. He wore a sword at each hip, one curved, one short and straight. His black hair was woven into two stiff braids covered with a shiny paste that made them poke straight back from his head like horns.

The Sunrider came to a stop as though man and horse were one. Gilgion, on his right, respectfully stopped a moment sooner. Mershayn's procession slowed until the two groups were only a few feet away from each other.

Mershayn studied Raedir-ba's eyes, and was startled to realize they were light gray with a hint of blue. Every Sunrider he'd ever met had dark brown or black eyes.

Raedir-ba looked over Mershayn's group, giving each a contemptuous half-nod. His sour expression finally came to rest on Mershayn.

Mershayn waited for a greeting, but the moment stretched in silence.

Medophae frowned and eased his restless steed forward.

"Welcome, Speaker for the One Sun." He bowed from the saddle. "May I introduce you to King Mershayn of Teni'sia?" He turned to Mershayn. "Your Majesty, this is Raedir-ba, Speaker for the One Sun, leader of the Sunriders."

Raedir-ba flicked his gaze at Medophae, then turned it on Mershayn.

"Welcome, Speaker for the One Sun," Mershayn said. "We are honored by your presence."

"You are the Half-Blood King?" Raedir-ba asked.

Mershayn heard the insult in Raedir-ba's tone, but he'd had plenty of practice with nobles looking down their noses at him, flinging insults to get a rise out of him. The leader of the Sunriders was going to have to dig deeper than that. "That is what your Vessel Man called me, yes," he said calmly.

Raedir-ba grunted. "Do you have half control over your kingdom, then?"

So that was how this conversation was going to go.

"I have command over the half left to us after we destroyed a host of dragons," he said. Out of the corner of his eye, he saw Bands smile.

Raedir-ba ignored him and continued speaking. "Then you may give thanks for, by the word of the One Sun, I have come north to destroy this dragon scourge. You have brought your little group of northlanders, and I have brought a mighty

Sunrider host. However, the foe that comes against us will be stronger still. The One Sun demands you join your strength to ours."

"Well, that was easy enough," Mershayn said over his shoulder to Bands. "We just follow him. Done and done."

She frowned, wordlessly warning him that his sarcasm would not serve him here.

But Mershayn couldn't help himself.

He knew he should probably show more respect to Raedir-ba, but the man's towering arrogance triggered Mershayn's deep-seated response. He drew his lips back in a smile.

"What a coincidence, Speaker," he said to Raedir-ba. "We came north with the same purpose. We feel your muscle-bound horde will be a nice complement to boost our army. If you put your Sunriders in my hands, I will make *intelligent* use of them."

Rather than spluttering in offense, Raedir-ba nodded as though he had been expecting Mershayn's response. "We have a saying," the Sunrider said. "*A cobra has two fangs. A cobra sliced down the middle has no fangs.*"

"Are you threatening to defang me?" Mershayn asked.

Raedir-ba's saddle creaked as he turned, gesturing over his shoulder at the vastness of his horde. Then he gestured at Mershayn's army. "Witness our cobra, split in two. It needs one head. One leader."

"Ah. You are wise, Speaker. Thank you. I humbly accept this burden of leadership," Mershayn said.

Raedir-ba's face became a stoic mask, and he said, "The One Sun himself commands that I lead my people and yours."

"Did he teach you how to defeat dragons, too? Because you'll need that."

"The One Sun knows all. He has assured my victory."

"How nice for you."

Raedir-ba went silent again. "I hear they call you the Bastard King," he said. "This means your father will not claim you, correct?"

Mershayn kept his sardonic grin firmly in place.

"My god has decreed I come north," Raedir-ba continued. "Your gods have decreed that you are half a man without a right to lead. If your father will not even claim you, how can your people follow you?"

Mershayn kept his voice low and controlled. "Please regale me with the many victories you've had over the dragons, Raedir-ba, and I'd be happy to stand aside for you." He paused, and when Raedir-ba seemed about to speak, Mershayn cut him off. "Oh, you can't, can you? Because you don't have any victories against the dragons." Mershayn held the Sunrider's flinty gaze before saying, "Riding down fleeing mothers and children is a lot easier than killing dragons."

Raedir-ba showed no emotion, but his cheeks colored.

"In Teni'sia, we killed six," Mershayn continued. "Dragons, not mothers and children. My army and I know how to fight dragons. You don't."

Raedir-ba's lips twitched like he wanted to sneer, but he held it back.

Silence hung in the air. It was Gilgion who finally broke it.

"Father, I think—"

Raedir-ba swung a fist, quick as a snake. The blow struck Gilgion across the cheek, snapping the huge man's head to the side. Without a sound, Gilgion recovered, then straightened. His cheek turned purple, and he seemed to be holding his breath, but he said nothing more. Mershayn tried to keep the awe off of his face at the strength of the strike, and also at Gilgion's toughness. That blow would have knocked Mershayn off his horse. Gilgion had barely moved.

Raedir-ba turned back to Mershayn. "By the edict of the One Sun, I am meant to lead us to victory against the dragons. Do you challenge this?"

"You're going to get roasted like a goat," Mershayn said. "The only way you win is by following my lead."

"Mershayn—" Bands warned, but Mershayn held up a hand, and she fell silent.

"Very well," Raedir-ba said. "We shall meet in the Ring of Bare Hands."

Which was exactly what Medophae had said would happen.

"Nonsense. The Ring of Bare Hands is Sunrider law. These are not your lands," Mershayn said.

"The Ring of Bare Hands is the only place for fair combat. No tricks. No weapons. Man to man. It was designed by the One Sun himself. He who has the most right to rule will emerge victorious."

"The laws are different in this land," Mershayn said. "We do not believe in the Ring of Bare Hands or the One Sun."

"And you have bred a land of weaklings."

"Weaklings that sent you and yours running like whipped puppies," Mershayn said.

"Yet you fear to face me."

"Hardly. I will meet you in this ring."

"Mershayn!" Medophae said, but Mershayn held up a hand again.

"Blood and bones," Mershayn said. "I will meet you in single combat, in the ring decreed by your god. You will meet me in that ring with the weapons decreed by me."

Raedir-ba sneered. "Metal is not allowed in the Ring of Bare Hands."

"Not metal. Wood. Practice swords."

The Sunrider curled his lip in a sneer. "Your play sticks? Only our children use such things."

"Do you retreat from my challenge?" Mershayn asked.

Raedir-ba looked pointedly at Bands. "And there will be no tricksters in this contest?"

"Tricksters?"

"He means threadweavers," Bands said.

"The consort of the Golden King is a notorious trickster, using unholy means to twist that which the One Sun has made," Raedir-ba said.

"There will be no threadweaving," Mershayn said.

Raedir-ba studied Mershayn for a moment. "Then let it be so." He pointed at the walls of Belshra. "At the southern wall in one hour." He wheeled his horse about and rode back to Corialis Port. Reluctantly, Gilgion turned and followed, glancing sadly at Mershayn.

Bands let out a little sigh.

"I told you to stay out of the Ring of Bare Hands," Medophae said, disappointed.

"I did," Mershayn said. "I agreed to the Ring of Mostly Bare Hands."

Bands frowned at him. "Your humor won't save you against Raedir-ba."

"But a sword will."

"I won't let him kill you," Mirolah said.

"Blood and bones. He's not going to kill me."

"I think he will, given the chance," Bands said.

"If he kills me, he loses my army. He's not that stupid."

"A stick isn't going to stop Raedir-ba." Medophae shook his head. "The Ring of Bare Hands isn't for temporary leadership. It's to decide who is most fit, who is the highest in the eyes of the One Sun. If you best Raedir-ba in the Ring of Bare Hands, you don't just lead this attack. You become the Speaker for the One Sun."

Mershayn's eyebrows raised at that.

"And the ruler of the entire Sunrider empire," Medophae finished.

27

MERSHAYN

AN HOUR LATER, the assembly of the Ring of Mostly Bare Hands got off to a rocky start. The sunset spread wide along the tops of the Spine Mountains, glowing reds and oranges bearing testament to the discussion. Galorman Balis's men lit tall torches stuck into the ground around the ring.

It took nearly another hour of discussion to form the ring in the first place. Apparently the contenders were not allowed to speak. The arrangements for Raedir-ba were made by Harael, his Vessel Man, who claimed he would stand in as speaker for the Speaker for the One Sun. When asked to choose his own speaker, Mershayn chose Bands.

That started off the first argument. In Sunrider culture, women were not allowed to be speakers. They were not allowed to be part of a Wind Ring. They were not allowed to even witness a contest for leadership.

Furthermore, the Ring of Bare Hands was traditionally made from Sunrider warriors linking hands, and Sunrider warriors were men. It was not traditional to have women as part of the circle, but Teni'sian warriors were sometimes women.

"You have no warriors who are women?" Mershayn asked Harael.

"Women are poor fighters," he said.

Before Deni'tri could unhook her hatchet and clout the man, Mershayn cut in. "Well, we're not in Sunrider territory. We'll do it half your way and half ours. Or we're going to put Raedir-ba into the ring with Bands to see how long he lasts."

"What?"

"There will be women as part of my circle, and Bands is going to be my speaker."

Harael turned red, then went back to Raedir-ba. There was a soft discussion. The soft discussion became a hard discussion. Finally, Harael gesticulated angrily, and Raedir-ba raised his voice, once. Harael went silent, turned stiffly, and came back.

"Very well," he said.

"And I want a hundred gold pieces," Mershayn said. Bands looked at him with sharp disapproval.

"Out of the question—!"

"Just kidding," Mershayn cut him off.

Harael looked at Mershayn hard. "Kidding? What is 'kidding'?"

"Joking. Not serious. Never mind. It takes a sense of humor."

"No gold," Bands said, putting a hand on Mershayn's shoulder. "And you can speak to me now. He will no longer speak."

Harael's face was dark red. "Very well," he said lethally. "Choose eleven."

"Eleven is fine. We will provide the wooden swords," Bands said. "Raedir-ba may have first choice."

Harael turned on his heel and returned to Raedir-ba.

After a moment, eleven bulky Sunriders, including Gilgion, came forward and linked hands. Apparently they were all Ring Leaders, like Gilgion. On Mershayn's side were Medophae,

Mirolah, Deni'tri, Grek'tas, Vullieth, Baerst, Galorman Balis, Bordi'lis, Grendis Sym, and, surprisingly, Ry'lyrio. Mershayn wasn't sure about the wisdom of that one, but the lady had insisted, and he couldn't come up with a reason less insulting than, "No, I don't want you to fly into a rage and start cutting Sunriders."

They stripped both contestants to the waist, the circle was made, and Raedir-ba made his selection from the two swords. He picked the closest without looking at it, as though he did not care. Then, Mershayn and Raedir-ba stood outside of the circle, waiting.

Once he and Raedir-ba stepped within, it was understood that neither could leave until the leadership was decided. Once a bone was broken or blood was let, the fight was over. Mershayn took a deep breath and made a couple of practice cuts with his wooden sword. He glanced at Mirolah and gave her a smile.

"It is time," Bands murmured.

Mirolah leaned forward and kissed him gently on the lips. "I will be waiting when you emerge."

Mershayn entered the circle between her and Medophae.

Raedir-ba entered the circle a moment later. The Speaker for the One Sun had been impressive when Mershayn first met him, but he was even more impressive now. There wasn't an ounce of fat on the man, and muscles rippled beneath scarred, sun-darkened skin. His gnarled fingers looked as though they could snap bone.

He stood with the athletic ease of a man in his twenties, but with the confidence of a man who had been to war and returned time and again. He was not afraid of Mershayn. No doubt that was why he had agreed to the swords, why he had agreed to break the traditions Harael fought for. Raedir-ba saw only victory for himself in this duel, and the quicker he finished it, the better, no matter how many Sunrider rules must be broken. To Raedir-ba, Mershayn was only an annoyance to be dealt with before the real fight with the dragons.

The Ring of Bare Hands closed.

Raedir-ba glanced down at the practice sword with contempt and cast it aside. It clattered across the packed earth and cobblestones and stopped at Gilgion's feet. With a feral smile, Raedir-ba crouched and extended his arms, hands open.

Time seemed to slow for Mershayn as it always did in a fight. "Only an fool gives up an advantage for no reason," Mershayn said. He leaned his head to one side, then the other, loosening his neck. Now the cares of kingship fell away. There weren't a hundred decisions to make here. This was combat, where he need only make one decision at a time. This, he understood. This was what he was born to do.

Mershayn brought up his sword and saluted.

Raedir-ba sidestepped like a cat along the edge of the Ring. Mershayn moved into the center, giving himself space to fence.

The Sunrider suddenly launched himself like a striking snake.

Even as prepared as he was, Mershayn was taken aback by the man's speed. Mershayn spun to the right, bringing his sword close to his body. Raedir-ba's hand grazed Mershayn's neck, caught a hank of his hair. Mershayn flinched as the Sunrider yanked it free.

Mershayn stepped back lightly, wincing at the sting on the back of his scalp, waiting for the second pass. With deliberate slowness, Raedir-ba put the lock between his teeth and bit down.

Mershayn waited.

The Sunrider came forward, slowly at first, then lunged again. This time Mershayn met the man's forehead with the point of the wooden sword. If he'd been using a real sword, Raedir-ba would have died then, impaled. Instead, the *thok* of the sword sounded loud, and Raedir-ba's head snapped back...

...but his hulking body kept coming as though it didn't need his head. Mershayn grunted and spun sideways, trying to evade those killing hands, but one caught Mershayn's side and clamped down with frightening force. Mershayn brought the sword down fast, striking the nerve clusters in Raedir-ba's forearm.

Whack! Whack!

The Sunrider's hand went limp, and Mershayn yanked his side from Raedir-ba's grip and stepped quickly backward. His side was on fire. It felt like he'd been smashed between two rocks. How could anyone be that strong? That had been a very near thing. A half second more, and those fingers would have cracked a rib. Medophae was right: Mershayn could never let Raedir-ba get hold of him.

The Sunrider looked up, impassive. A dark red dot stood out on his forehead, but the strike hadn't broken the skin. With the same cool composure, he came forward again.

This time, Mershayn was not content to wait. He stepped backward as before—

—then stepped forward in a quick lunge.

Raedir-ba dodged the point, but Mershayn had anticipated that. Spinning again, he slipped past those groping hands and brought the sword around with all the strength he could muster, aiming for the Sunrider's neck. But Raedir-ba shrugged, and the sword smacked into his meaty shoulder instead.

Raedir-ba's hand snaked out and grabbed the wooden blade.

Instantly, the Sunrider dropped to the ground, yanking Mershayn off balance. Mershayn knew he should let go. Clinging to the blade meant losing his balance, meant giving Raedir-ba the handhold he needed. But Mershayn couldn't do it. Once he lost the sword, his only advantage was gone.

So he held on, stumbling over the big man. Raedir-ba's free hand grabbed for Mershayn's ankles, but he danced between them then stomped hard on Raedir-ba's wrist.

Nothing. No cry of pain. No weakening of his grip. By the gods, his wrist should have broken! But the Sunrider held tight to the sword, rolled to his feet, and wrenched the blade in a circle, snapping it.

Mershayn stumbled away, looking down at the splintered wood.

His mind raced. Raedir-ba smiled and extended his hands,

as cool as before. He didn't lunge, didn't go for the quick win, as though Mershayn was no longer a threat. The Sunrider seemed content to let the icy reality sink in.

Mershayn clenched his teeth, looking at the broken piece of wood in his hand. With a battle cry, he charged. Raedir-ba's eyes lit with triumph, his expression betraying him for the first time. He shifted, hands outstretched, feet wide and ready.

Mershayn cocked back for a swing that would slash across Raedir-ba's chest, opening up a wound with the splintered shard of his sword. At the last split second, he abandoned the strike and dove to Raedir-ba's right. The big man's hands fumbled along Mershayn's back, barely missing once again.

Mershayn rolled across the ground and hit the impassive ankles of the Sunrider warriors on that side of the Ring—

—and came up with Raedir-ba's unused practice sword.

With a deft toss, he switched the broken sword to his left and caught the pristine sword with his right. He grinned and took three expert cuts at the air.

"Now I have two swords," he said.

Raedir-ba came for him.

With deadly precision, Mershayn hurled the broken sword at the Sunrider's head. The Sunrider ducked it with that amazing speed and brought his head up—

—right into the pinpoint accuracy of Mershayn's other sword.

The Sunrider's nose crunched. Blood exploded onto his lip. Raedir-ba's head snapped back, and his foot went out from under him. He slipped and fell to the ground. Mershayn sidestepped the tumble, taking himself out of range of those feet and hands, just in case.

"Yield," Mershayn said.

Raedir-ba spun to a crouch, and the blood from his nose flecked his chest, dripping onto the dirt. He looked incredulously at it, then at Mershayn.

With a roar, the Sunrider launched himself at Mershayn, arms wide.

Mershayn swatted the man's left arm down with the sword

hard, but Raedir-ba's hand still nearly got him. He stabbed the Sunrider in the nose again as he spun.

Raedir-ba's head snapped to the side, and it sent him off balance.

"Yield."

The Sunrider stumbled, caught himself and whirled around—

Mershayn stabbed his nose again, and Raedir-ba howled, swiping like an animal. Mershayn replied with a stout whack along the side of the Sunrider's head. Raedir-ba grunted, wobbled, swung again, missed again. Mershayn whacked him on the other side of the head.

The Sunrider's knees gave out, and he fell to the ground. He lurched up immediately, and Mershayn stabbed him in the nose again. It was a bloody ruin on his face.

"I've shed your blood. I've cracked your bones," Mershayn said. "The only thing left to break is your word. Yield."

Raedir-ba's clenched fists shook as blood dribbled down his lips and chin. Mershayn watched him coldly. He could drop the man on the next pass, but it might fracture his skull. The last thing Mershayn wanted to do was kill the Speaker for the One Sun. At best, that could only win him an army of enemies. He needed an army of allies.

"Fight with us, Raedir-ba," he said. "We need you. The One Sun demands it."

Slowly, the Sunrider descended to one knee, but his burning gaze never left Mershayn.

Half of the Ring erupted into applause and cheering. The rest remained in stunned silence.

28

SILASA

SILASA AWOKE IN THE CITY OF HER BIRTH. A human might have gasped, started awake, and scrabbled against the stone lid above her, but Silasa did not. One moment she didn't exist, and the next moment she did.

Life simply vanished during the day. She assumed her body became nothing more than a sculpture of flesh and bone, and the idea of someone finding her during the day continually terrified her. Even someone who was only curious, with no ill intent, could destroy her by dragging her into the sunlight.

Early on, while Silasa was still adjusting to her new life as a slave to White Tuana's blood, she had made many mistakes, but the biggest had been staying outside too long and being caught by the sun.

She would never forget that night. It had been only a week after she'd become a vampire. She had ranged farther from her cave than she'd meant, caught up in the wonder of the night, the exploration of new creatures, the acuity of her new eyes. When she finally realized dawn was imminent, she was too far from her cave to make it to safety. She had run so fast that the trees were a blur, but it had been too late.

She was still half a mile from her cave when the first rays of daylight filled the sky. She thought she could make it, could see the entrance. But then the sun's first rays struck her, and it was like she had jumped into a bonfire. She remembered the excruciating pain, remembered her arms bursting into flame, and then she remembered nothing.

It had happened so quickly.

She had awoken in her cave, unable to see, and it felt like her limbs were burning logs and a thousand men were sawing on her. She had screamed. The wail went on and on until she'd heard another voice, speaking softly in her ear. Eventually, her screaming had subsided and she'd discovered that the soft voice was Bands calming her, holding her, telling her that it would eventually be all right.

It had taken her a month to fully heal from the sun's damage.

By sheer fortune, Bands had seen Silasa running for the cave when she burst into flame. Bands had transformed into her dragon form, leapt into the air and shielded Silasa as Medophae carried her to the cave.

Silasa knew better now. Digging into the earth could save her, in a pinch. She didn't like to do that, but it was better than immolation.

She pushed at the heavy stone sarcophagus lid. It scraped until the opening was wide enough for her to emerge. She stepped out and looked at the engraving on the monolith at the head of the sarcophagus.

Silasa, Princess of Belshra.

So good to be home....

She traced the inscription with her finger. This was where she would have been buried if there had been a body to bury. At Silasa's request, Medophae had told her father there had been nothing left after the vampires had finished with her.

The tomb of the kings of Belshra was filled with her relatives, down through time until the destruction of the city

213

when Harleath Markin had capped Daylan's Fountain.

Mershayn had asked her to come here in advance, to do what she could to protect Galorman Balis from the Sunriders, to be his supernatural enforcer should things go sourly. But the Sunriders hadn't arrived last night—

A light breeze tickled her skin, there and gone. But there were no breezes down here in the tomb. She turned.

Ynisaan stood at the top of the steps at the far end of the long, dark room. She was in her human form, midnight black skin and white hair, eyes so dark it was difficult to tell them from the rest of her face.

Silasa started to deliver a scathing rebuke, but she stopped. Something about the woman was definitely off.

Ynisaan wore gray breeches and black boots, and a dark gray riding jacket, but her usually immaculate attire was stained and streaked with dirt. Her boots were scuffed, covered with mud, as were her knees, like she had been crawling. The woman's eyes were half-lidded, and when she stepped forward, she stumbled into the baluster at the top of the stairs. Her heel turned on the first step. She lost her footing and fell, thudding down the wide staircase.

Silasa jerked, her conscience wanting her to leap to Ynisaan's aid, but her anger still boiled, and she stayed where she was. She watched as the woman tumbled to the bottom, then rolled onto her back and let out a little breath.

"Heh," Ynisaan said, then she rolled to her knees, pushed herself upright, and staggered to her feet. She leaned heavily on the stone baluster at the bottom of the steps. "Found you." Her words were slurred.

"So you did."

"I can always…find you, you know."

"You're drunk." Silasa had seen humans get drunk before. For some reason, she hadn't thought Ynisaan was capable of such a thing. But really, why wouldn't she be?

"Yes. I have watched…" she hiccoughed, "…ssho many humans do this…when their hearts hurt. Ssho many… I had nothing else…to do, ssho I decided to see if it held any…any wisdom." She slumped against the baluster, breathing hard. "It does... It makes you care less."

"I'm happy it worked for you." Silasa walked toward her, then past her onto the stairs.

"It alsho makes you braver...braver," Ynisaan said. "S'why I went to the Coreworld. I...wassh going to let them kill me."

"What is the Coreworld?" Silasa stopped halfway up the stairs, turning.

"I walked right in like I didn't care. Didn't try to hide. Looked at whatever I wanted. I wassh just going to let them find me and kill me, like they did my mother. But they didn't come. Ssho, I raised my foot to splash a line. Y'can't shtep in the water," she whispered conspiratorially, cupping her hand to the side of her mouth like they were alone. "They know if you shtep in the water." Her head nodded forward. "Was going to do it," she mumbled. She took a long breath, then blinked up at Silasa. "But then I sshaw it. I had to look, didn't I? And I sshaw it. Everything that's going to happen."

Her knee wobbled. She overcompensated with her other leg, stepped on her own foot, and pitched forward. Her hand scraped on the baluster as she tried to grip it, but there was no handhold. She went down on her face. She grunted, and after a moment, she rolled onto her back, looking up at the ceiling. This time she didn't try to get up.

"Avakketh," she huffed. "Knows what you don't. He's going to kill them all. Medophae. Bands. King Mershayn. The others. All the Shunriders. The humans. The quickshilvers. Shtavark..."

"Stavark is alive?" Silasa asked. When she'd last talked with Mershayn, the boy was missing.

"Avakketh's going to recreate the world. S'what he always wanted. He's just too scared. He's always been too scared. But I think he's more scared of the GodSshpill coming back, more scared of threadweavers, than anything else. Little human gods, running around... Can't have that."

"Where is Stavark?" Silasa asked softly, coming down and sitting at the bottom of the stairs.

"Sho, he gets what he wants." She raised her hand. "Toast to him, then! Gets what he wants…" She didn't seem to hear Silasa's questions. "Yay for the fake god of dragons."

"Fake god?"

"It's only one ghost line goes where Avakketh doesn't win," she slurred. "Jusht one. But in that one, your friends don't die. And so…I couldn't die yet. Couldn't kill myshelf… Not yet."

"Ynisaan—"

"Ssho I came back. I swore to use what I know to stop those who are shelfish, shelf-serving with their power. Like Zilok Morth. Like Avakketh. I swore…. But I…wronged you." Ynisaan turned, and seemed startled to find Silasa sitting so close. "I was scared and shelfish, and I wanted to keep you. And I told myself I deserved to keep you, and sho…I abused the power. I became like them. Sho, I'm going to put it right. Just like I saved your life for me, I'm going to give my life for you. Gon' shave your friends. And then maybe…" she said softly. "Maybe you'll think better of me."

A hard lump caught in Silasa's throat.

"Avakketh's shtrong," Ynisaan whispered. "Sho shtrong. And he knows what Medophae doesn't know. Bands doesn't know. Medophae can shoot Oedandus at him all day long, can kill him over and over again, but he will always rise." She looked up at Silasa. "But I know his secret, and I know the little ghost line that shteals his victory. The only one…"

Ghost lines. That wasn't the first time Ynisaan had mentioned them. Were these lines how she saw the future?

"Tell me about the ghost lines," Silasa said.

"He has the GodShtone."

"What's a GodStone?"

"He keeps himself inside, invulnerable. Pure. As long as he keeps the shtone pure, he'll just keep coming back, can draw himself back out as much as he wants…. Sharaphazia doesn't know. Tarithalius doesn't know. But I have a piece of it." She patted a pouch at her side. "Shaturated with Tarithalius. Avakketh used it to destroy them, but it's the answer. I shaw.

Such a thin ghost line, but I know what to do," she slurred. Ynisaan rolled onto her belly and painstakingly pushed herself to her hands and knees, then climbed to her feet again. "Sho…" she said, swaying and starting up the stairs. "Think better of me, dear Shilasa… I was wrong, but I'm going to fix it."

Silasa leapt up the steps and put herself in front of Ynisaan. The little woman blinked her black eyes, and she swayed, almost falling down the steps again. Silasa grabbed her hands, steadied her.

"I'm sorry I was angry with you," Silasa said. "Tell me what you know."

Ynisaan shook her head. "You were right. You being angry…wash right. I hurt you. I was shelfish, and I knew better. Protecting others…it's more important than living. I knew that, but I was scared. What I did was…unforgivable."

"Then you learn," Silasa said. "I learn. And we do better next time."

Ynisaan blinked, and her hands gripped Silasa's. "We?"

Silasa nodded.

Ynisaan's lip trembled. "I…"

Silasa embraced her.

"I'm sorry." Ynisaan grasped her desperately, clutching Silasa's back and murmuring into her shoulder. "I'm so sorry," she whispered.

"I accept your apology," Silasa said. "We're going to start again. You're going to be straight with me, and I'm going to keep my temper. We're going to make things right. Together."

Ynisaan trembled and held her. "Thank you…"

Behind Ynisaan, a coffin lid scraped and fell to the ground. Bony fingers curled around the edge of the casket, and suddenly Silasa didn't feel like hugging anyone.

29

MERSHAYN

MERSHAYN DID NOT KNOW what the etiquette was after winning the Ring of Bare Hands, but he could guess from the scornful frowns on the Sunriders that Mershayn's half of the Ring was not supposed to dissolve into chaos and rush forward to congratulate him.

Mershayn looked around the circle. The sun was gone, and firelight from the tall torches played on the smiling faces of his nobles. Ry'lyrio's grin was maniacal.

"Well done, Your Majesty!" Lord Baerst clapped Mershayn on the back. Mirolah waited while Mershayn was mobbed, but she pointed over their heads at Mershayn and winked. Bands gave him a gentle smile and a nod of the head. Medophae nodded respectfully, but he gave a second meaningful nod at Raedir-ba.

"I have never seen anyone move so fast." Lord Baerst continued. "*That* was swordsmanship!"

"One moment, Lord Baerst." Mershayn signaled for silence and everyone about him went quiet. Raedir-ba still knelt in front of him, and that was not something to take lightly.

"Deni'tri," Mershayn said. "A cloth for his nose, please."

"Yes, Your Majesty."

Mershayn walked over to stand in front of Raedir-ba. "Rise, Speaker for the One Sun."

Raedir-ba shook his head. "The One Sun has spoken without me this night. You are now the Speaker for the One Sun."

"Not so," Mershayn said.

Raedir-ba looked up, his countenance emotionless.

"This contest was to see who leads the war against the dragons," Mershayn said. "And so the Ring of Bare Hands was altered. In order to speak for the One Sun, I would need to meet you with the rules laid down by him." Mershayn gave a wry smile. "And after witnessing your prowess, I would never agree to meet you with only bare hands. But this war needs both my expertise and your strength. Rise, Speaker, and let us face a common foe together." He reached out a hand.

Raedir-ba looked at the extended hand, and, for a moment, Mershayn thought he would refuse. With quiet deliberation, he reached out and took it in that powerful grip that could break bones.

"You speak like a Vessel Man and fight like a Sunrider," he said in a low voice. "I will heed your words, King Mershayn, and I will follow you in this war." He stood and, with a mighty gesture, he thrust Mershayn's hand upward in his own. His Sunrider warriors cheered.

Deni'tri arrived then with a white cloth, and handed it to Raedir-ba. He nodded gratefully, then pressed it to his bloody nose.

The group quieted and began walking toward Belshra's walls, Teni'sians and Sunriders together. Mershayn glanced at the small smile on Bands's face, and he felt gratified. He'd made the right choice, and he had emerged victorious. Now, all he needed to do was—

"Mershayn!" Mirolah's voice cut through the noise of talking nobles and Sunriders. He turned, and the crowd followed his gaze.

As though Mershayn and Mirolah were connected by a rope of fire, the crowd gave way, creating a lane between them. Mirolah stood with her fists clenched, her eyes closed and head bent. Mershayn ran to her.

"What? What is it?"

"They are working," she murmured. "A tremendous threadweaving. It infects the earth. Gods!" She turned her head upward to the night sky, and her kaleidoscope eyes splashed color across Mershayn's face, across the nearby nobles and Sunriders. Ry'lyrio gasped and stepped back. With curses, the Sunriders also backed away from Mirolah.

"What is it?" Mershayn asked.

"They're all around," Mirolah said. "We have to get into the city. We were expecting them to attack from the sky, but they're not. They're—"

A thin, muddy hand thrust through the ground and grabbed Mershayn's leg. He shouted, twisting away and stumbling backward.

Shouts went up from Sunriders and Teni'sians alike.

Dirt exploded upward around the hand, and a skinny, muddy man emerged, clawing his way out of the ground. Moist clods fell from the face, revealing bony cheeks, hollow eye sockets.

Mershayn watched the approaching horror, speechless. He knew he should grab a weapon, move away, but for the first time in his life, he froze.

The skeletal man grabbed at Mershayn with fetid hands—

Golden fire flared in Mershayn's face, and Medophae's flaming sword hit the skeleton's chest and knocked it away.

There was a sharp popping sound and a red flash of light. The skeleton's bones came apart and clacked to the ground in a scattered pile.

Mershayn stared at it, breathing hard.

"Your Majesty," Medophae said, steadying him.

Mershayn blinked, his heart racing.

"Your Majesty!" Medophae said fiercely, and it snapped

Mershayn from his daze.

"It was a dead person," he murmured.

"And not the only one."

Mershayn suddenly became aware of shouts and screams around him.

"They're coming out of the ground," Medophae said. "We need to get into the city."

"Mirolah," Mershayn said, pushing past his terror. "Where is Mirolah?"

"I am here," she said from behind him.

He whirled around. "What's happening?"

"Come on, Your Majesty." Medophae touched Mershayn and pointed him toward the walls. "Inside the city first. The bulk of your army is there; that's where we go."

Mershayn followed him. "The dragons are doing this?" he asked.

"Yes," Bands said.

"Why would they attack us this way?" Mershayn asked. "Why not directly?"

"A half dozen reasons," Bands said. "Let's ask questions later."

"I could...try to unravel the spell," Mirolah said.

Mershayn almost opened his mouth to tell her to do just that, but then he stopped himself. He needed to stop acting like a frightened rabbit. He needed to think.

"No," he said. "Save yourself for later. You're here for one reason: to bring the dragons to the ground. If you can't do that, we lose. I don't want you wasting your strength on anything else. The rest of us came to fight; let us fight."

Medophae grunted his agreement, and they ran over the field to the gate. More skeletons erupted from the ground to their left. To his right, a hand scraped against the wall, thrust up from the mud.

Sniff arrived, churning turf as he brought his huge, muscled body to a stop. A hand thrust up next to him, and the monstrous dog immediately pounced on it. He growled, yanking the hand and the entire skeleton out of the ground.

Sniff mauled the skeleton, his giant jaws snapping down on its neck, its shoulder, its spine, cracking bones. His growls and snapping bones came in a flurry. Finally, with a mighty shake of his head, he tossed the skeleton's splintered torso into the darkness.

He turned, jowls covered with mud, and he opened his jaws in a grin. His pink tongue lolled out.

"I think he's enjoying this," Mershayn said. Sniff padded protectively next to Mirolah.

"Yes," Mirolah said.

"Well, that makes one of us," Mershayn murmured to himself as they passed through the crumbling arch that used to be the main gate into the city.

The main army had settled in the city's center, a huge, circular area near the palace. To Mershayn's relief, Giri'Mar had already responded to the shouts outside the wall. Teni'sian soldiers stood ready, blocking the main roadways. Others manned the fortifications Galorman Balis had arranged to trap the dragons.

"Report," Mershayn asked as Giri'Mar approached, his cloak rippling out behind his armored body.

"Skeletons, Your Majesty," Giri'Mar said. "They are..." He shivered.

"I know how you feel."

"We are...fighting them, Your Majesty."

"Don't let them in here," Mershayn said.

"And don't let them touch you." Silasa's voice came from behind him.

He turned, feeling a deep relief. She'd done away with her typical old-fashioned dress in favor of black riding breeches and a long-sleeved burgundy tunic, belted at the waist. Silasa was ready for battle.

"They grab anything alive that they can reach. Don't let them. And especially don't let them bite you," she said, lifting open a rip in her long sleeve. An ugly wound swelled on her upper arm. "There is some kind of poison in it. I do not think a mortal would survive this."

"Are you all right?" he asked.

"No. It ruined my outfit."

That broke the tension for him, and he smiled. "It's good to have you here, my friend."

"You were smart to bring the army into the city. The buildings will help," she said. "But these skeletons are rising from the ground, and there are plenty of dead bodies in Belshra. Tell your soldiers to break bones. If you strike at their joints, they just re-assemble. But if you break a bone in half, it doesn't heal. Break their thighbone, and they cannot walk. Though they'll still try to grab you. And they know how to use weapons. If they see one, they'll pick it up."

"Thank you."

"You're welcome." She hesitated. "Your Majesty..."

"What?"

"I must leave you," she said, frowning as if she didn't like her words any more than he did.

"What?"

"Where?" Medophae, who stood nearby, interjected. Bands also watched Silasa intently.

She glanced at all of them, but her gaze finally rested on Medophae. "Fight him, Medophae. With everything you have. I'll be...helping from somewhere else."

"Where. Are you. Going?" Medophae asked, his brows coming together.

"I'm sorry. But cannot say. I just wanted to tell you so you weren't looking for me."

"Silasa—" Medophae began, but Bands put a hand on his arm. He quieted.

"Silasa, I need you," Mershayn said.

"I know," she said. She began to back away. "But you need me more where I'm going. I'm sorry you don't understand. If we make it through this, I'll explain."

Medophae tensed, like he was going to chase her. Bands still had hold of his arm. "Let her go," she said.

"Bands—"

"She knows something we don't know," Bands said. "Let

her go."

"Then why doesn't she tell us?"

"I don't know."

"That's not good enough—"

"Do you trust her?" Bands asked.

"I…" He hesitated, then he said, "Of course I do."

"Then trust her."

Mershayn watched Silasa vanish into the night.

First Stavark, now Silasa. I'm going to lose a lot more before this night is done. I can't spend time on this loss, on any of them. I have to focus on the battle to come.

Mershayn turned to the Speaker for the One Sun, who had followed them into the city, leading his horse. "Raedir-ba, bring your Sunriders inside the city—"

"No," the big Sunrider interrupted.

Mershayn's temper flared. The Sunrider had lost in the Ring of Bare Hands, had pledged his fealty to Mershayn for this battle, and yet here he was, disobeying Mershayn's very first order.

Raedir-ba cut him off before he could speak. "With respect, King Mershayn, our horses are worth nothing inside these walls. We must ride. We are not a walking army, like most of your warriors."

Mershayn blinked. This wasn't rebellion. It was a leader who knew his forces, knew their strengths and weaknesses. Mershayn would be a fool not to listen. He controlled his anger, barely, and gave himself a second to think.

"Of course, you're right," Mershayn conceded, trying to keep his voice from sounding like a growl. He was suddenly glad that only his friends had heard the exchange. "Protect the plains. Kill the skeletons outside the walls. Get them all, Speaker."

"At once, King Mershayn." Raedir-ba swung up onto his mount with practiced ease. The Teni'sian soldiers parted, and Raedir-ba galloped until the street ended at a broken section of the wall. A skeleton had climbed through the gap, and Raedir-ba leapt the broken wall, shattered the skull with his curved sword, and vanished into the night.

Sniff lowered his head and growled. Mershayn turned to face the wide darkness of the main street, perpendicular to the smaller street. Mershayn's soldiers created a defensive line, protecting the open circle.

"They're coming," Mirolah said.

Shambling skeletons appeared at the edge of the torchlight. Row after jagged row, dozens of them.

Bands bowed her head, looking like she did right before she'd transformed into a dragon.

"Wait," Mershayn said, putting a hand on her arm. "Don't transform."

Startled, Bands glanced curiously at him. She didn't transform, didn't say anything, but her unspoken question hung in the air.

"This whole attack might be for you," Mershayn said, the thought suddenly occurring to him. After reeling at one surprise after another, his brain was finally working right. "It might be to draw you out, so Avakketh can pinpoint you. We need you when the dragons attack. You wait. We can handle this."

Medophae's flaming sword burst to life in his hand. He grinned. "Then it's time for me to go to work," he said. "Let Avakketh pinpoint *me*."

Mershayn nodded. "Yes."

"I'll take the main street." Medophae roared and ran toward them.

30

SILASA

WITH A HEAVY HEART, Silasa left Mershayn in the midst of his battle. She had promised she would look after him, and she was breaking that promise. But according to Ynisaan, Mershayn's army, Medophae's strength, Bands's wisdom…all of them would amount to nothing if Ynisaan's mission failed. If this "one ghost line" did not prevail amongst a thousand other dark futures, then Mershayn's army would be slaughtered by a host of dragons. Medophae and Bands would die on Avakketh's claws. Amarion would fall.

In many ways, this was exactly what Ynisaan had done last time. On the eve of a battle, she had plucked Silasa from the battlefield and sent her on a different mission.

But this was different. Ynisaan was not closed-lipped and mysterious this time. She was broken and vulnerable, reeling in a drunken stupor, and it had caught at Silasa's heart. Silasa knew the dull, grinding bite of loneliness, and Ynisaan was caught in those jaws. And the woman finally seemed ready to reveal everything to Silasa: who Ynisaan was, how she could see the future with these "ghost lines." She'd mentioned something called the Coreworld, and cracks and water that couldn't be touched.

Silasa scaled the crumbling wall of the palace to the first walkway. Ynisaan leaned against the stone rail, hands clutching it. Silasa had carried her up here after the skeletons popped out of their coffins. The creatures had been brutally strong, but they were slow and stupid. They were horrible climbers.

Ynisaan's head bobbed about, and she focused on Silasa. "We're running out of time," she whispered.

"I withheld information from my friends and abandoned them the moment before a battle. Sound familiar?"

"But to save them this time. Not to save you," she said, then softer, almost to herself, she said, "You and I will mosht likely die."

"Such a comfort," Silasa said.

Ynisaan staggered toward her. She leaned to the side, stumbled, caught her balance. "I have never...done this...drinking before. When does it wear off?"

"I've never been drunk either," Silasa said. "But I've watched it often enough. I think you're in for another few hours."

She let out a long breath. "That is...dishappointing."

"Ynisaan, what are we doing, and where are we going?"

"Dear Shilasha," Ynisaan slurred. "I can tell you how I know what we must do. Or we can save Amarion. I don't think there is enough time for both. We need to be elsewhere very shoon. We may already be too late."

"Try."

She hesitated, her eyelids closing as if in thought. Or sleep. For a moment, Silasa thought Ynisaan had passed out standing up. But she suddenly jolted upright, her eyes opening. "There is one way." She thrust her finger in the air. "We can run, and talk, at the same time."

"Run?"

The air around Ynisaan became inky, and her silhouette blurred. Then, a black unicorn with a pearlescent horn and white mane stood where Ynisaan had been. It dipped its head, stumbled to the side. Its hooves clacked on the flagstone, and it caught its balance.

Silasa opened her mouth in shock and took a step back. "You're a...a unicorn?"

The unicorn bobbed her head, and it seemed that she was beckoning to Silasa. Cautiously, Silasa stepped forward.

Ynisaan stamped at the ground, lowering her horn.

Silasa narrowed her eyes and stopped. "What?"

The air around the unicorn turned inky, and suddenly Ynisaan stood there in her human form once more. She let out a long breath through her lips, much like a horse.

"I'm sorry. I should have shaid..." she trailed off, her eyes at half-mast.

Silasa sighed. The idea that Ynisaan was going to save Amarion by herself, in this state, was ridiculous. She was on the verge of passing out. "You should have said what?"

Ynisaan's head snapped up. "I cannot...talk in my true form. Not like humans talk." She nodded, which looked startlingly similar to the way she'd tossed her head as a unicorn. "We don't talk with our mouths. We talk with our minds."

"I don't know how to do that," Silasa said.

"Jussht touch foreheads with me, and I can show you."

"Okay..."

The little woman suddenly became the unicorn again. Like before, she lowered her horn.

Fine, Silasa thought. Tentatively, she lowered her head, too. The sharp point of the pearlescent horn touched Silasa between the eyes like a droplet of rain.

Suddenly, there was a hum in the back of her mind. Then it stopped.

The unicorn blinked, waiting. The hum came again.

Silasa tried to hum back. No response.

"What do I do?" she asked.

The hum came again. Silasa hummed back. "It's not working," she said.

In the city below, shouts rose. Steel rang on steel. The

battle with the skeletons had begun.

The hum in the back of Silasa's mind became an insistent buzz, like angry bees.

"What? What do you want me to do? This doesn't make any sense!"

The buzzing increased, and Silasa's head started to throb. She closed her eyes, imagining the buzzing like a big bee hive in her head, and she stomped on it.

"*...just have to break the barrier.*" Ynisaan's voice suddenly spoke in her head. "*Your mind creates a barrier. Break it.*"

"*I think I just did,*" Silasa thought.

"*Oh! There you are. Well done.*" Ynisaan's voice didn't slur now, in this mind-to-mind conversation, but Silasa felt a sense of...bubbles all around her, drifting and popping. Each pop sounded like a soft giggle.

"*How is this going to help us be faster?*" Silasa asked. Talking mind-to-mind felt thoroughly weird.

"*We can talk while we run. You wanted me to tell you about myself. And I will.*"

"*Well, you're a unicorn. That's new. I'll be chewing on that for a while. Where are we running?*"

"*I am running. You are riding.*"

"*I'm supposed to ride you?*"

"*You can't get where we are going on your own. Come.*"

Silasa hesitated, then leapt onto Ynisaan's back. She hadn't ridden a horse for centuries. Horses and other animals reacted to vampires like they reacted to wolves, or rock lions, or any other large predator. But once upon a time, Silasa had been very good at this. Aside from sneaking away to swim in the ocean, riding had been her favorite activity as a child.

The black unicorn looked over her shoulder, tossed her mane, and leapt forward, galloping toward the edge of the walkway. Silasa almost fell over backward, but grabbed a fistful of mane at the last instant and kept her seat.

Ynisaan's hooves sparked on the stones, and as they came close to the edge of the building, the sparks became little flames. Instead of flickering in the orangish yellow-red of a fire, they flared purple and revealed...someplace else, a dark and purple beyond, like they were creating little rips in the fabric of the world. As the little flames rose up, joining together, they became a portal.

Ynisaan reached the edge of the walkway, and leapt into the air. The flames enveloped them, and Belshra vanished. They landed on a flat, barren landscape. There were no trees or bushes or grass, just rocky outcroppings under a purple sky with a blue sun.

Silasa clung to Ynisaan's mane, hunched down over her neck. Silasa's knees squeezed Ynisaan's flanks tightly.

"What is this?" she asked.

"My imagination. How I travel from one place to another quickly."

"You travel through your imagination? How does that even work?"

"I can explain it, or I tell you what I know of Avakketh and the GodStone. We don't have time for both."

"Fine. Tell me about the GodStone."

"I learned about the GodStone when I was little. It was one of the many artifacts Natra created. It was once the centerpiece of Natra's treasure room, but it hasn't been for a long time."

Ynisaan's hooves sparked, creating the same rising flames, showing soft blues and iridescent pinks in the world behind the flames. The blasted landscape and its purple sky vanished as she leapt into the flaming pink gateway.

Suddenly, they were falling in a blue sky filled with giant pink bubbles. Ynisaan dropped onto one. The bubble gave beneath her hooves, but didn't pop. Then it sprang back into shape, launching her upward. Together they arced, fell, and Ynisaan bounced off another bubble.

"By the gods!" Silasa thought to her.

Ynisaan expertly bounced from one bubble to another, and Silasa hung on. She had no idea what would happen if she fell, and she didn't want to find out.

"Natra made many artifacts. Some were powerful enough to tip the balance between the gods, like the Crown of Natra, and the GodStone was the most powerful of them all. My mother suspected that, because of this, Natra took the GodStone away long ago and destroyed it."

"Because it could fall into the wrong hands."

"Yes."

"But she didn't destroy it," Silasa guessed.

"Yes. Mother was wrong."

"And now what Natra feared has happened. Avakketh has it."

Silasa found it unsettling to talk about the gods like they were squabbling siblings. But speaking mind to mind was getting easier. *"What does it do?"*

"Bring a god back to life."

"What?"

"I don't know why Natra created it. It stores GodSpill. Maybe that's the only reason she made it, a reservoir of power to bolster her while she was creating the world."

"It generates GodSpill?"

"It takes a little piece of a god, and it makes more of it."

"How does that resurrect a god?"

"Gods are made of GodSpill. Or rather, I should say that GodSpill is the residual essence that leaked from the gods themselves into the lands. Even the smallest amount of Avakketh will quickly multiply inside the GodStone. In moments, it can generate enough of Avakketh to recreate him. As long as a piece of Avakketh remains in the stone, he can't be destroyed like Dervon. He'll just emerge and heal himself, or he'll recreate himself altogether."

Sparks rose from Ynisaan's hooves again, bursting into flame with each giant bubble she hit. Green and purple flickered in the flames. When they grew large enough, Ynisaan leapt through...

...onto a giant rippling purple ribbon the size of a road, stretching out across a night's sky. Silasa looked all around, but there wasn't any ground anywhere. Green and purple ribbons the size of roads fluttered past them, coming up, going down, flowing behind, or rippling out in front of them. Ynisaan galloped hard down the undulating purple road.

"You like purple," Silasa noted.

"I do."

"So if Oedandus can't kill him, how are we going to kill him?"

231

"*Two gods can't occupy the stone at the same time. If Avakketh is inside, it belongs to him, but if someone else was inside...*"

"*We're going to jump inside the stone?*"

"*We are not gods,*" Ynisaan said. "*But I looked at the ghost lines...and while a thousand of them show Avakketh triumphant, one shows him dead forever, killed by Medophae's hand. In that one, you and I replace the piece of stone that Avakketh removed.*"

"*He removed a piece?*"

"*Yes. That was the stone Medophae carried around for four hundred years.*"

"*The gem that Bands was trapped in!*"

"*And Tarithalius. And once we replace it, we may dislodge Avakketh.*"

"*With what?*"

"*With Tarithalius.*"

"*But Tarithalius and Bands aren't even in the gem anymore.*"

"*Some of Tarithalius's GodSpill must linger in the gem. It's the only explanation for that one ghost thread. Even the barest trace of his essence is enough—and we are going to use it to replace Avakketh in the GodStone.*"

"*This...residue of Tarithalius could fight Avakketh for possession of the GodStone?*"

"*If we can make the transfer just as Avakketh dies, yes.*"

"*When he dies?*"

"*Yes.*"

"*So Medophae is going to have to kill Avakketh. Then we jam the ruby back into the GodStone, and that's supposed to stop him?*"

"*Just after he pulls all of himself out of the GodStone to resurrect himself.*"

Silasa shook her head. "*How do we time something like that?*"

"*When the color drains, we'll know,*" Ynisaan said.

"*And how do we know that Medophae is even going to be able to kill Avakketh? What if he can't duplicate what he did to Dervon?*"

Ynisaan paused. "*Well, yes. We can't know for sure.*"

"*You said the ghost lines lead to this path!*"

"*The lines are just possibilities. And while there is one line that shows victory, there are a thousand that show defeat.*"

"That's reassuring."

"It has been done before." Ynisaan galloped hard up a particularly steep ripple in the undulating purple road.

"So, you're taking us to the bottom of the ocean to look for the stone?"

"I have the stone. When I saw this single ghost line, I took it."

Silasa was silent. Finally, she said, *"One ghost line out of a thousand?"*

"One out of a thousand," Ynisaan confirmed.

"This is a really bad plan."

"Yes." Sparks leapt up from Ynisaan's hooves, and the flame gate revealed a rough cavern. She leapt through, hooves clacking on rock floor as she slid to a stop. She wobbled, then caught her balance.

"And we've arrived."

A large, ghostly dragon filled the cavern almost floor to ceiling, nearly as large as Avakketh himself. It turned, its slitted eyes focusing on them.

"And there's a guardian," Ynisaan said.

"A guardian? That might have been important to mention. Did it slip your mind?"

"I'm a bit drunk."

Perfect, Silasa thought. *I'm standing in a cavern in Irgakth, about to fight a ghost dragon for a stone that resurrects gods.*

And I'm riding a drunk unicorn.

Silasa could see through the hazy body of the ghost dragon, and just behind it was a ruby the size of a barrel, sitting atop a natural rise in rock floor. It was the same crimson color as the gem Medophae had carried for so many years.

That, she thought, *must be the GodStone.*

The dragon lowered its head and hissed. Its red eyes were the only part of its body that wasn't a translucent shade of gray.

"How do you fight a ghost dragon?" Silasa asked.

"I was hoping you'd know."

Silasa showed her teeth. *"Great. Okay. I'll take the dragon. You jam the stone back in."*

"Not until the stone changes color."

"Right," Silasa said, keeping her eyes on the guardian. *"Nothing could possibly go wrong."*

"Just distract the dragon."

The ghost dragon looked back and forth between the two of them, then decided it had waited long enough. It arched its neck like a snake about to strike, and ghostly flame blew toward them. Silasa didn't know how a ghost dragon's flame could hurt her, but she was certain she didn't want to find out.

She leapt from Ynisaan's back even as the unicorn charged the other way. The ghostly flame shot between them.

"Let's do this." *Silasa charged.*

31

GRENDIS SYM

BREATHING HARD, GRENDIS SYM BACKED AWAY cautiously. The stars shone bright overhead, and the thin moon lit shambling skeletons everywhere. Rich earth fell from them in clumps, and the dirty bones glowed sallow beneath. He'd already put three of them down for good, but they just kept coming.

Shouts of alarm, screams of horror, and the wails of the wounded filled the night. Another skeleton burst from the earth right next to him. He leapt to the left and slashed down. His sword caught it on the upper arm. Red light flashed, and the bone sheared in two. The skeleton staggered back, looking at its fallen arm.

This was not a battle for a real swordsman. There was no kill strike, no elegant lunge that could drop these monsters. Each brutal hacking of his sword took only a piece of these horrors, and they just kept coming until they were dismantled. Better to have a woodcutter, accomplished at ceaseless chopping, fight these creatures. Sym was a blade master. How did one skewer an opponent through the heart when there was no heart?

He thanked the gods he had one of Bands's enchanted blades. The Teni'sians with normal weapons were worse off, and they died screaming. Sym had watched too many soldiers strike mighty blows on the relentless, muck-covered skeletons and still die under their relentless grasping.

Sym's arm ached with all the chopping, but he couldn't stop. Another skeleton shambled toward him, head cocked like its neck had been broken. It slashed a rusty sword at Sym. He sidestepped and hacked at the arm again. Another red flash. The arm fell; the creature did not. It looked down, picked up the sword with its other hand, and continued forward. Gritting his teeth, Sym stepped backward over the uneven ground, trying to catch his breath. He shrugged his leaden shoulders, adjusted his grip, and prepared to hack again.

Five spikes closed around his leather shoulder plate, ripping through thick cloth and plunging into his flesh. Sym gasped. A skeleton had snuck up behind him!

Lurching sideways, Sym somehow yanked himself free of the cold grip. The new skeleton staggered, its hand still clenched, its index finger red with Sym's blood.

Don't let them touch you... The bastard's words echoed in his mind, a hasty speech delivered as they had formed ranks only moments ago.

Sym backpedaled, hit a low, broken wall, and barely blocked the rusty sword of his first attacker. The new skeleton grasped for another handful of his flesh.

"Ala'kus! Vendyn!" Sym shouted, looking for the guards who had been on his flanks. They needed to keep the perimeter, needed to keep him from being surrounded....

Ala'kus and Vendyn lay dead a dozen paces away, necks twisted, flesh gouged and bloody. Beyond them, the rest of the soldiers—who had surrounded him only moments ago—lay in heaps.

Sym's blood turned to ice. He was alone. Farther away, more than a hundred yards, the main battle raged in the center of the city. Somehow, he had been separated and driven down this empty street. A dozen skeletons had lumbered between him and the main army now, and all were turning their attention on him.

His wound burned, and he retreated down the narrow alley behind him, looking hastily over his shoulder. Nothing moving down there. Was it safe?

The skeleton with the rusty sword came into the alley first and swung again. In desperation, Sym ducked underneath and attacked, bringing his blade down hard on the skeleton's knee. The bone shattered, and the skeleton went down.

Two more staggered into the alley to take its place. He glanced over his shoulder again. The darkness of the alley resolved into a wall. Blocked!

He was going to die. Once he reached that wall, his retreat would be over. The skeletons would overwhelm him.

With a desperate cry, he threw himself forward and slashed at the skeleton, its bloody fingers outstretched for more. His sword glanced off the thing's shoulder with a red flash. The skeleton reached for his neck. Sym spun and slipped on the muddy cobblestones. He went down, and the grasping hand missed, raking across the armor on his back. He rolled to his feet and bumped into the wall.

Before him, a dozen skeletons filled the alley, swaying as they shambled forward.

Sym leapt to his feet, screaming as he hacked left and right. Red flash after red flash blinded him. One skeleton went down, its hips cracked in two. Another lost its head and staggered away, blind. A third lost its arm and that damned rusty sword. But soon, Sym's breathing grew ragged, his strokes weak. The sword chipped into the bones, but to little effect. He yelped and backpedaled as five hands reached for him, but tripped on a piece of broken wall. Sym fell.

Suddenly, golden fire erupted behind the skeletons, and one of them vanished as though it had been sucked up into the sky. Sym rolled on the ground, avoiding two grasping, bony hands, and then that skeleton was yanked backward as well.

The final skeleton exploded like a tree struck by golden lightning.

Medophae emerged in a nimbus of golden fire. The skeletons swarmed him, but he knocked them back like they were made of sticks. Loud popping sounds and red flashes accompanied each strike.

In moments, all of the skeletons in the alley were piles of scattered bone.

"Medophae!" Sym blurted.

"Sym," he acknowledged as though all of this was ordinary. "This is a bad place to be." He held out his left hand. Sym took it and Medophae pulled him to his feet. Wild, conflicting emotions raged within Sym's heart. He hated this man. Medophae had killed Sym's father. Sym would have been king of Teni'sia twice if not for this man and his interference.

And now Medophae had saved his life.

"Next time you want to take on the entire skeleton army by yourself," Medophae said, "let me know first. I'll go with you." He tipped his head toward mouth of the alley. "We should get back."

"Y-Yes," he said, cursing his shaking voice.

"Follow me."

Sym followed. The skeletons fell before Medophae and his burning sword like wheat before a scythe.

They reached the army in short order. To Sym's surprise, the Teni'sians were winning. The last pockets of the undead had been pushed back up the side streets. Tenacious soldiers hacked methodically amidst red flashes. Once Sym was safely in the midst of the army, Medophae ran back toward the nearest cluster. But before he could reach the fight, the remaining skeletons flashed red on their own, then dropped to the ground like marionettes with cut strings. Soldiers looked around, weapons up, waiting for the next surprise.

Silence fell over the battlefield.

Mershayn's voice roared over scattered soldiers. "Form up!"

Sym looked to the right. The bastard stood atop a broken

wall with his glowing blue sword thrust in the air.

Soldiers ran back to the wide, circular cobblestoned area, forming up ranks and facing the front of the city. Sym's vision blurred, and he blinked to focus his gaze. He felt like he should do something, but his body was reluctant to move.

"My lord?" a voice said.

He suddenly realized something had hold of his arm, and he jerked away, looking wildly to his right.

But it wasn't a skeleton. It was a bald woman with scars on her face.

"My lord," she repeated. "You've been injured."

"Deni'tri…" he said thickly. His voice sounded strange. He glanced at his shoulder. The skeleton's puncture had swollen huge and red beneath his ripped tunic. It looked hideous.

"My lord, come with me," Deni'tri said, her voice sounding thick and distant, like she was speaking from the other side of a tunnel.

"The battle…" he slurred. "The skeleton…"

Don't let them touch you….

Sym's legs wobbled. Deni'tri took his arm and steadied him.

"D-Don't let them touch you…" he murmured, and collapsed.

32

MIROLAH

MIROLAH LOOKED OVER THE BATTLE from atop the palace tower. Sniff sat next to her like some muscled sculpture. She'd left Mershayn behind and floated up to this one intact tower to search for Avakketh.

The last time she'd brought the dragons to the ground and insulated Mershayn, she had become the GodSpill itself. It had snatched her away and dragged her all over Amarion as the wind.

This time, there would be a hundred times that many dragons. But this time, she was also taking precautions. She imagined a thick, formidable rope lashing herself to her body. No matter where she went or what she did, this glowing rope would lead her back. Then, once it was constructed, she let herself seep into the GodSpill a little bit at a time. Her awareness expanded.

She reached out around her, feeling everything. She was part of the wind that ruffled Medophae's hair as he stood at the front of the massed soldiers, looking to the northeast. She swept past Bands, swirled around Raedir-ba and his mighty Sunriders. Mirolah lingered at last upon Mershayn. The King of Teni'sia and his guards stood at the forefront of the army next to Medophae, watching the broken front gate of the city and waiting for the dragons to arrive. Mershayn's nobles had urged him to go to the back of the army, but he would never lead from behind. He would give hope; he would show his people that they could overcome their fear.

I will protect you. Whatever else I do this night, I will protect you.

She moved on, sending a part of her awareness into the long town hall that Galorman Balis had prepared as an infirmary. Many had died in the skeleton attack, but she wasn't going to let the poisoned follow. She went into those who lay slowly dying from the poison, and she drew it from their bodies. She heard their babbled awakenings, the surprised cries of the healers, and then she moved on, stretching her awareness even farther.

Tall grasses bent in the wind, anxious to reach for the sky, waiting for the arrival of the sun. The Inland Ocean lapped against her shores, quietly determined to eat away at the rock and sand until there was nothing left. The old, crumbling stones of Belshra, the houses and the city walls, clung tenaciously to their tasks, stout reminders of the shapes their builders had intended for them. The Teni'sian soldiers paced at their posts, some with the fiery hope of glory, others resigned to death. She became part of the Sunriders forming up ranks on the field, and finally she brushed across the now-inert skeletons. She felt the last wafts of red GodSpill—Avakketh's GodSpill—trailing away toward the northeast. She followed it, and...

There were the dragons.

They were in flight, rushing toward the ruined city at a terrible speed. Avakketh led them, a terrible red GodSpill enveloping him in a burning nimbus. He was fully three times as large as the enormous white dragons that flew directly behind him. And then, beyond, the sky was filled with dragons. They went on and on, hundreds of them.

The GodSpill called to her, drawing her farther and farther out of her body, and this time she went willingly, the security of her stout cord trailing behind her.

She reached out, laying light fingers on the god of dragons—

Avakketh twitched, like he could smell her threadweaving. His great wings beat, and he turned toward her while the rest of the dragons continued toward the main army. Flame erupted from his mouth, and his baleful gaze pierced the intervening distance, through clouds, through walls.

"This is my land," Mirolah thought. *"And this is my air you fly upon. And you will not—"*

Red GodSpill flared from Avakketh, and an invisible blade slashed through the thick cord Mirolah had connected to her body. The blade then slashed through the attachment she'd made to Sniff, and also the one to Mershayn.

No one heard Mirolah's silent scream. In horror, she watched the city fall away below her as the GodSpill yanked her upward, shuddering in delight. It stretched her, pulling her over the land, and she became a part of everything from the Inland Ocean to the northern plains of Belshra, from the Corialis mountains to Denema's Valley. She became the earth, the trees, the people, the air itself.

Mirolah's body fell to the stone floor of the tower, dead.

Sniff's howl split the night.

33

MERSHAYN

EVERY MAN AND WOMAN in Belshra heard Sniff's long, mournful howl. It came down as if the sky keened, and it reverberated through the ruins of Belshra. Mershayn would forever remember it as the trumpet that began the battle.

A harsh, hot wind hit the city. Teni'sian soldiers squinted into the acrid blast, and the first dragon screech split the night, followed by a cacophony of screeches that shook the crumbling walls of Belshra.

Murmurs of fear rippled down the Teni'sian line.

Glowing mouths appeared in the dark. Black wings blotted the starry sky. At their head, a giant dragon resolved in the moonlight with crimson scales and a horned head that came from a nightmare. Five snow-white dragons followed closely behind the red, looking like children by comparison. After them, the sky filled with dragons of every color.

The red dragon opened its mouth, showing the raging inferno deep inside, and suddenly Mershayn's guts turned to water. His knees felt wobbly. Only Medophae's unflinching stance and implacable glare at the giant red gave Mershayn the backbone to keep his feet.

A Teni'sian soldier cried out and fled, pushing his way through the army. Another broke and ran. Then another...

"Hold!" Mershayn shouted, raising *Laughter* in his hand. "Have faith, Teni'sians! This is not their victory. This is where we pay them back!" But his voice was tremulous as he fought his own fear.

The soldiers didn't listen. Dozens fled, and then the entire army broke ranks, running away from the oncoming dragons.

"Your Majesty," Deni'tri cried, anguished, as her legs seemed to take her away from him. Mershayn jerked, about to go with her, but Medophae's hand closed on his arm. He, Bands, and Lord Baerst were the only ones standing their ground.

"Let me go!" Mershayn cried, gripped by sudden panic.

"It's a spell," Bands yelled over the frightened din. "Don't give in to—"

"Hold!" Baerst's mighty voice boomed into the night, and it stifled the frightened cries. That deep, rich voice echoed through the city, thudded into Mershayn's chest, and restored sanity. Suddenly, the overpowering fear vanished as if it had been chopped away.

The fleeing soldiers stumbled, their limbs once again under their own command. They shook their heads and turned around.

"Come on! They're just lizards. Where's your backbone?" Baerst boomed again.

Mershayn spun to his right and took a step back. Standing where Lord Baerst had been was, instead, a giant Lord Baerst. He was still the same stocky, purple-nosed lord in every way, except now he was eight feet tall.

"When the battle starts, put me up front, Your Majesty," Baerst boomed, echoing what he had said in the Teni'sian throne room. "And I'll do you right."

Mershayn gaped at him.

"Tarithalius!" Bands exclaimed.

"Tarithalius," Medophae echoed, less surprised and less enthusiastic.

Bands's surprise turned to annoyance, and she narrowed her eyes. "This is supposed to be funny? You appearing at the last second?"

"It is supposed to be useful." He grinned down at her. "Come now. They were *cheating*. I can't stand cheaters."

"You invented cheating!"

"I can't stand *other* cheaters. Look, if Avakketh makes all the humans run away, there's no battle. What fun would that be?"

Mershayn gaped, watching these gods and demi-gods have their discussion. He felt it had to be some kind of dream—or nightmare—from which he was about to wake.

"Fun?" Medophae growled, gripping the flaming golden sword at his side. "You think this is fun?"

Bands, ever the calm one, put a hand on the raging demigod's shoulder. "It's no use," she said. "He's not going to change. You're not going to change him, and this certainly isn't the time. He's here and, apparently, on our side. We need every bit of help we can get."

"She's right," the giant Baerst said, pointing at the sky full of dragons. "That's a lot of dragons."

Mershayn fought to keep his composure. He was king. He couldn't stand agape. Lives were depending on him. He shouted the first thing that came to his mind. "Reform the line!"

Behind them, Giri'Mar relayed the order, shouting at the soldiers, and the army's line began to reform.

The dragons had almost reached the range where they could begin blasting fire down on the city. Mershayn tensed.

"Wait," Bands said in an even tone.

"I am going straight for Avakketh," Medophae said.

"That's the big one in the front?" Mershayn asked.

"Yes," Medophae said.

"Say, that's an awful lot of dragons," Tarithlius repeated. Mershayn glanced at the god, then away. He absolutely didn't know what to think when looking at Baerst-as-a-god. It was damned unsettling.

"Knock, knock," Tarithalius said.

"What?" Mershayn glanced up at the god. He reeled from the idea that Lord Baerst had been Tarithalius all along. Mershayn felt he should curse the man...and also apologize somehow. He'd never really given much credence to the gods, and he'd never paid homage to Tarithalius. Never honored him.

"Knock, knock," Tarithalius repeated.

"No." Bands let out a grunt of annoyance. "Not now."

"What does it mean?" Mershayn asked her.

"It's a joke," Bands said, then shook her head. "It's *supposed* to be a joke."

"'Knock, knock' is a joke?" Mershayn looked quizzical. "I don't get it."

"He's imagining he's knocking on a door and you're supposed to imagine that you're answering it and say 'Who's there?' Except don't."

"Why not?"

"Because this isn't the time for jokes, and they're not funny."

"I think they're funny," Tarithalius said, not seeming to take offense at all. He put his fists on his hips and looked up at the wave of dragons flying toward them. "Say, that's an awful lot of dragons. Knock, knock."

Mershayn stared at the god of humans. If his god wanted him to play along with His joke, it seemed a bad idea to snub him. Just letting him stand there, joke half told, made him look...foolish.

"You don't have to do what he tells you," Bands said, as though she could read Mershayn's thoughts. "He doesn't care, and it won't make him like you any better. By the same token, he won't hate you if you don't answer him."

"Knock, knock," Tarithalius repeated, grinning.

"But he *will* pester you incessantly." Medophae growled.

"Say, that's a lot of dragons in the sky! Knock, knock."

Mershayn relented. "Uh, who's there?"

"Not us!" he said. "Not for long!" He laughed, and it sounded like thunder.

Mershayn felt a crushing letdown, like he was looking at his father and suddenly realized that his father was an idiot. He'd hoped Tarithalius's joke would at least lighten the mood, or bolster his spirits. He frowned at Bands. "Well...that's horrible."

"I told you," she said.

"Knock, knock," Tarithalius said again.

"Quiet, Thalius," Bands replied. "It's time to fight."

"Ah!" the giant god roared. "Good."

The giant red dragon could now be seen clearly, and its head suddenly twitched, as though it had sensed something to its left. With a screech, it veered from the main group, leaving the five white dragons in the lead.

"Where's Mirolah?" Mershayn muttered. The dragons were almost upon them.

"Dead, lad," Tarithalius said in a neutral tone. "Avakketh found her. That's why he broke away from the group. We're on our own."

"No..." Mershayn whispered. Sniff's baying hadn't been a call to war. It had been a lament.

"Tarithalius, can't you—"

"Eyes on the fight, lad. They're here."

The dragons swooped low, nearly to the gate. The white dragons in the lead drew in breath and—

Abruptly, the foremost white dragon dropped in a flutter of leather wings. It plowed into the earth with a thunderous boom a hundred yards from the broken main gate. Dirt rose like a wave, cresting and crashing into the walls and burying the gate.

Earth-shaking booms thundered across the northern fields of Belshra as dragon after dragon plummeted. The night sky spat them like thunderous rain. Impact after impact shook the ground, and a tall, half-ruined building crumbled under the strain, sending men and horses scurrying away.

Tarithalius began to laugh. "Guess I was wrong, lad! She is a surprise, isn't she! Come on, it's time to crack some dragon skulls!"

Relief flooded through Mershayn. She had done it! Mirolah had brought the dragons down!

"Now!" he shouted to Giri'Mar. Giri'Mar blew his shrill whistle.

Mershayn thrust Laughter into the air. "Our threadweaver is with us! Attack! Don't give them a chance to recover!"

He ran up the main street, racing to get to the hill made by the first fallen dragon. Hundreds of roaring soldiers came behind him. As he neared, he heard the *clunk* of one of the many catapults Giri'Mar had positioned on a stout building just behind the wall, and a barrel lofted high into the air. It arced perfectly, descending on that first white dragon that had landed in front of the broken gates. The barrel hit, exploding on the big dragon's back.

It screeched in pain as the water from the True Ocean splashed over it. Plumes of hissing steam wafted up from it from the killing water, and its flesh sizzled.

"Again!" Mershayn shouted. "Now!"

Clunk. Clunk. Clunk.

More barrels lofted into the air, spraying trails of water and descending expertly into crater after crater where the nearest dragons had landed. Pain-filled screeches went up from each smoking site.

Clunk. Clunk. Clunk.

Three more catapults sang, and the barrels dropped into the next group of nearby dragon craters. More dragon screeches pierced the night. Mershayn made a mental note to promote those catapult operators. They hadn't missed a single shot.

Clunk. Clunk. Clunk.

He heard the next round of catapults shoot, but he'd run out of time. Mershayn scrambled up the hill created by the first thrashing, fallen dragon, and leapt onto its back. The beast's scales sizzled and smoked, but when Mershayn touched the hissing water, it was just water. He found his footing on the bloody scales and stabbed Laughter deep into the white dragon's neck. Medophae, who had matched Mershayn pace for pace, landed next to him a second later, his flaming blade hitting the other side of the beast's neck.

The dragon's screech ended, and it went limp.

"One down!" Tarithalius boomed, running to the top of the hill and jumping over them, an enormous war hammer suddenly in his hand. His jump took him far past them, all the way to the next crater that hid a screeching, thrashing dragon. He vanished into it, but his thunderous voice could easily be heard.

"I shall call you Wanda the Wingless!"

A dragon's shriek split the night, and the shadowed figure of Tarithalius leapt into the air again, flying toward the next crater like a giant grasshopper.

Wind rushed past Mershayn, and he looked up in time to see Bands, finally in her dragon form, fly overhead, the only dragon in the sky. Fire spurted from her mouth at the next downed dragon, half-buried in the dirt of its impact and screeching at the acid water that ate into it. It shrieked as Bands's flame engulfed it.

The open field was littered with a thousand downed dragons, even Avakketh. He lay a thousand paces to the east across a shattered wall and three crumbled buildings.

"I'll see you at the end of the battle," Medophae said to Mershayn, sprinting toward the downed god.

Mershayn looked around. His soldiers, now encouraged by the fallen dragons, ran to catch up with him. The Sunriders, waiting along the outside of the wall, charged across the field like an angry storm, swarming over the nearest dragon.

"Attack!" Mershayn commanded, though he hardly needed to. He leapt down and raced at the head of his army.

The next dragon he found, also a white, had snapped its neck in the fall, and it lay sizzling and unmoving in a shallow pool of seawater. He ran past it, and his soldiers caught up with him, surrounding him.

Ahead, an enormous blue dragon shook, still stunned and struggling to rise. Mershayn leapt upon it, and drove his blade into its back leg. It shrieked, whipping around to bite him. He dove to the side, rolled to his feet and met the dragon's next bite with a nose full of Laughter.

It shrieked and jerked upward, pulling Mershayn into the air. The dragon shook him free, but he managed to hang on to his blade.

He flew through the air, but as before in Teni'sia, the wind met him, cradled him, and softened his descent.

He landed on his feet.

"Thank you!" he shouted to the wind.

Now surrounded by soldiers, the blue dragon roared, flicked its head to the side as a hundred angry Teni'sians with enchanted weapons rushed out of the darkness. They skewered the beast in a dozen places before it could draw a breath. It died thrashing.

Killing the dragon gave the soldiers confidence. Shouting like wild things, they rushed the next, and the battle began in earnest.

Some of the scaled horrors were found stunned and broken. Others had shaken off the fall and slithered forward on all fours.

Bands, the only dragon capable of flight, rained fire on her fellows, scorching the field and setting grass alight. Dragons shrieked and shot fire back at her, but she had every advantage. They were static; she was a green blur. She could see them clearly; they didn't see her until it was too late.

Mershayn ran with his army, seeking their next foe. The stench of brimstone and burning flesh drifted in a haze across the battlefield. Human and dragon screams mixed together, sometimes sounding close and sometimes far away. Bursts of orange light lit the smoky night as the dragons panicked and shot fire about themselves.

The haze benefitted the Teni'sians, who were much harder to find than the giant dragons, who thundered wherever they walked.

Mershayn and his group of soldiers found dragons, stabbed dragons, killed dragons. They pressed their advantage quickly before the dragons could organize themselves.

But even in confusion and pain, the scaled monsters were deadly. Men and women died all around Mershayn. One whip of a tail crushed the woman next to him. One swat from a claw impaled the soldier to his right. His fellows fell, but more Teni'sians rushed forward to fight by his side.

Soon, he found himself far from the walls of Belshra and alone with a scant handful of men and women in the drifting smoke. He had no idea in which direction the city lay. Ahead, he heard the thudding footsteps of another dragon. Mershayn whispered to his small troop, and they moved as one. He directed them to fan out when they saw the shape.

"Now!" Mershayn shouted, rushing through the smoke. A giant black dragon emerged, horns sticking out from its head like a fan, and Mershayn chopped viciously at the black beast's long tail. The dragon screeched, and his flaming breath roared around in an arc, engulfing Mershayn.

He flinched as the flames hit him...but felt only a warm wash of air, just like in Teni'sia.

"I love you..." he whispered to Mirolah, wherever she was. He thought he felt her sweet fingers on his cheek for one lingering moment, then one of his soldiers screamed.

The Teni'sians had charged when they saw their leader immolated, and the dragon retaliated by biting one of them in half and snatching up another.

With a cry, Mershayn launched himself onto the rear leg of the dragon and scrambled onto its back. He thrust his sword through the scales, through flesh and bone, straight down. The dragon screamed and reared, throwing him off.

He hit the ground hard and lay stunned for a moment. The giant black reared over him, brought its deadly jaws down—

Silver light flashed, and suddenly a hundred hands shoved Mershayn to the side.

The dragon bit dirt. The silver streak of light left Mershayn and raced to the dragon's head. A silver sword flashed out again and again, and the dragon fell, twitched, then lay still.

The silver flash returned to Mershayn, and suddenly Stavark suddenly stood there, breathing hard. He held out his hand and Mershayn took it, getting to his feet.

"Ha!" Mershayn shouted. Pure relief and giddiness swept through him, and he began to laugh. "Ha!" he said again. "I knew no fishy goddess could kill you!"

"Mershayn." He nodded solemnly. "You have many dragons here."

Mershayn laughed again. And then he laughed so hard he feared he wouldn't be able to stop. He hugged the quicksilver, and Stavark went stiff in his arms, then slowly embraced him. "You are a sight for sore eyes, my friend," Mershayn said into the boy's silver hair. "Gods, I actually thought we'd lost you this time."

Stavark began again, "You have—"

"Yes. I know. Many dragons here." He laughed again and released the quicksilver. "Let's thin them out, shall we?"

Stavark nodded.

Mershayn ran into the haze once more, and his soldiers formed up around him. There were scarcely more than a dozen Teni'sians now.

"We can't waste any time," Mershayn huffed to Stavark. "I don't know how long Mirolah can keep this up, or if Avakketh can reverse it. While they're down, we make sure they don't get up again."

"You cannot kill them all like this," Stavark said. "There are as many dragons as humans."

"We don't think about that. We just fight."

"Then we go that way," Stavark told him, his tall quicksilver ears hearing something Mershayn didn't. They jogged to the left.

Mershayn and his troop followed the quicksilver into the smoke—

Suddenly, a horrible, enraged scream split the night. Golden fire flashed behind the haze, burning straight into the night's sky. The smoke vanished, falling to the ground like dirt and exposing every soldier and dragon on the battlefield.

34

MEDOPHAE

MEDOPHAE CHARGED. Battle madness seeped into his veins, and he showed his teeth to the night as he sprinted toward Avakketh. At the same time, his heart pounded. He had fought a god to the death only once before, and it had almost destroyed him.

But he was the shield over humanity. No one else could fight Avakketh except Medophae.

The Teni'sians and Sunriders could make a battle of it. They had stacked their advantages.The dragons didn't know about Bands's enchanted weapons. They didn't know about Mershayn's seawater. They weren't prepared to be landbound while Bands blasted them from the sky.

But the shock and disorientation wouldn't last long. The humans might do unexpected damage while the dragons were disoriented, but the dragons would recover.

Once they did, a lot of humans were going to die.

In the end, there was only one battle that really mattered. If Medophae took down Avakketh, *that* blow would be devastating to his dragon army. It would strike at their very perception of truth.

Avakketh reared up from where he had crushed the eastern corner of the city. He had been heading toward the palace, toward Mirolah.

Good. But it's time to fight someone your own size, Avakketh.

The dragon god's red eyes were violent slashes on his horny head, and red lightning crackled around him. Red scaly lips peeled back from teeth as tall as Medophae, and smoke leaked between them. He opened that cavernous mouth and let out a thunderous roar.

Medophae's ear drums blew, and he stumbled backward, gritting his teeth as Oedandus repaired the damage.

"So, hatchling," Avakketh said. "You have elected not to heed my warning."

From beneath furrowed brows, Medophae glared up at Avakketh. "I've elected to end you."

"You," Avakketh said, smoke leaking out with his words, "are a fool."

Avakketh crept off the crushed buildings. Stones the size of carts tumbled off him like gravel. He was unbelievably graceful for a creature the size of a mountain, and he sinuously encircled Medophae, creating an amphitheater of scaly walls around him. "You are a shell, hatchling. Except that Oedandus had need of you, you would be nothing more than the dust of mortal bones. You are the cloak wrapped around the shape of his flickering self. You are nothing."

"Bold words from such a cautious god." Medophae kept the godsword blazing in his hand.

"I am a fair god, stripling," Avakketh countered. "More fair than you deserve. Now, for the last time, I offer you your life. Take any of these mortals you wish. Keep your kingdom by the sea, live in it, never leave it, and I will spare your chosen few. Live the rest of your stolen life for all I care, live until the end of eternity. Sleep with your traitorous dragon mate. All these, I will allow...if you leave this the battlefield now. Let us part as Saraphazia and I did millennia ago, two forces who need never meet again."

"You cannot have these lands, and I will not tolerate you here. Sate your bloodlust with the destruction you have already caused and abandon this field of battle. Never bother humankind again, and I will spare you Dervon's fate."

Avakketh hissed. "You did not kill Dervon."

"History speaks otherwise," Medophae said darkly.

"History lies. Posture all you wish, hatchling, but I know your secret. You fled into the recesses of your weak mortal mind when Dervon came for you."

A flicker of fear shivered through Medophae, and he stamped it down. "I've learned a few things in the last fourteen centuries," Medophae said.

"You've learned nothing." Avakketh whipped his tail away, opening the field behind Medophae. The god also opened his mouth, and an inferno burst forth.

Medophae shouted into the face of the god, and he cleaved the enchanted fire in two with his blazing sword. Fire flowed around him like a river split by a rock.

Medophae launched himself at the huge head and its deadly jaws.

Avakketh twisted. Medophae slashed out and caught the end of one tooth. Red fire met golden fire.

The explosion sent Medophae backward. Dragon claws snatched him out of the air, lifted him up. He shouted, about to hack at the claw when he saw the scales were green.

"Bands!"

"On your feet, my love." She dropped him to the ground, then transformed into her human form. His fear evaporated.

She wore what she always did, a green evening gown as though she was about to attend a ball, not join a battle. Perhaps that, more than anything, set him at ease. She acted as though this was just another fight, just like any number of battles she'd fought with him over the years. There was one thing different about her ensemble, though. She wore a crown of tall, thick crystals, each a different height.

He recognized it immediately, and it stunned him.

"That's Zilok's crown," Medophae said. "That's what he used to teleport me to Dandere. What is... Why are you wearing it?"

"I'll explain later, my love," she said.

Avakketh loomed over them, his front legs slammed into the ground to their left and right like towers, his giant head rising high into the sky on a neck that was as wide as Teni'sia's castle.

"You should have stayed in your real form to fight me, Randorus," Avakketh said.

"I'll fight you wearing the face you fear, and I'll kill you with Natra's might."

His enormous eyes narrowed, and now he seemed to recognize the crown. "Where did you get that?" the god asked.

"What matters is that you will lose. Go home, Avakketh."

Avakketh's laughter boomed down at them. "You're a fool," he said.

"Go and live. Stay and die. At the end, we will see who the fool is," she said.

Avakketh showed his teeth. "If that really is the crown, then it will destroy you."

"I will gladly give my life to take you with me, my lord and god."

"Bands..." Medophae said, tense. "What is he talking about?"

But Bands didn't answer him.

Avakketh smiled. "Your lover does not know, eh? Then let me educate you, Medophae. The Crown of Natra was made to devour gods. It will strip her faithless soul in a matter of seconds."

"Bands..." Medophae said. "Is that true?"

She didn't say anything; she kept her gaze upon Avakketh.

"Let's put it to the test!" Avakketh roared.

The dragon god's head came down so fast it was a blur. Medophae shouted and leapt in front of Bands, meeting the teeth once more with the godsword. Red and gold fire exploded, driving him into the earth and making Bands stumble backward.

Medophae climbed to his feet in a shower of dirt. His fiery blade blazed twenty feet into the air, a beacon in the night.

"Leave him!" Medophae said to Bands. "I will fight him."

But Bands stood before the god, Natra's Crown blazing red. The crimson lightning encircling Avakketh formed into a crackling funnel. It started at Avakketh's head, then thinned to a single point and entered the crown. The lightning fire flowed from Avakketh to Bands, just like it had when Zilok had pulled Oedandus from Medophae.

Avakketh hissed. He shifted his bulk, sweeping a giant claw at Bands.

Medophae leapt at the claw, hacking with the godsword. This time, instead of an explosion of red and gold fire, the sword bit flesh.

Avakketh howled, yanking his claw back. The crackling red lightning increased in a frantic dance between Avakketh and the crown, draining away from him. The crown blazed red, just as it had blazed gold when Zilok had attacked Medophae.

"You don't know what you're doing!" Avakketh roared.

"I know...enough," Bands said through clenched teeth. Her body vibrated, shimmering like a mirage.

"Bands, stop," Medophae shouted. "I'll fight him!" He leapt onto Avakketh's foreleg, sprinting up his arm. He had to end this, end it now. Medophae leapt into the air and stabbed the godsword into Avakketh's expansive chest. The sword drove through scales, through flesh and bone.

Avakketh screeched and thrashed to the side.

Below, Bands shouted, as though fighting to keep control of the power. Her shout became continuous, as though she had no end of air in her lungs. The red lightning rushed into the crown.

"Fool!" Avakketh roared as the red lightning coursed into her. He reached out again, and his tail lashed toward her.

Medophae blocked the claw with his back. It slammed into him, but he used Oedandus's strength to hold his ground. He slashed at the tail, keeping it from hitting Bands.

Bands's continuous shout became a scream of agony.

"Bands! Stop it!" Medophae shouted. Her attack was gutting Avakketh, but the strain was clearly killing her. Her body rippled like a banner made of mist, and her scream became a thin keen.

Medophae leapt onto Avakketh's neck, scrambled up, and drove the godsword into the god's skull, letting loose Oedandus's rage at last. A spear of golden fire shot down into the god of dragons.

Avakketh stiffened, then fell with a *thoom* that shook the earth. The red lightning crackled feebly one last time, then vanished. The god lay unmoving.

Bands looked at her dead god. She was barely visible now, a wispy ghost of herself. She turned, disoriented, and her gaze fell upon Medophae.

My love, she mouthed, but no sound came from her lips.

"Bands!" He threw himself from the height of Avakketh's corpse and landed next to her. She staggered, and he caught her as she fell.

She was as light as a silk gown, and he laid her gently across his knees.

"Bands, what did you do?"

"What needed to be done..." she said. Her voice was a whisper. Smoke drifted around them, and the sounds of distant battle raged to the north where Mershayn, the Teni'sians, and the Sunriders still fought.

"He called it the Crown of Natra," Medophae pressed. "What does it do? Tell me how to undo it."

"It steals the power of a god," she said faintly, as though her voice was coming from a long distance. "But there is a heavy price."

"How do I undo it?"

"There...is no way to undo it."

"There *has* to be a way! Tell me how to stop it."

"It can't be stopped," she said. "Someone must pay. You. Or me."

"Then let it be me," he said, crying now.

"No…" she whispered. He could barely hear her now, and he leaned close to her insubstantial face.

"I'll take it," he said. "It won't kill me. Oedandus will—"

But she shook her head.

"Bands—"

"Kiss me…" she said softly. "Be quick. We saved…humanity. Kiss me, and I will know it was worth it…"

He kissed her, holding her ghostly form to him. He could barely feel her arms around his neck, barely feel her chest against his, her lips on his…

…and then he couldn't feel her at all.

The crown thumped to the grassy earth. Bands was gone.

Medophae growled and grabbed the crown. His growl turned into a scream.

"Bands!" He yelled at the sky and let Oedandus's rage loose. A pillar of gold fire shot into the heavens. The haze of smoke across the battlefield dropped like it had been flattened, revealing every dragon and human on the plains of Belshra.

He cocked his arm back to hurl the crown into the wall—

Thunder boomed, so loudly that it drove Medophae into the ground. He stumbled, barely kept his feet, dropped the crown, and spun around.

Red lightning snapped and lanced over Avakketh's body and then, unthinkably, the god began to move.

Avakketh lifted his giant horned head, and those hateful eyes glowed red once more. The two deadly wounds in his chest and head had vanished.

"Now," Avakketh said. "Let's try this again."

35

SILASA

SILASA QUICKLY LEARNED how ghost flame could hurt. She'd been hit twice now.

With a grunt, she leapt clear of the next ghostly fire blast. It bathed the wall where she'd had just been, catching the tips of her fingers as she dodged. She hissed as it seared her. The pain lanced up her arm, lodged in her chest, and she felt that sinking feeling that had come with the first two times. Her legs and arms became heavier, harder to move.

Silasa had learned a lot in the last five minutes.

First, she had learned that there was a GodStone, and that it could resurrect gods. Second, she'd learned that Ynisaan was a unicorn, and that she could travel in her imagination to wherever she wanted.

Third, she had learned that ghost dragon fire didn't sear your body. It seared your soul.

Silasa wasn't sure if she had a soul anymore, but whatever she had was vulnerable to ghost dragon fire. It didn't burn; instead it drained her, sapped her physical strength and her will to live.

She ran up the side of the wall, defying gravity for a scant moment to stay out of the ghost dragon's next fire burst, but the edges of the blast caught her. That was three. Worse, it had caught Ynisaan three times, also.

Each time Silasa was hit, she became a little slower and a little more certain they were doomed. She tried to shake off the doom, but even though she knew the despair was an attack, it was almost as hard to shake as the sluggishness. She could only imagine what Ynisaan was feeling.

This battle had started with the thought that Silasa would distract the dragon. During that time, Ynisaan was supposed to dart in, keep her hand on the GodStone to feel for the change, then jam the gem in as soon as Avakketh drained his life force from the stone to resurrect himself.

But the ghost dragon was too fast. Silasa couldn't distract it long enough to get it away from the GodStone, and she hadn't found a way to hurt the thing, so the battle had turned into Ynisaan and Silasa dodging toward the GodStone, then leaping away, waiting for the color to change.

"We can't keep this up," Silasa said in Ynisaan's mind.

"There is no other plan," Ynisaan said. *"We must keep it up until—"*

"We're both getting slower, and we can't hurt that thing. Eventually it's going to catch us with a full blast, and we're done."

"We can't—" She paused in mid-sentence.

The GodStone flickered, then the red color began to sink like a glass cup being drained, leaving clear diamond behind.

It's happening! It's now. Silasa, it's now! Medophae has slain Avakketh. He's pulling his life-force from the stone to replace what he has lost."

Silasa looked up at the ghost dragon, standing with the barrel-sized GodStone right in the middle of its insubstantial chest.

And that was the fourth thing Silasa had learned: Ghost dragons weren't stupid. It knew what they wanted.

"We're going to have to charge it," Silasa said. *"I'll look more threatening. You sneak through."*

Ynisaan nodded.

"Go!" Silasa said in Ynisaan's mind, then screamed aloud, running to her left so fast that she ran up the wall, then started onto the ceiling between stalactites. The ghost dragon tracked her with its slitted eyes, drawing a breath, but it also kept an eye on Ynisaan.

The unicorn tapped her hooves fiercely, created doorway from purple flames, leapt through it, and was gone.

Silasa reached the top of her arc and leapt just before gravity claimed her. Her momentum carried her right at the dragon's face, and Silasa extended her hands, fingernails gleaming as though they could do something against a ghost.

Ynisaan appeared through a sudden purple flame doorway behind the ghost dragon, transformed into her white-haired, black-skinned human form with the gem in her hand, and rushed through the insubstantial haunches of the ghost dragon.

The ghost dragon blew fire at Silasa. Gray and white flames billowed out just as Ynisaan slapped the gem into a tiny divot on the right side of the GodStone.

Flames engulfed Silasa, and she screamed.

36

TARITHALIUS

"AND YOU SHALL BE KNOWN as Frederick the Fallen!" Tarithalius brought his hammer down upon the head of a purple and yellow striped dragon. It twitched and lay still.

Tarithalius looked up, scanning the hazy battlefield for more foes. This was a delightful little fracas. The refreshing young threadweaver Mirolah had taken to the winds, made them her own, and created a battlefield ripe with bloody pickings. Dragons were an intransigently arrogant lot, and it was about time they'd had the wind knocked out of them. Ha. His smile stretched so wide it hurt his face. And then Bands had created a wealth of smoke and confusion by burning her fellows from the sky. Confusion. Chaos. Battle. Delicious.

Another dragon appeared through the smoke in mid-air, pouncing on Tarithalius. Finally! A dragon willing to attack. Dragons were used to fighting from the sky. Losing that ability must have been a blow to their confidence. But they were still immense and strong. They ought to act like it.

Tarithalius felt the threads of his mother's tapestry all

around him, and he pulled against the fabric to relocate his body, moving faster than a mortal could. The dragon's jaws snapped where his head had been. In a blur, Tarithalius twirled his hammer—bringing the axe head to bear—and buried it in the underside of the dragon's chin.

He grunted as he hauled on his axe, using the tapestry again to hold his body in place. The surprised dragon flipped over itself entirely and crashed, breaking its wings beneath its immense girth.

"I dub you Carl the Crushed!" Tarithalius cried, leaping on top of the dragon and ending its life.

Two more dragons emerged from the haze, bearing down on him. They'd seen the threat now, and were trying to gang up on him.

Tarithalius laughed. He loved this part best. Hissing, arrogant, frightened dragons converged on him, and he laid about himself with abandon.

"Have at you, you ignorant, arrogant, blustering bullies! I name you Daniel the Disemboweled!"

"Sally the Severed!"

"Benny the Beheaded!"

"Polly the Ponderous!"

"Leo the Late and Lacking!"

By the time the golden fire of Oedandus the Binder shot into the sky, Tarithalius stood on a mountain of dragon corpses. The haze of smoke vanished, and he clearly saw the battle raging all around him. He felt a flash of pride at his humans, so outclassed, so determined. They rushed bravely to their deaths again and again, and they took a dragon or two with them from time to time. They might actually *win* this fight. Simply marvelous!

And Medophae, the serious-minded child who had taken up the ragged and ill-fitting mantle of Oedandus, had slain Avakketh with the help of his beloved dragon lover. She had died in the attempt. Tarithalius had liked her, but then, true victory wasn't victory at all without cost.

Best of all, Avakketh was dead. Ahhhh, that tasted so very

sweet. Avakketh had always been a giant bully. If dragons were arrogant, it was because they drank from Avakketh, the fountain of all arrogance. It felt glorious to see him taken down by a human with a big, burning sword.

And now he was gone, creating another enormous shift of the natural order. There were so many new possibilities to explore. Would his sister creep out of her oceans? Would Zetu reappear? Would Tuana come down from the mountains? A glorious new age was about to—

He felt a sudden wrenching, a tugging, like a half-dozen hooks had yanked on his guts. He turned. That had come from the north. It tugged again. How curious. New possibilities already!

And this was... *Important.* That tug wasn't simply on this body he'd created, it was pulling at the heart of him, at his life force itself, what the humans called GodSpill.

During Tarithalius's preoccupation with this tugging sensation, an enormous dragon the color of mud had scrambled up the corpse mountain. But Tarithalius was finished with this battle. The tide had turned, and it was no longer interesting. He leapt into the air as the dragon's jaws snapped where he had been.

"Monty the Muddy and Mashed!" he declared, bringing his hammer down on its head.

Then he let this body unravel, joined the threads of the air, and shot after the tugging sensation like an arrow. It took him all the way to the north, to Avakketh's land of Irgakth, and into a little cave that contained a vampire, a unicorn, and Temeralis, the sad ghost of the first dragon. Avakketh had enslaved her ghost as some kind of attack dog. And...

Oh! And... *The GodStone!*

If Tarithalius had taken the time to form a body, he would have gasped. But he was only the wind at the moment, and so he silently stared at his mother's most powerful artifact. The unicorn, in the fake form of a human, had jammed something into the GodStone, and it was this that tugged at him.

There was a story here. And it obviously had to do with the

battle at Belshra, but how…?

Tarithalius loved puzzles. In the flashing second that he absorbed the scene, he began to work it through.

His mother had created the GodStone to store bits of herself so that she would not be tired as she created the world. Avakketh had obviously found the GodStone. Why else was his sad little slave, Temeralis the First, guarding it? Undoubtedly, Avakketh was using it to make himself more powerful, so that he could create…something. What had he created? Some juggernaut to eliminate Medophae?

Except Avakketh didn't create. He had almost no imagination. So why would he need…?

Oh!

Avakketh was going to recreate himself. Of course! That was exactly the kind of boring, colorless thing the arrogant god would do. The GodStone could conceivably work in that way. It could take a very small piece of Avakketh and remake him. And so Medophae's victory was worthless. Bands's sacrifice was for nothing. No matter how many times Medophae killed Avakketh, he'd always return, unless…

Tarithalius looked at the human unicorn, pressing her hands to where she had jammed something…

No. Not *something*. A gem. *The* gem. The red gem that had been Tarithalius's prison for four centuries.

Of course! That gem had been a piece of the GodStone. If Tarithalius had a body, he would have smacked his own forehead at the sudden obviousness.

Solving that mystery was like eating a bite of rich, sweet cake. What else could have held Tarithalius except a piece of his mother's most powerful artifact? He really should have seen that before.

And then, instantly, he knew what the unicorn was doing. Avakketh had emptied his recreated self from the GodStone just now when Medophae had killed him. No doubt he intended to put another small bit of himself back inside once he'd been recreated, but only one god could fill the GodStone at a time. While Avakketh was out, the clever unicorn wanted to put someone else in, barring Avakketh from re-entering, making him vulnerable again. To do it, she was trying to swap Avakketh's presence with the thinnest, barest residue of Tarithalius left behind in the gem that had held him for four hundred years.

What a ridiculously unlikely plan...

It was brilliant! Who *was* this unicorn?

Tarithalius watched, feeling the GodStone tugging at him, almost as though it was asking permission to begin filling itself with his life force. It would make Tarithalius invulnerable. He would not be able to be killed by anyone, not his overbearing sister or his absent grandfather or the fascinatingly creepy White Tuana, nor any other god who might come along. He could have power enough to control anything he wanted.

Ick. What a bore.

But the unicorn, now *she* was interesting. She had woven such an intricate plan that he hadn't even understood it at first. She'd given it so much thought, crafted such a daring hope.

But I have a better idea. How about...I refuse.

Tarithalius pulled the residue of himself from the gem, from the GodStone itself. He denied the artifact permission to recreate him, and he took away any chance he could displace his brother's hold on the GodStone.

There. Much better. This will be more interesting....

37

MEDOPHAE

FOR A BOY WHOSE FATHER HAD DIED on the claws of a maggot monster and a mother who'd died under the sword of a despot, Medophae had experienced a number of moments he would have considered the most frightening of his life.

When he had seen the maggot monster descend upon his city, the first real spark of terror ignited in his heart. He could barely understand what the monster was, only that he was helpless to stop it.

It was worse, after remaining in hiding with his mother for years, when she didn't return from the local village on a normal, ordinary day. He had raced through the forests of Dandere, lungs burning and legs aching, to find her, to stop his worst fear from happening a second time. Icy water had pumped through his veins with every beat of his heart, because he knew she could be taken from him in an instant.

And she had been.

And yet, that personal, gut-wrenching tragedy was nothing compared to the gibbering terror he'd felt as Dervon had towered over him. The god's cruel gaze had flayed hope from Medophae's mind, stolen his confidence, his will, and any reason to keep living. Dervon had reduced Medophae to a babbling boy.

That same unreasoning fear coated Medophae with frost as Avakketh's many-horned head rose above him on its long, scaly neck. It was as though Dervon's grotesquely fat, many tentacled form was superimposed over Avakketh, vast and dark and invincible.

Medophae's mind skidded sideways, unable to understand why the dead god had risen. Medophae had rammed the godsword through Avakketh, had sent a torrent of Oedandus's rage into the dragon god's body. It should have killed Avakketh. It had killed Dervon, and he'd been the more powerful of the two.

If Avakketh could recover from that...what more could Medophae do?

Avakketh roared, stamping down, and Medophae forced his frozen limbs to move, but he was too slow.

The god's claw plunged into Medophae's thigh and pinned him to the ground. With a shout, Medophae twisted and drove the godsword into Avakketh's knuckle.

Avakketh roared and yanked back. Medophae staggered to his feet. Oedandus wreathed him in flame, healing the hole in his leg, and Medophae limped backward.

He tried to shake off the fear. Avakketh wasn't Dervon, and Medophae wasn't that boy from so long ago. He had to remember that this was just a battle like any other. He had to keep moving, find the solution. He swung the godsword at the dragon's leg.

Avakketh jumped straight upward, astonishingly quick. Medophae's sword swiped through empty air—

—just as Avakketh's razor-sharp tail drove into him from behind.

Medophae screamed. The tail yanked back, pulling him up high into the air, and Avakketh snapped his jaws down on Medophae. Ivory spears rammed through his body. He screamed.

Oedandus's fire fought back, healing the wounds around the teeth, keeping Medophae alive and in agony, just like he had when Dervon had impaled Medophae with his black tentacles.

Panic blossomed. It was happening all over again.

"No..." he growled, trying to keep control.

Avakketh ground his teeth, and Medophae screamed again.

He retreated inside, away from the overwhelming pain, the fear, and the hopelessness. He felt that deep well right behind him, and he stood at the edge of it. Down there lay safety, oblivion, a cessation of the pain.

But he knew that once he fell, the only way out was to let Oedandus have his body, to let the god take control. During the horrific moment of Dervon's death, Oedandus had roared up out of Medophae, trammeling over him, shoving him into that dark well inside his mind.

Oedandus had taken Medophae's body from him.

Medophae had no recollection of the week after Dervon's death. Only that he woke up seven days later, weak and confused, with Bands at his side. He didn't remember the intervening days, but he had been left with the certainty that if he ever let Oedandus take control again, there would be no Medophae left.

Since then, he had fought to keep control, to keep Oedandus securely leashed. Oedandus had to remain Medophae's tool, never the other way around.

I'm not going back there.

"Die, hatchling," Avakketh growled through his clenched teeth. "Die."

Avakketh blasted fire over Medophae. His skin melted, his flesh bubbled, and he lost his precarious handhold on the edge of that well. Medophae pitched headlong into the chasm of his own mind. He fell and fell, and the pain faded behind him.

Cool, quiet darkness.

It was over then. He was dead. What he had begged for during those long, empty years bereft of Bands had finally come to pass. And he was glad. He'd forgotten what peace felt like...

A golden light flickered in the dark.

No... It's over. I'm dead. Let me be dead. I don't want to struggle anymore. I don't want to hurt.

The golden light grew, as if coming nearer, and it traced the silhouette of a muscled man. He was taller than Medophae, larger, with thick plates of armor covering his arms and thighs, flaring wide at his exaggerated shoulders as he strode forward. He carried a helm under his arm. His thick, blond eyebrows hunched down over deep-set eyes, and his lips pulled back, giving a thin glimpse of clenched teeth.

In quiet times, Oedandus had always been a growling voice in the back of Medophae's mind. In times of stress, he became a raging monster, but Medophae had never met him face to face. He had always envisioned Oedandus as a floating cloud of furious golden lightning and fire, stretched out over all the lands of Amarion.

"It's over," Medophae said. "I'm dead. Let me go."

"Justice..." the angry, towering god said in the same dark voice that had haunted Medophae for centuries.

"There is no justice."

"You are the hand of justice."

The same old words, repeated over and over. The mindless Oedandus only knew how to hate, how to rage, how to kill.

"Stop it! You talk of justice as though you know what it means, as though justice is slaying whatever angers you. It isn't! I'm dead, at last. Let me die."

"Destroy them," Oedandus said, extending his wide, gauntleted fist and opening it. "Kill them all."

"No!"

For fourteen centuries, Oedandus had striven to bend Medophae to his will, but Medophae had kept command. It was a constant siege, tearing at him, but with only momentary lapses, Medophae had succeeded in keeping the raging god locked away, had used him only when needed.

Medophae prepared to brace Oedandus's rage, but he was

too weak this time. At long last, Oedandus would get what he wanted.

But his god didn't attack.

Instead, he let out a long breath. In the darkness of the well, there was no floor for him to sit upon, no walls to indicate a room, no sky or horizon, but he sat down anyway, wreathed in golden flame. Together, the two of them floated in darkness, a tiny pinpoint of red light far above.

"I…" Oedandus said, seemingly struggling to come up with a thought that wasn't *Hand of justice! Kill! Destroy!* "I am angry."

"You're always angry," Medophae said. "It's *all* you are."

Oedandus went silent, and his baleful gaze turned down at his huge, metal-encased hands. "Not…" he said thickly, "…always. I was not always."

Medophae was stunned. Oedandus had always demanded. Raged. There was no real sentience behind the force that tried to dominate Medophae. Oedandus had never actually *spoken* to Medophae.

"You…fight me," Oedandus said. "You always fight me."

"You want to take my body."

"I wanted to make you a god. To replace me."

"You wanted to make me *into* you."

Oedandus pondered that. "No," he said.

"I'm not your replacement."

"But…" the god struggled. "But you are."

"When you killed Dervon, you stole my body," Medophae said through clenched teeth. "Bands said I wasn't myself for days, and I remember nothing from that time. You nearly erased me!"

Oedandus paused, his ridiculously wide shoulders hunched. His hands lay, palms upwards, on his knees. "I am…nearly adrift," he said. "You have been my anchor, but I am slipping away. A little more each year. Soon, I will fade. The effort to…appear to you like this, to actually have a mind, it will spend the last of me, I think." He seemed to be gathering momentum, as though fighting to talk coherently had given him more clarity, and his thick words became smoother. "Without you," he continued. "I cannot even form words. And I must...tell you many things before I fade. Help me..." he said, reaching out one of those huge, gauntleted hands, "...to tell you."

When he'd gone searching for his god in the first place, this was all he'd ever wanted. To speak to Oedandus. To understand what had happened to him. But still, he hesitated. He'd learned to distrust the power inside him, and he wasn't sure if this was some kind of trick. He'd never had a conversation with Oedandus before.

Medophae reached out, his fingers appearing from the darkness as Oedandus's golden light illuminated them, and he clasped the god's hand.

Oedandus took a deep breath, and his angry gaze softened. His words came even more coherently. "Thank you," he said, glancing up at the red pinprick high above, then back at Medophae. "We may pack a conversation into a second in this place, but time is short. In moments, Avakketh will slay you."

"Then let me die, now, with Bands. If there was a fitting time for my death, it is now.

"There is no fitting time for your death. You must take my place."

"If you need a shell, take Raedir-ba. Take Gilgion. They have your blood. You could use them as you wish to use me."

"You think I wish to use you."

"You chose me because I am descended from Avanda Roloiron. Because I was the only Dandene on Amarion."

Oedandus grunted, then shook his big head. "You think there were no others here with my blood the day you set foot on this land? You think you were the only one?"

Medophae hesitated.

"I *chose* you, Medophae. There were others in the lands I could have used, but they didn't have all that I needed. Anger, yes. I needed a mortal whose anger matched my own, but I needed more. A desire for justice, yes. A compassion for others, god and mortal alike. But above all, I needed a mortal with *will*."

"Will?"

"Your will, Medophae. A mortal mind is as fragile as an egg. I needed something stronger. I looked. Oh, I looked for many years before you came. When I found you, I rejoiced, and you have exceeded every one of my expectations. You have wielded the remains of me and not been overwhelmed. That..." he said, "is unique. Every time you fought me, it frustrated me, but it also made me proud, made me know that I had chosen correctly. It meant you could channel my anger, you could choose the right despite my lapses of sanity. Only to you did I dare connect myself."

"But you suffused Vaerdaro. You gave him your power."

Oedandus sighed. "You must understand that I am not coherent most of the time. This is the most I have spoken in a millennium and a half. I spend my time only in the most animal state. There are years I go without knowing who I am or what is needed. Yes, I was fooled by Vaerdaro. He very nearly fulfilled my worst nightmares. I did not see him clearly until he tried to kill an innocent."

"Mirolah."

Oedandus nodded. "If I gave myself to Vaerdaro, he would have split open like an egg. Or, if he had managed to wield me, he would have become a horror akin to Dervon himself. I cannot allow that." He shook his head again. "No, Medophae, son of Jarod. You were not a desperate grasp, some gulped goblet of chance. I chose you carefully. There is no other who can take up this mantle."

Medophae was stunned.

Oedandus looked up at the pinprick of red light above. "I could fight Avakketh for you, as I did Dervon, but I think I would lose. I am not as potent as I was when I destroyed Dervon, and the killing strike you used against Avakketh has depleted me."

"Then we die."

"No," Oedandus said. "If you stop fighting me, if you finally join with me...it may be enough. We could yet prevail.

We could protect Natra's world. We could save your beloved humans."

"Join with you…"

"Become the god we were meant to be, the god that only *you* can be. Take my power and carry on the duty I dropped when Dervon and his traitors stretched me across this land. Preserve Natra's order."

Become a god… He thought of Bands, thought of living an eternity without her. Eternal. Invincible. Alone. The pain of it was like a barbed wire dragged through his insides.

"You're thinking of Bands," Oedandus said. "I loved, too, Medophae, and it was my undoing. My preoccupation with Avanda Roloiron killed me, in the end. I was given a sacred trust, and I abandoned it for love. You are lucky that Bands is dead. You no longer have that bond to pull your gaze from your duty. You can pick up the burden without distraction."

"I join with you, and I become a god?"

"The one you were meant to be."

"I don't become you?"

For the first time, Oedandus gave a ghost of a smile, there and gone in an instant. "It is already your will that holds me together, not my own. I am nearly gone, and it falls to you, and no other. Serve Her, Medophae. Wield my power for those in need. For gods and mortals alike, as she intended."

Those words… Medophae had heard those words in the dream on Dandere, when he was shown how to get back to the mainland. The woman, floating through the clouds, had given him the information he needed, then said: *"…wield your power for those in need. Gods and mortals alike…"*

For a moment, he struggled. He longed for the carefree days with Bands, flying over the countryside, choosing where to intervene, creating hope, fighting despots. He could do this, what Oedandus asked of him. He could be a shield over humanity. If he was the only one who could do it, then he must.

It was what Bands would have done.

He felt a change within him, a tight-fisted squeezing of his heart, and then a release. He let go of Bands, and a piece of his heart dislodged and floated away.

"I'll do it."

Medophae reached out and clasped Oedandus's other hand.

Oedandus's crouched brows evened out, and his fierce eyes lost their fire. He let out a long sigh. "It has been a long time convincing you...." Golden fire and lightning started in those eyes, spread out across his long, wavy golden hair, down his wide shoulders and arms, and then leapt to Medophae.

The pinprick of red light above them began to grow, and Medophae realized they were rising. The pinprick became the size of a ball, then the size of a wagon wheel, then he could see the red scales of Avakketh's face, Medophae's blood on his teeth—driven through Medophae's chest—and the red fire moving slowly over his body, as though he was almost frozen in time.

The red circle engulfed Medophae, and he came back to himself in a ball of golden fire. Oedandus's power exploded in Avakketh's mouth like a miniature sun, blasting his jaws open.

Avakketh raged, yanking his head away as Medophae fell.

Medophae's body was barely more than a burnt skeleton with muscle and flesh hanging off it, but a thousand threads of golden lightning crackled inside him, around him, filled in the gaps, and flesh formed again. He landed heavily on his feet. The power coursing through him was different his time. Before, Oedandus was a pool of power Medophae could draw from, but now that pool was his entire body. He wasn't using the power; he *was* the power. The difference was startling. The immensity of it staggered him.

Golden fire and lightning leapt and snaked at the inside of his legs, his belly, his chest. Images, flashes of Oedandus's memories rushed like a river through Medophae's mind as the two of them joined. Medophae saw the creation of the world. He stood beside Natra as she wove the great tapestry together. He felt Oedandus's regard for Natra and her plan. Medophae's own memories swirled like rose petals on that flood. The raging flow filled him, and his soul stretched. It felt like he was dying and being born at the same time. It felt like Oedandus's boundless fire would burst free, destroying Medophae's pathetic mortal form.

He howled, hanging on, hanging on...

...and then it stopped. The flow ceased, and Medophae blinked, fists clenched.

He had held it; he had contained it.

He looked down at himself, and he towered over the battlefield, suddenly a giant. To his left, the ruins of Belshra spread out like a tiny model. Avakketh's immensity didn't seem large anymore. Compared to Medophae, he was the size of Sniff.

A breathless moment hung between them, and Medophae realized that Oedandus's dark voice was gone. He felt the god's rage, but it was mingled with Medophae's own rage, just as the memories had been. He remembered Dervon both as Medophae and as Oedandus. Medophae had met and killed the god fourteen centuries ago, but he'd also known Dervon from the first moment they'd arrived here in Amarion.

Avakketh sucked in a breath and breathed fire over Medophae again.

Medophae held out his hand, and a shield of golden fire formed, protecting him. The red flames hammered into it, but they did not touch him.

"I warned you, Avakketh," Medophae said, and his voice boomed deep and low, half his own and half that dark voice of Oedandus. "Now the warnings are done." He held his fists together in front of himself, and he knew exactly what to do. Oedandus knew how to kill a god.

Golden lightning crackled, and fire swirled in a ball of power around Medophae's clasped fists.

The dragon god showed his teeth. "You cannot win. Grow as large as you like. Deplete Oedandus's rage. I will come at you again and again, hatchling, until you have nothing left!" He flicked his tail toward the north, as though that had some significance.

Apparently, whatever the tail flick signified did not work, because Avakketh's vicious smile faded. His eyes went wide, and Avakketh turned to stare in the direction as he'd flicked his tail. "No…" he whispered, then he roared. "No!"

He spun back to Medophae, suddenly desperate. He leapt into the air, flapped his wings, but he'd forgotten about Mirolah's spell, and he fell back to the ground. "Leave off! Or you will suffer, hatchling," Avakketh threatened. That chilling, overwhelming voice that had frightened Medophae suddenly sounded reedy and thin.

Avakketh hastily surrounded himself with a protective egg similar to Medophae's shield, then turned and loped toward the mountains.

Medophae aimed, pointing his crackling fists, and he let the fire loose. He thought of Dervon. He thought of Bands.

The golden lightning struck Avakketh's protective egg, shattered it, and hit the dragon god so hard that it lifted him and spun him around.

"No!" Avakketh shouted. "Medophae!" He desperately opened his mouth and breathed fire, but he missed. Medophae poured all of his rage into his strike, burning Avakketh, breaking him down, tearing apart his threads.

"Justice," he said.

38

MERSHAYN

WHEN THE HAZE on the battlefield dropped, events moved quickly, yanking Mershayn's hopes and fears back and forth. For the dragons, the disorientation from falling out of the sky had already worn off, and the scant advantage that Bands had given them with the smoky haze had vanished. Mershayn tamped down the fear within himself as he prepared for the dragons to turn the tide of the battle.

That didn't happen.

When Medophae and Bands teamed up on Avakketh, there were half a dozen dragons within striking distance of Mershayn, but none of them could tear their eyes away from Avakketh's fight. The dragons could have attacked Mershayn or his people, could have burned or impaled them with claws while they gawked. Instead, they stood stunned as Avakketh lost, fell to the ground, and died.

And yet, somehow, that didn't happen either.

Either Avakketh faked his death, or Medophae hadn't finished the job, because as screeches of despair arose from the dragon horde, Avakketh shuddered, came *back* to life, rose up, stamped on Medophae, then snapped him up in his jaws.

Mershayn felt he should turn and face the many threats all around him, but, like the dragons, he couldn't tear his gaze away. Perhaps it was simply impossible to look away when two gods were trying to kill each other.

Avakketh's jaws exploded with golden fire. Medophae dropped to the ground, and he grew to a hundred times his normal size.

"By the gods," Mershayn murmured. His numb mind screamed a warning that he and all of his soldiers were exposed to the enemy, vulnerable, that he should have them attack or retreat, but he kept watching. No dragons assaulted them.

The two giant gods faced each other. Medophae clapped his hands together and created a miniature sun. Avakketh fled, and Medophae shot him with a fire so bright that Mershayn winced and covered his eyes with his arm.

The fire flashed and vanished, and again Avakketh lay limp and smoking on the ground. Mershayn expected him to rise again and continue the battle.

That didn't happen.

Enough. Do something. This could be your one advantage. Attack the dragons!

Mershayn tore his gaze away from the dead god to look at the dumbfounded dragons. Many of them flinched back and slunk away from the castle-sized Medophae.

The wild-maned demigod turned his baleful gaze toward the dragons, each one about the size of a cat to him now. He clenched his fist, and that miniature sun began to form again.

"Dragonkind," he boomed, his voice like a thunderstorm. "You have been poorly led by your god today. He has overstepped his bounds and pulled you with him. For him, justice has been done, but you need not suffer his fate. I give you this one chance. Go now, or face my wrath."

The closest dragon, one of the whites that had flown just behind Avakketh, leapt at Medophae, breathing fire at his legs.

Medophae stretched out the fist bearing that miniature sun

and blasted the white dragon from the sky. It screeched and plowed into the ground like a falling star, then lay still. Medophae turned his gaze to the rest of the dragons.

"Flee," he said calmly.

And that actually *did* happen.

The dragons turned and ran. Several of them flapped their wings, trying to get airborne, but apparently Mirolah still prevented them. Instead, they galloped and loped and slithered away as best they could, heading northeast toward the Corialis Mountains.

Stunned, breathing hard, Mershayn watched them go, scanning all around him. The only dragons that remained were corpses. The battle was over.

"Your Majesty?" Deni'tri said.

He turned to find her at his side. Her left arm hung limp and crooked, broken by a dragon's strike. Blood covered half of her face and her clothes.

"Is that... Did we win, Your Majesty?"

He looked around, stunned.

"I..." he said, hope trickling hesitantly into him. "I don't believe it..." He spun around again. The giant Medophae was gone. The dragons had left the field. It was over.

"Yes," he said. "We won."

"Captain Medophae was..." she said, struggling with the words. "He turned into..." She trailed off.

"Where did he go?" Mershayn asked.

"I didn't see, Your Majesty."

Mershayn stared dumbfounded at the mountainous corpse of the dead Avakketh, then shook his head. He couldn't stand here amazed. The battle might be over, but there were still many who needed him.

"We need to take care of the injured," Mershayn said, snapping out of his stupor. His soldiers had done him proud, but for every dragon they'd felled, a dozen Teni'sians had paid the ultimate price. The casualties would be high. Curls of smoke drifted over the corpses of dragons and humans alike.

His heart caught in his throat as he saw Ari'cyiane, barely a hundred feet away, hunched over a figure. "Come with me," he said to Deni'tri and the remaining soldiers who had followed him, and he went to Ari'cyiane's side. Deni'tri and the soldiers followed at a respectful distance. Lord Vullieth lay in the dirt, unmoving.

"Ari'cyiane..." he said softly.

"He's dead," she said in a flat tone. She gripped her husband's limp hand.

"Ari'cyiane... I'm so sorry. He was a good man and a true ally."

"The was the best of men," she whispered. "*He* had conviction and purpose. *He* never abandoned those he loved."

"Ari'cyiane—"

She turned and lanced him with her gaze. Tears streaked her dirty cheeks, and her eyes blazed. "You failed me, Mershayn," she said. "But I am to blame for trusting you in the first place. I am to blame...for this." She pushed Vullieth's hand against her cheek.

"Let's get him inside the city," he said.

Ari'cyiane let go of her husband's hand and stood up. She waited like a statue as Mershayn and his soldiers lifted Vullieth gently and carried him toward Belshra. They entered the city and laid the lord on the ground of a wide, ruined building. It had no roof, and the walls had crumbled into a crude stair, but Galorman Balis had cleared the debris from the floor. It was flat and clean, and prepared for this purpose.

Ari'cyiane stood over her husband's body, looking down in a daze.

"He gave his life so that Teni'sia could live on," Mershayn said to her, trying to find the right words. "We will honor him."

"I don't care what you do," she said in a dead tone. "What you do doesn't matter to me anymore." She walked to the far corner of the ruined building, then looked out toward the northeast where the dragons had gone.

Mershayn watched her for a moment, then turned to Vullieth. Mershayn removed his kingly cloak, knelt in the dirt, and laid it over the lord up to his neck.

"Be at peace, Lord Vullieth," he said. As he stood, he glanced again at Ari'cyiane, but she kept her back to him, as though she was searching for some kind of answer in the stars. Quietly, he left and went to look for other survivors.

39

GRENDIS SYM

GRENDIS SYM SAT UP IN BED. He had never been so surprised, so grateful, to be awake. He glanced at his shoulder, wrapped in white linens. It felt normal again. It still hurt, and a spot of blood had soaked through the cloth, but that horrible rotting feeling was gone. He peeked underneath. The ragged wound looked almost healed. Miraculous. How had...

Then it came to him. Threadweaving. It had to be. Sym had felt the hand of death close about his throat when that skeleton gouged him, and now he was fine. For once, Sym was the beneficiary of Mershayn's powerful allies.

Healers were ushering in more injured now, and the makeshift infirmary bustled with activity. Some were burned, some sliced by dragon claws. The healed victims of the skeleton assault rose, clearing off their pallets to make room for the victims of the dragon battle. The town hall filled, so many coming now that the wounded were being laid upon the floor.

Sym gingerly eased his feet over the edge of the bed and

found that he could walk without dizziness. Two healers bearing a bloody man on a stretcher stopped at his pallet.

"Take this one," Sym said. "I'm fine."

"Our gratitude, my lord," one of the healers said, and they began transferring the wounded soldier to the bed.

Sym pulled on his boots, worked his way up the long hall and into the night air.

The street to the broken gate was filled with soldiers coming and going, busy tending the wounded. The gate itself had been buried in a mountain of dirt, and the white wings of a dead dragon stuck up in the air at odd angles, like bones in the moonlight.

But no dragons attacked. There were no sounds of battle. Aside from the clamor of human activity, it was silent.

He put a hand against the stone wall next to him, staring out at the field beyond. He could see Sunriders galloping back and forth, and he saw several hills much like the one that had buried the front gate. Each hill was a fallen dragon, but none moved.

"By the gods…" he murmured. Had they won? Against the odds and all common sense, had Teni'sia and the Sunriders actually repelled the dragons?

For the first time in Sym's life, he began to believe in destiny. The Bastard King was favored by the gods. Maybe he actually belonged on the throne. That feeling had been growing since that night in Teni'sia when Sym could have killed Mershayn and did not.

Sym closed his eyes and let out a sigh. If he believed that, it changed his whole view on life. What was his purpose, if he was not trying to gain the throne of Teni'sia? It was what had driven Sym's father, and ever since he had been killed, Sym had thought of nothing else. But over the last week, that desire had slowly seeped away like water into the ground. Sym had dug deep to chase it, to find it, to bring it back by thinking of the many ways the bastard had slighted him since he'd become king, but in doing so, Sym had discovered something curious about himself…

He wanted Teni'sia's prosperity more than he wanted its crown, and he knew that without Mershayn, Teni'sia would have fallen. Only the Bastard King, flanked by his strange and supernatural allies, could have won this impossible battle.

Instead of concocting plans to unseat him, Sym began to envision aiding Mershayn, being a true advisor, guiding him. Despite Sym's captivity, Mershayn had come to trust him. It was possible.

There could be new plans. New ambitions. By the gods, this dragon war had changed Sym; it had changed them all forever. The world was larger than the squabbling nobles of Teni'sia had ever imagined. Teni'sia's concerns should not revolve around political positioning and fear of Sunriders. The panorama of possibilities stretched out before him.

In this new fertile land, filled with GodSpill, free of the shadow of a dragon war, where might the kingdom of Teni'sia turn its gaze if led by a strong king and a united nobility? Teni'sia could expand to the north, resurrect the ruined kingdom of Diyah, rebuild Corialis Port. They could claim it all for Teni'sia, and elevate new nobles to rule the outlying areas. Perhaps they could even expand as far as this ruined city of Belshra. With Mershayn's threadweavers, they could build a kingdom to rival the empires of long ago. And Teni'sia could be the first to embrace the threadweavers again, ushering in a new age, becoming a power in Amarion.

Sym opened his eyes and smiled. He could create a new story for himself. He would not be king, but he could be the strongest influence upon the king. He could dedicate himself to service. With his expertise and Mershayn's charisma, together they would create a kingdom that had not been seen in a hundred years.

Soldiers shuffled, close together, up the street toward a large ruin of a building. There were torches stuck on each side of the collapsed archway that led into the roofless building, and in the firelight Sym suddenly recognized Deni'tri's bald head among the group. She and the five other soldiers carried a body between them. They brought the body in and left it on the ground.

Once Deni'tri and her soldiers deposited their burden, they left, followed shortly by Mershayn himself. Sym barely recognized the king. He looked just like the rest of the soldiers, smeared in blood and looking as though he'd been dragged through the dirt. He was missing his telltale, ostentatious cloak with the fur shoulders, but it was indeed Mershayn. He looked exhausted, and his gaze swept right over Sym without seeing him. Sym thought of calling out, but he hesitated, and the king left, striding back up the road toward front gate.

How many died this night? Sym wondered.

Without really deciding to, he walked across the street and into the ruined building. There was only one body there, and Sym recognized the long, pale face instantly.

Lord Vullieth, once the strongest noble in Teni'sia, was dead. King Mershayn had laid his fur-shouldered coat over the noble who had been the greatest obstacle to Sym's plans aside from Mershayn himself. Vullieth had been incorruptible and frustratingly immune to Sym's persuasion. And now he was gone.

Sym had no doubt this ruined building would be full of corpses in mere minutes, but for now, it was just him, Vullieth, and the long shadows cast by the crests of broken wall. It was perhaps the only moment he'd have to honor his opponent privately.

Sym walked to the body and knelt next to it. Like Sym's previous plans, Vullieth was representative of the old Teni'sia, of the struggle between the nobility, and, as Sym stared down, all his anger and frustration toward Vullieth seeped away with those old plans.

"Your death will not be in vain, Lord Vullieth." Sym touched the fur of the cloak gently. "Your sacrifice will allow Teni'sia to rise higher than ever before. Rest well. You helped us through the night. A new day will come."

Sym stood, giving a final glance to the man.

Enough, he thought. It was time to begin the new day. It was time to offer his services in the aftermath. He turned, intending to chase after Mershayn and—

Ari'cyiane stood before Sym. She wore her decorative leather armor, but tonight it obviously hadn't been just a fashion statement. It had been well-used in the battle. Blood spattered her left shoulder, and claw marks marked the hard leather. She wore dirty bracers and leather greaves over her shins. Her hair was tied back severely, and it glittered like strawberry gold in the torchlight. Her blue eyes gleamed, as cold as ice, and she clenched her jaw.

He glanced down and saw the dagger too late. She plunged it into his belly, under his ribcage.

Sym opened his mouth to gasp, but he had no breath. He grappled with her hard arms, but his fingers had lost all strength. She watched him without pity as he slid down the front of her, face pressed against the leather of her chest.

He gaped, tried to speak, but everything had gone cold.

A new day...

He thudded to the dirty flagstones and died.

40

SILASA

SILASA FELT WIND RUSHING PAST HER, and her eyelids fluttered. Hunger and thirst gripped her body.

"Thank the gods!" a woman breathed. Silasa didn't have the strength to say anything, not even to open her eyes. The woman's voice was familiar, but she didn't care to unravel the mystery. She needed to feed, and there was blood nearby. Soft. Subtle. Pumping behind a veil of flesh.

She lashed out blindly, trying to reach it, to make it hers. Her fingernails ripped into someone, and the woman gasped. The sharp scent of fresh, exposed blood struck her nostrils.

"Stay back," someone else warned, her voice deeper, matronly. "She is disoriented. Give her another moment."

The wind continued rushing past her, and Silasa suddenly realized it was rushing *through* her. That breeze whispered through her veins, her organs, her muscles. As it did, she felt better. The thirst eased. She still wanted to feed, but at least now she could think straight.

"She needs blood," the younger woman said. "I have to get

her away from here, somewhere she can feed."

"Approach her," the matronly voice warned, "and it is you she will feed upon."

"I can't just leave her there," the young woman said, and Silasa finally recognized the voice.

"Ynisaan," she croaked.

"Gods, Silasa," she whispered. "I'm so sorry."

Silasa licked her very dry lips. "I am...okay. I won't hurt you now." She blinked her eyes open. The wind continued to rush through her, and she recovered enough strength to sit up.

Ynisaan stood five paces away in her human form, gripping her upper arm as blood leaked between her fingers. The ghost dragon loomed over her.

"Ynisaan!" Silasa cried. "Behind you!"

Ynisaan looked up at the dragon, then back. "It's okay. It's okay now."

"What do you mean?"

"Avakketh is dead," the ghost dragon said in her matronly voice. "I am no longer driven by his whims. For that, I thank you." The ghost dragon bowed her head, then took in a deep breath. The wind coursed through Silasa again, and she realized the ghost dragon was creating it with her indrawn breath. Little flickers of ghostly fire streamed out of Silasa's chest and into the dragon's mouth. When the ghost dragon had a lungful, she spoke again, "This will not heal you, but it will keep you from death. The rest will take time."

"Who are you?" Silasa asked.

"Her name is Temeralis," Ynisaan said. "She's quite nice, actually, once she stopped trying to kill us."

"But who *is* she?"

"I am the first dragon to wake," she said. "The first among my kind to think, to begin to understand the world that Natra made, and I encouraged the rest to do the same. When Avakketh decided he should stand as lord and god over my kind, I opposed him. He killed me, and then he kept me in this...half life, drowning out my will and setting me to protect whatever was most precious to him."

"Forever?"

"Until this moment, yes. I am deeply in your debt. Whatever I can do for you, it is yours for the asking."

Silasa still felt like someone had spooned out her insides, but she grunted and looked about the cavern. Several yards away, the GodStone glowed emerald green. The fierce crimson light it once had was gone.

"What happened?" Silasa asked.

"Avakketh is dead," Ynisaan said. "The GodStone is filled with another."

"Tarithalius?"

"I...don't know. I do not think so."

Silasa looked at the green stone, then back at Ynisaan. "Then who's in there?"

41

ZILOK MORTH

ZILOK FLOATED, invisible and incorporeal, just above the tower where Mirolah had let go of her body. Beside him stood Orem, cloaked and cowled. Zilok gazed at the bloody battlefield where dragons and humans met.

Impressive.

The threads thrummed around him, awaiting his command, but he'd had no cause to use them. He'd told himself that, if he was needed, he would step in at the right moment, but once Bands sacrificed herself, the battle turned. As Zilok suspected, it gave Medophae the necessary rage to best Avakketh.

It was Zilok's victory as much as anyone else's. After all, if Bands had not been tricked into taking the crown, had not known she was dying either way, she would not have found it so easy to sacrifice her life fighting Avakketh. And if she hadn't...Medophae would not have found his spine.

You see, old friend? I serve the people of Amarion even more than you. Once again, I was the final push you needed.

293

"Well...that worked out just fine," Zilok said to Orem, who stood silently next to him. "Except for the end." Zilok pondered the meaning of Medophae growing to such an enormous size.

"Yes, my master."

"Medophae didn't quite look like himself, did he?"

"No, my master."

"I didn't like that. Not one bit."

"Yes, my master."

"He has never grown large like that, not even when we killed Dervon. What do you think it means?"

"I do not know, my master."

"It is...worthy of study." Zilok sighed. "We shall have to find a way to match him. It is a new complication."

"Yes, my master."

"But other things are simpler. Bands is finally out of the way, as is that troublesome novice, Mirolah."

Zilok had watched when Avakketh cut Mirolah free of her necrotic anchor. He hadn't seen her fly to her afterlife, but the Godgate—which churned eternally overhead—had no doubt devoured her by now. If the girl had been properly instructed, she might have crafted a lasting anchor. Instead, she had clung to the silly notion that she was still alive, and she had mistakenly bound herself to dead flesh.

Well, she had been a refreshing study, but like all the powerful threadweavers who had ever challenged Zilok, she had not outlasted him.

He looked down at the building where Mershayn had just left the dead Lord Vullieth. He watched Lord Sym approach, watched Ari'cyiane stab him. Sym crumpled to his knees, then fell over.

Splendid. That was well done.

"Excellent," he said to Orem.

"Yes, my master."

"The Lady Ari'cyiane has fangs. I think I'll keep her. She will be a serviceable back-up in case you and I ever get separated." Zilok reached out, testing the threads of the Lady

Ari'cyiane...then he withdrew.

"Ah, no," he said distastefully. GodSpill swirled in her. The woman had threadweaving talent. Curious that she hadn't manifested it yet. "Never mind. She would make a horrible anchor." Those filled with GodSpill made the worst anchors. It was why Orem was such a find. Despite his passion for threadweaving, the man had the talent of a stone. When a human's threads were dry, it was much easier for Zilok to saturate them with his own color of GodSpill. To attach to someone like, say, Mirolah, was impossible. It was like trying to hug a greased pig.

"Never mind. It was a pretty thought," he said.

"Yes, my master."

"We will have to look for a more suitable—"

The threads thrummed all around him. Zilok whirled, but there was no one there. No mortal threadweaver, no spirit positioning to attack.

He immediately hardened the threads of air around himself, searched around, ready to direct his will and burn them to ashes.

"Orem," he said. "Did you sense that?"

"Yes, my master."

Then where did it come from?

The threads thrummed again, and he felt a feathery touch on his cheek. Except he didn't have a cheek. The impossible touch sent a shot of cold dread through him. There was only one person who might do something so unexpected, and she should be dead.

"Mirolah?" he said.

The feathery caress came again, then turned into a knife blade, dragging across his skin. Except he didn't *have* skin. He recoiled at the impossible pain, searching madly now, but he couldn't see anything.

He spun, and that's when he noticed the giant Skin Dog emerge from the arched stairway. It had its head down, and it growled.

She would have to do better than threatening him with the

dog. A Skin Dog might be able to follow GodSpill, but it didn't have any ability to fight a threadweaver like Zilok.

But Mirolah herself was another matter. How could she make it seem like he was being cut with a knife? It was as though the threads themselves were attacking him. He focused his will and twisted the threads, shoving the ghostly sensation away. It vanished.

"Impressive," he said aloud, trying to calm his fear. It had been a long time since Zilok had faced something so foreign, so unknown, an opponent he could not find with his threadweaver sight. He hadn't thought it was even possible. "I see you've lost your body." He made a flare of fire burst over her corpse. "I can help you. I can show you how to make a true anchor, just as I showed you how to kill Ethiel."

A whisper spoke in his mind. *"But it's you I want to kill...."*

The touch returned, except this time, her ethereal fingers were monstrously strong, and they snatched his insubstantial throat.

How?

The hands shoved him to the ground, and he struggled like he would if he was human.

"I never underestimate you...but you never cease to underestimate me," she said into his mind, and he recognized the tone and the words. He had spoken those words to her in Teni'sia when he'd caged her, right before he'd made Stavark stab her to death.

Zilok stopped struggling. There was more than one way to fight a threadweaver, even an invisible one. Matching brute power was for amateurs.

Instead, he reached into his own threads. Long ago, he'd discovered a complicated spell that could speed his perceptions and his reactions, enabling him to do a thousand things in a second, while others moved at their normal slow pace. It was what he'd done with Mirolah in Daylan's Fountain and again in Calsinac. She had erroneously thought he'd stopped time somehow, and he hadn't seen the need to correct her misperception.

Of course, it wasn't an easy spell. It required pulling a vast amount of GodSpill from his environment into himself and making a hundred minute twists and subtle color changes in his own threads. A single misstep, and he could rearrange himself incorrectly. If he'd occupied a flesh-and-blood body, such a failure could result in hideous deformity. In Zilok's case, it would disrupt his natural composition and would almost certainly cut him free from his anchor.

But Zilok had done this spell many times. He took hold of his own threads and pulled from the GodSpill around him—

Suddenly, the threads were gone. The GodSpill was gone. Mirolah had yanked them out of his reach, leaving him in a dry bubble.

That was his spell! He'd cast it around her in Teni'sia. Somehow, she'd moved faster than him.

As a spirit, Zilok was comprised entirely of GodSpill himself. He couldn't stay in this bubble for long, or it would drain him. But there was always a way to solve the problem. Making a victim seem helpless was half showmanship. When he'd trapped Mirolah in Teni'sia, she'd thought herself helpless, confined by narrow thinking and her human body.

Zilok was not so gullible, nor so inexperienced.

The thread of his connection to Orem, twisted and thick and glowing blue, pierced the bubble. Zilok plunged his fingers into that cord, prepared to pull himself along it, shrink and emerge next to his anchor. He shoved himself into it—

Mirolah's impossible, monstrous fingers grabbed him, yanked him out of the cord, and threw him back into the center of the bubble as if he had a body that could be thrown around.

It just wasn't possible!

A tremor ran through him, and he felt like a rug that had been shaken. In horror, he looked at the cord that connected him to Orem. Outside the bubble, she was unraveling it, fraying it strand by strand.

"Mirolah, stop! I give you full marks. You are an astoundingly powerful threadweaver, but don't forget that it is

I who taught you this spell. There is much more I can teach you."

"You have nothing I want to learn," she whispered inside his mind.

The unraveling continued. With every strand she stripped away, he jerked and diminished a bit more. He tried to reach the edge of the bubble, but it moved with him, keeping him in its center.

"No!" he screamed.

Then the deed was done. She removed the anchor and cleared the spells Zilok had set over Orem's mind to cloud it, to make him pliable. Orem gasped and stumbled away, and Zilok floated inside the bubble, adrift. Only his prison held him to the mortal plane now. Above, the ever-present Godgate swirled—hungry, waiting.

With the last of his waning strength, Zilok dove for the tiny hole in the bubble where the cord had been. He slithered through, and suddenly he could feel the threads, could feel the power of the GodSpill filling him.

He was free!

The Godgate loomed larger overhead, filling the entire sky as though sensing he had no anchor at last.

Zilok would have thrown himself into the threads and traveled away from this spot, but he didn't have enough strength to get far. And wherever he emerged, the Godgate would be waiting for him, hungry. Without an anchor, he could not resist it.

He needed Orem back. Then he could flee and take the man with him. Brutally, he shoved himself into Orem, who spasmed, trying to fight. Zilok gripped the man's threads, began to sink into him, to bind him—

Zilok's ethereal fingers slipped from Orem's threads as a maelstrom of GodSpill rushed into the man. Zilok grasped hard, but the GodSpill was like grease, and it saturated every thread in Orem's body.

Mirolah had pushed the GodSpill into him; she had filled his talentless body full to bursting with it!

Zilok grabbed again, using the whole of his formidable will, using every ounce of his power to shove Mirolah out and take hold of Orem's threads. Once he had a good hold, he would flee this place and go where Mirolah didn't dare follow—

His fingers slipped off.

The Godgate yawned overhead, and Zilok began to float upward.

"No!" he screamed. He tried one, last desperate attempt to grab Orem, but the man was brimming with GodSpill now, and Zilok was weaker than he'd ever been. There was nowhere for Zilok to gain purchase.

Too late, he looked for some other nearby human. Ari'cyiane. She had talent, but he might be able to overwhelm her. He reached out...

...but he didn't have the strength. He could not cross the distance.

He slipped and fell upward. The Godgate churned, drawing him in.

"Not yet!" he screamed. "I am not meant to die! I am meant to live!"

He wailed as he stretched. His spirit became a long strand of gray, joining with the swirling maw, then he was swept into its center.

42

STAVARK

THE BATTLE WAS OVER. The dragons had fled. As though in response, a storm had gathered over the Inland Ocean, coming this way. Lightning flashed among the clouds.

Stavark wiped his bloody sword on a small cloth at his waist, then sheathed it. A dozen paces away from him, partially hidden by this last dragon's corpse, Mershayn recovered his breath, surrounded by his loyal Teni'sian soldiers.

Before Mershayn could talk to him, Stavark stepped into the silverland and ran away from the Sunriders and Teni'sian soldiers, away from the field of battle. He had to think. Helping slay the dragons had damaged his balance once again.

He stepped out of the silverland next to the shattered wall where Avakketh had fallen to earth, where Medophae had stood against the god of dragons and prevailed. Blood slashed the ground like it had been flung from a giant brush. Claw marks and burn marks gouged the turf, but Medophae was nowhere to be found.

Natra's Crown lay on the bloody ground, the artifact of a

goddess discarded like a broken sword. He had recognized it. Zilok Morth had worn it when he took away the *Rabasyvihrk's* power. He had recognized the same effect from afar. He wondered if Bands somehow took this from Zilok Morth and used it against Avakketh.

Stavark's people had many stories of Natra, kept in memory and stored in writing from the most early days. He had seen paintings of her with this very crown on her head, walking through the lands, creating, bringing beauty to life.

He stood in the midst of this battle of mortals and gods, and he could barely comprehend what it meant that a god was now dead, nor what it meant that the *Rabasyvihrk* seemed to have become a god himself. In all the stories Orem had ever told Stavark, in all the stories Stavark had ever read, and in all of his interaction with the *Rabasyvihrk* himself, never had he displayed such raw, godlike power.

The lands had changed today, and the change was not over yet.

Stavark had become the slayer again today to help his friends, and with that act arose the same conflict that he had not been able to resolve in the garden at Teni'sia. He wanted to stay pure, he wanted to bring balance, he wanted to flow with the natural order of the lands. He did not want to kill. Only abominations to nature deserved to die, and the dragons were not. They were created by Natra and fed by the lands, just like all of her creatures.

But neither did he want his friends to die. He'd thought when he became Vee's champion that he would never face that choice again, whether to slay the living or watch his friends be slain in turn. He could not have stood by and let Deni'tri or Grek'tas or Mershayn die, but neither did he want to take the life of a dragon. His soul had been cracked, creating an imperfect edge.

He wanted a third solution, but he could not see it. Perhaps the only way to resolve the problem was to not care about killing. Or, like his mother advised, to stay away from humans altogether.

He could do neither.

Stavark felt the sublime answer was not as simple as one or the other. Neither his mother's way nor the way of the warlike humans was the answer.

I must find the right, even if it is hidden from me, even if it is hidden from everyone else.

Stavark looked down at Natra's Crown and thought about the balance of the lands. Though Vaisha the Changer had changed his people from humans into the silver-haired, silver-eyed beings that all others called quicksilvers, it was Natra who had given them life in the beginning, and it was she who also gave them the word *syvihrk*: the people who love beauty.

The word *syvihrk* came to be the way Stavark's people saw themselves. A true *syvihrk* cherished beauty, and they saw everything Natra had created was beautiful in its own way. The dragons. The Skin Dogs. The humans. All of her creatures. The *syvihrk* worked to protect, to create, not to kill or destroy.

He blinked, staring at the crown, and suddenly he understood why it had killed Bands, why it had probably killed Zilok Morth before that. They had used it to destroy. An artifact of the Natra the Creator could not ever be used in such a way. It could only be used...

...to create.

Neither Bands nor Zilok had used it as a *syvihrk* must.

He heard the padding of small feet, and looked up to see Vee step lightly over the tumbled stones and across the broken wall.

"My champion," she said, and her voice filled him, smoothing his most recently broken edges.

"*Maehka vik Kalik,*" he breathed, and he knelt before her.

"You left me."

"My friends needed me," he said, standing again. "In serving the right, I...could not let them die. You were safe, so I needed to take the moment before it was too late."

"But I am not safe. My body rages. The lands suffer." She nodded toward the nearing storm. "And Mirolah is moments away from claiming my body permanently."

Stavark had not put it together that the storm was anything but a storm, but suddenly he understood what she was saying.

"It is Mirolah," he murmured. "She fights with the GodSpill. That is why there is lightning."

"She has left her human body, my champion. Soon, she will try to bind herself to my body. Or she may try to steal another mortal's body while maintaining her hold on mine."

"Mirolah would never steal another person's body. The only reason she stole yours is because she does not understand what it is."

Vee shook her head. "She is human. She is desperate. That is what desperate mortals do. Look at what she does to the land in her effort to remain alive. She has used *my* body to keep herself in this strained half life. She has twisted the lands. Soon, she will bond with my body. Once she does, my quest is over. I shall never get my body back, and the lands will suffer her struggles forever. Raging storms. Decaying, neglected pieces of the lands. Mirolah still thinks she is human, still *wants* to be human. Her mortal mind is strong, but it cannot comprehend how to use my body, nor what is needed for the lands."

He nodded. "I understand."

"So you will help me?"

"My life is yours, *Maehka vik Kalik.*"

"She must be expelled from my body."

"And if we expel her…she dies."

"She is already dead, my champion."

The impossible choice had come again. They always did when he didn't know the answer. Nature teetered off balance, and Mirolah stood at the tipping point. If he expelled her, Mirolah would die. Then Vee could have her body again, and nature's balance could be restored. Vee could become Vaisha the Changer again, the patron goddess of the *syvihrk.*

But…

"I cannot kill my friend," he whispered.

Vee raised her chin. "You are my champion. Only together can we expel her. I will show you how—"

"She will not do this thing, bonding with the GodSpill. If

she understands, she will do what needs to be done. She will do the right thing."

Vee bit her lip. "She won't," she whispered. "And the lands will suffer."

"She will."

"My champion, she has not chosen rightly since she freed my body from its prison."

"There must be a third solution…" he whispered.

"What?"

"Something that is not killing her or letting her bond with the GodSpill."

"There is nothing," Vee said.

Even Vee did not see a third solution. If a goddess didn't see it, then perhaps it did not exist. He clenched his teeth, banished his fear and his doubt.

Vee wasn't a goddess, not yet, and perhaps he could best serve her by finding the solution she did not see. Perhaps it was up to him to show it to her.

"I will not help you kill her. She will choose to restore the balance."

"My champion, she won't!"

"*Syvihrk* work for the good of others, always. *Syvihrk* do not use violence to remove those who are inconvenient, even those who are dangerous. Neither do *syvihrk* turn their heads and pretend those people do not exist or are not worthy. A true *syvihrk* must help *all* people to grow. That is what it means to be a *syvihrk*. Natra the Creator taught my people this long ago."

"How can you believe that when Mirolah has proven, time and again, that she would rather tear the lands apart than let herself die? How can you believe that when she is the cause of this imbalance?"

"Because if there are only two choices, to run away or to kill, then I do not wish to live in this world."

"Sometimes we must kill."

"Sometimes we must create," he said. "We must make a new solution." He looked down and, impassively, he picked up

Natra's Crown.

Vee hissed. "My champion! Drop it! That is Natra's Crown. It is death. It will slay you as it slew Medophae's consort."

"I know what it is." He offered it to her.

She recoiled. "You would slay me? That is a god-killer. Only Natra could wield it."

"I know why. I know its secret."

"Secret?"

"It was made to create. When it is not used that way, it reflects the intentions of those who use it. How you use it comes back at you. A true *syvihrk* knows this, would use it this way."

Lightning struck the wall to the south and far to the west, and Stavark flinched, looking that direction. "The time is here. Mirolah needs me," Stavark said.

"*I* need you. I cannot expel her without you!"

He shook his head. "I will find a third solution. In this, if in nothing else, I will be *syvihrk*."

"My champion, she will bond with my body forever!"

"No. She will give it back to you. She risked everything to bring your body back to the lands." He looked into the eyes of his goddess, and he said. "What will you risk for her?" He held the crown out to her on one finger.

Vee watched him, stunned. But for the first time, Stavark's doubt and uncertainty were gone. He felt full of the right. He had found the balanced solution. He'd found the path of the right.

"Like Mirolah, I know you will choose the right in the end."

Stavark let Natra's Crown go and stepped into the silverland.

The crown hung in the air for a breathless moment, then fell to the grass.

43

MIROLAH

MIROLAH WATCHED until Zilok's spirit swirled into the black maw of the Godgate. She remained vigilant for some last trick, but it appeared that he had run out. He floated through the Godgate like he should have long ago.

You won't hurt anyone ever again.

Orem stood at the edge of the tower, blinking. He brought his hands up and stared at them. Pushing back his cloak, he turned, gazing out over Belshra. He saw the archway of the staircase, and he staggered toward it. She thought of following him, of speaking into his mind and telling him what to do. But she supposed he'd had quite enough of that. No, Orem was free. Orem's mind belonged to him once again. Let him sort through his sanity.

She had her own sanity to sort through.

"Come," the GodSpill called to her. *"Leave this place, these humans. Fly to the Spine Mountains, flow with the tides of the Inland Ocean, sweep along the sands of the Red Desert...."*

Mirolah looked down at her desiccated body. Avakketh

had cut the cord, and weeks of decay had occurred in mere moments. Only now did she realize how much power she'd had to spend to fool herself, to make her body seem alive.

She could repair the damage, perhaps even push the flush of life into those limbs, but she could not make it truly alive. She had tried. And every moment she poured more and more of her power into keeping that body in the semblance of life increased the risk that the GodSpill would overwhelm her with its will, with its agenda.

Now, rather than just being an obstinate voice within the GodSpill's flighty mind, she was clear, and strong. Avakketh had given her an unwitting gift. She didn't need a body to continue being Mirolah within the GodSpill.

"Come," the GodSpill beseeched again.

No.

"The Spine Mountains... The Inland Ocean..."

"No! I am Mirolah. I am not the Spine Mountains or the Inland Ocean or the Red Desert. I will see to my friends."

The GodSpill railed against her, but this time, she was in control. She didn't have the hindrance of keeping her body alive. She made the GodSpill obey.

Wind blew. Thunder cracked overhead. Clouds began to blot the sky.

Mirolah ignored the GodSpill's anger. She turned her attention below.

Mershayn strode toward the large, ruined building that Zilok Morth had been watching. Far behind him, dozens of soldiers were doing the same, carrying the dead into the city from the battlefield. Mershayn entered the building alone...then he saw Ari'cyiane standing over the body of Grendis Sym.

Mirolah flowed closer.

I love him...

"Come," the GodSpill urged. It yanked at her. Lightning forked down, striking the water a mile off the coast. The GodSpill fought her, but Mirolah kept control.

Wind whipped around her and the soldiers below. Rain

began to sprinkle down as the GodSpill raged, but Mirolah descended to hear Mershayn's words.

"Ari'cyiane," Mershayn said, his voice sad. "What have you done?"

"What you clearly could not," she said.

Ari'cyiane wiped her dagger on her cloak without a hint of remorse, then sheathed it. Sym lay next to Vullieth as though he had been laid out intentionally, another casualty from the war.

"You killed him," Mershayn said sadly. "Ari'cyiane, you stabbed him."

"Justice is served." She watched him with fiery eyes.

"You can't...just kill someone because you want to."

"Want? I didn't *want* any of this!" she shot back. "I didn't want that traitor to strip me naked and tie me to a pillar. I didn't want my husband to die. Don't tell me what I want!"

"Ari'cyiane—"

"We can't choose what villains do, Mershayn, but we can stop them. Grendis Sym was a traitor, a schemer, a liar, a murderer. He deserved to die."

"I had already decided his penance."

"Your penance was *nothing*." She spat the word like poison. "Bring your brand of justice to those who will listen to your lies. I do not recognize your authority!"

He hung his head, and the angry wind blew his hair about his face. "You don't know what you've done. Sym was the Lord of Buir'tishree. When his supporters find out what you've done...it will fracture the kingdom. Perhaps he deserved to die, but it wasn't for you to decide!"

"I say it was!"

He glanced to the side, hearing the approach of the soldiers who had followed him, bearing the dead. He pressed his lips into a firm line, then he gave one terse nod. "Very well. You've taken your revenge. I will...look the other way. Let it appear he died in battle."

"How *kind* of you." Her words dripped sarcasm.

His gaze became stony. "Take your *victory* and go, Lady

Vullieth. I hope it is enough to sate you, but know this: I consider us even."

"I don't need your absolution," she hissed. "If you want my blood, take it. What is this life to me now except pain?"

"We have all suffered tonight, my lady. But our foes are defeated, and the sun will rise on a new day. We will rebuild. *You* can rebuild."

"Feed your honeyed lies to someone else."

The soldiers' torches bobbed above the broken wall as they approached. Mershayn glanced again at the entry way. "Go then," he said. "While there is no suspicion upon you."

"I hate you, Mershayn," she said. "The only person I hate more is myself for trusting you, for giving myself to you, for ever betraying my husband." She stalked from the broken building, head down as rain began to fall.

The soldiers entered the broken building, carrying bodies, and began to lay them out alongside Sym and Vullieth, creating a row of corpses.

The GodSpill wrenched at Mirolah again. It tried to haul her up into the clouds, but she kept it under control. Lightning struck just outside the wall to the south and again to the west. The clouds darkened the night sky, coming closer with every second.

Mershayn spun, facing the broken archway. Sniff had followed Mirolah down the stairs from the tower, and he stood in the flickering torchlight, head low, watching. The soldiers who carried the dead in from the battlefield backed away, alarmed.

"Mirolah?" Mershayn gasped, shielding his face from the rain and peering at Sniff.

"Yes, my love," she said into his mind. *"I am here."*

He winced, as though it had hurt him, but then he shook it off. "Are you okay? What can I do?"

"Your Majesty!" Deni'tri shouted. Sniff had slunk closer, and he looked like he might pounce.

"Stay back, Deni'tri," he shouted over the wind.

"Is it Mirolah?" She started to interpose herself between

him and the enormous Skin Dog.

"Back!" He held out his hand, palm toward her. Then to the air, he said. "Are you okay? Where are you?"

"I can't... I can't go back to my body. It is...dead."

Her heart hurt, thinking about that. She couldn't love him like this, not just as some voice on the winds—

Suddenly, the wind yanked Mershayn and Sniff into the air like leaves, whisking them twenty feet off the ground.

"Your Majesty!" Deni'tri shouted, running forward.

Mirolah shouted, grabbing hold of the GodSpill. It wanted to kill Mershayn and her Sniff. She felt its malevolence and its intention. It wanted to hurl Mershayn and Sniff hundreds of feet into the air and let them fall, anything to destroy her connection to them. With a shout, she bent the GodSpill to her will and lowered both of them to the ground. Deni'tri and two other soldiers leapt to steady their leader. He gained his feet gracefully and shouted at the wind next to Sniff.

"Mirolah!" Mershayn called.

Sniff howled.

She watched Mershayn and Sniff as she floated higher. She had to take permanent control of the GodSpill so that it would never do that again. She couldn't let the GodSpill be this dangerous, willful child. It had to obey. She had to *make* it obey.

Down the street, Mirolah saw Ari'cyiane lean against the wind and rain as she crossed the wide-open space of the city center. She reached an alley with tall walls on either side, and vanished into the darkness. Mirolah hesitated, then followed.

In the dark alley, Ari'cyiane fell to her knees. She slipped her dagger from its sheath, set the point against her chest. Mirolah watched, transfixed, as Ari'cyiane took deep breaths, working up her courage.

She's going to kill herself.

Mirolah reached out, about to fling the knife away from Ari'cyiane's grip. stop the suicide...

But she didn't.

A thought occurred to her, and it stunned her into

inaction. No matter what Mirolah had tried, she couldn't give life back to her own body. She had healed it again and again, had filled it with GodSpill, had filled it with warmth like a living body, but in the end, it was still just a corpse she had forced to be animate. She could heal flesh, but there was some difference between that and giving life. Whatever the secret to giving life was, Mirolah didn't have it.

But what if Mirolah was nearby when another's soul made the trek to the Godgate? If she timed it right, if she got to the dying body in the instant before death, she might be able to go inside...

Horrified and excited, she floated closer.

Ari'cyiane doesn't want her body. She wants to die.

The lady was sobbing, her hands shaking as she held the hilt with both hands.

She doesn't want to live, and I want to live so badly.

Ari'cyiane gripped the hilt hard.

Don't...

She shoved the dagger into her heart and gave a squeaking little scream that the howling wind stole away instantly. She slumped forward with a long sigh, and fell to her side.

Ari'cyiane's spirit wafted up from her body like steaming snow, forming a ghostly mimicry of her living body. The Godgate swirled overhead, its gray strands twisting into the black maw, and Ari'cyiane's soul floated toward it.

Mirolah could stop the suicide. Even now, she could snatch the knife away and heal the wound before Ari'cyiane's soul reached the black maw at the center of those gray swirls. She had done it before.

But Mirolah hadn't killed Ari'cyiane. Could she be blamed if she simply waited, took the body for her own? If Ari'cyiane wished to die, that was her choice. But it would be a crime to let her body go to waste...

It is my only chance to be human again.

Mirolah moved closer to Ari'cyiane's dying body. She could do it. Then she could be with Mershayn, live the life she'd always meant to have.

She reached out with her ethereal fingers, caressing the body's shoulders. Yes. It was shorter, curvier than Mirolah's, but it was a beautiful body. It would do nicely.

She imagined touching Mershayn with Ari'cyiane's fingers, imagined him brushing Ari'cyiane's cheek with his, looking into those blue eyes. She imagined him kissing her...

And suddenly she cringed. She saw Mershayn's face twisted in disgust at what she had done, stealing another's body. She felt ill.

No. I can't.

With the speed of thought, Mirolah reached out, creating a net above Ari'cyiane's soul. The spirit struggled, gripping and twisting the strands of her net and wailing silently. Mirolah pulled the dagger out of Ari'cyiane's chest, reached into Ari'cyiane's body and healed her punctured heart, the slashed muscles, veins, and skin.

The Godgate retreated, and Ari'cyiane's spirit descended slowly at first, then faster. In a final rush, it slammed back into her body. Ari'cyiane gasped, and she sat up like she'd been poked with a spear.

"Gah!" she said. She stared aghast at the bloody dagger. "Whuh... By the gods! What happened?" She stared up at the sky, searching for the yawning Godgate, but while Mirolah could still see it plainly, the living could not.

"Cherish..." Mirolah whispered into the tangle of Ari'cyiane's frightened thoughts.

Ari'cyiane jumped, scrambled to her feet, and spun around, looking for who had spoken.

"Cherish the pain, Ari'cyiane. Cherish the joy. Live...."

Mirolah drifted higher, away from the alley into the sky.

And I, she thought to herself, *have but one option left. This monstrous body of GodSpill, stretched out across all of Amarion. I have to bend it, become it, make it obey....*

"Mirolah." The soft voice rode the winds.

It was spoken from a distance away, but Mirolah was everywhere, and she heard it like a soft whisper behind her ear. She rose above Ari'cyiane and looked back at the tower where her corpse lay. Stavark stood there, his long hair whipping like wet silver ropes in the wind. Lightning struck the palace behind him. A chunk of rock fell, crashing through a broken ceiling. Lightning struck behind her, one street away from Ari'cyiane. Thunder cracked.

"Mirolah," he said softly.

"*Stavark,*" she said into his mind.

"Look," he said. "Look around you."

"*It's angry,*" she said. "*I'm trying to control it, but it wants me to leave, wants me to blend with the lands.*"

"I'm so sorry," he said.

"*I have to…break it, become one with it, I think. I have to make sure it listens to me. I've been exploring it. I think I can…bond with it. If I do, I think I can control it.*"

"And then what will you do?" he asked.

"*What do you mean? I'll live.*"

"You will live. But after you have bonded with the GodSpill, will it be less angry? Or more? Will you finally give it what it needs?"

"*Give it… What do you—?*"

She suddenly realized that he was crying. Glimmers of silver came from his eyes, mixing with the rain.

"*Stavark…*"

"You are the hero of heroes, Mirolah," he said, his face a mask of anguish. "You gave your life to return the GodSpill, to give hope and life back to the lands."

"*You know… You know that my…body died in Daylan's Fountain.*"

"I know. You cannot be blamed for what you did after. You were given the power of a goddess without the ability to wield it. No mortal could have done better, but…"

She suddenly realized what he was saying to her. "*But it doesn't belong to me….*"

"Look," he said. "Look around you."

The GodSpill raged. Rain lashed, and lightning struck the city all around, again and again. Buildings shook. Debris fell. The Sunriders fled, riding farther north onto the plains.

Mershayn and his soldiers ran for the infirmary, trying to get out of the dangerous weather.

"But if I…let it go, it's just going to continue raging. It wants me to take charge of it".

"There is another."

"Another? Another what?"

"Another who can give the GodSpill what it needs, who can restore balance to the lands. She is the goddess from whom this GodSpill was taken. What you call the GodSpill is her body. She has returned, but she cannot claim it with you holding on so tight. She is Vaisha the Changer."

Mirolah had read that name. She knew it to be one of the seven gods. The legend Mirolah had read told of how Vaisha had been destroyed by Dervon.

"This…belongs to her?"

"Yes."

"And she can take it back?"

"If you let her."

"If I let her… If I let go of it."

"Yes."

"Stavark, I…don't have a body anymore. I…"

He kept his gaze on her, his eyes brimming with silver tears.

You're saying… I…should just die?

"It is not fair that you should be given this choice, but it is yours. You can save the lands again, Mirolah. You can save them for all time."

The unfairness of it ripped at her. This was not how her story should end. All the struggles, everything she had tried to do for the good of those she loved, even for the good of the lands. Now, at the end of that long road, the only option was to destroy the lands or to die herself.

Three more lightning strikes lanced into the city, thunder booming with them.

"Stavark…"

"I'm so sorry." Silver glittered across his wet cheeks. His hair was plastered across his face.

He stood there, unspeaking, as the sky opened up around them. She wondered if this freakish, powerful lightning storm had already killed someone, maybe many people. And how many more would die if she continued fighting with the GodSpill?

"I didn't want any of this," she said to Stavark.

"I know."

"I'm scared."

"I am here," he said.

"So this is…it? This is the end for me?"

"I will be with you. I won't leave your side."

"I don't want to go."

He was sobbing now, but he never took his gaze from her. "I will stay right here with you.".

She turned away from him. Streaks of lightning cracked down, one after another after another, and she screamed her frustration into the raging winds. The rain turned to ice. Below, Sniff howled above the storm. Mirolah spit her fury into the teeth of the GodSpill…

…and she pulled herself out. It was like pulling out the roots of a tree. Her chest was the ground, and the roots went through every part of her. She screamed again, and the pulling seemed to last an eternity. The storm circled around Belshra like a tornado, flattening grass, knocking over brittle walls.

Then suddenly, the GodSpill flung her away like a catapult. Her strength vanished, and she felt like a brittle leaf on the raging wind, blown upward toward the ever-present Godgate. She couldn't feel the wind anymore, couldn't feel the cowering soldiers or Sunriders below, couldn't feel Stavark crying on top of the tower.

All that mattered now was the softly swirling grays, whites, and blacks that flowed past her. The Godgate. The dark, black maw yawned above her, and the closer she came, the better she felt.

She was dead. This was where she belonged, and all the cares of her mortal life drained away. She didn't fight. At last, she could rest—

Suddenly, strands of burning white crisscrossed in front of her face. She tried to push past them, but they were in front of her hands, too, against her chest, tangling up her legs. She struggled, but the strands formed into a net and seared into her.

She screamed, trying to get past it, but the net held her tightly. The fire cut into her, forcing her down, away from the maw of the Godgate.

It hurts, I know, a voice whispered to her. *I'm sorry. It will be over soon.*

Suddenly, the pain faded, the net loosened. Her spirit floated above the palace tower where Stavark stood.

Next to him lay her body, but it wasn't the desiccated wreck she had left. Her face was no longer sunken against her cheekbones. Her skin was pink and plump and healthy. Her lips parted, drawing in a breath.

Mirolah's soul was drawn toward her rejuvenated body, but something made her look up.

Floating above her, descending gently, was a little girl with blue hair. She wore a white and blue dress and that crown of thick, irregular sized crystals that Zilok had worn when he'd captured Mirolah in Teni'sia. Rainbow colors swirled around the girl like ribbons of light.

Mirolah was so near to joining with her body that it was all she could do to resist. She could hear with her body's ears, feel with its skin. The wind had calmed. She heard booted feet coming up the stairway to the tower.

Mirolah held her spirit still, poised above her body. She focused on the girl and spoke into her mind as she had with Mershayn, with Ari'cyiane.

"Who are you?"

"I am Vaisha," she said. *"Thank you for letting my body go."*

"You're the one he said was meant to rule the GodSpill."

"He's a sweet boy." She glanced to her right, smiling. *"I always liked the* syvihrk. *And he is exceptional, even for the* syvihrk.*"*

"You're...a goddess," Mirolah said.

Vaisha grinned. *"I am now. Go. Be a girl, Mirolah. Be a woman. Be what you were meant to be before you righted the mistakes of the gods."*

"How did you...bring me back to life?" Mirolah asked. *"I tried, but I couldn't."*

"An exceptional syvihrk *showed me the truth."* She winked.

Mirolah found herself thirsting for that bit of knowledge, but the call of her living body was a sweet, glorious thing.

"Thank you," she said.

"You are welcome, Mirolah Rith. Love go with you, and a cherishing of all things large and small. You have given this goddess a second chance, and I thank you."

Finally, Mirolah stopped fighting the call of her body, and her spirit floated down. Her soul lay in the same pose as her body, and it was like being pushed into wet clay.

She drew a long, sweet breath. As she blinked her eyes open, she saw Mershayn appear at the top of the stairs. His were the booted feet she had heard, and now he ran toward her. He crashed to his knees next to her and took her into his arms.

For the first time in an eternity, she could not hear the whispers of the GodSpill all about her. She did not see with its kaleidoscope eyes. It was as though a veil had been laid over her eyes and muffs pulled over her ears. She felt her threadweaver sight, sensed the threads around her, but they did not appear as starkly as they had before. But at the same time, she did not feel the doom that had come along with all of it, either.

She was mortal again, with all the joys and foibles that came along with it. Mershayn hovered over her. She reached up and put her arms around his neck. After all, it was an order from the goddess, to cherish the small things and the large. "Kiss me," she whispered, and he did.

44

TARITHALIUS

TARITHALIUS SAW HIS DAUGHTER standing in the air above the milling humans. They couldn't see her, of course, because she didn't want them to. But he could see her. She wore Natra's Crown, the artifact Bands had used to kill Avakketh.

"It's going to destroy you, you know," Tarithalius said.

"Father." She turned to look at him. "Is this my welcome, then, after so many years?"

"What better welcome? A father expressing concern for his daughter. How do you plan to rid yourself of it?"

"I don't," Vaisha replied.

"No?"

"If you and Avakketh had spent half as much time thinking as fighting, you might also know what I've learned about Natra's Crown."

"Impertinence!" he said. "What do you mean?"

"If I tell you, what then would keep you from taking Natra's Crown for yourself?"

"I could have been lord and god of dragonkind and

humankind alike tonight. I could have kept all of Avakketh's power, taken control of Irgakth *and* Amarion."

"Why didn't you?"

"Blech. Can you see me as a 'lord and god'?"

She smiled. "No."

"Give me something new instead. Show me the surprising. Have an outlaw dragon kill her god. Turn a peasant into the strongest threadweaver Amarion has ever seen. Break an assault of dragons with a bastard and his ragtag human army. Show me *these* things, and I'll pay attention."

"Then I'll tell you the secret, Father."

"I like secrets."

"You can't use Natra's Crown to destroy. You can't use it to conquer, to imprison, or to dominate. If you do, it devours you."

"That's no secret. I saw what it did to Bands."

"The secret is what you *can* use it for."

"Something not having to do with destroying, conquering, imprisoning or dominating, I'll wager."

"As clever as always, Father."

"What does it do?"

"Natra made it to create life."

"Ah…" he said.

"She only used it for that, though Dervon and Avakketh saw it as a god-killer. Their own fear kept them at bay, when Natra was here. Natra did not discourage their ignorance. It was a feint."

"You get your smarts from my side of the family."

She laughed. "You haven't changed."

"So you used the crown only to heal Mirolah's body?" he asked.

"Mirolah herself could heal it. I gave it the spark of life with Natra's Crown. Nothing else can, you know, not threadweaving, not even the gods. Avakketh never created life. Nor Dervon. Nor Zetu. Not even me, until now. All we could do was change the creatures Natra had already made."

"So, will you go gallivanting around the countryside like

Wildmane now, righting wrongs and bringing people back to life?"

She gave him a wry smile. "No. Natra created the balance of life and death for a reason. I don't fully understand it, but until I do, it seems best to preserve the balance She intended."

"What about Mirolah?"

"She did the right thing, Father. It was worth an exception."

"There is a *right* thing?"

"Look at this land, Father. Look at what we've done to it. We have set a poor example. The dragons stew in arrogance. The quicksilvers in seclusion. The humans in bitterness. Have you looked?"

"I have looked. It's all very fascinating."

She sighed. "We must show them beauty."

"You always did like change."

"For the better."

"Blech. It's unseemly for a god to appear too noble."

"Mirolah destroyed Daylan's Fountain. She set me free. She held my body together when it wanted to fly apart. She did the work of a god. I owe her."

"You think she did it for you?"

"She did it for everyone."

"She did it for power. She took the GodSpill that belonged to you and used it for her own selfish mortal purposes."

"And she gave it back."

"She had no other choice."

"But she did," Vaisha said softly. "Two choices. She could have taken my body, but she gave it back. And before that, she could have taken Ari'cyiane's body."

"Who?"

"You know who Ari'cyiane is, Father. You need not play the fool so strenuously. Mother isn't here. Mirolah could have taken Ari'cyiane's body, but instead, Mirolah helped her."

"You sound like a bad Buravaran romance ballad."

"And you try too hard to sound like a bloodless rapscallion."

"Thalius the Bloodless. I like it."

"Mirolah could have stolen that poor woman's body. She didn't, even when she knew she'd die if she didn't. Then she did the same with me. That is something special. That is the kind of behavior a god should encourage. It's no wonder my body chose her to replace me."

"So you'll keep the crown?"

"It is too dangerous for anyone else. And I like what it will...remind me to be."

"Better you than me." Tarithalius looked around. There wasn't a single conflict in Belshra now. He half hoped the Sunriders would suddenly attack the Teni'sians, but they didn't. From what he could tell, Mershayn and Raedir-ba were going to shake hands and part friends.

It made the space between his shoulder blades itch.

"I have business to attend to," he said. He had just one more item to take care of, then he could leave this ever increasingly dull place. Perhaps he'd venture to Irgakth. It had always been so difficult to explore the north lands with Avakketh constantly snapping at him. He'd best go now before it came under new leadership.

"Be well, Father," she said.

"You're going to stay?"

"It's been a long time since I was whole. For now, I am content to simply be myself. I will watch over the humans for a while. Or perhaps I will take pity on Mother and let her know I'm okay."

"What a dutiful daughter. Tell her 'snooty Sara sucks on a sour patch' from me."

"Goodbye, Father."

"Goodbye, Vaisha."

45

MEDOPHAE

MEDOPHAE DIDN'T KNOW WHY he grew to giant size when Oedandus filled him. Perhaps his mortal mind couldn't comprehend how to absorb the god's power without making a larger body. Perhaps he felt threatened at Avakketh's enormous size and unconsciously grew to match him.

There was much about his new power that he didn't understand. He didn't feel Oedandus trying to sway him anymore, to fill him with rage, to push him toward the god's idea of justice. The dark voice was gone. It was just as Oedandus had said. The strength of a god was his to use now. For eternity. Alone.

When the dragons fled, Medophae shrank to his normal form near a small stand of trees to the west of the Belshran plains. Avakketh's body lay unmoving and horribly burnt off to his left. He inspected it, and it did not rise. The wounds did not heal like they had the last time, and Medophae knew that this time, Avakketh was truly gone.

Medophae kept walking, into the forest, feeling the

swelling of power that was a part of him now. It wanted to make him large again, wanted him to expand. His mortal mind couldn't conceive of it, but his mind wasn't just mortal anymore. Oedandus's memories, his experience, had blended with Medophae's own, and certain things he could never understand before now made sense to him. Gods were finite, like humans, but their limits were so far beyond a human's limits that it was difficult for a human mind to encompass it.

But now, somehow, Medophae could. He didn't know how long he stood in those woods, seeing new things inside his own mind, inside his own body, seeing old things with new eyes. It was like his new form was a vessel, and he methodically poured his consciousness into it like water, exploring the experiences of Oedandus, the vast knowledge and understanding. Only when it was full did he blink and look around.

Time had passed. The Teni'sian soldiers were hauling their dead away from the battlefield, and the starry skies had clouded over. To the south, a storm bunched, throwing lightning down at the water and moving closer to Belshra.

Medophae left the forest, passing the body of Avakketh, and walked toward Belshra until he stood over the bloody patch of earth by the broken wall where Avakketh had first fallen, where Bands had died. There was nothing left now, just ragged earth and the blood of a god.

This is the choice I made.

His heart felt raw and broken. But at the same time, he found a steadiness he'd lacked before. She was gone, but she'd died to save humanity. He could have died with her, but he didn't so that he could serve humanity. And that was worth something. Combined with Oedandus's view on life and time, he understood now that single lives came and went. Time came and went. But a purpose—serving a greater cause than one's own desires—lasted forever. If he could not be happy about Bands's loss and his choice, he could at least be proud of it.

He glanced over the battlefield. The Sunriders rode across the grass, looking for dragons that might still be moving. Mershayn and a group of his soldiers were walking back toward the crushed gate, carrying a body.

Medophae looked back at the bloody ground, then suddenly realized Natra's Crown was missing. After Bands faded, it had fallen to the ground right here. He searched the grass quickly, but there was no sign of it.

"Yes," a deep voice said from behind him, as though reading his mind. "It's gone."

There wasn't a soldier within five hundred yards of Medophae. No one could have snuck up on him or closed the distance so fast, except a quicksilver...or another god.

"Thalius," Medophae said without turning.

"If you're looking for Natra's Crown, it's not here."

"Did you take it?"

Thalius made a hissing sound between his teeth. "I'd rather pick up a snake."

"I think you'd enjoy picking up a snake," Medophae said, and he finally turned.

Thalius wore his real face now. Or, well, the face Medophae had most often seen on the god when he wasn't imitating someone else. He had curly black hair, mahogany skin, and formidable muscles. He stood over seven feet tall and wore a thick belt with a loincloth made of linked golden squares. He held a long-handled war hammer—which was nearly as tall as he was—lightly in his hand, like it weighed no more than a piece of straw.

"So..." Thalius tipped his chin back and inspected Medophae like he was a prize war stallion. "You're a god now."

Medophae said nothing. Thalius talked often; he rarely offered anything of substance.

"What do you think you'll do first?" Thalius asked, planting the handle of his weapon in the ground and leaning his bulging forearms on the hammer's head.

"Where is the crown?" Medophae repeated.

"Safer than in your hands, I'd wager. Don't you have enough to learn at the moment without trying to handle Natra's Crown?"

Medophae felt Oedandus's anger roar like an ocean in the back of his mind, but fighting one god in a day was plenty. If Thalius wanted the crown, let him have it. What would Medophae do if he had it, anyway? Use it? Oedandus had memories about the crown. It was a godkiller, an artifact from the age before humankind, when only gods roamed the earth. Those memories warned him that donning the crown would be a bad idea.

"Keep it. Look, Thalius, I have a lot to think on. It has been...an overwhelming day. I'd rather be alone."

"Would you really?" Thalius said, conspicuously studying the bloody ground where Bands had fallen.

Medophae's shoulders tightened, and a golden ball of fire formed around his right fist.

"If you've come to mock me, reconsider," Medophae growled. "Go now, Thalius, while I still consider us friends."

Seemingly unperturbed, Thalius continued to stare at the spot where Bands had died. "I've always liked you, Medophae. I liked you as a young man, going toe-to-toe with Dervon's maggot monstrosity like you had a chance. I liked it when you kicked Dervon in the teeth. I liked you when you flew about this little piece of the world on your dragon lover, knocking over petty kings. You were one of the most interesting mortals around...." He paused. "Well, except for the last four centuries, that is. Thank Natra I wasn't around. You were a horrible bore without Bands."

Medophae clenched his teeth, and the ground lit up gold as the fire of Oedandus surrounded him. "Once again, I say: Leave, Thalius. I'd rather be alone just now."

Thalius beckoned. "Come with me," he said. "I want to show you something."

"I don't want to see what you have to show me. So go. We can talk about what you'd like to discuss later. I daresay we'll have the time." An eternity of time. Alone.

Thalius smiled, white teeth flashing against his dark skin. Thalius had always enjoyed the effect of his dazzling smile in that face. It was the kind of smile Medophae had seen on the god of humans before. Thalius wasn't going to give up. He was going to pester Medophae incessantly, following him about, delivering bad jokes one after the other until he got his way.

Medophae sighed and decided to skip to the end.

"Fine," he said through his teeth. "Where are we going?"

"Just relax," Thalius said.

There was a wrenching in Medophae's gut, and the battlefield of Belshra vanished. The sky, the ground, the ruined walls, the distant Corialis Mountains...all of it twisted about Medophae like it had been spun into a rope. The well of Oedandus's memories told him this was one way to travel through the lands of Amarion and that, as a god, he would have access to it. On the heels of that memory was the knowledge that he could stop this any time he wished. He went along with it.

Just as suddenly, it untwisted, and Medophae stood in a cavern. He blinked. He sensed that, as a mortal, he would have been exceedingly disoriented. As a god, he demanded his faculties be sharp, and the disorientation vanished.

Silasa was here. *This* was where she'd gone. A small woman with white hair, dark eyes, and skin the color of the night sky between the stars stood next to Silasa, supporting the vampire underneath her arm. Behind them loomed a ghostly dragon, and beside them was an emerald stone almost as tall as Medophae. It lit the cavern with a green glow. Naked and facing away from Medophae crouched a third woman.

"My point," Thalius continued as if they hadn't just teleported into a cave. "Is that you don't *want* to be alone. And anybody in their right mind wouldn't want that, either. You're just...horrible at it."

The woman stood, and Medophae's heart began to pound. He'd know that silhouette anywhere.

"Gods!" he whispered.

"Also my point," Thalius said gleefully.

"Bands!" He ran to her. She turned, disoriented, then smiled as he wrapped his arms around her and lifted her up. Then he held her, just held her. She was real and warm and beautiful, and he didn't want to let her go.

Finally, Thalius cleared his throat.

Medophae put Bands back on her feet, but didn't let go of her arms. He didn't want to stop touching her. He didn't even want to blink for fear she'd vanish. "You didn't die. H-How?" he asked.

She shook her head. "I...don't know. I remember kissing you. Then...I was here."

Silasa and her white-haired friend looked at each other, obviously just as mystified. Medophae turned his gaze to Thalius. The incorrigible god grinned, like he had a mouth full of satisfaction.

"He looks like he's going to burst," Bands noted.

"Maybe that's not a bad thing."

Bands gave Medophae a playful tug around his waist.

"Fine," Medophae said. "Thalius, do you know anything about this?"

"In point of fact, I do." He said. "Bands *did* die. These young ladies." He pointed at Silasa and her friend. "Had a brilliant idea. I just...changed it a little." He turned his finger to point at the giant emerald. "Avakketh resurrected himself with the GodStone."

"The GodStone?" Medophae repeated.

"That's what it's called." He waved a hand as though that was unimportant. "Only one god can use the GodStone at a time. If one god's in, the previous god is out. The unicorn and the vampire were going to cut Avakketh off from the GodStone using me. Then I would possess the stone, and Avakketh couldn't resurrect himself. But I refused." He grinned those shiny white teeth. "I gave them Bands instead. The GodStone now belongs to her. And that means a great number of things, not the least of which is that it's going to be hard to kill her any time soon."

"Is that why I...feel different?" Bands asked. "I'm so..."

"Full?" Thalius asked.

"I...yes."

"That isn't the only reason, no. That stone was created by

Natra to, essentially, duplicate her vast power. She used it as a giant reservoir for everything she was. Avakketh used it as a place to duplicate himself so he could die and come back. I gambled that it wouldn't just duplicate the power of a god, and I stuffed you in there. And it...filled itself with everything you are."

"It made a duplicate of me?"

"It made you a thousand times larger."

Her eyes widened. She looked down at her hands, then around the room, as though she was seeing things no one else could see. "The threads are... What are you saying?" she whispered.

"Medophae." Thalius bowed to him. "May I present the new goddess of the dragons, Randorus Ak-nin Ackli Forckandor?"

"What?" Bands said.

"The GodStone...grew you. That's what it does. It took the essence of your mortal self and made it...unfathomably larger. You are more than you once were."

Medophae turned to Bands, took her face in his hands. "I don't care if you're a goddess or a dragon or a fish," he whispered. "I love you."

She pushed her hands into his wild mane of hair and pulled him down into a kiss.

Thalius clapped his hands, and it sounded like thunder. He laughed a deep, good-natured laugh that filled the cave.

"Eternity," Medophae murmured into her ear. "With you."

"Whatever shall we do with all the time?" Bands whispered back.

Medophae's laughter mixed with Thalius's, and he hugged her tight.

46

SILASA

FIRELIGHT BURNED in the center of Belshra, creating a glow that could be seen for miles. The celebration was in full swing. During Silasa's sleep during the day, Mershayn, his army and the Sunriders had buried the dead. She'd awoken to the party's preparations. Tonight, the humans and their gods ate, sang and danced for those who had departed, for their victory over the dragons, and for happy endings.

Silasa stood on the beach before the incoming waves, far away from the center of town, gently holding a glass globe in her hand. It swirled with pearlescent colors.

The waves rolled in low and gentle. She used to come here when she was a little girl, when she was alive. She'd slip away from the watchful eyes of her nanny, strip down to her bare skin underneath the summer sun, and swim in the glorious warmth of the Inland Ocean.

The dawn wasn't very far off. She could feel its approach. The sky would begin to lighten at any moment.

An ambitious streak of surf tickled her bare foot, then

receded. Her best friends were gods now. Bands and Medophae had taken one step farther away from her. Silasa felt joyous for her friends, joyous that she had been a part of bringing Bands back from the dead. But it had been yet one more division between them, one more reminder of what she was.

Bands and Mirolah had been absent at the beginning of the celebration tonight. Medophae had informed Silasa that the two of them had been working on a project during the day, and that they had not yet completed it. Bands and Mirolah appeared at the party when the night was nearly over. Bands arrived radiant in her green dress, and Mirolah was fetching in a simple brown dress. She had glanced at Silasa with a self-conscious smile, then had gone to sit next to Mershayn. Bands had then approached Silasa and taken her aside.

"This is for you," she had said, and she'd pressed the pearlescent globe into Silasa's hands. "When you choose, if you choose, hold it high above your head and speak the words, 'I am ready', and the spell will take effect. Simply know that once you use it, you cannot undo it."

The recent memory faded away, and she was left once again staring at the pearlescent globe Bands had given her.

"It's a difficult choice," Ynisaan said softly, suddenly, from behind.

Silasa smiled. That woman loved to sneak up on people. Silasa knew how she did it now, though. Silasa had ridden through Ynisaan's imagination to different parts of Amarion. No doubt, the unicorn woman had stepped out of a portal right behind her. Now, of course, Silasa could smell her: fresh air, a hint of grass, the lightest musk of horse.

"You were there? You heard?" Silasa asked.

"My apologies," Ynisaan said. "Eavesdropping has been my life for as long as I can remember."

"I don't mind."

"You're the only friend I have." Ynisaan moved closer, and she slid a hand into Silasa's. "I'm…rather addicted to being near you." The tiny woman only came up to Silasa's shoulder.

Silasa looked down at Ynisaan and squeezed her hand.

"It's good to have you here," Silasa said. She hadn't been able to think about anything else since Bands made the offer.

"Can she really do it?" Ynisaan asked. "Make you human again?"

"Bands wouldn't make an offer like that to me unless she was sure."

Ynisaan seemed to hold her breath. "It's what you want, isn't it?" she said softly.

"Yes," Silasa said without hesitating. And yet, even as she said it, the thought of becoming human terrified her. It had been easy to rail against her vampirism when she could do nothing about it. Tuana's curse had been forced upon her: the ghastly need to drink blood, the hunger that sometimes made her want to drain those she loved the most, the loss of the sun.

But for six centuries, she'd lived as a vampire, with heightened senses, phenomenal strength, and immortality. The memories of her childhood were golden dreams, but it had been so long since she'd been *mortal*. She thought of facing someone like herself, a vampire, if she was human, and the idea terrified her. Humans were so fragile, weak, so easily killed.

"You hesitate," Ynisaan said.

"I'm filled with hope, excitement. I was a girl when I was taken. There was so much I didn't get to do. A first love. A family. Now, I have the opportunity... But the more I think on it...I'm scared. I can't really go back. I'm not that girl anymore. I might reclaim her human body, but I'll never be that girl again. My mother and father are long buried. My sister, brothers. All dead. Their children. Their children's children's children. I would have to start over again."

"You could start all over again," Ynisaan said with a different, encouraging inflection.

"And I'll be...weak. I will live and die by aging in the next fifty years."

"Is it really so frightening?"

"How long do unicorns live?"

"Centuries." Ynisaan nodded. "I see your point."

Silasa sighed. "What do I do?"

Ynisaan stayed quiet, and her presence was a balm.

"No really. Tell me," Silasa said. "You can see the future. What do I actually do? What do I choose in the end?"

Ynisaan glanced up at her, perhaps not knowing if Silasa was serious or not. "I probably shouldn't use that ability for personal needs. It was a hard lesson I learned from a dear friend." Ynisaan winked.

"But you've looked, haven't you?" Silasa asked. "At the ghost lines. At the future. *My* future."

Ynisaan hesitated. "Yes."

"So you know what I'm going to do."

"I think you know, too, Silasa. You do not need to see the ghost lines of the Coreworld to know your own heart."

They watched the waves roll in for a time. Silasa glanced east, to the brightly limned Corialis Mountains. The moment was upon her. She had to make the choice now, or run and hide.

Ynisaan followed her gaze. "I'm here," she whispered. "I'm with you. I won't let you go." Her hand clasped Silasa's.

Silasa felt the familiar pain in her skin, in her organs. The sun would rise any second. She held the globe before her and looked at that distant eastern horizon.

As the first ray of sunlight streamed over the mountains, Silasa made her choice.

47

STAVARK

STAVARK GAVE ONE LAST LOOK to the city of Belshra. They had buried the fallen, and Mershayn had thrown a feast last night to honor them. Stavark had said the goodbyes that needed saying. He'd come to the human lands to bring back the *maehka* for all the lands. He'd come to restore the *Maehka vik Kalik*. He had done both.

Mirolah had told Stavark how she'd freed Orem from Zilok Morth's grip, and how he had left immediately. It saddened Stavark that he could not say goodbye to his oldest friend. He would like to have seen Orem before he went home. But Orem was finally free, and that was enough.

Nothing had turned out the way Stavark had expected. When he had joined Orem on his quest, Stavark had felt invincible, more than a match for the perils of the human lands. Since then, he had been broken down and rebuilt.

He tried to let it flow away, his failures and successes. The path of beauty created itself from the moment, not nostalgia for the past nor worry for the future.

Yet he felt jagged inside, as though his once-smooth soul had cracked and healed, and cracked and healed again. Now it had bumps and edges and imperfections. Was this what the elders talked about? Was this what it meant to grow up, that your soul could no longer be smooth and untroubled?

He didn't know the answer. He knew only that he needed to leave the human lands. He was done here, and he missed his home. All he wanted was to stand beneath the familiar Killik trees, to make peace with his mother, to extend that peace to the rest of the *syvihrk*.

He turned his face into the wind. It was light and pleasant, reminiscent of summer.

He would miss them all, his human friends, but he had served the *Maehka vik Kalik*. He had served the right. He had done his part.

He had not seen the *Maehka vik Kalik* since the dragon battle began.

That was a bittersweet joy, a rough edge of his soul. The balance had been restored, and She had no more need of him. She must turn her attention to healing the lands, and that was as it should be.

Likewise, it was time for him to return to the life of a mortal. He could not expect to be kept by Her side at all times, feeling the glorious flow of Her presence.

But, when his mind was quiet and his heart open like now, he thought he could almost hear her voice on the wind.

He turned to the huge yellow dog towering over him and patted Sniff's skinny side. The dog turned and licked Stavark on the side of the face.

"You may return to your mistress now," Stavark said softly, but he knew now that the dog would not. It was his third time asking, and he suspected this was Mirolah's way of saying goodbye. Stavark was certain the great Skin Dog would accompany him all the way to Sylikkayrn.

Sniff panted, and his tongue lolled out as he looked at the plains and the distant forest to the west. Stavark started out across the field...then he drew up short.

Ahead of him, a figure stood silently, cowl low over his face. The man had not been there a second ago. Sniff raised his long snout with its bramble of teeth and tested the air. He let out a low whine, but he didn't growl.

"I'm sorry I didn't say hello before now, my friend," the man said. "I had…a lot to think about."

Stavark's breath came faster. He tried to retain his calm, but it was difficult.

"Orem," he whispered.

"I have walked a dark path of late," Orem said.

"And now?"

"I didn't dare to hope at first… But I think the sun has finally risen."

"And have you found the day as you hoped?"

"Stavark…" His voice caught in his throat. "It is…like a dream."

"Worth the suffering?" Stavark said.

Orem's hands stayed hidden by the sleeves of his robe, but his cowl drew up and back as if moved by invisible fingers. His face was just as it had always been, weathered by the sun, wrinkles at the corners of his eyes. But Stavark could see something more about him, a dancing of barely perceptible light. Orem watched Stavark with sparkling eyes and a happy crook to his mouth.

Stavark couldn't suppress the grin that spread across his face. "You are a threadweaver."

"A gift from Mirolah…when she was still a goddess. I think it was how she removed Zilok's hold…" he said, then paused. "I feel as if I can begin my life's story all over again."

Stavark walked forward until he stood beside his friend. He looked up. "You have dragged me all over Amarion, Orem. This time, let me drag you. Come with me to Sylikkayrn."

"Okay," Orem said instantly. Together, Stavark, Orem and Sniff began walking toward the distant trees.

"I saw almost everything Zilok saw," Orem suddenly said. "I remember many of the spells he crafted. Plus everything I ever studied in Denema's Valley, the libraries at Buravar and

Teni'sia. I could go on and on. There are a thousand things to practice."

"I met a goddess," Stavark said.

Sniff howled as though offering a third story.

Orem glanced at the Skin Dog. "Maybe we should let the monster go first."

"He's a dog."

"Don't presume to educate me. I'm the most well-read man in Amarion, and I know a monster when I see one."

Stavark grinned. He wanted to move, so he began jogging. Orem matched him. Without entering the silverland, Stavark ran as fast as he could, enjoying the feel of his legs churning, of his feet hitting the ground. Orem ran with him, and Sniff kept pace with a lazy lope.

Stavark and Orem laughed together, and they ran until they were tired.

Mailing List/Social Media

AUTHOR LETTER

Dear Reader,

This book was never supposed to be. *Threadweavers* was intended to be a trilogy beginning with *Wildmane,* continuing with *The GodSpill,* and culminating with *Threads of Amarion.* I wrote the ideas and much of the rough draft years ago in New York City. In rewriting the series, I went farther and farther afield as I moved through the meta-story. While *Wildmane* stayed almost completely true to the original manuscript, the other volumes evolved dramatically.

The GodSpill (originally titled *The Humanlands*) kept about 70% of its original form. The basics remained the same, but as I combed through it, I found places to tell more of the history of Amarion. I built the relationship between Mirolah and Medophae more thoroughly and laid down thicker foreshadowing for Avakketh's arrival in the (as of then) final volume: *Threads of Amarion.*

Then I got to work on *Threads of Amarion* and discovered it was a holy mess. Not only was it the roughest of the three drafts, but each adjustment I'd made to *Wildmane* and *The GodSpill* took the meta-story further away from the original path that was supposed to finish in *Threads of Amarion.* I started in by cutting a full third of the manuscript. Wildmane's journey originally involved Gilgion the Sunrider and a plateau in the desert. That got chopped and rewritten to Wildmane's journey of discovery to his home island of Dandere, and that was just the beginning of the rewrites. In the end, I only kept about 30% of the original material, mostly the scenes with Mershayn (which held up quite well), and lopped off half the book to be the next final volume, newly named *God of Dragons.*

And so *God of Dragons* began with about 40,000 words cut from the end of the very rough *Threads of Amarion.* That quickly got reduced to 10,000 words, which got whittled down to a mere 5,000 usable words.

Then I began writing in earnest.

But what started as a threadbare fabric of frayed story lines became my favorite book of the series. I lovingly wrapped my arms around these characters for the last time and gave them my all. It was vital to me that each of them, even the supporting characters (especially the supporting characters. Who *doesn't* like Stavark and Sniff?), have satisfying and full arcs by the end of the book. No cliffhangers, no unresolved plot lines, and, yes, a happy ending.

My editor tells me happy endings went out of style with the rise of *Game of Thrones*, but she loved it, and I hope you did too. Thank you for joining me for this journey. It was my pleasure to guide you through Amarion. So much has happened for Mirolah, Medophae, Bands, Stavark, Mershayn, Silasa, Ynisaan, and Orem. I wish them the best as they walk into their happily-ever-after. I don't expect we'll be seeing them again.

Then again, I did have this unbidden idea hit me in the shower the other morning...

What if, a few years from now, Mershayn and Mirolah's daughter (Shiralayn maybe?) and her playmate stumble across a bubbling pool of black oil in the caves north of Teni'sia? What if Shiralayn's playmate slips and falls in, and it consumes him. And what if, only then, does Shiralayn feel the powerful sentience and realize that the god, Dervon the Diseased, is rising again...?

-Todd Fahnestock

ALSO BY TODD FAHNESTOCK

Tower of the Four Series
Episode 1 – The Quad
Episode 2 – The Tower
Episode 3 – The Test
Episode 4 – The Nightmare
Episode 5 – The Resurrection
The Champions Academy (Episodes 1-3 omnibus)

Threadweavers Series
Wildmane
The GodSpill
Threads of Amarion
God of Dragons

The Whisper Prince Series
Fairmist
The Undying Man
The Slate Wizards (Forthcoming)

Standalone Novels
Charlie Fiction
Summer of the Fetch

Short Stories
Urchin: A Tower of the Four Short Story
Royal: A Tower of the Four Short Story
Princess: A Tower of the Four Short Story
Parallel Worlds Anthology: *Threshold*
Fantastic Realms Anthology: *Ten for Every One*
Dragonlance: The Cataclysm – *Seekers*
Dragonlance: Heroes & Fools – *Songsayer*
Dragonlance: The History of Krynn – *The Letters of Trayn Minaas*

ABOUT THE AUTHOR

TODD FAHNESTOCK is a writer of fantasy for all ages and winner of the New York Public Library's Books for the Teen Age Award. *Threadweavers* and *The Whisper Prince Trilogy* are two of his bestselling epic fantasy series. He is a finalist in the Colorado Authors  League Writing Awards for the past two years, for *Charlie Fiction* and *The Undying Man*. His passions are fantasy and his quirky, fun-loving family. When he's not writing, he teaches Taekwondo, swaps middle grade humor with his son, plays Ticket to Ride with his wife, scribes modern slang from his daughter and goes on morning runs with Galahad the Weimaraner. **Visit Todd** at www.toddfahnestock.com.